A Very Modern Hero

Mark Cullen

Copyright © Mark Cullen 2018

The moral right of the author has been asserted

All characters and events in this publication, other than those clearly in the public domain, are fictitious and any resemblance to real persons, living or dead, is purely coincidental.

All rights reserved.
No part of this publication may be reproduced, stored in a retrieval system, or transmitted, in any form, or by any means, without the prior permission of the publisher.

ISBN 9781980616283
ASIN B07BMWW6YW

Published by etv productions limited 2018

www.markacullen.com

@markacullen

"...a thing is true at first light and a lie by noon."
Ernest Hemingway

Part One

Chapter 1

'Hello, for those who don't know me, my name is Jonathan Lomax. I think you all know that I'm here today to present my ideas about where your television networks should be going.'

Jonathan looked around at the dozen people in the room. The Executive Board, some Heads of Departments and a few advisers of probably the least successful media company in Britain. It was just as he expected - a few over-promoted editors who were past their sell by dates, a couple of adsales guys full of their own self-importance, and a sprinkling of non-execs from blue-chip companies who looked as if they would rather be somewhere else. In the corner of the room sat the recently installed Chief Executive, looking impassive. He was really the only one that mattered, Jonathan knew, but he also understood that he had to win a few hearts and minds today. The real power lay outside this room in the hands of the four largest shareholders, all hedge funds, who had plunged into UK media a year or two ago and watched their investment in GBNewsmedia PLC tank in spectacular fashion. Hence the new Chief Executive and today's presentation for a new Managing Director of television. It was Jonathan's dream job and he knew he wasn't the favourite to get it.

'You don't need me to tell you that you've ploughed some 380 million pounds into your three TV channels and you've got nothing much to show for it. You haven't built any decent brands, you don't have any must-watch programming and you are still losing lots of money.' Jonathan knew his presentation by heart and he watched the audience respond to his first few slides on the screen. 'You've got impressive carriage deals with Sky and Freeview but despite this you've failed to make any breakthrough with audiences and I'm sorry to tell you that when you really drill down into your viewers today they're made up of the sort of people advertisers don't really want to reach: students, single mothers, bored housewives and the aged and infirm. The factual programming is dull, inoffensive and repetitive. I'm here today to tell you all that has to change and change now.'

As he often found when presenting, Jonathan was able to hold the room entirely in his grasp. He loved the theatricality of presentations and had full confidence in himself to deliver. He often tried, when presenting, to look at himself from a third party's viewpoint. He would see a tall (six foot two) slender guy with good hair, slightly too long for a fortyish man, with a warm broad smile that was his single best feature. He used it a lot and it generally got him what he wanted. He was dressed in his media executive regulation uniform: an expensive dark blue suit with white shirt and no tie. Black loafers and black silk socks. He wore the same uniform almost every day but this was his favourite suit and reserved for special occasions when he needed to feel at his very best. This was his moment to shine. The other candidates might have better spreadsheets but Jonathan was convinced he could out-present them all. He sought out eye contact with the most important of the non-executive directors, Jenny North from HSBC.

'You don't have enough resources to re-develop all three channels so you need to concentrate on your number one network and make it something worth investing in. So, let's look in detail at what I propose to do with Circus 1. First of all, the name. Yes, I know you paid a fortune to an ad agency to come up with a funky whimsical name that would show you understood post-modern irony but I'm afraid you were well and truly shafted. It researches terribly and drags down your audiences, it has to go. I've got a name to replace it but I'm going to hold that back for a while whilst I tell you how the new channel will work.'

This was his first test. The Chief Executive had told him, over dinner at Locatelli's last week, that everything was up for grabs except the name of the channels, and now he, Jonathan, was trampling that advice underfoot. No point being the underdog unless you were prepared to be radical, he had thought whilst preparing his presentation - and it was a truly terrible name for a television channel.

'Circus 1 seems to pretend that the internet doesn't exist. It's an old fashioned mix of me-too original programming and third-rate acquired stuff that the other networks have picked over and said no to. You are spending a lot on it and seeing no return. Of course, only two things really drive ratings: great drama and great sport. Between them, Netflix, the BBC and Sky have made sure you can't afford to compete in those markets so you need to do something different. Here's my plan to change everything about your TV channel.

'First, let's look at the world today. It's lurched to the right, on both a minor and a major scale. It's not just Brexit, it's across Europe and the States and we are seeing a major realignment of behaviour and ideas. Trump's election showed how uninformed social media can drive opinions and change behaviour. We live in a world where opinions have become facts and rejection of expert analysis is commonplace. Outsiders are dominating political debate and politicians are compromised by charges of elitism, corruption and the public's weariness of never-ending austerity. Television news has never been less powerful than it is today. People are not misled by false information and fake news but simply overwhelmed by the vast amount of information that is pushed onto them and they can't focus or filter out the truth from the fiction. many of them have given up even trying.

'Circus 1 carries a lot of political and current affairs programming today but it is incoherent and mixed up, no-one knows what the channel stands for. That just can't work in today's world. The channel has to reflect and shape the new thinking of popular conservatism and steal back the ability to form opinions and show leadership, just as newspapers did before electronic media came along. Your own newspapers played a major role in supporting Brexit and, along with the *Mail* and the *Telegraph*, have continued to champion the conservative right agenda. There's a gold mine of public support and the floodgates are open, here and around the world. However, if we are not careful, the conservative agenda will be swept aside by a populist over-reaction that will be every bit as corrosive to traditional conservatives as it has been to the centre left of British politics. The liberal centre is already in full retreat and its leaders in complete disarray. Socialism is dead if not yet buried across Europe. The conservatives could be next if we are not careful, as there will be no EU to blame for our misfortunes any more.

'It's time for television to catch up with the new world we find ourselves in and I am aiming to change everything on the channel. Imagine a television channel that leads public opinion, on politics, religion, health, sport. It will create a new agenda that the real people of Britain, not the media intelligentsia, can relate to. We will start making news on television, not reporting on it. We probably won't be popular with the Government as we lead our audience down new paths and new ways of thinking but we will be very, very powerful and influential. Our channel will adopt exactly the same approach as social media - we will lead with insight, speculation and opinion. It's not news, it's not impartial - it's comment, all the time, and it's in everyone's face, fighting the good fight. We will not be trying to change people's opinions but will concentrate on building and subtly altering them. The great thing television has over the web is that we can control the flow of news instead of being swept away by it. We will also ensure that the agenda we lead on is one we can all believe in. We will bring some orthodoxy to the new maelstrom we currently find ourselves in.

'I can hear you saying, what about Ofcom? How can we break the rules of television impartiality? Believe me, the new political re-alignment has changed everything. Do you really think that a Conservative Government, with no opposition to speak of, is going to close down a populist and successful TV channel that speaks out and often says what they would secretly like to say themselves? I don't think so either. You know how the Prime Minister feels about the liberal left and the UKIP wing of the Tory party.'

Here he paused to allow everyone in the room to remind themselves that Jonathan was until recently media adviser to the Prime Minister and still had access to a very wide range of political contacts.

'The gloves are off and we can make something new here that's a lot smarter and more influential than the right wing shock-jocks in the US promoting radical Republicans. I'm talking about running the agenda, not following it. Sure, we will eventually drag TV news programmes along with us, but they will always be caught up in news whilst we will be free to explore whatever we want to as we push the barriers ever further forward.'

Jonathan was beginning to sense that the mood of the room was warming, and thought he might have caught the right tone and could have something here. He told himself to calm down, keep smiling and not over-promise.

'You have great production facilities, good outside links coverage and a few good people. You also have around sixty too many staff.' He stopped to let that one sink in. There was nothing like headcount reduction to get the finance department salivating. 'I can make the channels described in the documents,' he waved in the general direction of the dozen bulky folders on the table, 'for a minimum of 10% less than you are spending today.' Excluding all those redundancy costs, he thought to himself.

'And what about Circus 2 and 3? Well, here's where we save some real money to spend upon the number one channel. I have a three year deal ready to sign with all the UK police forces - as you know, they are under strict orders to raise some real money from the private sector - to exclusive and live rights to all of their chase video footage, car, helicopter and bodycam. It's live, it's cheap and it will do good ratings. Chase TV will be a winner and we can run it on a staff of twelve. These savings alone will accelerate the financial breakeven of the TV business by over a year.'

The presentation moved into some technical details looking at viewership and advertising revenue projections and Jonathan could feel that he was on a roll, there were some nods of approval around the room and he wanted to finish quickly before the mood changed.

'I'm sure you have lots of questions,' he said, 'so why don't I stop here and let you fire away for a while.' He reached across the table for a glass of water and while raising it to his lips looked around the room for a first response.

Predictably it was the adsales director who was first off the mark. David Jonas was a thirty year veteran of UK adsales and had seen newspapers move from a licence to print money to a financial basket case. His reputation in the industry was as shabby as his dress sense. He had moved to run TV and online advertising in order to extend his own career and was just about holding on to his job by all accounts. He supposedly knew less about online advertising than a first-year intern at Google.

'Great presentation, Jonathan. But I don't know, however, how you make the case for the increase in audience and ad revenues in your plans. I think we all know how hard it is out there in the real world today to sell television advertising and I can't see that this new channel will make it any easier...' Jonathan interrupted across this ramble before any real damage could be done.

'Well, I don't say it will be easy, David. I will be bringing in my own dedicated Sales Director to focus on selling television, so that will allow your guys to concentrate on selling online for the rest of the group. I know you are at your happiest there. We need a fresh approach and some new faces too.' Silence for ten seconds before the next question, this one from Jenny North, the non-executive from HSBC. Nice legs, he thought in passing.

'Jonathan, thank you, a most thought-provoking presentation. As a non-executive director,' (Jonathan mind-yawned), 'my role is to query and question the direction of the company and I wondered if you thought your plans were consistent with the objectives the PLC has set itself for the next five years?'

Call that a question, he thought. 'I'm not applying to be on the PLC board today,' he began, 'but I do understand the problem here. The company has to be in TV to have a stake in the future and keep its share price performing, but if it has a serious TV underperformance, as it does at the moment, then the share price falls because TV losses eat away at diminishing newspaper revenues. We all know that online revenues are not growing fast enough to fill the advertising gap. This is compounded by the fact that no-one knows if old media can really succeed at online. Most importantly, the major shareholders and analysts worry about drift, and a lack of direction and strategy. My central play here is that I will make TV profitable and popular and exciting and this success will be amplified by a television channel that has a clear sense of its own identity. If we can make this transition, the television division will be fully supporting your PLC long-term objectives for the first time.'

I give you lot two years at most before another hedge fund or internet billionaire buys you as a trophy asset and takes the company off the public market, he thought to himself. Just long enough to get my channel up, running successfully and maybe even making a small profit.

The next question was from the Finance Director. Andrew something. Charmless, non too bright but powerful was Jonathan's information. Clearing his throat and limply waving Jonathan's presentation document, he asked, 'I see that you have reduced manpower costs in your spreadsheet and you've talked about sixty fewer staff but you seem to have put up staff numbers quite considerably at the same time. Would you mind telling us,' and here he nodded patronisingly around to his fellow directors, 'how you've managed to pull off this neat little magic trick?'

'It's really quite simple,' Jonathan replied. 'You, like most of the TV industry, use unpaid interns to reduce your costs. I've simply gone one stage further. To become a two year postgrad intern on the channel costs £15,000 a year. After two years, one in four gets a paid job. Just like daddy has had to pay for Tabitha to go to prep school, gap year travelling and university, he's now got to pay to get young Tabitha into "a really interesting job in London media",' and here he apes an upper middle class accent to smiles from a few in the room. 'As you will see in the revenue projections on page 14, Andrew,' he nods to the Finance Director, 'this revenue source is quite significant and brings breakeven forward by approximately eight months.' You can catch me out on a few things, he thinks to himself, but not on the big numbers.

The next question came from Andy, the Online Director. He is ten years younger than anyone else in the room but already overweight and prematurely balding. He had spent most of Jonathan's presentation scrolling through messages on his phone. To denote his online guru status he is wearing faded black jeans and a decorated black T-shirt that makes him look like an ageing heavy metal fan.

'I can't help but notice you haven't mentioned how our centralised online operation for all traditional media fits in your presentation. Do you see us as part of your plans or is this TV declaring independence?'

Jonathan was ready for this one and decided to fire both barrels. It would not be possible to work with Andy going forward so why bother to worry too much about offending him. He already had inside information that CEO Drew was casting around for a replacement.

'Of course, online is central to the channel's success,' he began, 'but used in a completely different way. Firstly, it will be fully integrated. We will elicit responses from the audiences through real time interactive voting and forums and push out additional material that will be, shall we say, too partial ever to make it onto the big screen. Online will show our highlights from the week alongside live streaming and an internet radio station that will make sure everyone on the move can hear us too. We will be the new Talk Radio. Every time you get into a cab you will be listening to us or hearing the cabbie talk about us. We will be everywhere and available on every platform. This will all be managed by the channel. Our approach to the web will be entirely different from the standard media owner model, even yours. We won't use syndicated photos of D-list celebrities showing a flash of under-boob or drive traffic to dodgy clickbait sites for a few fractions of a penny of revenue. Instead, we will generate opinion and this will drive audiences who will choose to interact with us rather than browsing through like a pack of aimlessly wandering wildebeest.' Andy had looked up, startled by the reference to his own editorial policy which was driving huge numbers of users looking for titillation (in many cases literally), but not even beginning to deliver the online revenues the PLC was hoping for. He slowly slumped back into his seat, deciding that now was not the time to have this fight with a guy who, after all, was only an outsider for the job of running television.

The questions continued for another ten minutes but Jonathan batted them back confidently and was feeling pretty pleased with the way things were going. Then Chief Executive Drew Smith asked his first and only question. 'So, in your plans, Jonathan, it's goodbye to Circus but you haven't told us what the new name for this radical new channel will be?'

'You're right, Drew, thanks for bringing me back to the central proposition. What we are trying to achieve is something that makes ordinary people feel they belong, that it's ok to think as they do and not be ashamed of their inner feelings. Together we are stronger and all that stuff. The channel will be called CATALYST. Not CATALYST TV, just CATALYST. It's about us, together, making the country a better place.' Jonathan paused and then pulled the large laminate board out of his briefcase and held it in front of him, white letters on a dark blue background, all upper case. CATALYST. Lucinda Grande (he'd found that on his Mac yesterday and thought it was the only font he had ever heard of that sounded like a hot woman). There were some nods around the room. He was on his way. Perhaps. The questions continued to flow.

***

'You didn't really say under-boob?'

'Lottie, some of the guys in that room think ripping down trees and smearing ink on them is a twenty-first century technology. I'm sure they didn't take it in. I didn't know it was even a thing until I read it in a magazine last week.'

Jonathan is standing outside the offices of GBNewsmedia talking on the phone to his publicity guru Lottie as he had promised he would do after the presentation. 'Anyway, they all know their online business is floundering, pretending to be a cut-price *Mail Online* and doing it badly. I didn't tell them anything they didn't already know.'

'When will they tell you about the decision?'

'Drew says he will be ready to talk again in a couple of days. I know they have two more presentations because the headhunters told me I was down to the last three. I'm pretty sure I was first on stage.'

'OK. Thanks for the update, Jonathan. See you when you are back at the office.'

Jonathan then called his wife, Ellie, another promised call. 'Ellie, darling, hi. Just calling to say it's all over and I think it went pretty well.'

'Sweetheart, thanks for letting me know. I'm so glad for you. Let's keep everything crossed. What time will you be back tonight?'

'Late. I have to get some work in on my paid job and it's been suffering badly whilst I've been preparing for today. I'll call you later. Love you. Bye.'

His next call was to the headhunters, Robinson, Pietro and Schmidt, RPS for short. A breakaway from one of the biggest headhunters in the world, RPS had quickly risen to become the go-to guys in London for all the big jobs in media. Jonathan dials Adam Robinson's direct number -in reality hits number 3 in his favourites list - but only gets through to voicemail. 'Adam, hi, it's Jonathan. Just to say it all went pretty well. They seemed to like the radical stuff but we will have to see what the other candidates come up with before we know more, I guess. Thank you for all of your help in putting this plan together. Give me a call when you have a chance.'

Having made these three calls, Jonathan flipped through the missed calls and emails on his phone. Seeing nothing of any importance he walked across the road, hailing a black cab as he did so. I really must get this Uber thing sorted out, he thought to himself, as he climbed into the taxi and gives the Soho address of his current employer.

Chapter 2.

Jonathan Lomax is a forty-five year old career media man. He started out, after dropping out of university two years in (seven years studying to be a doctor, what was he thinking?), as a trainee journalist. He found he was quick-witted and literate enough to hang on to a regional newspaper job that then gave him an opening at a London newspaper when the regional paper slimmed down its editorial operation and almost left him out of work. He had hated life as a junior London journalist. He worked long hours for little money and was surrounded by smug leftie liberals who despised his centrist Tory views, lack of a degree, and the fact that he lived in an Islington flat bought for him by his parents. He had become bored of saying, 'It's not really Canonbury, more Highbury, I think,' to try and help cover up his perceived lack of personal struggle, and generally shunned his male colleagues when not at work. Women, however, were a different matter. At university, Jonathan had floundered a little with women, but once he moved into the world of work, his confidence grew and he found that he could use his charm and winning smile to devastating effect. He did so on a regular basis and zealously worked his way through most of good-looking women in the editorial department, many of whom were a little repelled by his politics but charmed by his looks, humour and generosity with his credit card.

When he later looked back upon his time in print journalism, he felt it had given him three things: an ability to talk intelligently and convincingly upon any subject for a full five minutes, the self-confidence to do so, and most importantly the start of a great contacts book that he realised was the real key to success in the UK media industry.

Three years in newspapers was enough for him and television was calling. He had done a little front of camera stuff whilst working at the newspaper, but never felt comfortable staring into the lens while thinking of a pithy comment to end a report. He started applying for news producer roles, and after starting at Sky, he rose quickly through the editorial team on the main news show to an increasingly influential executive position. He enjoyed the meritocracy he found there and realised he had a real talent for managing people and getting them to do what he wanted. One rival there at the same time said that Jonathan's great skill was that he could walk into any crowded room and everyone would immediately look up, sensing that leadership had just arrived, all wanting to know what they could do to help him. Jonathan was likeable and tried hard to be liked; he listened carefully to input from even the most junior of his staff. Sky was a fiercely competitive place and full of equally ambitious and talented individuals. Jonathan thrived there and drew parallels with his schoolboy passion of middle distance running; he was never the best athlete or the fastest finisher but through discipline, training harder than those around him and really wanting to win, he had succeeded way beyond the expectations of his coaches and rivals. He did the same at Sky and drew admiring glances from those around him as he was promoted through the ranks without making any real enemies on the way.

It was obvious that Sky was grooming him for a top job, but very shortly after a three month stint in New York on a job swap with his opposite number at Fox News, he jumped ship to become Director of Television for one of the three major US networks then running TV channels across Europe.

His new job was a complete change of pace and style. At WBC he was effectively running a branch office for a US media giant and he found decision-making slow and ponderous. He missed the excitement of making television news and yawned his way through interminable scheduling meetings where senior executives agonised over moving the start times of their imported US dramas. He was used to extended days but he disliked the requirement to work to LA time as well as UK time which meant he was never free from the burden of long evening conference calls where nothing ever seemed to be decided without an offstage referral to a phalanx of US media lawyers. He sometimes wondered if they spent more on lawyers than they did on marketing. His boss was also a problem. A forty year veteran of the US TV industry, Bob North was on his final job for his one and only employer and spent most of his time in the UK shopping for expensive antiques. He had worked out long ago that if he could avoid making any business decisions, then no-one would tell him he had made the wrong ones. His slow mid-West drawl and frequent pauses in conversations left his colleagues wondering about his mental sharpness, but there was nothing slow about Bob North, he just spoke slowly and thought about each word in turn. Jonathan had been parachuted in without his knowledge or approval and their relationship was difficult from the beginning and only became worse as Jonathan started to shake up the bizarrely named EMEA operation.

'Do Americans all think that Europe, Middle East and Africa is really one place where a single set of decisions will work equally well?' he would ask Bob as the latest guidance arrived from California. 'I can't even see how they think that Germany and Spain have similar media habits never mind Nigeria and Finland.'

Bob would slowly murmur his disagreement, remind Jonathan they had the best TV content in the world, and go back to browsing for Georgian dining tables on the web. It was never going to be a happy relationship.

Jonathan's plan was twofold: he would revolutionise the TV channels across Europe, and secondarily ensure that he became one of the best known names in UK media in case it all went wrong with the Americans. To this end, he hired Charlotte Dukes as his personal PR machine (on the Company payroll, of course) and soon there was not a media conference or media story where Jonathan Lomax was not giving his opinions and sounding knowledgeable. Before long, Charlotte, or Lottie as everyone knew her, had positioned him to sit on one of the Government's think-tanks on the future of the BBC and his place in the media hierarchy seemed assured.

Lottie, he often thought, was his greatest ever hire. Short, slender to the point of skinniness, and with an aggressively short if expensive haircut, Lottie was a world away from Jonathan's usual choice in female hires. He often thought she reminded him of a fox and he was never sure if it was her narrow face or her shrewd decision-making that made him think so. In the early days of their working relationship, Lottie had pledged her complete allegiance to Jonathan and she had never let him down, working industry contacts and opinion-formers tirelessly, and watching his back in the office when he was out on the road. Smart, sophisticated and utterly loyal, Lottie was his confidant and indispensable supporter. She had been approached about several jobs in the industry but had turned them all down as she concentrated upon building Jonathan's career path. In turn, he ensured that Lottie was one of the best paid PR's in the industry and protected her from the corporate LA publicity machine which was retained to promote the TV channels and hated any local input or interference.

Lottie had impressed him at their first meeting and was clearly head and shoulders above the other shortlisted candidates. When he met her for a second interview over dinner, he was pleased by the way she had turned the meeting around and interviewed him for the whole evening. Over coffee she told him that she thought she could work for him and he had no hesitation in offering her the job there and then. Although she had a month's notice to serve at the BBC, she started working for him that very evening and there had never been a moment when he had regretted hiring her. Lottie for her part saw in Jonathan a rising media executive and one blessed with charm and talent - which marked him out from many other high-flyers in the industry. She genuinely liked him and trusted him and shared his values whilst also enjoyed her significant role in his growing success. She laughed at him over his ineptitude with social media and took over managing his image and output immediately after she joined the payroll - he regularly found himself checking Twitter and Facebook to see what he had said about things. In media interviews however he excelled and Lottie rarely intervened. Journalists liked interviewing him - he had strong and impassioned views and was always good for a quote on any subject. He also remembered journalists' names and was charming and courteous. For a young trade journalist passing through the industry and making their own career, this courtesy was unusual and welcome, again marking him out from some of his more self-important contemporaries.

At the same time as Jonathan's personal ratings were rising fast, the TV channels, under active management for perhaps the first time in their history, were showing real audience gains and starting to make some serious money. It was all looking good and Jonathan felt he was in a strong place to take over from Bob North. However, Jonathan had underestimated Bob's dislike of his young high-profile pretender and a carefully orchestrated whispering campaign back in LA began to undermine Jonathan's authority and increasingly reduce his room for manoeuvre. It became obvious to Jonathan that Bob's successor would not be him but another time-serving American - a safe pair of hands that Head Office could trust not to rock the boat.

It was at this moment that Adam Robinson, newly crowned CEO of start-up headhunters Robinson, Pietro and Schmidt, entered his life and things began to change again. Jonathan was used to headhunters and their craven ways and thought himself immune to their flattery, but Robinson was different. He had managed the careers of several top European media executives and demanded and got the highest fees in the industry. After several meetings at top London restaurants they had sworn exclusive loyalty to each other. Jonathan never expected to keep his side of the bargain but somehow it all clicked into place and Adam Robinson became, after Lottie, perhaps the most important figure in Jonathan's career.

Adam was a good ten years older than Jonathan and not in great physical shape. Heavy set and of less than medium height with almost no neck, he looked fatter than he really was. Always in a striped suit and patterned tie he looked out of date and out of place and slightly shambolic. His shirt usually bulged uncontrollably at the waist as the buttons strained to hold together and his haircuts looked as if they had been done hastily in the dark. Two divorces in rapid succession had pretty much destroyed his personal finances and his private life but once he started talking it became obvious that, professionally, Adam was at the very top of his game.

'The first thing we need to do is get you out from under Bob North,' Adam began, 'I've got the right job for you coming up and you are a shoe-in. It's another US network with lots of money and no ideas, but this time you will get to run the UK operation all by yourself. No more than two years there though, I've got plenty more commissions to make out of you.'

It all seemed to be that simple. Jonathan breezed through the interviews in London and LA. The inside information from Adam Robinson gave him the edge over rivals but in truth the fit was pretty good anyway and before long Jonathan found himself installed as UK MD of rival US network SBC. Different dramas, different problems, but essentially the same job as the network he had just left. His personal entourage, Lottie and Carol Smith, his PA, moved with him along with Tom Rabanski, the channel scheduler and Jonathan's secret weapon. No-one at his previous company had rated Tom. Tall, mild mannered and happy to be helpful, Tom was a million miles away from the typical channel scheduler in that he really liked television, watched a lot of it and understood how audiences made their viewing decisions and moved around the programme guide. He commuted from the Kent coast daily and spent both journeys on his laptop consuming the television that he hadn't managed to watch the day before. He was happy to be left alone by management and more than content to let Jonathan fight his battles. Carol had followed Jonathan from Sky and was everything anyone could want in a PA. Frighteningly efficient, intensely loyal and a great networker, Carol was Jonathan's eyes and ears around the building, reporting back snippets of information and gossip and making sure he was fully dialled in to what the workforce was thinking, who were the winners and losers, the shirkers and the strivers. Carol's insight meant that Jonathan could reward talent and lose the time-wasters. This generally went down pretty well and outsiders often commented that Jonathan ran a happy ship and it was hard to prize away good talent from his operation.

In his first year at SBC, Jonathan and his team succeeded spectacularly well. Ratings were up, revenues were up, and Jonathan had outwitted his boss who ran the international channels and carefully cultivated the Americans who really mattered in LA. His bonuses kicked in and life was good. Lottie continued to network him around town and he was an established figure at every media event worth going to and on first name terms with most of the people in the *Guardian's* Media 100 hotlist. A list he had just entered for the first time at number 72. 'Caught between Kirsty Walk and Alan Yentob if you can believe it,' was his amused comment to Ellie as he dismissed the list as cheap fiction of the worst kind. Of course, he was actually delighted. He was on his way and he realised, for perhaps the first time, that he could make it to the very top of the industry.

The second year was inevitably harder for the team. Targets were revised upwards and most of the early scheduling and manpower gains couldn't be repeated in year two. Work began to be a grind and the team laboured hard to keep any momentum. Everyone agreed it was less fun but no-one was expecting Jonathan's resignation just eighteen months into the job.

It was, of course, Adam Robinson who was behind the move.

'This next job is the one that really marks you out as a high flyer. Running overseas channels for US networks is fine and you can earn good money and have a enviable lifestyle but you will always be an outsider when it comes to the top jobs in the US. If you really want to make it to the very top, and I think you are good enough to get there, then you need to do more than network your way around London. You need to display the intellect and authority you have and you need to do that in the boardrooms around London and not just in the conference rooms.'

And so Jonathan was added to the shortlist to become CEO of media consultants and advisors Tangentially. Tangentially had grown rapidly over ten years by employing the brightest and the best young talent to advise media owners on their future strategy. This team of bright young things, all with MBAs or doctorates, found themselves trying to explain the uncertainty of the future to traditional media owners, most of whom were terrified by the changes they faced to their existing business models. Of course, the truth was that no-one knew anything about the future and that included the bright young things, but they were impressive and slick and reassuringly expensive. Repeat business levels were high and their publications about future technology were eagerly awaited by media owners, analysts, private equity companies and advertising agencies. Over time, Tangentially had expanded to cover European markets, advertising, and marketing, and numbered many of the world's largest companies as their clients. They went public and then were almost immediately acquired by WPP, making the three founders millionaires several times over and most of the senior partners seriously rich. It was at this point that things began to unravel. The founders were concentrating on their earn-outs, the bright young things were showing off their new found status and moving into interesting new areas in new consultancies they were setting up to compete with their former employers - and some clients were moving with them.

After two years of declining profits and unhappiness all around, Johanna Davis, one of the three founders and generally reckoned to be the real brains of the outfit, organised a management buyback of the business supported by a Silicon Valley private equity fund. Once more independent, the business started to rebuild, rediscover its roots, attract new young talent and win business from new and former clients. From chic new offices in Soho Square, Tangentially started rebuilding its reputation as the top media adviser in London. And then one day, just twelve months after the buyback, Johanna, only 41, dropped dead of an aneurism and the business found itself in turmoil once again.

The private equity fund realised two things after Johanna's death: there was no succession plan and there was no-one else in the Soho Square building capable of running the business. Clients, after a brief period of mourning that lasted for about five days, began to worry about 'future direction' and muttered about moving their business. The private equity fund promoted Paul Kafferos, a brilliant brain unfortunately attached to a man entirely lacking in empathy or human warmth, to the position of temporary MD and appointed RPS to find them a new CEO quickly.

After a flurry of interviews and extensive help from Adam, Jonathan was offered the position and took some time to negotiate his salary and stock options whilst simultaneously expediting his exit from SBC. Whilst the private equity owners realised they were desperate and rolled over on Jonathan's salary demands and agreed to take on Lottie and Carol, SBC were rather more difficult in releasing Jonathan from most of his notice period. He had no obvious successor and SBC were not keen to let him go early. Eventually, the head of the PE firm in Silicon Valley talked to the CEO of SBC in LA and a deal was done and he was installed in a fortnight. Lottie ensured that everyone in European media knew that Jonathan Lomax was the new CEO of Tangentially and just how significant a position this was.

In truth, the move scared Jonathan. He had a team of thirty-five and twenty of them were consultants with further degrees and doctorates and backgrounds in astrophysics or philosophy. In one case, astrophysics and philosophy. They were to a man and woman scarily bright and sceptical of a high-profile media man with no background in consulting and not even a BA to his name. It took a month or two to win them over and Jonathan's charm and winning smile were much in demand. Eventually, it all started to work out as the team began to understand that Jonathan was really the front man and the salesman of the business whilst they would supply the rarified intellectual input. Their academic insight was tempered by Jonathan's pragmatism and experience and mostly the blend worked well and impressed the clients with whom they met.

He was surprised that Paul Kafferos became an immediate ally. Paul never wanted the top job and knew he couldn't do it. He loved thinking through complex problems and developing solutions and together they made a formidable pair. Paul was admitted to the inner circle, joining Lottie and Carol in what was increasingly known by them as Team Lomax. There was never a formal induction or even a Whats App group of that name, but everyone on the inside knew they were on the inside and there for the long haul. One team member who didn't make the journey across town was Tom Rabanski. Even Jonathan's salesmanship couldn't persuade the private equity guys that a strategic consultancy needed a highly paid programme scheduler on their payroll but Jonathan made sure that Tom didn't feel neglected.

'Tom, I want you to stay working at SBC and learning stuff but you are on my team and very soon I will be calling you for something really big. You can't see me consulting forever, can you?'

So Tom remained on Team Lomax, just on someone else's payroll. Every few weeks, Jonathan would squeeze a quiet coffee with Tom into his diary (Tom didn't drink alcohol or do socialising) and make sure that he continued to feel the love.

Another new recruit to Team Lomax was Ben Zinneri. Although a relatively junior consultant at Tangentially, he was the most insightful of the bright young things when it came to the future of media and had some really radical ideas as to how the world might change. Jonathan encouraged Ben to keep these ideas to himself for the time being, mostly because Ben's ideas suggested media owners should close their doors as soon as possible and sell the office furniture before switching off the lights and giving any remaining money back to shareholders. Tall, with an unruly mound of curly black hair betraying his Italian origins, Ben was quickly renamed "Benzina" by Jonathan, who thought it a good pun on Ben's incendiary ideas on the future of the media business. Jonathan shortened, sweetened and changed the names of most of the people he worked with and most of them thought it a sign of his affection for them. The one exception was himself. If anyone called him Jon or Jonny he simply ignored them until, in order to get his attention, they were forced to revert to his full name.

One of the biggest changes that Jonathan brought to Tangentially was to expand outside of the media business and embrace both banking and politics. As the power of media grew to touch all parts of daily life, Jonathan realised that they could recycle much of their insight and repackage it for other markets. Adam Robinson was especially helpful in reaching into the higher echelons of the Tory party machine, and before long, Tangentially was advising Conservative Central Office on media strategy and development. Although a natural Tory himself and reasonably well connected from his journalist days at Sky, Jonathan had not really developed his political links and Adam pointed out this shortcoming. Jonathan began to court politicians from the centre to the right wing, leaving the Labour Party to a younger and more radically minded colleague who woefully reported back that Labour still thought they could do everything for themselves and didn't want professional help. They all agreed it was just too hard to even think of working for the Lib Dems.

Tangentially's work for Central Office led to them helping some individual ministers with their future media strategies and Jonathan offering his own private media advice to the newly elected Prime Minister. Jonathan had several meetings with the PM and found himself struggling to explain how out-of-touch the Tory party was with younger people in Britain. The PM listened, but Jonathan never got the sense that he was getting through. Although Jonathan and the PM got on well enough together, Jonathan never felt he understood what the PM really wanted from him. Most of the work was through the PM's officials, but when the *Guardian* ran an exclusive story outing all of the 'shadowy figures behind the new Prime Minister', Jonathan's mugshot was prominently displayed along with some Google-inspired copy that suggested Jonathan's past employment by two US television networks made him unsuitable to be a secret political adviser. Surprisingly, they didn't mention the *Guardian* Media 100 hotlist where Jonathan had by then climbed to number 55. Lottie was delighted with the story and unusually claimed no knowledge in its genesis (although the keener-eyed observers did notice that Jonathan's photograph was of rather better quality than the others in the article and the only one not previously available on *Google Images*). Lottie span the story well and Jonathan's brief foray into prime ministerial politics left him considerably more famous - even if the Tory party was very slow at settling their invoices. The article resulted in him being sidelined by the Prime Minister, and when he was eventually dropped as an adviser it was a junior SPAD who passed on the news to him by email.

Jonathan enjoyed running the consultancy. He enjoyed the intellectual rigour of working with his smart colleagues and liked the fact that his working hours were far more civilised so he could spend a little more time with his young family. He still packed in a sixty hour week, but a daily 6am swim followed by a 7.30 start every morning allowed him to get away from the office by 6pm most days. His driver would then take him on a brief round trip around the best media events in London and he was home by 8pm having shown his face and pressed the flesh. His weekday socialising rules were simple: meet only the interesting people, try not to drink more than one glass of wine per event, never eat the canapés, and never stay more than twenty minutes. To which Lottie would have added 'and then call Lottie so I can find out who you met and tweet about the useful bits.'

Then it was off home to Richmond. Unless, as was often the case, there was a dinner, or a conference somewhere, or a presentation that really needed re-writing overnight. In which case, Ellie would eat with the children and leave him to sort himself out.

Chapter 3

Jonathan had met Ellie whilst he was at Sky and they were living together within a month of their first date. Ellie was a lawyer at one of Sky's outside legal firms and she joined her team as a late replacement in one of the many legal meetings he had become increasingly involved in. Sky was trying to do some complex restructuring and although Ellie was not a media lawyer she had some relevant experience in working with EU regulators that her boss felt could be helpful to the discussion. Jonathan was naturally courteous around Sky's outside legal teams, knowing that the company only used the brightest and the best, but Ellie's entrance into the meeting room upset his equilibrium. Taller than average but not tall, with long and wavy dark blond hair and an open and friendly face, Ellie didn't fit the description of the corporate lawyers Jonathan was used to. Her movements were languid, loose and relaxed and her smile warm and inclusive. She was wearing casual dark trousers and a loose white shirt, all very different from the close fitting, Chanel-inspired two-piece suits that women lawyers used as a uniform at that time. She was very quiet in that first meeting, listening intently and making furious annotations to her legal pad. When she did finally speak it was to ask a short but penetrative question that went to the heart of the complex issue Sky was consulting upon and showed just how European lawyers would undercut their proposed case.

As the meeting broke up, Jonathan followed her out of the meeting room and complimented her on her insight. Her shy smile was an unusual reward and Jonathan made a mental note to follow up with her after the next meeting. From long experience, Jonathan knew not to move too quickly in the pursuit of women - and anyway, he knew it wouldn't be long before they would meet again.

For over ten years Jonathan had had a succession of elegant girlfriends. Generally they were of a type - tall, good looking, younger than him - and dropped by him after a few weeks or a few months. He avoided long term complications and joint living arrangements but mostly remained friendly with discarded girlfriends and sometimes revisited them for dinner, occasional sex, weekends away, and even holidays. They all tended to remember him with affection as a missed opportunity and they all bought into his mantra that he was not of the marrying type. Some of the women he dated were work colleagues, but his increased profile across the industry and his networking skills and easy charm meant that he met many eligible women from across the media business. He often felt that he enjoyed the chase, the seduction, the first kiss, the promise of discovery, rather more than the consummation of the affair itself. He enjoyed women and they enjoyed him. He was charming company, chivalrous, generous, and interested. Indeed, his ability to listen attentively marked him out to many women as something unusual. These listening skills combined with a good memory for facts and names helped him out in many a nascent conquest.

    He further avoided the complexity of long-term relationships by building something of a myth around a former girlfriend who had died whilst they were on holiday together. In truth, Alice and he were never meant to go the distance, but in the midst of a week's holiday in Turkey they had rented an open-top jeep for the day against the advice of the car-hire salesman and when Jonathan realised he had forgotten to bring his driving licence, Alice stepped in with hers. After a pleasant lunch in the mountains, Alice had lost control of the jeep going around a sharp corner and in the resulting rollover she had broken her neck and died instantly. Jonathan, not wearing a seatbelt, had been thrown clear, and apart from a broken wrist and a small scratch on his cheek that needed a few stitches, had suffered only cuts and bruises. On a deserted mountain road with a very obviously dead girlfriend and no mobile signal, Jonathan waited for over an hour before another rental car appeared and helped him notify the police. Very quickly, there were paramedics and policemen everywhere and Jonathan was being helped into the back of an ambulance. In the days that followed he struggled to deal with the demands of Turkish bureaucracy and the grief of Alice's parents who arrived on the first available flight and stayed at the villa Jonathan and Alice had rented. Jonathan was deeply affected by Alice's death, but couldn't pretend even to himself that they had had more than a brief encounter. To Alice's parents, however, he seemed to represent something more and they ended up building a story around their love affair that Jonathan reluctantly bought into because it was easier than the truth that Alice was a fun girl who liked to drink heavily and was refreshingly indiscriminate in her sex life. He doubted they would have lasted much beyond the week's holiday.

Eventually, he managed to smooth over the issues about the alcohol levels in Alice's bloodstream and the body was released to be flown home. He travelled with the coffin and Alice's parents and accompanied them all from Stansted to their home in Norwich. He stayed in a nearby hotel, refusing their kind offer to stay in the family home. At the funeral found himself playing the part of the grieving boyfriend as he tried to help Alice's delightful parents cope with the death of their only daughter. Even now he remained close to them and visited them in Norfolk for the odd weekend and telephoned when he remembered.

He found the myth of the long-dead girlfriend very useful in detaching himself from problematic women and, although he used the story sparingly, it had grown in the re-telling into an even more harrowing experience, helping him gently slough off the more difficult relationships. Although he never said that Alice might have been the one for him, the implication was left floating in the air and he never disavowed it. He was happy dating women but even happier without the inevitable complexities of meaningful relationships, and he also enjoyed his own company; as an only child he had spent much of his early years on his own and he rather enjoyed solitude from time to time. He didn't see this changing anytime soon. He knew that family life wasn't for him and saw no reason to conform even as his contemporaries started to settle down around him. He enjoyed weddings though, he had to admit. Everyone was always in a good mood and there was usually at least one pretty bridesmaid to flirt with.

Ellie didn't attend the next two legal meetings on the European issue and so it was a couple of months later at one of the legal firm's client networking events that they ran into each other again. After several minutes of easy conversation, Jonathan asked her if she would join him for dinner that night and was gently rebuffed.

'I'm sorry, but I just don't do one on one dinners with clients. It can lead to all sorts of misunderstandings and I think it's just best avoided. I also happen to have a date for dinner tonight so it's impossible anyway.'

Despite Jonathan's valiant efforts, Ellie refused alternative dates and after a few more minutes they parted to both network the room in the time-honoured fashion. Twenty or so minutes later, Ellie noticed that Julia, one of the legal secretaries, was far less familiar with the client/attorney 'no fraternising' rule than she should be. Julia was collecting her coat and leaving with Jonathan, presumably with a similar sort of dinner invitation on their agenda. Something inside snapped. When asked by friends to reveal how they first met, Ellie's recollections were straightforwardly simple.

'I walked into this dull European law meeting and was introduced to the team from Sky. Last of all was Jonathan and my jaw just fell open. Here was the first drop-dead gorgeous client I had ever met and so I kept very quiet through the meeting so as not to make a fool of myself. After the meeting he had a few quiet words with me and then was gone. I was moved onto another project and didn't meet him again for another six weeks when the firm had a drinks party. He was, of course, full of charm and as good-looking as I remembered and when he asked me out to dinner I decided to play hard to get and pretended I had another date that night. Within minutes, he had another girl in the firm lined up for dinner and I just decided to go for it. As they left, I ran after them and said my date had been forced to cancel and I could now join them for dinner. Jonathan was amused and gracious but Julia, the other woman, looked pretty confused in the taxi and across the table at dinner where we all made polite small talk. After what seemed to be a meal that lasted forever, she made her excuses and left and within minutes Jonathan had paid the bill and we were in a taxi heading west kissing for all we were worth. The rest as they say is history.'

They tried to keep their dating a secret for the first few weeks but before long the intensity of their relationship became obvious to those working around them and they were finally outed as a couple by one of Jonathan's bosses who spied them at a late night club together and spread the gossip around both offices. No-one mentioned client/attorney personal relationships to Ellie so she surmised that it was a rule that many had already broken. At Sky, Ellie was seen as just the latest in a long line of Jonathan's girlfriends. They were both a little frightened by the passion they ignited and the pleasure they took in each other. Three weeks after their second meeting, they flew to Crete together for a holiday and enjoyed a week of sightseeing, sun-worshipping and, well, mostly each other. Jonathan later joked that apart from the food and the wine it was the most perfect holiday he had ever been on.

Jonathan was both pleased and somewhat mystified by his new relationship. When he tried to examine things rationally he kept coming up short as to why he was so taken with his new girlfriend. Sure, Ellie was very good-looking and quite lovely, but he had had affairs with stunningly beautiful women who had not had this affect upon him; sex with Ellie was good but again he had known more resourceful girls in that area too. She was funny and witty and clever but other girls had been equally interesting. He thought about the way her shy smile would sometimes blossom into a broad grin that would light up her whole face and bring out the young girl in her. That very thought made him smile. With Ellie, he felt that somehow everything just worked for him in a new and very different way and decided to stop trying to analyse his feelings. When, in those early days of their relationship, he found himself at a conference in Berlin turning down the advances of a rather beautiful blonde who was keen to give him a private view of the inviting areas of her body not on public display, he realised that something had changed in him and for the first time that night he told Ellie on the phone that he loved her.

Ellie was more cautious in the relationship stakes. She knew a little of Jonathan's reputation and was determined not to be too hurt if it all cooled off after the first blush of romance. She had been badly dumped once before when she thought everything was going well and was keen not to make the same mistake twice. She loved his cavalier attitude to life and his ability to surmount obstacles and his enthusiasm for everything. Despite her reservations, she found herself falling completely for him and her relief, when he told her he loved her, was intense. Now she began to feel that she could reciprocate by telling him of her emotions and after a short while she began to confide her feelings to him and they both felt their relationship move up a gear.

Within a month, Ellie was spending every night at Jonathan's Fulham house and several weeks later rented out her own flat, which somehow made the moving-in seem much more permanent. When they began to come up for air, they introduced themselves to each other's friends and won universal praise for their suitability and compatibility. They now began to recognise themselves as a couple. They met each others' parents and in both cases were approved of. Ellie's parents were of a similar background to his own; replace Surrey with Sussex, stockbroker with investment manager, golf with tennis and gardening with painting and not much else needed changing, although Ellie's family home outside Horsham was considerably more relaxed than his own. Jonathan did note with interest that Ellie's mum was still strikingly attractive and thought that boded well for Ellie as she grew older. Unlike Jonathan, who was an only child, Ellie had an older sister called Anne, but Anne was several years older and had left to go to an American university where she married and rarely came back home. She was only distantly in touch with the family and something of a stranger to Ellie. Functionally, Ellie was therefore also an only child and her parents treated her accordingly. They were initially suspicious of Jonathan but within half an hour of meeting him they were both charmed and converted by him. He enjoyed their company too and found he didn't have to work too hard to make that first weekend in the country a success.

Jonathan's parents instantly warmed to Ellie and saw in her a stability and likability that had perhaps been missing in the several girls Jonathan had paraded in front of them over the years. Jonathan's father in particular hoped that Ellie would provide the steadying influence over his son that he often felt was missing. Despite Jonathan's only child status, father and son had never been close, and Jonathan's mediocre school record, his dropping out of university and a career in journalism had done nothing to bring them closer together. Both looked back to a time before Jonathan went away to school with a fondness that was probably more imaginary than real, but Jonathan's mother had taken all of the emotional space between the three of them and left no room for a meaningful relationship between a father and growing son. They retreated to a formal, not unfriendly, but restrained relationship, and often found they had little to say to each other when they were left alone by Jonathan's mother who liked to dominate the conversation in any room she was in. Especially if her only beloved son was in the same place too. Ellie was dutifully quiet in her presence and won brownie points for her demeanour and un-flashy appearance.

Despite her new relationship, Ellie was determined to hold onto some of her single girl activities. The main one was her girlfriend Saturdays where every three weeks or so she would take herself off for a day of pampering followed by shopping and dinner with a girlfriend or two. Having her hair carefully cut and coloured was a religion for Ellie. Naturally mousy coloured hair had been a trial for her through school and university and now the best salons in London were affordable and available. Her blonde hair was so well coloured it fooled all the men and many of the women she knew and gave her new confidence in her appearance. She also used her girlfriend Saturdays to catch up and gossip, whilst trying out new massages, treatments and organic juices across London before undoing all of the good work with a boozy dinner which often extended into an overnight sleepover watching chick-flicks.

Outside of the small fortune she spent on her hair, Ellie was unconcerned about clothes or fashion and was happiest in a pair of jeans and a T shirt. Jonathan would buy her expensive lingerie, but often when he undressed her he would find her wearing washed out M&S underwear that had seen better days. It always made him smile. With his encouragement she began to buy more expensive clothes and shoes and spend more of her hard-earned money on herself. Before they met, Jonathan had traded in the Islington flat his parents had bought for him, for a terraced house in Fulham with a relatively small mortgage. The rent from Ellie's flat more than covered her mortgage and they both held well-paid jobs. London was a hip and stylish city again and Jonathan and Ellie were playing their full part in making it work for them. They partied with friends and tried many of the new fashionable restaurants as they opened. They began to hold dinner parties in Fulham and

Ellie's carefully precise cooking and Jonathan's expensive and eclectic wine choices made them a hot ticket in their social circle. Ellie encouraged Jonathan to start appreciating contemporary art and before long they were a regular feature at London gallery openings and private views. They began to dabble in purchasing art from up and coming artists. They were living the life of the upwardly mobile, young, upper middle class couple and life was treating them well. They skied at least twice a year and took exotic summer holidays in Vietnam or Mozambique. They frequently drove away from London in Jonathan's convertible 911 to spend weekends in exclusive boutique hotels in the Cotswolds and the south coast and occasionally speculated about selling Ellie's flat and buying a bolt hole in the country.

Superficially, their lifestyle seemed idyllic, but in fact they barely had enough time to live together in one house never mind two. They both worked hard, with long hours and frequent trips away. Ellie was often in the Brussels office working with EU colleagues and Jonathan was spending more time in the States. Some weeks passed by with them hardly seeing each other at all and they were forced to leave post-it notes around the house to communicate with each other - and especially with the Polish cleaner who repeatedly refused to engage with them on email. Sometimes they would just spend weekends completely crashed out, recharging their batteries and eating take-aways before the bedlam of another week began again.

When Ellie announced tearfully that she was pregnant, the news took Jonathan completely by surprise. He knew that Ellie had come off the pill on her doctor's advice but had blithely assumed that the alternative contraceptive precautions would be just as effective. Both of them had carefully skirted around any talk of marriage or life-long commitment even as they went to weddings of friends who would pointedly ask when they would join the club of newly-married late thirty-somethings. It wasn't that they were opposed to the idea of marriage, Ellie would later say, it was just that they were very happy as they were and didn't want to risk that happiness by changing anything.

Now everything had changed, and once they had their heads around the issue of Ellie's pregnancy, they began to make plans and take practical steps to turn themselves into a family unit. They sold the Fulham house and Ellie's flat and bought a much larger house in Richmond that needed a fair bit of restoration. Ellie organised to take extended maternity leave, and four months into her pregnancy they flew to Barbados where they were married on the beach with a few hotel staff acting as witnesses. Upon their return, they held a post-wedding party at Soho House and were fully inducted into married society by their friends and work colleagues. Ellie threw herself into the restoration of the new Richmond house and had just managed to say goodbye to the last of the builders when she went into early labour.

George was born a couple of weeks prematurely and after an extended stay in hospital proceeded, as all first children do, to turn their world completely upside down. He slept badly and, consequently, so did they. The two of them researched baby sleeping problems and read endless books on the subject but nothing they tried worked, and Jonathan would find himself missing large parts of meetings as he dozed through the dull bits and for the first time in his working life struggled to stay one step ahead of his colleagues. Ellie took to motherhood as the proverbial duck takes to water. Her world centred upon George and she re-organised her life completely around him. She took to sleeping to his timescale and would often be asleep when Jonathan returned from the office, waking only to snack and say hello to her husband who was most likely to be found grazing on a ready-meal he had found in the fridge and watching Sky Sports. After several months of 'baby max' as they would later describe it, their life began to re-adjust to the new normal. Jonathan was working harder than ever and rarely home before nine, social events and dinners now a full part of his new executive status. Ellie became a west London yummy mummy with a wide gaggle of old and new female friends. They found they socialised almost exclusively with couples who had similarly aged children and whilst the women were meeting several times a week at various social events, Jonathan and the other husbands would often find it difficult to develop meaningful friendships.

Ellie returned to work at the end of her maternity leave and fell pregnant again almost immediately. This time it was not a surprise. They had both agreed that two children was the right answer and when Albee arrived in the October of that year, Ellie decided that she would give up her career for the time being and concentrate upon the children. The second pregnancy was tough for Ellie. She was not always well but continued to work and had to manage without Jonathan for three months when he was seconded to the New York Fox News operation through the summer. Although he flew home every other week, she felt the separation keenly. The live-in nanny was a godsend but Jonathan's enforced absence created a problem for both of them. Jonathan struggled to make the New York posting work for him. If Ellie had not been pregnant it would have been a great adventure, but splitting life between a sterile company apartment in Manhattan and long haul flights for a weekend at home with a pregnant wife and young son took its toll upon him. On top of everything, he struggled to make any impact at Fox and Sky didn't seem to miss him as much as he had hoped.

When Jonathan did return from New York just a month before Albee's birth, it was with the news that he was moving jobs and would be starting with his new employer before the end of the year. The new job came with a sizeable salary increase and, although they both agreed the timing was awful, they started to talk again about a second home somewhere out of London where they could all escape for weekends.

In the summer after Albee's birth they would often be found early on a Saturday morning or sometimes late on a Friday night, loading children and luggage into their new Porsche SUV and heading off to the weekend home Ellie had found several miles outside Winchester. Isolated and more than a little rundown, the cottage was a sanctuary with a large garden and lots of potential – at least according to the local estate agents. Jonathan liked the fact that it was not in one of the hotspots for Londoners looking for holiday homes; the last thing he wanted was to meet up with media rivals at the local farmers' market when he was trying to get away from them for the weekend. For the first time, they found themselves financially challenged. The cottage was swallowing huge amounts of renovation money as local Hampshire builders took their silent revenge upon the 'glamorous yuppie couple from London', and the loss of Ellie's salary was significant. They tried but failed to rein in their expensive shopping and eating habits. Luckily, as Jonathan joked, the financial crash at least meant mortgages had never been cheaper; which was just as well as theirs seemed to be growing rather than diminishing.

Ellie still maintained her girlfriend Saturdays even if now they only took place monthly. On the first Saturday of every month, Jonathan and the nanny were given the boys to look after and relegated to Richmond for the day whilst she travelled into town and indulged her hair and beauty regime, although boozy dinners and sleepovers were by now replaced with early and healthy dinners at chic organic restaurants in up-and-coming corners of the capital with two or three of her closest friends. She would normally be home by ten, glowing healthily and ready for another month of full-time mothering.

Unlike Ellie, Jonathan had few really close friends outside of work colleagues. His oldest friend, David, was an old school friend, but David had dropped out of school at sixteen and drifted around Europe for some years trying out several different lifestyles before settling down to run a Land Rover repair business in North Devon. The business had been owned by David's new partner Caitlin and, when her husband had died, Caitlin had tried to run it on her own and eventually came across David (drunk, face down in a ditch, the story goes) and he ended up working in the failing business and later sleeping with his boss. Neither their business nor domestic life together could be called a success. He was as unlikely a friend as Ellie could imagine Jonathan having. David was disorganised, clumsy and often rudely drunk, but Jonathan would not hear a word against him.

They had spent a couple of weekends down there but the obvious hostility of Caitlin towards her had made Ellie uncomfortable in the rambling and damp farmhouse which was full of wet dogs and dis-assembled engine parts. Their metropolitan appearance, clothes and even the car they drove marked them as outsiders, and North Devon didn't take well to outsiders. Caitlin was North Devon through and through. Jonathan had tried to laugh it all off but even he found the atmosphere difficult. A disastrous weekend in London where the pair arrived with three large dogs and Caitlin proceeded to spend the weekend shredding their lifestyle and arguing with their friends over dinner, persuaded Ellie that it would be best if Jonathan started going down to Devon on his own. He did that infrequently, usually when Caitlin was away, and spent those weekends rough shooting and drinking copiously with his old friend. David was chronically short of money and more than once Jonathan had lent him some money so that he could pay the next month's rent on the farmhouse or the garage. Sometimes it was re-paid, sometimes not.

Devon David (as Ellie began to call him) would telephone Jonathan once a month and spend an hour talking about whatever happened to be on his mind. Often, it was the wayward Caitlin who would take off for days at a time without notice and refuse to discuss her absences upon her return. Even Jonathan began to dread these rambling and often alcohol-fuelled phone-calls and would take them in his study so Ellie didn't have to endure the full nightmare.

Jonathan's other friends were mostly rowers. They all seemed to be of the same social strata and all enjoyed nothing more than getting together, drinking lots and talking about rowing. Jonathan had rowed successfully at his school and then for a mid-ranking team on the river at Henley. He loved rowing and all things about it. He was now an active social member of The Leander Club and an occasional committee member, having stopped rowing when he felt his back starting to suffer. Ellie very consciously didn't intrude into this world of rowing and rowing mates; she thought it was important he kept this male bastion to himself. He would often spend rowdy evenings dining at Leander, reminiscing about former glories on the water before being returned home by minicab, often still wearing the worn-out stripy blazer that only just fitted him. Regatta week at Henley was hard-coded into his diary and he would often spend two or three days there staying at some local hotel with fellow enthusiasts. Ellie had gone along one year but was mystified by the apparent inattention to the actual racing displayed by most of the visitors and also by the public schoolboy side of Jonathan that she hadn't seen before. She had decided that once was enough and this was something Jonathan should do without her and he seemed happy with her decision. Occasionally, rowing friends would stay over at Jonathan's invitation as they were passing through West London. Usually, Jonathan would round up a couple of other local rowing mates and they would go out for a curry before returning late and drunk. Ellie would usually make herself scarce at these times and let the boys be boys.

House responsibilities between the two of them were divided up much like their own parents had divided theirs. Without any formal discussion on the subject, Ellie was most definitely in charge of all things to do with the children. It was an easy decision; Jonathan worked hard with long hours and was often away for days at a time and she was always several steps ahead of him about things that needed doing for the boys and decisions that needed to be taken. He followed along, happy to agree. Shopping trips to the Kings Road were now more likely to end in the baby and toddler department of Peter Jones than buying expensive clothes in Hugo Boss or Joseph but they both felt they had settled into family life pretty well and both took real pleasure from the steady development of their children.

Ellie had given up alcohol during her pregnancies and hadn't really started again in earnest. A couple of glasses of champagne, maybe a dry martini and, when socialising, a few glasses of white wine, was as much as she would normally drink. Whilst Jonathan did not follow her down this route, he drank modestly by the standards of their friends, perhaps half a bottle of good claret or burgundy when they were alone for dinner, considerably more when they were socialising, but never enough to lose control, although like most of their friends he became noisier and more argumentative as these evenings drew to a close. The rush of cocaine-fuelled sex that had briefly featured in the early days of their relationship was now firmly off their grown-up agenda and Ellie ensured that they tried to eat healthily; although Jonathan made it clear when he spotted the detox cookbooks taking over the kitchen that giving up meat was not part of his agenda. He started running or swimming every weekday morning at 6am before work. Although he had always been slender, his fitness drive helped him fight off the thickening waists that many of his contemporaries were developing and cleared his mind wonderfully for the rigours of the working day ahead. After Albee's birth, Ellie started running too and soon became hooked, running up to three times a week with a women's group in the park.

Richmond socialising was based around dinner parties. Conversations tended to be light and frothy; the men avoiding talk about work and the women trying to be vivacious and entertaining. The favourite subject for gossip was always the trials and tribulations of any local contemporaries who were richer than the dinner party group gathered together. Tales of wildly expensive divorces, drug habits and gratuitous and pointless expenditure would always set the room buzzing with schadenfreude. Heads would be shaken and smiles exchanged as those in the know regaled their eager audience with these tales of super-rich woe. At duller moments, conversations could drag on interminably about school choices and the latest trends in child rearing.

Politics were not often discussed around the dining table. Most of their social circle were, by nature or selection, conservative, and shared similar views about hard work and ambition, thrift and self-help, but they would normally only get excited about problems that affected them directly, such as the ridiculously high hurdles in employing domestic help. Although they could all be encouraged to agonise over big issues like climate change or the world's poor, they were generally not politically motivated. They would joke about *Guardian* readers and the unwashed proletariat from time to time, but as long as politics didn't impinge too directly upon their lives, work or interests, they were content enough to let their political leaders carry on and do their jobs. Jonathan, however, could and would argue politics with any of them if the need arose and Ellie was often surprised by his knowledge of political issues and policy detail, his ready grasp of facts and figures and his single-minded determination to win any political argument.

Other fathers around the table were much like Jonathan, although he felt luckier than most of them. They all worked long hours in banking, insurance, commodity trading, law or the media, spent little quality time with their children and allowed their wives to organise their social lives. Exhausted by the time the weekend came around, they socialised with people leading similar lives and often drank too much at a Friday night dinner party and suffered for it on a long Saturday as they ferried their little darlings between rugby / ballet / fencing / drama / art / sculpture / mindfulness / judo / soccer or, for the very unlucky, horse riding. Sticking to a strict timetable they had been given by their wives over breakfast, they spent their waiting time sitting in their cars or drinking over-priced lattes in trendy coffee shops whilst reading the newspapers or, more probably, catching up on the week's unanswered emails.

For these fathers, Saturday afternoons were sometimes spent slumped in front of the TV watching sport for an hour or two if they were lucky, and a few times a year they were excused family duty to spend quality man-time at Stamford Bridge or Wembley or Twickenham. However, Saturday afternoons were far more likely to be spent in smart shops on the Fulham Road discussing interior design trends or home improvement ideas with the current builder of the moment. All houses were seen as works in progress and one new kitchen or loft extension in a street could start a small explosion of copy-cat development. Everyone in their social circle was over-extended financially although it was considered vulgar to talk about money and weak to admit any financial constraint. Most of them lived on the hope that the next bonus would pay off the growing debt mountain, or at least keep it manageable.

Saturday night would be a repeat of Friday; a dinner party locally or a restaurant on the west side of town, and Sunday would involve hangovers, child exercising, a social lunch and an evening slumped in front of the TV worrying about the start of the week ahead. For many of these fathers, the working week was more predictable and more stable than the weekend and many dreaded the role reversal of being bossed around for two days by their wives and children. For some of the wives, the weekends were similarly disconcerting. During the week they could dominate their domestic helpers and their children, fit in some shopping with girlfriends and then play host to their returning husbands in the evenings, leaving them to babysit once or twice a week for book club or mindfulness or high intensity gym evenings with girlfriends. At the weekend, there were more complications and juggling their husbands and social lives became stressful, especially if entertaining at home was on the agenda. Dinner parties were a competitive sport in certain areas of west London and to be assured of success it was essential to be organic, eclectic, innovative and locally sourced. Celebrity chef cookbooks were distinctly frowned upon. Wines had to be expensive and showy. It was stressful and exhausting for these wives, and they too would often be glad when the simpler regularity of weekdays returned their lives to normality.

The cottage helped Jonathan and Ellie escape some of these pressures, and a full weekend in the country, especially if they managed to escape from Richmond on a Friday night, helped keep them sane. Ellie noticed how Jonathan was closer to the boys on these country weekends and how he took as much pleasure from an entirely ordinary country pub lunch as a Michelin starred restaurant in town. He was happy working in the garden although he had no idea about plants or planting and could often be found undoing the good work of their locally sourced gardener. His childish delight at producing his first ever crop of broad beans was one of her happiest memories from these early family trips away.

At other, less happy, moments, Jonathan could be short with the boys and take himself off to his study for hours to escape their noise and exuberance. Although he loved them both, he sometimes struggled to cope with them on a daily basis and often seems to be fonder of them in abstract than in reality. On Ellie's girlfriend Saturdays he started slipping the nanny an extra £20 to take charge of the boys for a few hours whilst he went off and enjoyed the Saturday newspapers in a coffee shop or lunched with a similarly absconding colleague. Thus fortified, he would return home with a vengeance and lavish full attention on the boys until their bedtime.

As his career responsibilities grew, work started to intrude more and more into weekends. There were often two or three conference calls and trying to find a quiet place and a good mobile signal at the cottage was difficult, so that he might well spend an hour in the car on his phone talking to New York or LA. Sometimes he spent most of the weekend sitting in front of his laptop emailing his distant colleagues. On these weekends, he would often tell Ellie that this was the price they had to pay for all the other things that made their life so desirable. As she nosed the car back to London along an almost stationary M3, Ellie would reluctantly agree to his analysis and mentally start her own preparations for the week ahead.

Ellie started work again when Albee reached his third birthday. Although she wanted to stay working in the law, she was keen to work locally and have flexibility in her hours. She knew that all of the large law firms treated returning mothers badly and had several friends who were working fifteen hour days whilst trying to juggle motherhood at the same time. She was determined not to fall into this trap and so she changed direction dramatically and began to provide pro bono legal advice for a women's shelter in Kingston. This quickly expanded to also working for a homeless charity in Ealing and before long she was working four full days a week. She found herself completely dependent upon a succession of Polish and Czech nannies for childcare and school pick-ups. Despite the many challenges of nanny management, she thought that her work was far more interesting and rewarding than her corporate work in the City and felt she was putting something back through helping people a lot less lucky than herself. For the first time, she began to appreciate just how hard life could be for some people, many of them living less than half a mile from her own front door. A comfortable middle class upbringing, a smart day school in Sussex, followed by three years at Cambridge and a move into a legal graduate scheme at a top London law firm had done little to prepare Ellie for the harsher aspects of modern Britain and in those early days of volunteering she was often shocked by the things she encountered. Almost inevitably, her new work began to change

Ellie's views on life, politics and money. Although always a little to the left of Jonathan in her political thinking, she generally agreed with the broad thrust of the ideas he and others shared around the dining table from time to time. As her views began to change, she began to realise that her circle of friends knew little of the real world her new clients were forced to live in and had no concept of the challenges that many ordinary people faced in their daily lives.

Chapter 4

Jonathan didn't hear from GBNewsmedia for some days after his boardroom presentation. He was surprised to get a call from Drew Smith the CEO directly rather than Adam Robinson the headhunter.

'Jonathan. We've decided that your proposals for the channel, with some modification from us, are the best hope and most interesting avenue for us to explore. We've had Deloittes going through your business plans today and I have to say they are very impressed. Can you come in and see us this afternoon?'

Jonathan arrived at the Paddington HQ as requested. Ushered into the glass boardroom to meet Drew, he was surprised to see Adam there too; he had tried but failed to reach him after Drew's earlier call. Sitting alongside Adam was Tom Schalke, the American hedge fund manager who really called the shots at GBN. Whatever Tom decided, the other three hedge funders would agree to and, consequently, whatever Tom wanted to do, the board was powerless to resist. Although the four hedge funds owned only 38% of the public company between them, the rest of the shareholders were in effect without a voice. He had met Tom on three occasions before when Tangentially had advised his firm on a failed acquisition for a Spanish internet company. Tom had refused to meet the price Jonathan and his team suspected the company would demand and had walked away from the deal without a backwards glance. Unlike other billionaire hedge funders, Tom made no pretence of being interested in the visual arts or donating to struggling opera companies. He was interested in media, or rather, he was interested in media companies and deals that could make him money. In his late fifties and with a strong Brooklyn accent, there was no small talk with Tom. A heavily muscled man of six foot four, he looked as though a month on a health farm was the only thing that could prevent a second heart attack. His neck bulged over the top of his too-tight shirt collar. He was the only person in the room wearing a tie. He started speaking even before Jonathan sat down in the only vacant chair in the room.

'So, Jonathan, your presentation makes good sense to me, although if it fails, it will fail spectacularly badly. How do I prevent that?'

'You can't. There are only three reasons for the channels to fail. The first will be restricting the budget I need and that's why I have asked for your financial commitment to the channel as one of my employment terms. Number two is simple: am I the right person to lead the channel and make it happen? That's for you to decide. The third reason is the hardest to predict. The world is changing dramatically and pretty damned fast. We have to surf those changes and stay ahead of the wave. If we do that we prosper, if we don't, we drown. Can any media organisation do that? I don't know and I don't think anyone else does either.'

Tom shifted in his chair and stole a glance at Drew and Adam. 'We think your gameplay can lift us out of the hole we are in at the moment and we are ready to give you everything you need. We've sorted out your remuneration and benefits with Adam and we want you to start yesterday. I can talk to the backers of Tangentially to get you out of there quickly. What else do you need?'

'Unconditional support from the GBN newspapers and websites...'

'Done,' said Tom. He was interrupted by Drew.

'You know how hard it is to keep the editors in line on these things...'

'Drew, if you can't control your editors on this one I will get someone in here who can. It's a reasonable request and we will not take any prisoners. Make sure this happens. Jonathan, what else?'

'I've got a small team of five. They are all at the top of their game and I want to make job offers to all of them this week. Is that ok?'

'Done. Is that it?' Without waiting for an answer he stood up from his chair and, buttoning up his jacket, he advanced across the room and shook Jonathan firmly by the hand. Leaning in to him, he placed his other hand upon Jonathan's shoulder and said quietly, so that only Jonathan could hear, 'Don't fuck up'. Then in a louder voice for the benefit of the other two he added, 'If we can make this model work I want to expand it with local media partners right across Europe and maybe back to the States. Let's get going!' With that, he was out of the room and gone and the other two visibly relaxed at his exit.

'Shall we get some coffee and work through the detail?' said Drew, and without waiting for an answer, picked up the phone and ordered coffee and the Head of HR into the room.

'Bob, this is Jonathan. He's the new MD of television and will be hiring and firing like crazy when he arrives in a few weeks. He's the boss and he needs your help. It's your job to keep the HR problems off his back and make it all happen. I don't want any roadblocks appearing that might slow us down.'

The meeting wound on for twenty or so minutes as they discussed details before Jonathan called time by telling them he had another appointment across town that he could not afford to miss. He left the building with Adam but they were silent until they were well outside the glass and marble foyer.

'So, Adam, how did the money talk go?'

'I think you will be pretty pleased with the numbers. There's a lot tied into performance bonuses and big stock options that could make you rich if the share price moves in the right direction. Your base salary is about fifty percent up on your current earnings. As you requested, they've agreed to a car and driver on call and a big contribution to your pension fund as a welcome present. Everything works well. I will email you all the details and get going on the contract front for you. Yes?'

'Give me a few minutes to think it through. I want to make sure in my own mind that this is what I want. We both know this is the big job that will define my career. I just want to be sure it's the right move for me. I will give you a call.'

'I thought you had an important meeting?'

'No. I just wanted to bring the last one to a close at the right time.'

With that, Jonathan shook Adam by the hand and marched off quickly towards the canal side. Once by the water's edge, he slowed down and strolled along the towpath looking closely at the five or six brightly painted canal boats tied up alongside.

Adam watched him go and then reached inside his pocket for his mobile. He hit a speed dial key and said simply, 'Our man is in place. The plan is coming together.' Without any further discussion, he stabbed the phone to end the call and walked off in the opposite direction to find a taxi to take him back to Mayfair.

Jonathan was in no real doubt about taking the new job. He knew it would be a tremendous challenge and there was a reasonable chance of failure but it was a rare opportunity to create something new and something built entirely around him. Adam had helped him plan out the strategy for the channel, but the execution would be completely down to him and if he could make it work, or at least spin it to appear as if it was working well, he would be the biggest star in London media and could name his own price for one of the four or five big jobs in the industry around the world. Of course, it would mean more absences from Ellie and the children and less weekends away from London. There was no doubt about just how much hard work this project was going to be. Smiling to himself, he took out his phone and called Ellie. The call went to voicemail which presumably meant she was in a meeting with some poor unfortunate, he thought. When her recorded greeting had finished he left his message, 'It's all agreed. Big money and bonuses to follow. We will be rich. I'll call you again later. Bye honey.' He then texted Lottie.

Pack your bags we are moving again. Wandsworth is lovely at this time of year. Jx.

He then sent a shorter text to Adam.

Let's do it. Jonathan.

Messages sent, he used his new Uber app to request a ride back to Soho. Another thing I won't need to do when I move, he thought to himself, as a silver Prius appeared after a few minutes of waiting time.

***

The Circus channels were not based at GBN's swish Paddington headquarters but at a converted factory by the side of the Thames in what was traditionally the grittiest part of Wandsworth. The brick built early-Victorian factory was unusual in that it remained zoned only for industrial use and television just about qualified. Everything around about was in the process of being converted into, or knocked down to build, riverside apartments for wealthy foreigners who wanted a London property investment. For these new 'buy to leave' owners, the 'River Factory', as it was now called, was a modern blot on the landscape that echoed the area's original roots as London's tannery when local worthies had complained about the smell and the pollution leather-making had brought to what was then a leafy outskirt of the city. Many of those same land-owners had made fortunes when the streets around were swallowed up by rows of identical Victorian villas as London expanded across the river.

Now, you were as likely to hear Russian or Greek or a hundred other languages spoken on the streets of Wandsworth alongside English, and GBN was amazingly the biggest private sector employer locally. Unfortunately, few of the company's employees could afford to live in the borough and most commuted in from Leytonstone, Silvertown and other far flung corners of London's rapidly expanding canvas. Jonathan had visited the River Factory several times for industry functions and was drawn to the exposed brickwork, high ceilings and shabby industrial feel of the building.

The next six weeks passed in a blur. Tom Schalke was as good as his word and the private equity backers of Tangentially were remarkably amenable to his early departure. There was obviously some bigger picture between these private equity guys and they even agreed to the early release of Paul Kafferos to join him at GBN. A high-flying American was parachuted in to replace them both. Team Lomax took shape quickly, even though most of them worked two jobs during this period. Jonathan organised for Lottie to leave Tangentially within twenty four hours of his contract arriving and Team Lomax HQ was set up at her terraced house in Wandsworth, handily just half a mile from the River Factory. They covered the downstairs walls with lining paper and then with multi-coloured magic markers they devised channel strategies, hiring ideas and revenue models through the nights that followed. In addition to developing the media strategy, Lottie provided food, encouragement, occasional beds and floorspace alongside endless coffee to keep them all going.

When the six of them looked back on this period, they were all struck by their incredible energy and motivation and how they complemented each other so well to develop raw ideas into viable plans. Ben Zinneri, "Benzina", was particularly strong at finding logical flaws in their thinking and suggesting new ways of working, and Paul's intellect and strong knowledge of Conservative policy ensured they never deviated too far from their overall direction of travel. Carol could bring them all back to earth by pointing out their financial inconsistencies as she turned their scribbles and sometimes rambling expletives into something that resembled a manifesto; and quiet Tom Rabanski planned out the nuts and bolts of the channel's operation and timing. Even as tiredness overcame them, the six were reluctant to go to their respective homes and miss out on the energy that was being shared in Lottie's sitting room. Consequently, their various partners saw little of them in this period apart from brief trips home to nap or change their clothes.

As well as hiring the five team members of Team Lomax, Jonathan was busy using the GBN chequebook to entice some leading TV presenters away from their current employment. Using all his charm and persuasive powers, he wined and dined them, stroked their insecure egos and tried to persuade them to join him in a wonderful future where, even though the ratings might be smaller, their influence would be greater and the grass greener and their bank balances bigger. He succeeded with about fifty percent of the people he really wanted - which was considerably better than any of the team thought he would achieve.

Four weeks into their shadow roles, the media got hold of the emerging story from one of the presenters Jonathan had failed to persuade. Lottie had been waiting for this moment and her pre-agreed plan swung into action. Nothing was denied but nothing was revealed. Lottie announced that the new channel would be unveiled to the world in ten days' time, just three days before Jonathan officially started as the new MD of television. Of course, the news of major changes and new bosses threw the existing Circus channels into chaos as employees rightly feared for their jobs in this latest upheaval for the failing business. Although everyone knew there was a vacancy for the top job at Circus, none of the current employees had had any idea of the scale of the changes that would be taking place in the next few weeks. Jonathan had already established that not one of the existing management team would stay when he took over. Bob Jones, Head of HR, had plans in place for a swift and early exit for the whole management team and was offering jobs out to new employees almost as quickly as Jonathan identified and secured them.

The only senior person he didn't hire personally was Paddy Duffy, the new Finance Director, who was seconded from GBN's finance department and clearly there to keep more than one eye on the money as they laid waste to the existing order. Paddy reported not to Jonathan but to the PLC Finance Director and was a loyal and long-serving member of the group finance team. A softly spoken, thoughtful Irishman of thirty-eight, Patrick had thought he really only enjoyed playing rugby and drinking craft beer but, given this new degree of freedom and an inspirational figure like Jonathan to work for, he began to love his work too and over time he quietly made the journey over to Team Lomax, although he was careful to keep his new loyalties away from the prying eyes of the GBN board.

Jonathan's biggest success was to poach Angie Smith as Director of Television - effectively his number two and the day-to-day manager of the channel. Angie was a neurotic fifty-five year old television veteran who had worked for most of the major UK news operations. Acerbic, loud and foul-mouthed, Angie had moved to the UK from Melbourne thirty years ago but had never lost her accent or her ability to call a spade a fucking big shovel. She could drive a production team harder and better than anyone else in British television and inspired fierce loyalty from her team. She never appeared to sleep or eat but could drink her team under the table on a regular basis. Angie ran on nervous energy and had a rasping laugh that could frighten horses at thirty paces. Her major problem had always been that she ended up despising her immediate bosses, and in the later stages of her career, came to feel the same about authority figures generally. This had led to countless arguments, disciplinary meetings and hurried departures as her career lurched along under various despairing managers. Angie was a risk, but Jonathan knew that if he could control her, she would move heaven and earth to make the channel a success. As she was between jobs when he approached her, she was able to start immediately and her wide network of contacts meant that soon she was hiring key staff to work directly for her. Jonathan was happy to let her make all of her own important staffing decisions.

As the reveal date approached, Lottie ramped up the media suspense. Rival media owners were keen to find out more and quizzed current employees for insight. Unfortunately, they knew only what they were reading online and not much of that made any sense at all. There was speculation that the channels would be devoted to adult Manga-type cartoons (all this because GBN had unwisely made an investment in a Japanese cult feature film that had bombed at the box office), and an equally unlikely rumour that the channels would only show subtitled East European thrillers in an attempt to find a successor to Scandi Noir drama.

The night before his launch presentations, Jonathan made it home by eleven, early for him at this time. Ellie had already gone to bed after a long day with several needy clients and Jonathan quietly undressed and slipped into bed with her. She acknowledged his arrival with a grunt and then, waking more, asked him if he had written his presentation yet.

'You know how it is with me,' he said, 'I've got lots of notes and I will hoof the rest of it in the morning. I've got the staff presentation to do first and then an abbreviated version for the press and city analysts shortly afterwards.'

'I don't know how you manage to ad lib these speeches you make. I couldn't do it without a whole lot more preparation.'

'That's because you are a lawyer, darling, and I'm not,' he smiled and cuddled around her back, gently cupping her breast as she sank bank into sleep with an appreciative murmur of physical contentment.

Ellie had not been as enthusiastic as he had hoped when he detailed his plans for the new direction of the channel. She was worried about how much he was taking on his own shoulders and had a low opinion of GNB's newspaper business. She also disliked the political slant of the channel. His frequent absences didn't mean that Ellie hadn't made her views clear to Jonathan about the direction his new life was taking him. Unusually, they had argued several times about his long hours, with Ellie asking what was the point of all this money if he was never around to see the children and she was required to do everything as if she were a single parent.

Jonathan tried and failed to fall asleep. Normally he could sleep anywhere and had a great knack of switching off from work problems. But not tonight. He tossed and turned, thinking through his speech, but most of all wondering to himself about what he was taking on with the new channel. What made him think he could do something as radical and different as this, and with such limited resources too? After what seemed an eternity, he crawled out of bed at five am and slumped into the shower to wake himself up. He looked in on the sleeping boys and then, dressed in his favourite suit, went downstairs to find some coffee before the GBN pool driver arrived at six to take him to the Riverside Club for his morning swim.

Although he had yet to formally start his new job, GBN had provided a car and driver for him from the moment he signed his new contract. In the mornings, he would have a pool driver and a car from the GNB HQ, but from 11am until whatever time he finished, he would have a dedicated driver who would work only for him. He had liked Eddie from the first meeting and found time to take him to dinner at one of his favourite Sardinian restaurants where he knew he could talk freely without being overheard. Eddie, prematurely balding and chubby through spending too much time sitting down in his expensively upholstered Mercedes, listened attentively as Jonathan - he had insisted that Mr Lomax was his father's name - explained the rules of the game going forwards.

'There will be lots of people who contact you trying to find me when I don't respond to them. I don't care who they are, they must learn to understand that you will never put them through, take messages or tell them where I am or what I'm doing. We will be doing lots of high level meetings and many of them will be secret. You can politely but firmly tell them I will return their calls if they text me and no more. That's everyone, even my wife or Drew Smith. No exceptions.

'You will also be spending a fair bit of time in the River Factory waiting for me during the day. You will almost certainly hear stuff from the staff and if it's relevant to the business I want you to feed it back to me. If there are things going on I should know about then you must tell me. I don't mean grubby little affairs between workmates, but real grumpiness, or managers who can't earn the trust of their teams or anything where I can intervene to make the operation run more smoothly. Anything like that. I also want you to read all of the newspapers and then as we sit in traffic you can tell me what you think about things going on in the UK and around the world. I think we shall get on famously and I shall make sure that you have a great time on this job. Now, you look like you are struggling a bit with this menu. Do you like seafood? Yes? Well then I recommend the stuffed polpetto and the linguine granchi. That's what I'm going to have. How about a decent glass of Gavi di Gavi to go with it? Just the one as you are driving. Now, whilst we wait for the waitress, tell me why you think it is that Chelsea are doing so badly in defence this season, I'm completely at a loss to understand why things are going so wrong.'

By the end of the evening, Eddie was a fully paid up member of Team Lomax and went home to his wife with the pass for Jonathan's rarely-used three season tickets at Stamford Bridge in his pocket: 'Why don't you keep these and manage them for me. I hate to see them go unused and I never have time to go there these days. I will probably use them for staff treats from time to time but you can fill the seats with your friends and keep them warm for me.'

When Jonathan emerged from his swim, it was Karl, one the GBN early-start drivers, who delivered him to the River

Factory where he had a meeting with the Circus TV executive team before his presentation to all staff. It was only 7.30 am when he arrived at his new office and, after closely inspecting his letter of authority, the security guard looked surprised to see his new boss arriving at this time in the morning. Although the channels were already on air, all the programming at this time of day was pre-recorded and, with a robotic play-out system running the shows, there were very few staff in the building. Jonathan wandered around the almost empty studios and found his bearings. He admired the views over the river and thought of the offices he would have torn down and spaces re-arranged upon his arrival. Although he would make some significant changes, he had to admit that, physically, this was a pretty slick operation, and ideal for the type of television he intended to make.

The existing six-strong management team arrived at eight accompanied by Drew Smith, there to lend authority to the morning's proceedings and to introduce Jonathan, alongside Bob Jones who was there to manage exits. Assembled in the large boardroom, the team listened as Jonathan explained the requirements for the new channel and then told them all that they would be leaving the company that morning.

'It's quite simple,' he said, 'you've tried your best and it hasn't worked. We need to do something new and we all feel it is best if we bring in an entirely new team to make it work. GBN will honour all of your contractual entitlements and give you generous exit terms and outplacement help. You will all need to sign new non-disclosure agreements but from today you will all be free agents and we wish you the very best. Bob will take you through the paperwork now and Paddy Duffy will take over the day to day running of the place until I arrive in a short while. Thank you.'

He turned and left the room. Long experience of firings had taught him that keeping the initiative was vital and that leaving all of the questions to a subordinate usually took the temperature out of the meeting. He hoped it was the last but one mass firing he would have to do in this building.

He then sat down in the canteen area to wait for the staff meeting. Actually, it wasn't much of a canteen. There were big long oak benches and trestle tables and some coffee and snack vending machines lining one wall. This will be the first place I change, he thought, as he watched the workforce start to arrive, most having shunned the low-cost coffee available in the building and carrying large-lidded mugs full of coffee flavoured milk from Starbucks or Costa. Some glanced in his direction, not sure who this guy in a suit was, others recognising him from the stories in online news sheets and social media. Drew Smith came and found him just before nine, and together they walked into the main studio which was the only place large enough to accommodate the nearly three hundred people working for the three channels.

After Drew's warm introduction, Jonathan stood up and addressed the hushed and expectant audience. There were lots of young and worried faces in front of him and he smiled at them all to show he was not the grim reaper about to throw them all out onto the street.

'You all know that I'm the new guy that Drew and the Board have entrusted to lead the channel going forwards. I'm now going to tell you of our plans and ideas and, at a high level, how everyone fits into this new world.

'Despite everyone's best efforts, the Circus channels have not been performing and we are going to radically change them to make them work. Nearly all of our effort is going to go into one channel and this channel is going to shake up the world. We live in confusing times. We are seeing the rise of populism right across Europe and the Americas and no-one knows where it might end. It's possible we are looking at the end of democracy and we just don't realise it yet. The ruling elites are at a loss to understand, never mind counter, these new narratives as they dominate our political discussions today. We intend to become a major part of that new narrative. Cutting through the incoherent shouting of social media and the relentless carcass-picking of rolling news channels, the Board and I believe there is a real gap in the television market for a channel that tells viewers straight what is happening in the country and across the world. The new channel will deal with complex subjects and look for real answers for real people. That's why we are calling the new channel CATALYST. Popular but not populist, honest but not complicated, we will talk intelligently with viewers and encourage their interaction with what we produce.

'We live in a world where the reporting on news and current affairs quickly becomes the story, and how stories are controlled and shaped by us, and how the twenty four hour news cycle weakens politicians and strengthens the news media is part of our burden today. We must be very careful to make sure we are always doing the right thing. In 1946, the German scholar Ernst Benda, who would later become the head of Germany's Constitutional Court, was looking at the rise of communism as Russia occupied East Germany where he lived. Fresh from the horrors of Nazism, he had helped found the youth wing of the Christian Democrats and he developed a new doctrine. I quote. "Simple truths: be honest, do not lie, be fair to your political opponents, be just, deliver social justice." I can't think of a better way to describe the channel we intend to build. Seventy years on, it's a dialogue that is more needed now than ever. It's also a warning for us, however, because within a year the Christian Democrats were snuffed out in East Germany by the communists and Benda had fled. I don't look over at Drew and see Eric Honecker by the way' (nervous laughter around the room), 'but there are powerful forces that will not enjoy us shedding light on complex areas that they would prefer to remain as crude slogans that they can manipulate.

'We are in a unique position in that we are part of a public company; we are not owned by a foreign media magnate or corporation or, as in the case of the BBC, financially fearful of the Government of the day. We are responsible to our shareholders and to our staff and we can take risks that others would not. Of course, we face challenges too: we don't have a fraction of the resources of Sky News or BBC News and we will not attempt to compete with them. There will be no late-night live crosses from reporters standing outside windswept offices trying to look relevant. We will not follow the tyranny of the rolling news cycle. Instead, we will be taking the stories apart, explaining them and encouraging our viewers to think through the implications, whilst at the same time keeping them entertained. We will have some of the highest profile presenters around and we will also be growing our own talent who will become the stars of tomorrow. We've already recruited some key players and whilst I want to keep most of them secret for the time being I can tell you that Melissa Bell, chief political editor of ITV News, will be joining us from day one of the new operation.'

This did produce gasps and whispers from the audience. Melissa Bell had brought glamour and passion to her news reporting and, despite her reputation for being a complete bitch, she was a catch, a name that would help put the channel on the map. Jonathan had recruited her using Lottie's inside information that Melissa's husband was in serious financial difficulties. Jonathan had offered to double her salary to sort out the money problems and suggested putting her name on a prime time show to massage her considerable ego. This two-pronged approach had sealed the deal.

'Of course, you all want to know "what does this mean for me?" I understand that and will attempt to explain. You will all have to live and breathe this channel to stay here. It will be all-consuming. You will look back at this launch time and describe it to friends as the most exciting and challenging period of your adult working life. You will forge friendships with colleagues that will last a lifetime. You will never work as hard again. It will sometimes be fun; it will often be tough; it will always be relentless. That's the nature of the beast. If you can see your future here, then my new management team want to sit down and discuss your career and your ideas. If you don't think this is for you, and that's fine too, now is the time to decide and then Bob and his guys will organise your departure, paying up your contracts, writing your references, etcetera. You will leave with our good wishes; we know this new channel is not for everyone. You should know that the current management team – you might have noticed their absence already – are leaving today and again, they go with our thanks and our best wishes for their future.

'There's a whole lot to take in and we will aim to keep you all as informed as we possibly can over the coming days. I will be here in eleven days and the new channel, which will by then have a clear structure and identity, will launch in seven weeks' time. There's a huge mountain to climb before then. I will take questions on another day soon, but that's all for today. Thank you.'

With that summary, Jonathan walked out of the studio with Drew at his shoulder. Later that morning, he gave a truncated version of the same presentation to journalists and analysts and Drew played more of a role here, talking up the importance of Catalyst to the PLC and how he had great confidence in Jonathan's ability to deliver something radically different and financially successful. They split up after the second presentation ended and Jonathan found himself in the back of Eddie's Mercedes wondering if he really could do everything that was being asked of him.

The next ten days carried on in much the same pattern: working two jobs and getting no sleep. Lottie had organised several feature interviews and Jonathan had to fit these in around his many other commitments. Although used to dealing with journalists, these were difficult meetings as Jonathan needed to project positivity without revealing anything important about Catalyst that would detract from the launch itself. This meant that whilst the first couple of journalists were happy to write mainly glowing personal profile pieces, the later interviewers wanted something more meaty to add to the story and there was nothing more that could be revealed before the launch. Jonathan was forced to name a couple more high-profile presenters just to get journalists to bite on the rest of the story.

Jonathan assiduously avoided meeting any politicians in this period. Lottie and Carol had been flooded with requests for meetings and drinks and dinner invitations from special advisers, political PR's, party apparatchiks and elected politicians but had, as per Jonathan's instructions, turned down every meeting, saying that it would be inappropriate to have meetings before Jonathan actually started work for GBN. He did accept a lunch invitation from Adam Robinson, however, and after a brief celebratory glass of champagne, Adam, as usual dressed in a suit designed for someone slimmer, turned immediately to a discussion of Conservative politics.

'Now you have the channel roadmap out there, I suspect you and your team are besieged by politicians of all shapes and sizes?' Without waiting for a reply he went on, 'I know that Lottie is a great PR for you but I'm thinking that I can help here too. As you know, I'm pretty close to the centre of power in the Conservative Party these days and I know where most, if not all, of the bodies are buried. So, for instance, Lottie might be very pleased if the current Justice Secretary asks you for lunch, whereas I can tell you that the PM despises him and is determined to have him out at the next re-shuffle. I can also ensure that you meet some of the really important people who will shape the future even if they aren't in the public eye.'

'You mean the grey men who really control Britain.' Jonathan laughed, but he knew Adam moved in the highest circles of Westminster power, and if he was to succeed, he would need Adam, or someone like him, to help him enter this closed circle of influence.

'Of course, that's all overdone in left-wing conspiracy theories but it's true that many of the most important people in the Conservative party have never stood for election and never intend to. I can get you in to see these people and you can find out what is really going on.'

Lunch broke up with an agreement that Jonathan would brief Lottie and that she and Adam would liaise to ensure Jonathan's political meetings were the right ones and taking place at the right time. Yesterday's buffoon could be tomorrow's foreign secretary was how Adam described the importance of timing in politics. As he left the restaurant, Adam took out his phone and texted

Lomax: all good and under control.

Pressing send, he watched the screen as the green send line moved from left to right and the text was reported as sent to "Prime Minister, private phone". He wondered how his message would be received. He did not expect and nor did he get a reply.

Chapter 5

Day one at the River Factory was a blur of meetings and decisions against the backdrop of a dull January mist and intermittent snow showers. Carol had arrived there a couple of weeks before Jonathan and had set up his office and generally organised things for him. His large office now sported a large chrome Gaggia expresso machine on top of the drinks fridge and a long leather sofa, designed to be long enough to cope with Jonathan's outstretched frame as he fully expected to pull frequent overnighters as the channel took shape. Ben, Paul, Angie, Tom and Lottie had all started in the weeks before and had taken over offices ranged around Jonathan's. The one exception was Angie; he found her an office at the far end of the building near the main studio space that he felt would give her some room away from him so that she could rage in relative privacy from time to time. Her office was also soundproof enough for her to tear strips off unfortunate staff without the rest of the company hearing her unparalleled choice of Australian expletives. Paddy's office was along the corridor in the middle of the Finance Department and Andy Smith the Sales Director was in the office next to Paddy. Jonathan had little time for the excuses that adsales teams usually brought to meetings to explain their underperformance and had outsourced television advertising sales to Sky. If he delivered ratings and page views, Sky delivered revenue. Andy's job was simply to meet advertisers and agencies and talk up the channel to encourage them to spend money and to put occasional pressure onto Sky to do everything else.

One of Jonathan's first tasks on day one was to meet with Paddy and Andy and break the news to Andy that he would be reporting to Paddy from now on. Everybody wanted face time with him, he told them, and he just didn't have the bandwidth. Paddy would be in charge of money, both spending it and bringing it in. He could see Andy saw this as a personal slight but thought to himself that he didn't really care, there were legions of adsales managers out there struggling to cope with how technology was making their jobs redundant. They had enjoyed good lifestyles in the past but Google and advanced advertising algorithms were taking over and soon it would all be done by machines. Bring it on, he thought.

Lottie had taken over all of the press and publicity for the channels and had recruited a small team to help her cope. She still saw her main preoccupation as promoting Jonathan personally whilst her team was fully dedicated to the channel. At his first meeting with them all, Jonathan was surprised that Amber, Lottie's new deputy, a redhead with a small, slight figure just like her boss, was almost a clone. He liked her pushy personality and her warm smile and thought, if these two can work together for a few years we will not fail for a lack of publicity. He left that meeting feeling good.

By the time seven pm came around, Jonathan was ready to leave. The stress of the first day in the office had taken its toll and he was tired, concerned by the amount they still had to achieve and worried about the resources they were missing. He had promised Ellie dinner to celebrate his first day in the new job and he was ready to go. Leaving his team hard at work and with the River Factory production crew at full stretch on the existing channel's doomed output, he called Eddie from the canteen and together they drove back to Richmond in silence to pick up Ellie and then go on to dinner at her favourite restaurant in Barnes.

Ellie had gone to a real effort with her outfit, he thought, as she emerged from the house looking both elegant and desirable in a short dark dress and coat and wearing her highest heels. He climbed out of the car and greeted her with a kiss and a lingering hug on the pavement. He complimented her warmly on her appearance and received a pretty smile to show she was pleased her efforts had not gone unnoticed. They had spent no quality time together for the last four weeks and had lots to catch up on. Carol had chosen the Barnes restaurant over flashier rivals for exactly this reason, and as they sat down at the table with a dry martini each, early conversation was mostly given over to Ellie giving Jonathan information on the children's progress, both good and bad, alongside the domestic updates he had missed in his enforced absence. By the time they had finished their starters they had worked through this essential information exchange and were ready to really talk. Helped along by a quickly gulped glass of white burgundy, Ellie began.

'You know how much I worry about this new job of yours. I worry about how hard it is for you and how you might burn out, but I also worry that if you are successful you will help to prolong the future of this Government, and God knows I see the dark side of what their policies mean. So, I'm in a real trap, darling. Our friends think you are the new face in securing the future of Conservative Britain and I worry that might be true because I know how good you are at achieving things. At a time when we need more compassion and more money at the bottom end of society, we are on a path to do less and less and the Government panders to the loony wing of the Tory party in order to keep their majority intact. It's very frightening and I don't want you to become part of that right wing cabal that appears to be running this country. I'm sorry; I don't want to be making a speech, you know I'm no good at that sort of thing, but I do worry and we do need to talk about this stuff.' Running out of steam, she paused and looked at him for a response.

'Darling, you know I'm just as scared as you are by the rise of the extreme right in this country and the channel will be one way of redressing the balance so that the sensible middle way gets a voice again. We can't depend upon a bunch of useless politicians to win arguments anymore and so we have to look at new ways of combating the populist nutters before they take over the asylum. Everyone has to realise that the old ways and the old loyalties are meaningless these days. Outsiders are taking over the debate and whilst that can be good it can also be terrifying. I don't think I could do anything more important than this job and if I can make it work editorially and financially, and that's a big if, then I will really have done something worthwhile with my life. Apart from you and the boys of course, that goes without saying. Enough speechifying though, let's have another glass and toast to us and how lovely you look tonight. We are so very lucky. To us.'

They clinked glasses and the rest of the evening's conversation lightened as they unwound together through the main course and the coffee that followed.

At the end of the evening as Jonathan waited for the credit card machine to arrive, he said, 'Let's try and do this every couple of weeks. You know the next twelve months will be a nightmare and we need to spend some quality time together. I'm going to have to work every weekend for the next few months - Sunday looks like a really important day for us - and I'm not going to be home early any night unless it's in the diary like tonight, so let's hold onto these special occasions and remember why we are doing all of this.'

As Eddie drove them the short distance back to Richmond, Jonathan caressed Ellie's thigh and, finding no resistance there, explored further until Ellie's hand stopped him. She smiled and kissed him warmly and later, when they were safely inside, the babysitter paid and chauffeured home by Eddie, he undressed her quickly in the kitchen and they had urgent sex across the dining table. It was a long time since anything like that happened and, inspired, they went to bed and made further passionate and gentle love for an unusually long time, even though it was a school night and they would both need to be up before dawn.

'We must do this more often,' said Jonathan before he fell asleep and Ellie wondered if he meant dinner and sex or just sex and thought she really must make more of an effort to get him away from work and win some time back for just the two of them. And more time with the boys too. She wondered about how she was going to achieve this as he was so focussed on getting everything right with this new job and that meant family life and her needs were becoming ever more difficult to fit in. As Jonathan lay sleeping contentedly beside her, Ellie's last thought before sleep was that she must try and get up extra early in the morning and retrieve her lacy underwear from the kitchen floor before the boys came down for breakfast.

The next few days at the River Factory continued as a kaleidoscope of meetings and hirings and firings as the new order was established and the old one swept away. Paul and Ben presented their detailed editorial strategy to the team and Tom revealed his plans for scheduling on the channel and online video players. It was all beginning to take shape but time was short and the workload frightening. Not one of the management team was leaving before midnight. Angie was a whirling dynamo striding through the factory shouting instructions and demands and rubbishing proffered artwork, copy and ideas with monotonous and profane regularity. If Jonathan ever had a chance to sit back and think about progress he would have been mostly pleased but it wasn't until his Friday afternoon meeting with Group CEO Drew that he had a chance to draw breath.

'I think things are going quite well Drew,' he said, 'I'm sure Paddy will have told your finance people that we are managing to stick within the budget - just, and we are migrating from one team of people to another and making that work. It's hard but there's a real sense of energy about the place and I feel optimistic about the future. It will be a bit rough around the edges on the first few nights and we will inevitably change things around as we learn from our mistakes but on the whole we are doing better than I thought we might at this stage.'

'From here in Paddington it all looks something of a hurricane down in Wandsworth. As you know, you have my complete trust and I'm counting on you to deliver. My biggest fear - and this was shared by a City analyst I lunched with yesterday - is will the channel find an audience of any real size and will it ever make money? I know the projections look OK but there's an awful lot riding on your success and the company share price is the most important. How do I sell the dream to analysts that this will be a commercial as well as an editorial success?'

'You know that the sort of channel we are making here can never be a ratings winner, but that's not why you agreed to it in the first place,' Jonathan countered. 'We will be in profit within two years and our daily reach will be bigger than the newspapers in the group in a similar timeframe. If we can follow Tom Schalke's model and syndicate this channel concept across Europe with other media partners, we will have a roaring success on our hands. Why don't you put me in front of analysts to help with these questions?'

'I'm afraid we have a Board policy of only allowing PLC directors to speak directly to analysts and advisers. That came after a couple of editors made fools of themselves and us, so I would need to get approval from the Board before agreeing to that idea. I'm not against doing that. In the meantime, can you draw up a crib sheet of positive answers so that I can drum them into the heads of my fellow directors? TV is all anyone in the City wants to talk about at the moment; you are creating quite a stir.'

The meeting broke up shortly afterwards, with Drew heading off for a weekend with his wife buying art in Paris and Jonathan heading back to the River Factory for a long night of rehearsals for what he hoped would be the prime show on the channel, snappily titled "Tonight with Melissa Bell". So far, everything about the show, from the host's test performances through to the set design and the entertainment interludes, had been a disaster and the production team were tearing their hair out whilst Angie was incandescent about the lack of progress. Jonathan had personally had to beg Melissa to give up a Friday night to put in some extra rehearsal time and it was vital to get a semblance of order into the show. Apart from anything else, the show featured heavily in their launch promotions and Melissa had been interviewed by most of the UK's media who were excited to learn about her new role. She had even done an underwear shoot for GQ. PR Amber had ridden shotgun on all of these press meetings and reported back that the GQ shoot had been the easiest as Melissa was only required by the photographer to keep smiling and her mouth shut - and it was when Melissa talked that trouble really began.

'She has no control,' Amber reported, 'She bigs up her ability to get guests on the channel just through the power of her name, for heaven's sake. Journalists are going away believing we will be seeing Henry Kissinger, Vladimir Putin and the tooth fairy all on her show in the same week!'

Everyone knew that the real problem with Melissa's show was Melissa. She had made her name as a key journalist on ITV News, breaking big political news stories and using her undoubted physical charm to seduce politicians and viewers alike. The problem was that she was good in small bursts; two minute pieces to camera were her forte but anchoring a one-hour show four times a week needed a different skill set. She had to learn how to share the screen with her guests and give them a chance to shine. Jonathan was stepping in to make this happen. He suspected that it would be a long night. He was stuck in Friday night traffic for quite a while heading back from Paddington, and rehearsals were already well underway when he arrived so he stood at the back of the control room and watched the stand-in guests - spare members of staff pretending to be politicians - making conversation with Melissa. After just four or five minutes of chat, Angie burst on to set, stopping everyone in their tracks.

'Mel, darling, you've just got to stop dominating your guests like that; you've really got to give the poor fuckers a chance to speak.'

'But, Angie, it's clear they don't know as much as I do about this.'

'They are only stand-ins, darling. Just pretend you have the Foreign Secretary in that chair and try to look interested when he talks.'

'I definitely know more about everything than he does, believe me. All he knows is how much he wants to shag me.'

It was time to intervene. Jonathan walked onto set and asked everyone to take five. He took Melissa by the arm and gently led her to the edge of the studio floor. 'Mel, darling, is it really true that you know more about politics than most front-line politicians?'

'Of course it is,' she haughtily replied, 'I've a first in PPE from Oxford, I've reported on politics all of my life and I'm not held back by special advisers and PR's telling me what the party wants to hear. Most of them are pretty useless and just rabbit out what they are told. They are terrified of the whips and their voters and the media.'

'In that case, why don't we turn the whole show around? Why don't we get politicians, and not just politicians but celebrities and viewers too, to ask you questions of real importance and get you to answer them thoughtfully and at whatever length you want, right down the barrel of the lens. Your politics fit the brief of the channel and we might get some extraordinary debates, the politicians couldn't help themselves from challenging you and you would wipe the floor with them. We can get a couple of high powered researchers working flat out to give you the ammo you need and by limiting each week to a few subjects we can stay on top of the workload. What do you think?'

Stopped in her tracks for a moment by Jonathan's outburst, she visibly thought it through and then finally responded. 'It's brilliant, I will be the centre of things and the viewers will get real answers to issues with all of the politics knocked to one side. The only flaw I can see is that I will never be able to work as a journalist again, having crossed the great divide and become a pundit.'

'This will be such a success that I don't think you need worry about your career.'

He gathered the team around him and explained what he wanted to try.

Angie was the first to get her head around the changes and smiled at Jonathan whispering, 'You clever fucker. I can see why you get paid the big bucks.'

They rolled the prototype credits again and straight-away saw that the new show could work. True to her word, Melissa really did know her stuff and took no prisoners. When they had some real guests, and it was always easy to get politicians anxious for broadcast time, she would get some real opposition and occasionally lose an argument but she wouldn't be an easy person to beat. This could be a winning show. It would provide endless tabloid and broadsheet fodder and that ongoing publicity would drive ratings. He gave some more instructions to the production team and then thought he would leave them to get on without him.

'Mel, Angie. Come and find me when you've had enough and we'll crack a bottle of champagne to celebrate. Well done, everybody; let's get this show up and running.' With that, he left the studio and returned to his office. There was a mountain of other stuff he could be doing and he wanted to let Angie control the actual production of the show; he must be careful not to try and do everything himself.

Sitting in his office with just his laptop and angle-poise illuminating the otherwise dark space, he attended to the huge pile of emails that needed reading and responding to, invoices requiring signature, and projections and forecasts from all of the departments. There was a week of work just here, he thought to himself, and I've probably only got an hour before Mel and Angie arrive demanding praise and reassurance in equal measure. He clicked open the first important email.

Chapter 6

Launch day arrived with Jonathan reckoning that only about four of the main shows were really suitable for viewing, but he felt that at least they fitted into a coherent schedule, and with work and some re-arrangements would all be better after a few episodes on air. Luckily, or more probably thanks to Lottie and Amber's efforts, Melissa's show was getting all of the publicity and they had been able to book both the Home Secretary and the leader of the Liberal Democrats onto the opening night's show. If that went well, all the other shows could have some time to grow and no-one would notice their shortcomings for a little while. He had persuaded Drew to postpone the launch party until the end of the first week, he had worked his magic on every television journalist he knew, and he had everyone rehearse their shows until they were at least technically proficient. Everyone was dog-tired and only the adrenaline of launch was keeping people going. He knew from experience that night two was going to be the real test as people came down off their launch highs and tiredness caught up with them. A television channel was an insatiable animal and every day would create a new series of challenges to overcome.

The first new show went on air at 3pm as the team aimed for a quiet introduction to their new roster of programmes. The new schedule of pre-recorded shows, channel idents and graphics went off fairly smoothly through the early evening as they headed towards the 8pm start for Melissa's live show.

Team Lomax had all kept themselves busy as the pre-recorded shows went to air, but now, as the clock counted down to the show that would define their launch, all of them started to congregate together in the boardroom as they had been, quite rightly, banned from the control room by Angie. Jonathan was hosting the Home Secretary and the Lib Dem's leader in the Green room and trying to put them at their ease with the unusual format they would shortly face.

'Just think of Melissa as an everywoman,' he said, 'She will lead on the big issue of the day, control of immigration, and develop ideas that could form some sort of future policy. You have the luxury of shooting her ideas down and, as you have been told, she will expect that and refine her thinking to meet your criticisms. It will freewheel from there and, who knows, we may even end up with something that can work. We will have viewer interaction in real-time along the way so you can see how the public responds to the ideas. As she is leading you into these areas, you can leave your party politics behind and argue about her ideas, using the public's response as a guide if you wish. No-one's here to score points off each other or do each other down, just to see if we can unlock thorny problems with some new and different thinking.'

Both participants looked somewhat puzzled and apprehensive and were probably thinking they should have listened to their advisers and not volunteered for the first episode of an unknown show with a difficult and fiendishly bright presenter like Melissa.

As the credits rolled (the show name had morphed into a much simpler "Melissa"), the noise in the boardroom dropped and anxious faces watched as Melissa introduced herself and her guests with a warmth and friendliness that surprised them all, even Angie who had spent days trying to get her star to smile more and frown less. As the show rolled into its first pre-recorded segment they all glanced at each other: perhaps it was going to be alright and it could actually work as a format. By 9pm, they were triumphant. Melissa had been brilliant and had coaxed some real issues out and moved the Home Secretary much further along than a traditional format would have achieved. The Lib Dem's leader had been both something and nothing but that was OK as she was really just there as filler anyway. Melissa and her production crew entered the boardroom to cheers and applause from the assembled team and very quickly Jonathan was opening champagne and toasting the success of the launch night. The Home Secretary was putting on a brave face and congratulating everyone whilst surreptitiously looking at the steady stream of emails and Whats Apps from Conservative Central Office. Government policy had shifted just a little bit during tonight's show and that was all the team needed to declare that "Melissa" was a media success. It was true that the viewer contribution had been poor and unashamedly right wing - and more than a little racist, but as Jonathan argued in his impromptu speech, you can't get everything right on day one and, most importantly, Melissa was a star in the making. Relief rather than alcohol was the intoxicant of the evening and by the time Newsnight reported on the success of the opening night, the team were cheering every single comment, positive or not. It was party time at the River Factory.

Jonathan made sure there was enough, but not too much, to drink and quietly left the party and returned to his office where he started to grapple with the hundreds of emails that had arrived during the day. He concentrated on ones from journalists looking for information and background who had dared to circumvent Lottie and Amber. He wanted to reward them for their direct approach and make sure they had the information they needed to write their pieces in time for their deadlines. He had been quietly writing away for an hour or so when there was a knock on the door and a slightly tipsy Melissa entered his office.

'Jonathan, darling, it's been such a night. I really think we have something here, don't you? Just between us, were you happy with the show and my performance?'

As usual, the insecurity of the performer was all too evident in her and Jonathan took the proffered glass of champagne and sat down on the sofa next to his new star.

'Melissa, my lovely, that was terrific. Just wait until the newspapers follow up the story tomorrow. You were wonderful and, just as you said, you led those politicians right down the garden path to the point where they ended up agreeing with you and making new policy on the hoof. It was fabulous and you were wonderful.'

'Oh, darling, you are too kind.' She leant forward and kissed him on the cheek and as she did so he felt her hand gently grasp his thigh. She whispered into his ear, 'After all that excitement and a few glasses of champagne, I'm feeling rather randy. How about we slope off and celebrate somewhere quieter in more style and with fewer clothes on? You know I've always had a soft spot for you.'

Alarm bells were ringing loudly as Jonathan stumbled over his excuses, 'Melissa, I can't think of anything I would like to do more. You know you are a very beautiful woman and I'm very attracted to you. I'm terribly flattered that you would even consider me. But you know, we might both regret it in the morning. We are both married and all that and colleagues and it could be a real mistake. Let's instead celebrate your success with some dinner. How about that sweet little Greek place in Kensington that you like? I will get Eddie to bring the car around and after dinner he can drive you back to Chiswick before taking me home. We've got it all to do again tomorrow.'

She smiled in a tipsy agreement. Crisis averted and her ego protected, Jonathan switched off his laptop and escorted the slightly unsteady Melissa towards the lifts. Christ on a bike, he thought, as he pressed the down button, I didn't see that coming. Day one, and already struggling with the bloody talent. He was careful, in the lift, in the car and in the restaurant, to keep a small physical space between himself and Melissa, whilst all the time lauding her performance and her genius. He made sure she was delivered safely into the somewhat reluctant arms of her property developer husband and then headed home where Ellie was already fast asleep after a difficult day at the housing charity.

He switched on the laptop in his study and saw that Lottie had compiled all of the early newspaper reviews into a single email and had circulated them to all of the management of the company. Broadly, the coverage was good, especially for Melissa's show, with the *Mail* and the *Express* leading the way in praising her plain speaking and non-political approach. The *Guardian* and the *Independent* were a bit sniffy, but that was to be expected, and the *Times* was sitting on the fence, no doubt waiting for word from on high to see what position it should take upon this potential media competitor.

There were also congratulatory emails from Drew, Tom Schalke, Adam Robinson and a dozen other high profile names from the world of politics and media. Now that day one was over, he could begin a slow transition from worrying about the programmes all day long to working his political contacts and making sure the channel had real access to decision makers. He could then start making the news rather than just recycling political stories like everyone else. He wrote short but personal congratulatory emails to Angie, Amber, Melissa, Ben, Paul, Tom and Carol and then a rather longer email to Lottie. Broadly satisfied by day one, he switched off his laptop and quietly crept up the stairs, as usual using the spare bathroom so as not to wake Ellie, before he crept silently into bed with his sleeping wife.

Chapter 7

The first few weeks on air sped by almost without a second glance. Jonathan was splitting his time between multiple meetings at the River Factory and endless meetings with Conservative politicians, apparatchiks, advisers, grandees, pollsters and the recently retired and ennobled. There was no problem getting meetings; indeed, the real problem was that everyone wanted some of Jonathan's time, and having made a conscious decision to concentrate upon the Government, the other political parties were increasingly anxious at being left out and ever more noisy in their demands for access. Let them stew, thought Jonathan, they need to realise they are not that important and when I do take time to see them I will start at the very top and ration my time with them so they learn the rules of the new game.

In truth, Jonathan was being stretched almost to breaking point. He was in the office by 7.30 am and rarely home before midnight. The only time he had to himself was his morning swim and he came more than ever to relish that thirty minutes of exercise where he could switch off and just concentrate upon powering through his distance target with one eye on the clock to make sure he was keeping his speed up. Lottie had asked if she could meet him at the Riverside club every morning so she could have an uninterrupted twenty minutes with him in the car on the way to Wandsworth but Jonathan had pushed back; he needed that time to consider the day ahead, clarify his thinking about the big issues and, increasingly, use Eddie as a sounding board for his latest ideas. He compromised with Lottie: he would meet her in the independent coffee shop around the corner from the office and she could have her twenty minutes whilst he spooned up some granola or porridge and enjoyed his one and only cup of coffee of the day.

Occasionally, breakfast meetings with politicians got in the way of this routine, but even then Jonathan would find himself in an inferior coffee shop near to some Westminster hotel being briefed by Lottie on the meeting ahead.

Angie was completely dominant in the office. She ruled the production teams with a mixture of fear, charm and sheer bloody-mindedness that had Jonathan looking on in amazement. He had asked her to do the impossible and she just got on with it, and if the teams couldn't get it done she would just do it herself. She took no prisoners and several new starters were summarily fired with little regard for consequence or HR policy. She often reminded him of a rampaging elephant as she marched across the office, expletives flying and anguish written across her face as she dealt with the latest problem that dared to cross her path. Paul and Ben's editorial influence as editorial policy makers kept the channel broadly on track and Jonathan's main job was to stop Angie killing Ben and/or Paul as they dared to suggest changes to her shows. Paul and Ben would themselves argue all day long but Jonathan didn't worry about them. Paul was the traditional Conservative thinker and in tune with the mainstream of the party and probably the country. Ben was, as ever, the radical thinker, swapping left wing ideas on community with hard right views on freedom and individual choice. Their chemistry was solid and Ben would occasionally come up with something really exciting. Jonathan was quietly sizing up Ben to see if he could host his own show on the channel. If he could make it work, it could be the radical show that would take them forwards in a big and bold new way. There was no doubt Ben had the brains for managing such a show but Jonathan was unsure if he had the drive and the personality to make it compelling television.

The ratings for the channel's first two weeks on air were relatively encouraging and Jonathan knew they would buy him some time to achieve real awareness for the channel. As he expected, the 'catch-up' viewing online was the strongest element of the audience, with a relatively small number of viewers watching the channel live on air. Publicity was the key to keeping this audience and helping it grow. He knew that the channel could never actually make any money, but if he could keep it newsworthy and exciting he could call it a success and as long as the financial losses were not too bad then it would be very difficult for Drew and the investors to call time on the channel without themselves looking like fools. The police action-cam channels were performing well and advertisers seemed to like the format. As long as he could keep juggling the investors, the politicians, the publicity, the advertisers and stop Angie firing everyone in a fit of temper, he could make this work.

Political meetings were becoming increasingly dominant in Jonathan's diary. He would often have six or seven meetings a day; some brief catch-ups with rising stars and other longer meetings over lunch or dinner with the established grandees of the party. Adam Robinson was playing a formidable role in helping Lottie set up these meetings and privately advising, as he had promised, so that Jonathan could reserve his real charm and interest for the newly emerging elected talent and behind-the-scenes power-brokers who were often not so visible to the general public. Once Lottie had got to grips with Adam's gruff manner and blunt comments, she admitted that he was really useful in getting Jonathan in front of the right people. Adam even helped him with restaurant choices, gently moving him away from the cutting-edge new restaurants that Jonathan would naturally like to explore on his expense account to the more traditional and reserved places where his lunch and dinner companions would feel more comfortable. They unfortunately all tended to be heavier in both carbohydrates and portion size and Jonathan had to be as careful as possible with his choice of food to stop his waistline expanding. Dinners were the toughest as they often tended to be heavy drinking affairs with the elected politicians. There were usually aperitifs or a glass or two of champagne before dinner, at least one bottle of wine, and always a brandy or two to follow. For the guest, this was just freeloading on a media company, and selling influence and gossip in exchange for a good dinner and a glass too many was considered normal. For Jonathan, it was exhausting and he sometimes felt his natural enthusiasm flagging as he saw the warning signs of a second bottle of wine approaching. The only small benefits of these drunken evenings were the large number of political indiscretions revealed and occasionally a really useful piece of inside information. He had never realised before this charm offensive just how vindictive and petty minded politicians and their aides could be. Who was up and who was down but didn't know it yet was always the most popular topic of conversation, and whilst it provided useful insight for Jonathan, he was appalled at just how much pleasure his dining companions took in the looming downfall of their close colleagues and political allies.

Despite his best efforts in the first three weeks on air, he didn't make a single dinner date with Ellie. Carol made lots of appointments and every one of them was cancelled as some crisis or politician intruded. The house filled with apologetic flowers as Carol did her best to mitigate these failed attempts and Ellie despaired at ever sitting down with her husband for any quality time. He was never home before she was asleep and gone early in the morning without much more than a hello or a grunt depending upon his mood. He didn't see the boys at all during the week and the two of them began to communicate more by Whats App than by real conversation. After two weeks of seven-day working, Jonathan declared he would be at home at least every Sunday morning and lunchtime from now on and would dedicate himself to the three of them. The first of these family lunches was spoiled by young Albee behaving badly and being sent to his room and much of the rest of the meal was eaten in silence. George excused himself from the table as soon as he could and the two of them cleared the plates quietly, both wondering how this had ended up working out so badly. Later on, they retrieved the situation somewhat by playing a board game with the boys, and when Jonathan's phone rang to say that Eddie was outside to take him back to the studios they were all genuinely disappointed to see him go.

'Only two more Sunday evenings of working, I promise,' he said as he found his briefcase and pulled on his jacket. 'Honestly, only two more.' Ellie found herself doubting the veracity of this statement even though Jonathan made it in all sincerity. 'I won't be back late tonight either,' he said as he walked out of the door, 'darling, I will be home by nine, latest nine-thirty, just you see. Love you all.' And then he was gone. Again. Back home by 10.45, he was greeted by a short note on the kitchen worktop from Ellie:

S*orry, couldn't wait up any longer. Hope it went well tonight. The boys really enjoyed our time together this afternoon. Can we try for dinner midweek? Ellie XXX*

He crept upstairs to the second bathroom and, once washed, slid silently into bed alongside Ellie. Just two more weeks of this, he thought to himself as he fell into his usual deep and immediate sleep.

Chapter 8

By the time Catalyst was two months old, everything had stabilised somewhat and everyone was beginning to draw breath and relax a little. Ratings were ok, revenues were just about acceptable, and the critical response was still broadly positive. The audience reaction, however, was out of this world. Even though ratings suggested that watching Catalyst was a minority sport, the firestorm of social media response indicated otherwise. The channel found itself in the crosshairs of political debate with roughly equal numbers of lovers and haters. On a daily basis, new issues discussed on the channel would drive the social media world into a frenzy of rage, rejoicing, speculation and fantasy. This was exactly what Jonathan had prophesied and wanted and Lottie, Amber and their team stoked the fires expertly to keep the pot boiling. If only they could find a way to make money out of all of this they would be home and dry, he thought to himself when reflecting on the first several weeks of the business.

The social media reaction energised and frightened the politicians from the Government side and Jonathan was never more in demand for meetings and follow-ups. He accepted membership of a Conservative think tank, "The Pioneer Group", upon Adam's advice. He suspected that it was Adam who had put him up for membership in the first place. This was a group of right-leaning radical evangelists was loosely connected to the PM's office and specialised in discussing radical policies that were some years away from being adopted as Conservative policy. It was even better that membership of the group was a secret, with members taking a vow of silence over their involvement so that they could all talk freely without fear of being outed and their radical viewpoints exposed to the glare of publicity. Surprisingly, Jonathan was not the only media member of this club; an editor of a major national newspaper had been a member for several years and a senior BBC executive had also recently joined.

'It's a bit like being in the Masons,' Jonathan joked when he told Ellie over dinner about his first meeting. 'I had to swear an oath of confidentiality and I can't even tell you who is in the group. What's good though is that they all speak pretty freely and although some of them have some wild and wacky views, most are serious thinkers and they do drip their policy ideas into the PM's ear from time to time. It's amazing how many radical and unorthodox views have become part of the political mainstream recently.'

Ellie made an equivocal grunt in response to this news, deciding that now was not the time to challenge Jonathan, but she thought to herself that membership of this exclusive group of right-wing thinkers was exactly the sort of thing he would have loudly denounced only a couple of years ago. She kept her own counsel and moved the conversation onto smoother waters and away from politics. Although Jonathan's punishing workload had diminished a little and he was at home on Sundays now and occasionally even on a Saturday night too, tonight was only the third dinner date they had managed in the eight weeks since Catalyst's launch and Ellie could clearly see the change in Jonathan since he began to work at the River Factory. He was even more self-assured than usual, even slightly smug, and whilst she had always admired and loved him for his quiet certainty and self-confidence, she could now also see a hint of arrogance in his manner and this was new. Running Catalyst had changed the man she loved and even while he listened politely as she told him the sad tale of one of her mistreated legal aid clients, she sensed that he was feigning interest rather than showing the genuine concern he would normally have displayed in her work. She tried to dismiss this thought and the rest of their evening passed without incident. Later that night, however, when they were caressing each other in bed, she again felt a distance between them; he was going through the motions but his mind was somewhere else and when she turned and told him she was tired, he agreed and immediately rolled over to sleep. Disappointed by his response, she lay awake for a while, wondering if there was more to this than the obvious exhaustion and overwork. She was worried by him in a way she had never experienced before. They had never had secrets from each other and she didn't want to start now. They had talked at length over dinner about their imminent skiing holiday with the boys and Ellie thought to herself that she must make sure she used this holiday to restore Jonathan to his old self and drag him away from the caustic minefield of media and politics into which he had become so entangled. She felt sure that a week in the Alps *en famille* would work wonders for them all.

Part Two

Chapter 9

Jonathan's distracted mood with Ellie was caused by something he had heard earlier in the day from a member of the Pioneer Group. As usual it was not attributable and extremely opaque, but something in the way it was said puzzled Jonathan and left him wanting to find out more. The journalist in him was aroused and he couldn't let the issue rest. He couldn't be sure, but the implications of this snatched conversation could be explosive and extremely damaging to the Government, or it could be dismissed as yet more speculation and back-bench tittle-tattle. The next morning whilst swimming, he decided he wanted to investigate further and on his way into the office called Ben Zinneri to set up a meeting later that morning. Satisfied to be doing something, he sat back in the car and again pondered the magnitude of the story he was putting together in his head. He knew he couldn't trust Ben to keep anything quiet but if he carefully compartmentalised everything into several pieces, only he would know the full story and – who knows – it might well come to nothing anyway. He felt the rising excitement of uncovering a possible scoop that took him back to his days in the newspaper world and his early editorial meetings at Sky News.

'Ben, hi. Sit down. I want to talk to you about Sir John Cressley. What do you know about him?'

'Well, erm, Tory MP for Northamptonshire South East, sixty something, maybe seventy? Owns a great big monstrosity of a country pile somewhere near Silverstone and rather smart town house in Lord North Street. Made his money from property – family business – and more lately from oil and gas deals in the third world. Brexiteer. Generally right wing.

Knighted early on in the Cameron era for services to cronyism, two grown up kids, one of each, I think, maybe the daughter works in the business? Rather good looking trophy wife considerably younger then him who is on the social circuit, features in Tatler and the like. Seen to be one of the real power brokers of the party, content to keep his head down and out of the limelight but very close to the seat of power. That's about all I can think of. Why?'

'I think there's something going on there. I want you to take some time out and thoroughly investigate him.'

'I didn't think we were in the business of outing marital infidelities and shady business dealings by members of the Tory party.'

'No, we're not. I think there's something more fundamental going on here. I need a full understanding of Sir John. I want to know everything I can about him. I also want to keep this completely between the two of us. No exceptions. I don't want Paul to know what you are up to - he's too close to Conservative Central Office and we don't want to frighten our best friends in any way. So let's keep this entirely between the two of us. Work at it discreetly, spend as much time as you need to and then come back and tell me what you've found out. Ok?'

'Sure boss, leave it with me. If there's anything to be found, I will find it.'

Once alone again, Jonathan reached for a personal iPad from his briefcase and opened a new document. Across the top of the screen he wrote,

Quotation: "We can get Sir John Cressley to fix any delicate little problems we might have in francophone Africa. He has form there with regimes we want to keep in with but also hold at more than arm's length publicly." End quote. Minister of State, Foreign & Commonwealth Office in private discussion at the Pioneer Group meeting.

He dated the conversation. Underneath, he wrote:

Q. Sir John C. Does his work in Africa cover arms sales as well as oil and gas? Could he be the missing link in the Sunday Times Investigation? What could be more delicate than selling British made cluster bombs?

Three months earlier the *Sunday Times* had tried to stand up a story that the British Government had known about and turned a blind eye to sales of British-made cluster bombs to Mali, in contravention of stated Government policy and the UN convention outlawing their use. The paper attempted to make a connection by claiming that the Mali Government tried and failed to buy them from the French and when they were rebuffed they bought them quietly in the UK. Supposedly they were to be used in the fight to rid the centre of the country from Islamic terrorism but some enthusiastic general had used them to help put down a riot by an indigenous group who were protesting against illegal land appropriation. Seventeen tribespeople had been killed by the cluster bombs and over one hundred maimed. The general had later been revealed to be one of the land appropriators. Just one fragment of a single cluster bomb had been recovered and was clearly of British manufacture. The Prime Minister had stood up in the Commons and categorically denied any Government involvement. He blamed rogue and unidentified arms dealers re-routing old and now outlawed weaponry to third party states and promised to root them out and stop them operating in the UK. His strong performance killed the story and turned the attention on Britons involved in private arms dealing, but that quickly fizzled out too as these arms dealers were pretty good at not giving interviews and most of the British ones lived in Dubai or Monaco and their connections back to the UK were tenuous at best. Government action against British arms dealers never happened and the world and the ever-hungry news cycle moved on to the next story.

Jonathan called one of the best of the young political researchers on his staff and asked her to do some research for him.

'Khalila, can you pull me everything that's been mentioned in Parliament and Committees about Mali in the last two years? When you've done that, can you then put me together a précis of everything I need to know about the country: politics, tribal conflicts, Al- Qaeda etc. Edit it down so I don't have to read yards of stuff, please, and can you let me have it by the end of the week as a pdf before I head off on my week's holiday? Finally, can you keep this private and just between the two of us? If anyone asks just say you are doing some research directly for me but don't tell them its about Mali. OK?'

Satisfied with his progress on the project, he asked Carol to call a quick meeting with Angie and Patrick and when they arrived he told them of the changes he saw coming now the channel had, as he put it, got to first base.

'I want to hand over more day-to-day control to the two of you going forwards,' he said. 'Angie, you've done remarkable things with the production teams and the show formats and whilst we both know we will need to make more changes, I want to step back a little and let you make more of the decisions. Patrick, the same for you on the cost and revenue side. You've shown you have the skills to handle the ad sales business management and whilst we both know it needs to be a whole lot better to meet our first year targets, we are not desperately adrift. I don't want to cut Angie's resources at this point but we need to have very tight cost control to make sure we are on top of things. I'm stepping back a little from the day-to-day primarily because I'm doing too much and will end up killing myself, but also I have complete confidence in you guys to manage the business. I'm going to try to up the relationships with the political class so that we can get ahead of stories and not just compete with everyone else. If we can do this and use someone like Melissa to tease out some of the upcoming issues, we can drive the agenda and leave the rest of the media in our wake, reporting on what we are saying. Ratings will go up and so will ad revenues. The main casualty will be my waistline. Obviously, the responsibility will still be mine and our twice weekly meetings will be the main forum for sharing ideas and problems. The buck still stops with me. It goes without saying that you need to keep Lottie, Paul, Ben and the others in the loop too.'

After a brief discussion, the two of them made to leave the office but Jonathan asked Angie to stay behind for a moment.

'Angie, I know how hard you have been working and how tired you must be. I'm going to take next week off to recharge my batteries and I want you to do the same the week after. I hear that you are a winter sun worshiper so find yourself somewhere hot and expensive and use my company credit card to book it. Carol has all the details. I will make sure I don't screw things up whilst you are away.'

'But, boss, I don't think I can be away that week, we've got two new shows to bed in...'

'Angie, I'll manage. Take the holiday. I can't have you collapsing on me and you must be every bit as worn out as I am.'

With grudging grace, Angie took the bait and, after thanking him, left him alone in his office. After the week house-sitting for Angie, he thought, I can step back and I can make this work. I think. He saw that he was already late for a meeting with the streaming guys who wanted to demonstrate some new technology and then one meeting followed another until it was time to change suits, leave the building and head into Westminster. He was due at a small drinks event hosted by the Prime Minister and it would be the first time they had met in person since they fell out whilst he was working as an external adviser. It would be interesting to see how he handled their meeting.

Chapter 10

The private dining room in Westminster was already full of perhaps twenty people by the time Jonathan arrived. He knew about half of the audience: bankers, media commentators, chief executives, party fund raisers. There was a marked absence of politicians, he noticed, was that deliberate? The Prime Minister arrived shortly after him and worked the room with a few personal words for each of the invited guests. When he reached Jonathan he shook hands and they held each other's eye for a long time before the PM spoke.

'Jonathan. It's been quite a while. And look what you are up to now. I've always thought the fourth estate was there to reflect upon our decisions and hold us to account but judging by the little I've seen and heard of your new channel, you want to make our opinions for us as well. Oh well I suppose it's the new world we live in..'

'I'm sure that many of the ideas we discuss are central to your agenda Prime Minister.'

'Probably, probably. You knowhow old-fashioned I can be about the role of the media. Well, anyway, must circulate. Keep up the good work.'

Without waiting for a reply, he swept on to the next guest – an American banker whom Jonathan thought would have much more in common with the PM than he did. Polite conversation and drinks filled the next half hour but Jonathan realised that this evening was just a PR stunt and he was not going to hear anything interesting from the PM's speech. And so it proved. A forty minute ramble through the excitements and challenges of the new world, a bit of opposition bashing – which went down very well with the audience and showed the PM at his combative best – followed by a winding up where he promised less regulation and less red tape, more opportunity for entrepreneurs and tax benefits for innovation and job creation. This could be any Conservative leader's speech of the last forty years, thought Jonathan, and wondered if the PM had squandered this opportunity to say something radical or, more likely, had just run out of ideas and had really nothing to say. He favoured the latter argument. He spent the next hour networking and sounding out opinion on the matter from around the room. Broadly, the people he met agreed with him. They had come tonight expecting some insight from the great man – who of course had swept out of the room as soon as his speech was finished – and instead had been treated to a stump speech with no opportunity for posing the questions that mattered to them. Several of the invited guests were keen to find out more about his new television operation and Jonathan realised that he needed to do more to engage with this audience and bring their views and opinions onto the channel. If the PM wasn't interested in what they thought, he certainly was. He left the room with a handful of business cards and once inside his car he Whats App'd Paul and Angie and asked them to do some thinking as to how to bring non-political influencers and businessman and women onto the channel without making something as dull as Newsnight. He then called Lottie and discussed the evening.

'Lottie, hi. Well, as you rightly predicted it's been a pretty dull evening. Nothing new from the PM. I really think the cupboard of ideas is pretty bare there. He only survives because the party is supine and the opposition is so bloody useless. He was distant to me too – although nothing surprising there given our history. What was interesting is that several of our captains of industry are keen to meet and talk with me. I suspect they want to find out if Catalyst can help move their political agendas along in a way the Government can't. I've asked Angie and Paul to have a think about how such a show might possibly work. On the political front though, I think it's time I came out a little against the PM. Will you work out a tweet for me along the lines of "Drinks function with the

PM. Good canapes but no new ideas"? Will you text me something before you send it out?'

'That's no problem. Are you sure that the time is right to ally yourself with the rebels in the party?'

'No, I don't want to do that. I just want to mark his card a little. See what you can come up with and we will decide.'

Before he was home, Lottie texted:

Private drinks reception with the PM tonight. Great guest list but no insight from the PM. Ideas seem to be in short supply at Number 10. xx

He texted back.

Leave off the kisses but otherwise perfect. See you for breakfast. x

The next morning at breakfast, Lottie showed him the Twitter response to his post -he never tweeted himself and was often puzzled as to why anyone would without thinking it through and weighing up the consequences of their hasty interventions but, hey, look at Donald Trump. Several commentators had picked up on the tweet and added their thoughts along the lines of "Lomax falling out with the PM?", "Does the PM need yet more Tory doubters?", "Another leading Tory thinks about jumping from the leaking ship". Lottie thought they should respond with something conciliatory but Jonathan, spooning up porridge as he spoke, was less accommodating.

'No let's have him stew for a while and say nothing. We might get a couple of interesting calls today and we can always play friendly before the end of the day if we need to.'

Lottie, who despaired at convincing Jonathan to be as immediate as social media required, acquiesced and the conversation moved on to how they would communicate whilst Jonathan was away skiing.

'I'm flying off first thing in the morning, but inevitably I've got a pretty busy day today. I do want to spend some time with you before I go and this isn't the place for what I need to tell you. Could we meet in my office around 4?'

'Sure, what's so important that we can't talk about it here?'

'What I have to tell you can't be overhead in a Wandsworth coffee shop and I'm sure even these self-obsessed hipsters have ears,' he said glancing around the room. 'Now, I must get in to the office as I'm late for the finance meeting with Paddy. Have you finished your coffee?'

As they walked in silence the short distance to the River Factory, Jonathan reflected on his decision, earlier that morning, to tell Lottie the whole story about Mali and the possible Sir John Cressley connection. He knew Lottie was the one person, apart from Ellie, that he could trust absolutely and he knew that she would give him good political advice as to how best to handle the consequences that might result from the investigation. He glanced at her slight form, hurrying to keep pace with his striding walk and reminded himself what a strong team he had around him.

Just after four, Lottie came into his office looking concerned and sat down at one end of the long sofa.

'So, what's so secret you couldn't tell me this morning? Is it me?'

'No, no, nothing like that,' he smiled warmly to reassure her, 'I've stumbled across what could be a huge political time-bomb and I need to talk to someone I can completely trust whilst I investigate the whole thing and see what falls out.'

He then told her the full story, the overhead remark, making the connection to Mali and the *Sunday Times* investigation and setting Ben and Khalila to work on different parts of the puzzle to see if any more could be uncovered.

'If I'm right, and that's still a big if at the moment, this could be just the tip of the iceberg. It's not just the Prime Minister lying to Parliament but half the whole bloody cabinet lying too and where there are lies on this scale there's always money and money and secrets mean corruption. I need your help in piecing it together and with something this big I can't even trust the rest of the team to keep it quiet. Will you help?'

'Of course.' They both knew it was a rhetorical question and that Lottie would do anything to help Jonathan. She continued, 'What do you need meet do whilst you are away?'

'Khalila's research is the key here. I will send it on to you when she lets me have it later today and I need you to start pulling together some of the threads of the story, making connections where none are immediately apparent and trying to understand the scope of it all. Ben's stuff will also be really important but we need to keep Ben away from the rest of the story or God knows what might happen. Most importantly, however, I need you to be my political adviser on this one...'

They were interrupted by a repeated banging on the office door and the entrance of a breathless and agitated Amber.

'I'm so sorry to break in like this but there's a major problem I need your help with. Melissa's bloody property developer husband has just been rumbled for some tax haven nonsense four days after Melissa ranted on air about the rich using offshore tax companies to avoid paying their fair share. The *Observer's* got the story and I need help to see if we can smooth it over. You know how they always do the outreach on a Friday hoping we've all gone off for the week-end. Can you help?'

'Sure,' Lottie looked at Jonathan, 'We were just about finished anyway. I've heard nothing more on the PM tweet front since this morning, have you?'

'Not a thing. Let's just leave it out there and see if it grows at all. We can liaise if we need to take action whilst I'm away. See you both in a week.'

He ploughed through what remained of the rest of the day, struggling to apply himself to the various problems his team brought to him in person or via email. He was determined to get to the bottom of the Mali story and determined to bring out the truth – whatever the bloody cost. He was also determined to be out of the office on time today and spend some quality time with Ellie and the boys. He eventually made it home by eight-thirty with over-excited boys still running around in their pyjamas and Ellie looking frazzled as she attempted to keep order and pack bags at the same time. Eventually, they got both boys into bed and settled down in front of Netflix with a bottle of good Burgundy and a take-away from their local Thai. Jonathan fell asleep halfway through the film but was roused to go to bed as they had an early start in the morning and he still had to pack.

Chapter 11

When Ellie was organising the ski trip, Jonathan had some specific demands about the sort of holiday he wanted.

'First of all, no bloody Easyjet from Stansted at 5 in the morning. I will organise to use the company NetJets account and settle up with them. Second, I don't want to find myself in a chalet with a dozen viewers of the channel so let's have a place of our own, and most importantly, let's have a good cook looking after us.'

Having transformed a week's skiing from the expensive to the prohibitive, Jonathan left the details to Ellie. She booked a chi-chi three bedroom apartment at Courchevel 1850 and organised for Vanessa, their shared nanny, to join them for the week and help improve the boys' skiing outside of their ski school lessons. Vanessa lived in with the couple the Lomax's shared her with, and Ellie's biggest issue was buying off the other mother and persuading her she could manage for a whole week without Vanessa's presence. Vanessa was a strikingly pretty twenty-two year old with rich parents, a poor unfinished degree in hospitality and numerous skiing qualifications. She would ski with the boys and look after them when they'd had enough time on the slopes, allowing Ellie and Jonathan some freedom on the pistes together. Ellie had given Vanessa every evening off and fully expected her to live up to her local reputation as a party girl when she wasn't looking after George and Albee. This would also give the Lomax family some time alone together in the evenings when they could bond and be themselves.

An executive coach arrived at six am to pick up the five of them and take them to Northolt where the Netjets plane was waiting to take them to France. The boys were beside themselves at the prospect of flying on an executive jet and thought they had gone to heaven when they were allowed into the cockpit shortly after take-off. Even Ellie thought life was pretty cool as she,Vanessa and Jonathan sipped champagne with their breakfast croissants. She was determined to make this a holiday to remember and was delighted with the chalet she had rented and the staff who were there to welcome them. By lunchtime they were on the slopes and waving goodbye to Vanessa and the boys who wanted to ski more than they wanted food. Jonathan and Ellie lifted to the top and enjoyed some mountain food and a glass of wine before they ventured out on the slopes for some late afternoon skiing. Ellie was a better skier than Jonathan; she was naturally elegant and poised on her skis, but Jonathan was a more determined and fearless skier and could just about keep up with her. They had only just finished their first run when Jonathan's phone rang for the first time. It would be their constant companion for the week as problems, large and small, interrupted their time together. Jonathan started skiing with one phone earbud in place beneath his helmet so that he could take calls with less fumbling and glove removal. Ellie would often be found waiting at the bottom of runs after he had stopped to take calls halfway down a run and then would arrive, breathless and out of control, trying to catch up.

Despite these all too frequent interruptions, they enjoyed their skiing together and laughed more than they had for some time. They usually arrived back at their chalet in the dark, fortified by a post-ski aperitif and ready to hear extended tales of the boy's adventures. Their cook was talented, and whilst she generally produced different food for the boys, they all ate at the same time and mealtimes were noisy, fun and memorable. They would normally be followed by board games and then the boys would be packed off to bed, often with a DVD to watch whilst Jonathan and Ellie sat quietly enjoying a bottle or two of fine wine late into the evening. They would take to their bed around midnight, worn out from skiing and talking, and read until Vanessa came back from whichever bar she had been patronising that night. Only then did they them feel able to switch off their bedside lights and go to sleep. After the first two nights of listening for a key in the door, Ellie asked Vanessa to be back by midnight as they were struggling to stay awake. The days slipped by happily and it wasn't until the fifth day that Jonathan told Ellie about the investigations into arms dealing in Mali. Ben's report had arrived and having read it before dinner, he now felt there was enough circumstantial evidence to share his thoughts with his wife. He gave her Ben's memo to read first.

Memo: To Jonathan Lomax
From Ben Zinneri
Strictly Private & Confidential
Sir John Cressley (SJC)

Sir John Cressley, Conservative MP for Northamptonshire South East from 1997. Current majority 11,200 over the Liberal Democrats. Born 1950, age 68. Knighted by David Cameron in 2011 for services to charity. Chair of Transforming Young Lives, charity for improving the lot of socially deprived children who spent early years in care. School: Harrow and then the Guards. Saw active service in the Falklands. Retired as Major a few year later. Married with two children. Wife: Lady Annabel Cressley, 48, interior designer, second wife. First wife: Rose Cressley, 67, divorced in 1995 on grounds of his unreasonable behaviour. Children: Anna, 38 and James, 36. Country Seat near Towcester and town house in Lord North Street, Westminster.

Career part 1: After an early career in the Guards moved into the family business Cavendale Properties Ltd started by his grandfather and then operated by his father who left the business only a year after SJC joined it in 1985. SJC changed the business dramatically, including putting his own inherited shareholding into a BVI Company Crestamilk. Later, Crestamilk acquired Cavendale and the whole company moved offshore. Other minority shareholders, including his family, appear to have been bought out. Crestamilk moved domicile to the Cayman Islands in 2001 and became even more opaque. Son and daughter appear on the share register in 2005 and daughter Anna listed as Managing Director of UK operating company Cavendale in 2008. James listed as director. No directorships evident for Lady Annabel. Difficult to trace the money generated without a forensic accountant to help but obvious that the business has been throwing off at least £4 million a year in profits and probably a lot more. Mostly tax sheltered of course. Cavendale shows turnover of £288million in 2015 but small loss due to loan repayments to parent company Crestamilk and director emoluments. No corporation tax payable.

They own a shopping centre in Glasgow and two major office blocks in the City, all with good long term tenants. In addition, they own a series of residential properties split between some high end apartments in central London and a whole raft of rental properties in the Midlands and the North. They own a number of other commercial properties across Europe and Africa. Key markets are Sweden, Germany, Latvia, South Africa, Nigeria, Mali, Ivory Coast and Kenya. Major credit facility with banking syndicate led by RBS.

Career part 2: Cavendale always had property investments in Africa, mainly in South Africa and Nigeria and have expanded their holdings there over time. Moving into the oil and gas business there must have seemed a good idea in the early 1980s and SJC's father made the first investments under the Cavendale banner. When SJC took over, this was moved into a different company: Cavendale Exploration which was incorporated in the Cayman Islands through an operating company in Venezuela which later moved to be domiciled in Nigeria and then in Liberia. The real head office is in London in Mayfair, but Cavendale Exploration UK Ltd is a wholly owned subsidiary of the African business which is itself wholly owned by the Cayman Islands business, whose nominee owners operate behind another holding company in the BVIs. Confused? It seems most likely that the ultimate owners of the business are SJC and his two children. Anna is also MD of the UK Oil and Gas company so her interests mesh across both business areas. The London office on Conduit Street looks like it houses about twenty five employees in total. SJC and Anna operate from here but Anna is a frequent traveller to Africa, judging from her very active Facebook page. Her husband John is also listed as a non-executive director. He is a banker and an aspiring Tory MP.

SJC lists Cavendale directorships among his outside interests as an MP but does not make any other declarations about the BVI or Cayman Islands companies. I suspect, therefore, they are held in some sort of trust status to avoid scrutiny.

I've listed at the end of this report some of the key African contacts the business has there, and scouring through publications, many of them are subject to corruption allegations but nothing out of the ordinary for African businessmen.

SJC has been a contributor to the Tory party since the early 1980s and is obviously an admirer of Margaret Thatcher and her style. He has been a powerful influence behind the scenes and according to my sources has turned down junior cabinet posts on at least two occasions. He is definitely one of the powers behind the throne who likes to stay in the shadows. He is an active member of the Monday Club and, more interestingly, The Free Enterprise Group where he is something of an elder statesmen of the radical right wingers, most of whom are a generation younger than him. As you know, this group has been increasingly influential in shaping Conservative policy. He is an active Brexiteer. He is member of the Reform Club and White's. He has a reputation as a fixer of problems within the party and has acted as a referee on several occasions to bring warring parties together.

Outside interests include horse-racing – he owns, or jointly owns, several race horses – and building an arboretum in the grounds outside his country mansion. Country entertaining is a big part of his life with shooting and fishing parties often attended by prominent ministers and businessmen. African business leaders and politicians are also frequently invited. Wife Annabel is a noted hostess and seems to run that part of his life. There was gossip a few years ago about her extended trips to the Cote D'Azur with a younger painter and a whiff of scandal hung around for a little while but since then nothing outside of the usual gallery openings, first nights, society events, etc. She's quite a looker and often seen looking elegant in Tatler and other society publications. Her husband is rarely in evidence. Her politics are unknown.

In conclusion, there's nothing really remarkable about SJC. He has successfully partitioned his business life away from the oversight of the UK taxpayer and is secretive about his wealth but that could probably be said about twenty or thirty of his colleagues. His disclosures in the Members' Interests Register are economical with the truth. His politics are well to the right of the mainstream in the party but not exceptional. He has a poor attendance record in the House and is not known as a particularly diligent local MP. Again, pretty typical of the Tory shire parliamentarians.

Ben Zinneri

Below this memo Ben had scribbled

J- there's obviously something I've missed here or he wouldn't be of interest to you. When can you tell me more??

Ellie read the note carefully and handed it back to Jonathan.

'As your man Ben says, there's nothing here that's unusual and not a mention about arms dealing and only a single mention of Mali – and that's in relation to property. Are you sure there's something here?'

'I'm sure. I can't share too much with Ben as he's something of an unguided missile and also indiscreet. I've got to do the real digging myself.'

'As if you've got the time. This is the first week I've seen the real you in months.'

'I know. But I have told Angie and the others that they need to take on more responsibility and I'm using this break as a first step in not making all the decisions myself. I know the phone is ringing a dozen times a day but at least it's a start.'

He then passed over Khalila's report on his iPad. Mostly it was dull stuff about Mali, Government aid issues and disagreements with the French about the handling of their former colony. But buried away in the detailed report of the Foreign Affairs Committee meeting on Western Africa there was a single sentence from a witness – Andrew Gilmour, CEO of hostage recovery firm Secure Alliance – that Jonathan had highlighted.

'When you look at the widespread use of anti-personnel weapons by the Mali militias you have to wonder at the wisdom of the Western Governments who quietly sanctioned their sale.'

'None of the MPs on the committee picked up on this statement,' said Jonathan as Ellie placed the iPad down, 'but it appears to rebut the Prime Minister's statement that any anti-personnel weapons were there due to rogue arms dealers and not Western Governments. Now, we know the French refused to ship these sorts of arms and the one fragment found was of British manufacture. I think there's a puzzle here waiting to be unlocked.'

'It's a long way short of legal proof,' said Ellie the lawyer.

'I know, I know. But if the truth is even close to what I suspect, then this is a really big thing. The Government using Tory middlemen to illegally supply anti-personnel weapons and then the Prime Minister and half the cabinet lying to Parliament by claiming they had no knowledge. As you know it's always the cover-up that claims the scalps rather than the act itself. I've got the inside information on this and I've got to get to the bottom of it.'

'Is there anything you want me to do?'

'I don't think there's anything you can do. It would be great to have you as a legal sounding board when I do get fragments of information so that I don't get ahead of myself and then perhaps critically review any evidence before I take it to the company lawyers, but most importantly I wanted you to know what I am up to and why I'm so pre-occupied and so busy.'

'What's your next step?'

'I'm going to try and track down this Andy Gilmour character and see if I can find any evidence to back up his claims. Anyway, enough of this, I'm meant to be on holiday. Shall we try and do the four valleys circuit tomorrow? The weather looks pretty good and if we get an early start we can make lunch in that place I like above Val Thorens.'

The end of the skiing holiday finished happily for the Lomax family and they enjoyed their luxury transportation back to Richmond where a family pizza with Vanessa marked the end of the holiday and a return to business. The boys were back at school the next day and once Ellie had finished their preparations she sat down at her laptop and saw she had a long list of ignored emails to work through from both the homeless charity and the women's shelter. There were also several emails from her colleague Howard, which was unusual. She resisted the impulse to open them immediately and thought they could all be dealt with once the boys were packed off to school. Jonathan was immersed in his study but Ellie felt a satisfied peaceful air in the household – the sign of a good holiday – with all of her boys now happily in gear for the week ahead. As she settled down into bed with her book, she felt the family had never been a closer unit and although the boys were growing up fast and becoming scarily independent, they had really enjoyed spending a week with their father and he had reverted to his old happy self as the stress of the new job was lifted off his shoulders – even if just for the week and with a steady stream of work phone-calls in the background. Of course, he was now working away downstairs but at least he could return to work rejuvenated. Smiling to herself, she thought how lucky she was. Her thoughts returned to the emails waiting for her tomorrow. She re-instated her lawyer training as she switched off from that thought and returned her mind to her Lomax boys. Pleasantly tired, she gave up on her book, turned off her light and was fast asleep before Jonathan arrived from the study.

Chapter 12

The blue skies and sub-zero weather of the French Alps were replaced by a grey, drizzly London winter morning, but by the time Jonathan arrived feeling energised at the River Factory, he had already formulated a plan to push forward his investigation into the Mali connection. His morning and early afternoon was spent in a flurry of meetings as he struggled to resolve some of the issues that had come up whilst he was away and it wasn't until mid afternoon that he was able to sit down with Lottie and discuss the next steps on Mali. She had been through Ben and Khalila's reports and, like Ellie, was sceptical about the one line comment from Andy Gilmour being the smoking gun they needed.

'By all means meet with him,' she said, 'but not yet. You need to get further along with Sir John and his people. You don't know if talking to Gilmour will set alarm bells off everywhere and then you won't be able to make any headway with anyone else.'

Reluctantly, Jonathan agreed and they began to formulate a plan of how he might infiltrate the Cressley family. Lottie had done some further personal research into them.

'Obviously, Sir John himself will be keen to talk politics to you but I think we should be cautious of approaching him at this time. His wife Annabel is not involved in the family firms at all as far as I can see, so we've not much to gain by going there. James is mostly living in Antigua so I guess he has no active involvement in the business, so daughter Anna and her husband may be the best way in. Anna is ferociously bright and we probably need to treat her with caution but husband John Andrews may be a better entry point. He is a moderately successful corporate banker and is desperate to become an MP. He has been up for several safe Tory seats but hasn't managed to nab one yet. That gives you an opportunity to meet him without causing suspicion and then maybe you can get to Anna via him. What do you think?'

'Shall I get Adam Robinson to fix up a meeting?'

'I don't think you should. It strikes me that Adam always slants things towards the PM and his team and I don't think you want even the slightest whiff of this story getting out to Number 10 before we have some real proof.'

'You are right, let's not involve Adam in any of this. He's much too close to the Tory establishment. Would you mind doing this yourself? We can say we are trying to look at the ideas of the next generation of MPs or some such fiction and he'll probably bite at the thought of some publicity. Let's try for dinner, maybe even later this week?'

As they thought, John Andrews was only too keen to meet Jonathan and they met for dinner on the Wednesday evening, Jonathan shunting another dinner function away with a feeble excuse. They met at a quiet Mayfair restaurant Jonathan used a lot. He reserved his favourite table where he knew they could talk without being overheard. Lottie's research had thrown up the fact that John was 'known to like a drink or two' so it was fairly easy to put together a game plan for the evening. He had told Ellie he would be late back – even by his usual poor standards.

John was almost a caricature Tory of young/middle years. Slightly overweight, receding hair, a braying voice and a contacts book that reflected the right schools, the right university and a middling career in investment banking backing up a sizeable family inheritance. Jonathan had met many like him and knew the type well. After a couple of cocktails and general chat at the bar, they moved to their table and ordered. Jonathan carefully asked about John's political ambitions and gave some helpful advice. Once he had discovered that John had no great political insight or intellect, he steered the conversation around to the family business.

'So John, you are married? Yes? Tell me about your wife. Do you have children?'

'No, we don't have children. It's a personal sadness for me but that's the way it is. Anna, my wife, is a remarkable woman. She is the MD of her family business. It's called Cavendale, pretty big in property and energy, you may have heard of it?'

Jonathan said he hadn't but would like to hear more.

'Well, her great-grandfather started the business in the UK and she runs it today in tandem with her father – Sir John Cressley, do you know him? No? I'm surprised. He's a fairly heavy hitter in the Conservative party, very close to the PM. You must meet him, I will set it up. Anyway, back to Anna. She's a fabulous woman, much smarter than me and she's taken the business to new heights, especially in the oil and gas side of the business where she's doubled the size of the operation. Africa is the key and Anna bloody loves the place, she's always tripping over there to meet some dodgy dictator or shady businessman and of course the old man's influence does no harm; he's got this big pile outside Northampton and they use it for shooting parties and to impress Johnny foreigner and it works a treat. They're a real double act, her and her father. Sometimes I feel quite the outsider. Of course, I'm on the board too to provide some financial advice and City contacts but I'm not really involved in the way Anna is. I tell you what, we're having a big bash at the old man's place in Westminster on Saturday night, not that he'll be there, it's very much Anna's and my show. How would you like to come along? There will be plenty of interesting people and you can meet Anna yourself. I will email you an invite.'

Jonathan accepted the offer and steered the conversation away from Cavendale to avoid John's suspicion. Brandies followed dinner and the second bottle of wine and when Jonathan suggested a nightcap at his club, John was only too ready to accept. Already in his cups, John was open to a little more digging, thought Jonathan, and he worked the conversation back to Anna and the company.

'Africa must have huge potential for companies like Cavendale going forwards. Are you starting to be involved in anything outside of property and energy?'

'Not really. The old man, Sir John, he does a bit of this and that to smooth out the politicians and keep them happy, if you know what I mean.'

At this point John twisted his face into a cartoon impersonation of a nudge and a wink and with his index finger pulled down his lower right eyelid several time in rapid succession to further suggest knowing connivence. The effect was grotesque. Jonathan thought it must be an old school party trick and tried not to laugh.

'Best not to go there, Africa, don't you know. It's not like doing business here and best not to talk about it. Stuff goes on there that would make your hair stand on end. Some of the things Anna tells me...' He stopped rambling and hesitated, 'Anyway, enough of that. Shall we have a last one before we head off? I've got a thirst on and a cheeky glass of champagne might just be the perfect end of what's been a really enjoyable evening.'

After the last drink, Jonathan helped an unsteady John into the back of the car and Eddie dropped him off in Notting Hill before taking Jonathan home. Jonathan sat back and reflected on the evening. Clearly, John was not the sharpest knife in the set but he hadn't given much away. Some hints about dodgy dealing in Africa but no detail and certainly no smoking gun. He would have to spend more time with him and see if he could discover more. At least he had the invitation to the soiree on Saturday. He would not invite Ellie and see what he could discover there...

Much to his surprise, an email from John arrived in his inbox just after eight. John thanked him for dinner and a great evening and enclosed the invitation to the event on Saturday along with a hope that they could get together and do something else soon. Jonathan realised that John might be a better opportunity than he had realised: clearly the guy was lonely and in need of friends. He thought he would see what Saturday offered and make any further decisions from there.

The remainder of the week passed without incident as he managed Angie's new shows in her absence and kept everything on an even keel whilst they waited upon her return. He was surprised a little when, in his regular weekly meeting with his boss Drew, he was asked if there was anything going on that he, Drew, should know about. Drew then asked him if Tom Schalke, the hedge fund boss and the real power of the company, had been in touch with him. He truthfully answered that he hadn't spoken to Tom since the launch of the channel. He left the meeting wondering what was going on that he didn't know about.

Ellie had barely raised an eyebrow when he told her he was going to a black tie event in Westminster on Saturday evening,

'I could have got you a ticket darling but I know you would have hated it and there's no point both of us having to ruin our evening.'

'That's fine with me,' she said, 'I've got lots of work to do on a case for the women's shelter so it will be good to have some time to myself when I can really concentrate on the intricacies of the legal issues I need to deal with.'

Ellie's case load on her return from skiing had been much heavier than she had expected and she had been neglecting her duties at the shelter as she had been working hard on a complex homeless case with Howard. A young Nigerian family had been thrown out of their rented apartment along with their two very young children and were now in a squalid B&B and under threat of deportation because of some mix up in their residency paperwork. It was obvious to Ellie that they were entitled to stay but difficult to prove conclusively and the authorities were being deliberately obstructive. Howard had taken the case on as a personal crusade and now Ellie was almost as deeply involved. This one case was swallowing up huge amounts of time and she had needed to call up Vanessa and ask for extra childcare help twice this week. Vanessa had already agreed to take the boys out for the afternoon on Saturday so now she would have several hours to catch up and perhaps get ahead of things.

Jonathan worked all day Saturday at the River Factory and took his dinner jacket with him to change in the office and go straight to the Cressleys. After a week away and constant meetings through the week, he too had a chance to catch up on some paperwork and work in some peace and quiet. Lottie came into his office in the early afternoon and together they reviewed their lack of progress on the Mali investigation.

'I have to get past John and spend some time with Anna,' said Jonathan, 'I don't think that tonight will be the time as she's the hostess and will be busy but maybe I can at least meet her and then fix up to see her again next week and see where that takes us.'

'I'm sure you can,' said Lottie knowingly. 'Just be careful. If she's as smart as John says she is, she won't be easy to reel in and will wonder why you are interested in her.'

Later, Jonathan was reflecting upon Lottie's words as he showered before putting on his DJ and he thought he must work the room and be careful not just to concentrate upon Anna. If he didn't attract her interest tonight then at least she would see him as a collector of people and he was sure that he could use John to create another opportunity to talk with her. There would inevitably be some Cavendale people at the event so perhaps he could do some digging and ensure his evening wasn't entirely wasted.

He arrived by taxi as Eddie had the day off to watch Chelsea play and he walked into the delightful house in Lord North Street just around the corner from the Palace of Westminster. For many years the street had been the most desirable address for Conservative politicians although rising property prices had driven out all but the most affluent. The house was bathed in light and Jonathan watched for a moment as a well-dressed couple swept into the hall ahead of him to be met with cries of: 'Darlings, darlings, how are you? It's been simply an age.' These and other such blandishments typified a certain sort of upper-class London society and putting them together with the braying laughter coming from the back of the hall, Jonathan felt he had the measure of the place and the people inside. He had to admit that the house itself was as desirable a house as one could find in central London. He found himself idly wondering how much it might be worth. He accepted the proffered glass of champagne from the formally dressed butler and walked slowly into the broad hallway, scanning the room for friendly faces or the host. To his surprise, he recognised no-one. There were sixty or so people squeezed into three downstairs rooms, perhaps forty men and twenty women. The noise level was high and the crowd were being served champagne and canapés on large silver platters by tall and slender waitresses with hair piled high above their heads and all dressed in identical black catsuits and extremely high heeled boots. The effect was startling. The artful designs of the canapés themselves suggested that the most expensive of London caterers were in charge of tonight's event.

He sipped his drink slowly and looked about him. Before long John arrived at his side and greeted him warmly, again thanking him effusively for dinner earlier in the week. He introduced him to a few people in the immediate vicinity and then, making his excuses, he went to meet other late-comers along with a promise to get together soon and 'do something fun'. He extracted himself graciously from the dull group he had been introduced to and in his usual manner started to work the room. It was a skill he had learnt many years ago and enabled him to sweep in and out of conversations, picking up information and, most importantly, quickly identifying the key people in the room who would make the evening worth attending. He normally managed this exercise without too much effort but tonight was a little tougher as he had few touch points with the people he was meeting: bankers, lawyers, and that great catch-all, 'businessmen'. There was quite an international flavour to the gathering and alongside the usual US and European accents there were a sprinkling of African men and one or two African women as well as three or four Russian men, marked out by their bodyguards and loud voices.

Turning away from surveying the room, he finally caught sight of Anna Cressley walking down the central staircase. Tall and slender, she was wearing a long close-fitting and very low-cut cream silk gown that contrasted against the long chestnut hair that fell luxuriously around her shoulders. He was quite unprepared for this. He had seen a corporate picture of her online with her hair swept into a bun and conservatively dressed in a business suit and the transformation tonight was startling. Like him, she worked the room, greeting everyone as long lost friends and taking complements with grace and laughter. Eventually, she worked her way to where Jonathan was standing.

'Well, good evening. You must be Jonathan Lomax, the only man I don't know here tonight. I know you have befriended my husband but he certainly didn't tell me what a handsome man you are.'

Her voice was low pitched and he struggled to hear her clearly against the hubbub of the room.

'I am very delighted to meet you,' he said, a little lamely, as they shook hands but she smiled warmly at him and very obviously appraised his body whilst she pretended to sip her almost full glass of Champagne. 'John certainly didn't tell me what a beauty he is married to.'

She remained silent, continuing to study him so he returned the compliment and let his eyes wander over her. He thought they must look like two animals sizing each other up before making a move. She broke first.

'Enjoy the view, Jonathan. There's more tit tape holding these two up than is decent for a woman of my age.'

'Anna, I'm sure you have many years to go before you need to worry about showing your age.'

'How gallant. Handsome and charming too. Quite a deadly combination.' After a moment's silence she continued, 'John is so pleased to have made a new friend. He doesn't have that many real friends and even though he came back a little worse for wear the other night it was quite obvious that you and he really got on. I am so pleased. Don't let him down.'

'I don't think I was leading John astray in the drinking stakes – in fact I was struggling to keep up with him.'

'Yes, well, you are probably right there. His drinking can get a little wearing at times but he's a decent man despite that.' Again she paused and looked at him intently for what seemed an age before adding in a louder voice, 'I must go and circulate. It's been a real pleasure meeting you and I look forward to having a much longer conversation with you in the very near future.' She bent forward for a ritual goodbye air kiss and, as her mouth was alongside his ear, she whispered, 'Lunch Monday. Somewhere quiet. Keep the afternoon free. I'll be in touch.'

And then, with a shimmy of cream silk she was gone, leaving him feeling slightly dazed and surprised. Women had come on to him at events like this before but this was not what he expected from a woman he was trying to investigate for illegal arms sales.

He reached for a passing glass of champagne and tried to concentrate upon further networking whilst at the same time trying to work out Anna's approach. Was this just physical attraction or did she have some other motive? Could she know anything about his investigation? Caught in this conversation with himself he was a distracted networker and was less successful than usual at circulating and working the room. He found himself trapped by two German bankers for a while and smiled politely through their dull conversation. Across the crowded room he saw Anna looking at him but when he smiled and raised his glass in salute she turned away without a smile.

As the party began to break up he sought out the hosts to express his thanks and say goodbye. They were standing together near the main doorway. John was solicitous, asking if he had enjoyed himself and met interesting people whilst Anna was silent alongside him. However, as he said goodbye and again air kissed her she quietly whispered, 'Monday,' into his ear. He left feeling more than a little puzzled and as he Uber-ed his way back to Richmond his sense of disquiet stayed with him. He Whats App'd Lottie.

Anna C only came on to me. Wants lunch on Monday
Instantly he heard back.
WTF were you up to?
Talk Monday. Night x

Ellie was waiting up for him when he arrived back at the house.

'How did it go? Did you meet her and what was she like?'

'It was pretty dull, bankers and lawyers. Smart house though and delicious canapes. Yes, I met Anna Cressley. She was rather imperious actually. Social chit chat only though. She has agreed to meet again so perhaps then I will be able to a little digging. You are up late my darling. How has your work for the shelter gone? Shall we go up to bed?'

Chapter 13

When Monday morning came around Jonathan was perplexed to receive an early email from Anna's PA.

To: Jonathan Lomax
cc: Anna Cressley
From: Cressida Wilson
Subject: Lunch

Dear Mr Lomax
Ms Cressley has asked me to pass on her apologies but she will not be able to make lunch today after all. She is travelling to Africa later this week and I'm afraid there is no other free space in her diary before she leaves. She has asked me to contact you again upon her return to see if another date might be possible.

Regards
Cressida Wilson
PA to Anna Cressley
Cavendale Limited

So now he was being blown out by Anna. What the hell was going on? Sitting back and trying to analyse her motives, he was at a loss to understand where she might be coming from. Had she just backtracked and thought twice about her flirting on Saturday evening or was she suspicious? If so, who might have tipped her off? Without finding out more from Anna he knew he would struggle to move the investigation forwards. He wondered how he could make any real progress if Anna refused to see him. He thought of emailing Anna directly but instead hit the reply all button and acknowledged Cressida's email.

To: Cressida Wilson
cc: Anna Cressley
From: Jonathan Lomax
Subject: Re Lunch

Cressida
Thanks for letting me know so early in the day.

Anna
Travel safely and have a great trip and I look forward to lunch upon your return. I very much enjoyed the party on Saturday. Thank you for the kind invitation.
Kind regards
Jonathan

Jonathan Lomax
MD - Catalyst

Satisfied that he had at least kept the lines of communication open, he returned to the tasks of the day and was lost in the complexities of financial modelling with Paddy and his finance team when he was interrupted by Carol, who had been instructed not to put through calls whilst this meeting was ongoing.

'Jonathan, I'm sorry but I have Tom Schalke on the line for you and I thought you might want to take his call. I can get rid of him if you want.'

'No, Carol, I should talk to him'. Turning to the others in his office, he apologised and asked them for the room. 'Tom, hi, how are you? It's been an age since we last spoke.'

'Jonathan.' Tom's loud and brash Brooklyn voice rang out on the telephone, 'I just wanted to tell you that I've been watching the channel over the weekend and I think it is coming on leaps and bounds. How are the numbers looking?'

'We're never satisfied as you know Tom, but we are on target on the audience front. However we are still around 8%

below our predicted net revenue for the quarter so we may need to do some more revisions on the programming costs if that trend continues. As you know, the whole TV advertising business is down this quarter as Netflix and Amazon's growth encourages advertisers to switch out of free TV.'

'Yeah, I know, and that's a problem I predict will only get worse. If I were you, I would get on and look at those savings sooner rather than later.' He paused to let this advice sink home, 'but anyway, I'm sure Drew has filled you in on the broader picture of what's happening at GBN.'

'No. I met with him on Friday but we only talked TV. Is there something I should know?'

'Well, some of the investors, not us you understand, are keen to see faster progress on the transformation of the business. I keep telling them to be patient but you know how some of these private equity guys can turn on a sixpence and lose interest in a business plan they bought into only months before. The new revolving credit facility we are setting up for GBN is not going so well and Drew is looking a bit rocky. If I were you, I would be keeping my head down and my nose clean.'

So Drew was on the skids and Tom was phoning to give him the inside track: the king is dying, not yet dead, but keep your distance and get ready for change. Obviously, this succession plan was being led by Tom, despite his thinly-disguised denials.

'Tom, thanks for the heads up. I've purposely been keeping out of the rest of the business so I can concentrate just on TV. Do I need to worry about investor sentiment here?'

'No. I don't think so. Everyone seems to like the new format and see you guys as part of the future. Just make sure you hit your numbers so there's no room for any doubts to creep in.'

'Understood. Take it from me we will hit the first quarter numbers.'

'That's what I like about you Jonathan. Ask and it is delivered. How's that family of yours by the way? Are they seeing any more of you these days?'

'Yeah, a little. We had a great week away skiing so they were reminded of what I look like and we seemed to get along pretty well.'

'And a little bird tells me that you've been meeting the Cressleys...'

'Not much passes you by Tom. Do you know them well?'

'I know John quiet well. He was talking to me earlier about GBN, that's when you came up in conversation. Although his bank is not the biggest, he tends to follow my advice and so his outfit is in quite a few of our ventures. Having them on board early on helps some of the other bigger ones follow through. You know how sheep-like they can be. John's not the brightest of guys but he's ok. I wouldn't have thought he would be your soulmate though. I've always had him down as a chinless Tory, right school, right club and good contacts masking a third rate brain.'

'I like him a lot. I think he's probably got a bright future in the Tory party...'

'Maybe, maybe. There's a long history of not very bright people making it to the top in British politics. Did you meet Anna on Saturday night? She's a completely different proposition, what a knockout.'

'They are certainly very different...'

'Yep, I don't know how that marriage works and that's for sure. I've always thought John might be a closet queen and the rumour is that Anna has some young army officer who looks after her womanly needs when she's in Africa. One of those places where they have a problem with Islamists. West Africa. Can't remember the place. Name a country or two for me.'

"Nigeria, Sierre Leone, Ivory Coast..'

'No shorter, one word.'

'Ghana, Mali...'

'Yeah, that's it. Mali. She wanted us to invest in a gas plant there last year but there's no way a US fund would ever invest in a country where the words 'Islamist insurgency' are the first things that pop up on a Google search. Even at the rates of return she was promising. I think some French banks eventually bought in although they fleeced her too, I believe. I was kind of surprised as Cavendale is pretty risk adverse generally and Mali was not their usual profile. Maybe it had something to do with her young army officer...'

'So she spends a lot of time in Mali?' asked Jonathan.

'I don't know. She's always jetting to and from the continent but they have a lot of property interests in South Africa so I guess she spends a fair bit of time there too. I really only know what John tells me. Apart from the army officer, of course; that came from a different source.'

There was a pause in the conversation. Jonathan didn't want to appear too interested in the Cressleys and looked to change the subject.

'So, Tom, where should we be thinking about rolling out our franchise for Catalyst? Germany? Maybe France?'

'Maybe, maybe. I've sent one of the compilation tapes you sent me off to the biggest independent media company in Hungary and they have shown some interest.'

'I thought the right wing were already firmly in control in Hungary...?'

'Yeah, but that's just a few idiot politicians and that could spell big trouble for everyone there. I think Catalyst could be the way to create a really populist movement that can then start pushing those politicians around. That's what excites me – apart from the profits that is. If we can get that one franchise up and running and the model established, maybe then we can do a roadshow around Europe and see who else is interested. Could be fun. Anyway, can't sit around chatting all morning, work to do. Remember our motto, Jonathan: we want everything faster, better, cheaper. See you soon.'

And then he was gone, off to bully someone else and cause trouble elsewhere. At least he had given Jonathan some new information that directly linked Anna to Mali and indicated that she spent a lot of time there. He could see how the gas plant had slipped between the gaps of the two reports he had read. He has specifically avoided mentioning Mali to Ben to keep him off the scent and he hadn't mentioned Cavendale to Khalila, so she had no reason to include the gas plant in her report on Mali. He also filed away the news on Drew; he would need to tread carefully there. If there was to be a change in CEO he would need to make sure the new boss was every bit as keen on Catalyst as Drew professed to be.

Later that day, Jonathan emailed John Andrews and, after thanking him for the invitation to Saturday night's party, asked him if he was free for dinner towards the end of the week. An email reply quickly confirmed John's availability and he suggested dinner on Thursday at a Turkish restaurant in Clerkenwell that Jonathan didn't know. John said that they had great live music alongside really good food. They organised times and Jonathan left John to book his choice of venue.

In between other meetings, Jonathan found time to brief Lottie on Tom's revelations about Mali and they also discussed Anna's reversal on that day's lunch invitation.

'It could just be that she has had second thoughts about wanting to bed you boss,' said Lottie with a wry smile.

'Ha – I know it could be that simple but somehow I don't think so. Maybe her father told her to keep her distance; although he wasn't there and why would she have told him about me anyway?'

'Could it be husband John finding out?'

'No. By the sound of it they are pretty self-sufficient in that regard and he was only too keen to agree to dinner later this week. Maybe she did some research on me and decided it wasn't such a good idea after all.'

'But you know how shiny I keep your profile. If anything an online search would only have encouraged her.'

'That's probably true. Let's just keep her parked as a work in progress and see if we can make some tangible progress by the time she returns from Africa. We can then decide on our next steps with her. In the meantime, I think John is the weak link and I will see where some gentle questioning and a surfeit of alcohol can get us. Next week, I'm going to try and meet this Andy Gilmour guy too and see I can get his story to stand up. For now, I'm going to let the investigation lie fallow until I meet with John for dinner on Thursday.'

Thursday was a particularly busy day for Jonathan, with a number of minor production crises and a late afternoon emotional meltdown from Angie that required some serious mopping up over a glass or two of white wine at the end of the day. Consequently, it was almost nine o'clock by the time he arrived at the difficult to find and somewhat anonymous Turkish restaurant. John was already sitting down with a bottle of Raki that was already on-third empty. His glass, milky-white after dilution with water, was also half empty. This might be easier than he imagined thought Jonathan, as he sat down and accepted a glass of Turkey's national drink. Looking around, he was surprised as to how quiet the place was and how down at heel it looked. He had John down for a flashy see-and-be-seen type of restaurant-goer and this was certainly not one of those places. Their large table was out of the main body of the restaurant in a partially enclosed space that gave them a measure of privacy from the other diners, not that there were many there.

'Thanks for the text Jonathan. I knew you wouldn't be long so I've ordered a whole selection of mezze to go along with the Raki,' said John. 'It can knock you out completely if you don't have some food to go along with it. It's a drink that demands food.'

'That's fine,' said Jonathan, 'I don't think I've had Raki since I was last in Turkey three or four years ago.'

'It's my favourite of the Mediterranean aperitifs. Mind you, it can give you the mother and father of hangovers if you don't respect it. Anyway, I've had a week to forget so I've got my drinking boots on. How about you?'

'Oh, so-so. What's been the problem for you?'

'Not one problem, my friend, a complete bloody line-up of them.' Draining his glass, he continued, 'The bank is on my case for a couple of dud investments and in these straightened times you never know if that means one is only a step away from the dreaded pink slip; I've done two Tory selection meetings in the last two weeks and got neither seat; and Anna is in Africa again which means I've got her bloody father on my case barking demands about things only Anna knows how to deal with.'

'Why do you think the selection meetings are not going your way?' asked Jonathan, choosing the least interesting area to begin his evening of discovery.

'Well, for a start, it's not good if one's bloody wife can't be bothered to come along and support one. And then there's this idea that there should be more women candidates and that doesn't help, and finally I'm a bloody banker and that's not the most popular profession – even for a Tory party audience. If I turn into an unemployed banker then it will be even worse and I'll never get a seat worth having; they'll make me fight Rotherham North or some other Labour stronghold where I will be fighting to save my deposit and beat the bloody Lib Dems. I tell you Jonathan it's no joke and I don't know where to turn. You'd think my father-in-law would pull a few strings but he's as much use as a chocolate teapot when it comes to helping me out – although I've seen him doing good things for other people. It would look bad, he says, if he was to be seen helping his son-in-law win a seat other than on merit. Merit, I bloody ask you, what does that mean? He's so deep in some people's pockets it's a wonder he can ever see daylight.'

Waiting whilst mountains of delicious-looking food was unloaded onto the table, Jonathan asked, 'What can I do to help you, John? I've got a little influence in the party but not much down at grassroots level. But if I can help in any way at all you've only to say the word.'

'That's marvellous of you Jonathan, but I'm not sure either. What I'm looking for is a safe seat not too far from town where I don't have to keep turning up to please the bloody locals and can just wave the flag periodically between elections. It's not too much to ask, is it?'

'Have you ever thought of using the media? I've got a whole television channel devoted to conservative politics and we are always looking out for new talent. You could decide your political position to fit your potential constituents and make yourself famous. That could only help in the selection meetings, don't you think?'

'Would you do that for me? That would be wonderful. Name recognition does seem to be the thing these days, doesn't it?'

'I will organise a screen test in the next couple of weeks.' Jonathan thought he should push this out as far as possible; even John might realise what a buffoon he would be on TV when he saw the screen test, and a vague promise of future screen time was probably the best carrot to keep him on the hook.

'That's awfully good of you, old man. I am most grateful. I feel better already.' He took a long drink of his Raki and refilled his and Jonathan's glasses to the rim. 'Here's to the media and all who sail in her.'

'One problem fixed already then,' said Jonathan as he sipped gingerly at the fiery Raki, 'What's going wrong at the bank?'

'Well, that's quite a lot more difficult. Basically, the job works for me because I get the inside track on investment opportunities from a few private investors and hedge funds and then impress the powers that run the bank with my skills at finding great investments. However, my dearest friends have encouraged me and my bank into investing in a couple of turkeys – pardon the word whilst we are in here – and one of them could be very bad news indeed. It's a big enough investment to cause a real stink and if I'm not careful it will all be laid outside my door.'

'That does sound outside my pay grade,' said Jonathan, 'my only advice would be to say as little as possible in meetings and try and deflect the flak elsewhere if you can.'

'I know. That's what I would normally do, but this time I think it's a little too close for comfort and the City is such a small place. It's not easy to recover from an upset like this.'

'Hang in and keep your head down,' said Jonathan, unconsciously adopting John's idioms, 'Now what about your father-in-law? I don't know him but how can I help there? By the way, this chickpea and mint dish is delicious.'

'Anna's in Africa as I told you and the old man, her father, isn't really in the loop about all of her deals these days; he's obviously across the big property stuff and he can do those in his sleep, but the oil and gas stuff is too technical and too complex for him or me and Anna is the only one who can explain it all in ways that make sense to him. That doesn't stop him wanting to be in charge though. When she's not around he's always trying to Skype her and she's always in meetings or too busy to stop, and when she is in the UK they just argue like cat and dog. It's pretty miserable being caught in the middle of those two when things aren't going well.'

'Is there no-one else who can help carry the load?' said Jonathan, turning down a refill to his empty Raki glass and instead reaching for a glass of the red wine that John had ordered earlier.

'Not really. On the property side they have people who manage the business on a day to day basis, but on the energy side they are mostly technical staff and both Anna and her father treat them badly, so they mostly just do what they are told and read out their prepared scripts when we are trying to entice investors. Which we have to do because we are small fry in a world of big players. There's one chap called Donald Brown who is the COO but he's very cautious of saying anything to the old man without Anna there to back him up. He's in Africa too this week so he's no help to me anyway.'

'So, Sir John is not directly involved in Africa?'

'No, he's very involved. He is the one with the contacts, and at a very high level. It's just the financing deals are so complex. That's especially true when you've got tin-pot dictators and middlemen involved and everyone looking for a percentage. Some of it has to be kept below the radar too – especially when you've got the big multi-national energy companies involved. They can't be seen to be handing over suitcases of cash to smooth the progress of a deal. Anna's really good at all that side of things, keeping people onside and making deals work. The old man's name also carries a lot of kudos and that puts us ahead of some of the other players out there. It's the Wild West though, normal rules do not apply and some of the things we have to do would make your hair stand on end. Shall I get another bottle of this ready for later? It's rather good this Urla, isn't it?'

He motioned to the attentive waiter and another bottle appeared within moments, new wineglasses polished to accept what was probably the most expensive red wine in the restaurant's cellars.

Conversation moved on to discussions around John's real passions in life; Rugby Union and especially the intricacies of the England team-sheet, shooting and fly fishing. Jonathan knew just enough about all three to keep the conversation moving along and John only needed the smallest encouragement of the occasional question or nod of approval to keep going on his own. Whilst John rambled on about the decline in wild salmon numbers, Jonathan wondered how he could get John to open up further on Cavendale. He filled both glasses again and decided that copious alcohol was likely the only answer. He ate steadily to combat what he guessed would be a pretty awful hangover.

By the time coffee arrived, John had just about run out of steam on his pastimes and Jonathan thought it was his best chance to try and dig again.

'I did some reading up on Cavendale after meeting you last time,' he began, 'and what you've achieved in a short time in oil and gas is really impressive...'

'Thanks, old man, but it's really Anna and her father...'

'I'm sure you are a key operator too,' said Jonathan, 'but really, you've quietly become a serious player in African energy, especially in the Western Sahara region. It must be hard to run big plants like that one you have in Mali with all of the tensions that exist there.'

'Well, of course we don't actually run them, we sub-contract all of that out to companies like Halliburton, but in Mali it's actually a South African operator called DVBR. They have all the hassle and the Saffer's are pretty good on security and all the stuff that you need in places like northern   Mali. Anna loves the place but I can't imagine why. Timbuktu's interesting for an hour or two but when you've seen one old mud building you've seen them all, and Bamako is a swamp by a river and it's so hot there you can hardly even think straight. The flies are the size of hornets and bite great lumps out of any uncovered skin. At least you don't have to worry about the bloody Islamists down there though, when you get into the gas fields then you know everyone you meet wants to kill you. Even the bloody Foreign Office advises against going there.'

'Surely the army takes care of things?'

'No, once you get into the north it is really local militia leaders who call the shots whilst the national army swan around pretending that they're in charge. Everybody is in somebody else's pocket and everybody wants to put their hand into ours.'

'So Anna has to go over there with a sack of dollars?'

'If only it were that simple. In Mali it tends to be things: luxury yachts, apartments in Dubai, offshore bank accounts. Even guns and rockets are on their shopping lists. You'd be amazed.' Warming to his theme he went on, 'One local army commander even wanted us to supply him with anti-aircraft guns!'

'So you have to do these sorts of things to get the business?'

'You know how it is: you have to do what you have to do. Accounting for it all is the biggest problem. Ah, at last, the entertainment's arriving.'

Jonathan looked around as two long haired Turkish dancers dressed in flowing chiffon skirts split to the waist and heavily decorated rhinestone bras entered their area bearing two ice buckets and bottles of what Jonathan feared might be Turkish champagne. The heavily made-up girls were followed by a small man with a pot-bellied lute under his arm. Behind him, he pulled across an aubergine coloured velvet curtain that almost entirely shielded their table from public view. This was obviously a private performance area.

John introduced Jonathan to the two dancers, Esma and Ada. One of the girls poured champagne for all four of them whilst the musician tuned his lute.

'This is my favourite part of the evening here,' said John. 'Good food and wine and then beautiful girls to dance for you whilst you drink champagne.'

He sat back happily and demanded kisses from the two girls. Ada complied, shyly pecking him on the cheek but Esma happily sat upon his lap and kissed him hard and long on the mouth. She stopped as the music started and they both began to dance in a traditional Turkish style weaving their bellies, breasts and thighs into complex and fluid patterns whilst keeping their eyes fixed upon their two guests with their mouths locked into formal smiles that gave no sense of their real emotions. Both girls were impressive dancers and Esma's control of her stomach muscles was especially captivating as she rotated her hips in time to the music.

There was no doubt that the music and the dancing was erotic and Jonathan could see that John was transfixed by the two girls, especially by Esma. As their dancing continued, John leaned over to Jonathan and quietly whispered, 'Esma's my girl, you know. I often stay over with her when Anna's away and you can see what she does with her hips – well you can probably imagine what it's like to be in bed with her. A night of Turkish passion with my Esma and just about all of my problems disappear. Ada's a new girl but, my, she's pretty too. I can enquire for you to see if she's interested in a little extra-mural activity?'

Jonathan almost choked on his wine. 'No, no, I really have to get home tonight, I really do. Ellie's expecting me. But thank you. I very much appreciate the offer. As you say, she is certainly very pretty. Maybe another time when I'm more prepared?'

'Of course, I understand. It can be difficult for us married men. I should have warned you. We'll sort something out for a future date. Maybe the four of us for a weekend away? They love a little holiday with some luxury thrown in. Esma and I enjoyed a whole weekend in Brussels last month at the Kempinski. All paid for by the bank and I never even made it downstairs to the conference venue. Not a word about my little Turkish secret, of course. It's not something that I would want to be quizzed about at a Tory selection meeting in darkest Surrey.'

'Of course. Your secret is safe with me, and I'm honoured you shared it with me. I'm very tempted.'

'Don't worry. I will get Esma to smooth it over with Ada so she doesn't feel rejected. Proud people, you know. Doesn't do to upset them. Feuds can go on for years... Ah I think it's over. Girls come and join us. That was delightful. Here, Ada, come and sit on this chair next to me. You must be thirsty after all that dancing, have some champagne.'

The girls sat down, a sheen of sweat glistening across their exposed skin and they both smiled happily now their dancing was over. The musician left the room quietly, pulling the velvet curtain behind him to leave their area private. The girls quickly drained their champagne glasses and held them out to Jonathan to refill. He did so and wondered how he could extricate himself from the group now that any further chance of information was gone for the night. Ada obviously spoke little English and sat drinking and smiling at Jonathan sitting next to her. Esma was talking quietly to John with her head close to his whilst his hand slowly caressed her bare thigh. He tried to make small talk with Ada but the language barrier made that difficult. John and Esma were oblivious to them and it was fairly evident that they wanted to move on to somewhere quieter. This eventually gave Jonathan the opportunity he was looking for to stand up and announce his departure, thanking them all for a wonderful evening and leaving Ada looking inscrutable behind her heavy stage make-up. She looked away from him as he walked out. He hoped he hadn't hurt her feelings too much with his early exit.

Safe in a taxi, Jonathan reflected on what he had learned and wrote rapid notes into his phone so that he didn't forget anything when the inevitable hangover kicked in. Cursing quietly as the London potholes (and the copious alcohol) caused him to miss the right keys from time to time, he wrote himself a note. He and Lottie could go through it tomorrow morning.

Note:
Cavendale bribes Government officials and Army officers in Mali and elsewhere. Offers gifts including arms.
Anna the key person on the ground in Africa
Sir J still the driving force
J likely to lose banking job- opportunity?
check out Donald Brown -COO
check out DVBR
find out the name of Anna's Mali lover
organise a screen test for J

Once that was completed, he leant back against the seat and fell into a drunken sleep. He was woken up by the taxi driver gently shaking his shoulder after the taxi had pulled up outside his own front door.

Chapter 14

Jonathan met Lottie as usual at their normal hipster cafe for breakfast, although the over-consumption of Raki had prevented him from getting up for swimming that morning - much to Ellie's amusement as he rarely suffered from hangovers. He had decided not to tell his wife about the offer of a young Turkish belly dancer for the night.

'God, you look rough,' said Lottie, who as usual looked her groomed and elegant business-like self, 'what did he do to you?'

'Never let me drink Raki again,' pleaded Jonathan, as he sipped what would be the first of many macchiatos that morning. 'The things I have to do to find out the truth. Turkish food and drink followed by the offer of a belly dancer to myself for a night of gyratory passion. I ask you.'

Lottie giggled into her coffee. 'Seriously, he offered you a girl? I presume that means that he has one for himself?'

'Yes; she's called Esma. She has a tummy that can do a spin cycle both ways and gives our man physical comfort when his wife is safely out of the country.'

He passed his phone over to Lottie and she read through the brief notes he had written in the taxi the night before.

'So we've at least got grounds for believing that Cavendale trades arms for business favours. But nothing yet on the Government? Who is DVBR and what's the screen test all about?'

'DVBR are the South African company who actually operate the Mali gas plant on a day to day basis. I need to have them thoroughly checked out. John's about to lose his job from some failed insider dealing cock-up, so I'm trying to keep him onside and further his squalid political ambitions. He will be terrible in front of camera, of course – think Jacob Rees-Mogg without the funny haircut or intellect. Still, it will buy us a bit more time as he will feel he's in my debt, so it's worth doing.'

'What's the next step?'

'I will get DVBR checked out by Khalila and see if I can set up a meeting with this Andy Gilmour guy. We need to push things on as we are getting no closer to tying the Government into the Mali deal. Would you mind running a check for me on the Cavendale COO, Donald Brown? I don't want to get Ben to do it or he will start putting the pieces together for himself and that's too awful to contemplate.'

'Sure. What else can I do?'

'Can you shepherd John through the auditions? I hate to have to ask you to do it. I will introduce you by email but I don't want Angie destroying him before he's even started. We might have to promise him some outings next quarter – we can always rescind the offer later on.'

'No problem. Are you ready now for me to fix up a social meeting with Sir John? He's one of the few senior Tories you haven't met.'

'No, not for a week or two. I need to have my ducks in a row before I talk seriously to him. I suppose there's a chance he will be at the Pioneer Group meeting on Monday evening. It's a sort of social event so it would be a good opportunity to shake hands and say hello, maybe even fix up a further meeting for a couple of weeks' time.'

'OK, and how about Anna?'

'Let's see if she reaches out when she returns from Africa. I don't want to be seen to be chasing her.'

They strolled towards the studios together, Jonathan's head still beating like a drum, and split up in reception to head to their respective offices. Although he really wanted to spend time thinking through his Mali investigation, he, as usual, had a full day of meetings and was soon lost in the myriad of minor and major problems that generally made up his working week. He had realised after a few days on air that the nature of the channel's programming would always require him to referee between warring factions within his production teams and that this constant conflict would be the thing that really kept everyone on their toes and the channel moving forwards. It made for exhausting days but until he could train Paul, Ben and Angie to take more informed decisions he was stuck with making too many himself.

It was after four when he arrived at Drew's offices in Paddington for his weekly meeting. Unusually, he had Paddy in tow with him as Drew wanted to go through the first quarter finances and he knew that Paddy's analysis would convince Drew of the veracity of his plans. By some trimming and some cutting of the fat which he had carefully built in to his first budget, he could cut costs to ensure that he reached his first quarter numbers and make up for the shortfall in advertising revenues. At this stage no-one would be looking too closely at the detail of the numbers so the disappointing advertising revenues would not trigger any alarm bells. Jonathan knew that it would not be so easy in future quarterly analyses. After Paddy's run-through of the numbers, he was excused and the talk turned to a more general conversation about the business.

'I'm getting lots of grief from my Tory friends about the channel so I guess it means you are making an impact out there,' said Drew as the door closed behind Paddy. 'Even the PM said to me that you were stirring things up when we spoke earlier this week. He seemed quite positive though.'

'We are certainly starting to make some noise,' agreed Jonathan. 'We are also beginning to provide some good openings to the GNM newspapers so it's a virtuous circle at the moment. I'm sure the opposition newspapers will turn on us as we grow; at the moment it's only the *Guardian* that really sticks it to us and that's obviously good for business. *Private Eye* have even started a column called 'Catalyst Crap' which is really very funny and well-written. I wish I had thought of it myself. The production team's Whats App group loves it too, so it's great for staff morale.'

'Well, I'm pretty pleased with the way things are going. The editorial is ok and at least we look like hitting the business plan numbers, which isn't true in every part of the business. Have you had Tom Schalke on the phone to you yet?'

'Yeah, he called me on Monday but only to say that he had been watching the channel and he had liked what he saw. We chatted about a couple of mutual friends, nothing more than that.'

'He's an evil bastard but I guess you've already worked that out for yourself. I'm in the crosshairs at the moment so I'm biased, but be very careful what you say to him as you never know how it might be used against you. He chews people up and spits them out pretty quickly. I was the blue-eyed boy only months ago and now I'm seen as part of the problem here,' his arm motioned around the room. 'I don't know how it will turn out over the next couple of months but I've certainly seen how deadly he can be when he feels the need.'

Drew was interrupted by the Circulation Director, whom Jonathan only vaguely knew, bursting into the office, 'Boss, sorry to interrupt. Hello, Jonathan.' He paused and Jonathan asked Drew, 'Do you want me to step outside? We've nearly finished.'

'No, stay. This will only be a quickie I think.'

The Circulation Director hesitated for a moment with Jonathan still in the room and then went on, 'Look, we've got a problem over the weekend. I need to dump several tens of thousands of the Sunday paper straight over to Ireland and have them pulped. I know you've come out against it publicly but our circulation figures will be in the toilet this month if we don't do something. Can I have your agreement?'

Drew hesitated for several seconds and then said, 'Yes, ok. No paperwork please. Just do it.' Turning to Jonathan he added, 'You didn't hear that obviously. Nothing to concern you, every paper has to get up to these sorts of tricks from time to time.' They turned back to talking about the next steps for the channel.

As Eddie fought with the Friday afternoon traffic on the return journey to Wandsworth, Jonathan thought about the conversation on the newspaper pulping in Ireland. It had been common practice up until a few years ago, indeed Irish contractors lined up to formally bid for the rights to meet aeroplanes at the airport and immediately recycle the newly printed newspapers. An agreement between publishers had supposedly outlawed the practice as the industry tried to clean up its act and come together to take on the advertising juggernauts Google and Facebook. These two were steadily destroying the advertising base of the print industry even as young people stopped buying newspapers and circulations diminished. Things must be worse than I feared, thought Jonathan, if we are resorting to these tactics again to keep numbers up. Even more puzzling was Drew allowing him to listen in to this conversation. What was his game there? Drew must have expected the conversation to be about circulation issues and why have a witness to an improper if not downright illegal decision? He couldn't puzzle this one out and instead checked his emails. There was one from John, replying to Jonathan's earlier thank-you email.

From: John Andrews
To: Jonathan Lomax
Subject: Re: Last night

Jonny
It was a pleasure. Don't thank me, it was nothing. You did well to bail out as early as you did. It all ended a bit messy with the two girls. Esma gets very jealous and after she decided I fancied Ada it was all I could do to win her over and stay the night. No doubt it will take something from Tiffany's (again!) to win her true affection back. Bloody awful hangover today too. How much Raki did I drink? Anyway, really enjoyed it and will repeat soon. Off to the country for the weekend for a spot of rough shooting with the old man whilst

Anna is away but around next week for a return match. Venue up to you this time.
Best regards
John

Jonathan smiled to himself. There was no doubt he had John right where he needed him. He just had to decide how to play his hand to get the greatest return. He would reply tomorrow when he hoped that he might just have a plan. It was 6pm by the time he got back to the office and he was lost in the middle of a complex technology meeting when he had a text from Ellie.

Don't forget dinner out tonight. Be home by 7.45. E xx

Of course he had forgotten: he had promised Ellie he would make dinner with some of her work colleagues and partners even though it was Friday and she knew how he hated socialising on one the busiest days of his very busy week. He had promised, however, and texted Eddie to be ready in fifteen minutes for the trip west, which would inevitably take much longer than it normally would. He spent the whole journey on the phone to various colleagues and ended up having an unfortunate argument with Angie just as the car reached Richmond. Angie had returned from her week's holiday full of angst and was becoming ever more fractious to deal with as her stress levels increased. He was still arguing his case with her and simultaneously trying to calm her down as he walked in through the front door. Both boys were running around screaming and shouting and Vanessa was trying to calm them down. He quickly made his way upstairs where Ellie was sitting in her dressing gown, putting on her earrings and almost ready to go.

'Have I got time for quick shower? You look lovely by the way.'

'Hi. Thank you. Yes, if you are quick but don't shower whilst that phone is still attached to your ear.'

He made his apologies to Angie, promising he would call her back in fifteen minutes to resolve their dispute. He pulled off his suit and discarded it across the bedroom floor as he made his way into the shower. Ten minutes later, he had pulled on a new shirt and suit trousers and was almost ready to go out. Ellie walked back into the room looking elegant and understated in a close fitting black dress with a low neck that he didn't recognise.

'Wow. When I said you looked lovely I hadn't realised just how lovely. Have I seen this before?'

'No. I thought I needed something new for evening wear. Do you think it's too low here?' She brushed her neck and cleavage with her fingers.

'No. It looks great. Really good. I will just finish getting dressed and then I must give Angie a quick call back. Once I've done that I'm all yours.'

'We are late already so make it as quick as you can. Can you call from the car as we go?'

'Sure. Two minutes. Call Eddie, will you, and have him ready to go.'

Their host tonight was Howard, the driving force at the Ealing homeless charity where Ellie volunteered. Tall, painfully thin and super fit despite his sixty years, Howard was a retired in-house lawyer from the Department of Work and Pensions and had spent most of his working life inside that department. Taking early retirement, he joined the charity and quickly Howie, as he was known to all, became its leading advocate. He knew most of the tricks of the DWP and its forerunners and could run rings around the local Housing Officers. He cycled everywhere on a carbon fibre racing bike entirely unsuitable for London's potholes, and would usually arrive at meetings sweaty and late, but, as Ellie had noticed, as soon as any meeting began, everyone deferred to his judgement and rarely contradicted him. As lawyers, the two of them were drawn together, and over several coffee breaks in the local Costa, Ellie began to understand him a little better and like him a lot more. He was driven by a burning need to see justice for his clients and wouldn't stop until he had achieved it. They gently flirted with each over cappuccinos but there was nothing sexual in their relationship; he was divorced and seeing another woman and anyway he was far too old for Ellie and she definitely wasn't looking for an outside relationship. It was Howie who encouraged her to be more radical in her thinking and realise that things could be different if enough people demanded it.

Howie was committed to changing the relationship between the rich and the poor of the UK, and although he could sound like a *Guardian* editorial at times, he was a persuasive speaker. He began to share his ideas with Ellie whenever they had time to talk and in time Ellie began to develop her own theories as to how social change could be brought about. Howie listened attentively to her ideas, occasionally offered additional insights or contradictions, but generally just encouraged her to keep on exploring these new ideas for herself. She was fully aware of the upper middle class and affluent position she enjoyed but joined the Labour Party anyway and began to interact with local members via email - although she didn't dare attend any of the many meetings to which she was invited. She also decided that she would keep these new views to herself for the moment and see how things developed. She decided early on not to tell Jonathan about her regular chats with Howie, although she could never really understand why she had made this decision in the first place. Once it was made, it was increasingly hard to undo. It was probably the first real secret she had kept from Jonathan. Joining the Labour Party was the second. Tonight would be a real test as Jonathan would be outside of his comfort zone and exposed to some radical and forceful individuals.

They arrived at the house at the other end of Richmond some thirty minutes after the deadline to find the other six guests already drinking in the large Victorian kitchen. Jonathan knew none of Ellie's work colleagues and was introduced to them by Ellie as she was introduced to their respective partners. He hungrily drank the proffered glass of Champagne; he was still a little hungover and he suspected tonight might be a long night amongst a group unlikely to be soulmates. He promised himself he would be on his best behaviour so as not to upset Ellie. She didn't ask him to do a lot of these sorts of things so he must be good tonight and not get offside with her or any of her friends.

A couple of glasses of Prosecco later (he had realised his mistake at the first taste) the host invited them to move to the table at the other end of the knocked through kitchen. Jonathan hadn't really had a chance to talk to him, but Howie seemed to be the most interesting guy at the event. Ellie had told him on the way over that Howie had been a big deal at the DWP and had taken early retirement to work as a volunteer. He knew that Howie was divorced and the woman playing hostess for the evening evidently didn't live at the house but more than that he didn't know. Most of the other guests were, frankly, uninteresting. He could make small talk all night with them and by tomorrow he would have forgotten everything about them. Looking at them, he knew they would talk schools, local planning issues, their children, books, theatre and films. He could do this standing on his head but it didn't mean he would enjoy it. Howie's larger than life girlfriend Bathandwa was the exception. A strikingly tall woman with hair piled high above her head in an impressively tall beehive, she was dressed in what he presumed was tribal dress but found himself too polite to ask about. He sat at dinner between her and Sally, the manager of the local Sainsbury's, with Howie one along at the head of the table.

Bathandwa dominated the conversation through the first part of dinner but mostly ignored speaking directly to him. After the expected small talk with Sally, who was married to one of Ellie's co-workers, a couple of glasses of unexpectedly good white Burgundy that complemented the only-ok goats cheese and endive salad, he was working his way through the main course duck whatever-it-was and a rather thin Pinot Noir before he was able to start up a conversation with Howie.

'You must find life very different now from your days at the DWP. Ellie tells me you were there for most of your career.'

'Well, it's had several names over the years as you know, but yes, it's been quite a change. I saw so many poor results to policies we tried to push through that I was determined to do some good work in the community and early retirement has allowed me to do that. It's great that we are able to bring in wonderful people like Ellie and Susannah.' He used his fork to wave at Jonathan's wife and co-worker who were at the other end of the table and deep in conversation, oblivious to his comments. 'I like to think we are making a difference to people's lives and when you look at the homelessness issues, even in affluent places like Richmond, it makes you weep. I know you may have different political views to mine but it's hard to believe this Government actually cares about the poor.'

'I'm sure that's not right. I just don't think anyone has any answers these days that make sense.' Jonathan reached over to refill his water glass, hoping he might be able to steer the conversation away from the minefield of contemporary politics. The last thing he needed tonight was an argument. 'So what else do you spend your days on, when you are not working?'

'Honestly, I'm busier now than I ever was as a civil servant, but I'm also a keen cyclist so I do various sportive events around the south of England and I'm also heavily involved in the Labour Party here and on a London wide basis.'

So much for trying to steer the conversation away from politics. Cycling it would have to be, he thought. 'I've often thought about doing a sportive. Do they cater for all levels? I'm a beginner really.'

'Yes, there are lots suitable for first-timers and you are competing against yourself rather than other riders — many of whom are a lot younger and fitter than you or I. From what Ellie tells me, though, I must say I'm surprised you think you might have time to do any cycling. I would have thought you are up to your neck in it trying to drag the country further along towards right-wing conservatism.'

'Hey, hold on a minute there. I'm just part of the mainstream media and as that has changed we now have to take on issues rather than just report on them. If there's a criticism to be made of us, it's that we are not radical enough and we need to change this country faster...'

'I don't think many of the people we help would buy your brand of global capitalism any more, Jonathan. It simply doesn't work for the vast majority of the population. I do agree, however, that we need radical change and a Conservative Government is never going to make that happen.'

'Well, Howie, where's your precious Labour Party when it comes to suggesting alternatives? It seems to me they can't even agree what day of the week it is, never mind provide coherent opposition or a different world view.'

'Yes, I know there are issues with our party but at least they are trying to grapple with the problems the poor, the young and the under-employed face today. We will, as part of this ongoing conversation, renew and re-invigorate the party...'

'I'm sorry but what are you smoking? We are watching the Labour Party return to 1970's statism right in front of our very eyes and the only reason it's still going is the inertia of our rotten voting system that gives it a whole load of safe seats where people are too lazy to consider anyone else. What we need is a modern social democratic party that has shrugged off the unions and restrictive practices and a hundred years of celebrating organised labour. That world is over; it's gone and will never come back. The coal mines have all closed down. My channel is actually a bigger force in opposition to the Government than the whole of your shadow cabinet put together.'

By this time, silence had descended on the rest of the table and all eyes and ears were turned to the heated discussion.

'I'm sorry, but I don't recognise that statement: how can you be in opposition to a party you support?'

'We support their philosophy, it's true – but we challenge them on all of their thinking and policy ideas. By doing that we ensure that these policies are well thought through and where they are not we will attack them as inept.'

'But what gives you the right to set yourself up as the arbiter of what's right and what's not?'

'The failure of the political system and your Labour Party in particular to offer any viable alternative solutions.' Jonathan's voice was even and precise but underneath his cool exterior he was beginning to be riled by Howie's attacks. 'And remember, no-one has to watch our channel. If it doesn't deliver anything interesting it will wither and die. Much like the Labour Party.'

'We are re-building the party after the disaster of the Blair-Brown years and we will continue to do so. It takes time. We're recruiting thousands of new members and not just students and left wingers but sensible people like Susannah and Ellie here, who realise that your way works only for the richest and leaves nothing for the rest of society. You look surprised. Perhaps Ellie didn't tell you she's a member? I'm not, given your political outlook.'

'We are not the first couple in West London to have different political viewpoints and I don't suppose we will be the last,' said Jonathan, glancing down the table where Ellie avoided his gaze and reached for her wine glass.

An awkward silence descended upon the table for a moment and then there was then a concerted effort around the room to change the subject and drag the discussion away from politics. Within a few moments, a veneer of bright conversation had covered over the awkward conversation and the rest of the evening passed off without further incident. Jonathan was quieter than usual and drank a little more of the thin Pinot than he would usually have done. Bathandwa kept up a barely interrupted monologue at their end of the table about Xhosa society and virtues which Jonathan found impossible to follow, even if he had been in the mood to do so. They called for an

Uber as soon as it was polite to do so and were only just inside the Prius when Ellie turned to him.

'I'm sorry you had to find out about my Labour Party membership like that. I have tried several times to tell you. You know I don't always see the world in the same way that you do.'

'It's fine,' he said through tight lips. 'It's your life. I don't have a problem with it. I just wished you would have told me so I didn't have to find out from someone like your friend Howie.'

'He's a good, kind man.'

'With an outdated view of where the world is and a poor taste in red wine.'

The rest of the short journey passed in silence, and once home, Ellie retreated to their bedroom whilst Jonathan went into his study and switched his laptop on. Later, when he went upstairs, Ellie was asleep or feigning sleep and he got into bed and switched the light off. He wanted to think about something other than their disastrous evening and turned his mind back to the Mali investigation. He wondered what he might find out at the Pioneer Group meeting on Monday. Luckily, it was to be one of Ellie's pampering Saturdays tomorrow so he could concentrate on having some fun with the boys and avoid any more frostiness with his wife. He would make a definite attempt to smooth it over with her when she came back from dinner. On that thought, he fell asleep.

Chapter 15

Jonathan was woken by the boys demanding breakfast and, leaving Ellie in bed, he went downstairs and started to make French toast with them. It was a slow process and they were all still deeply involved in the sticky mess in the kitchen when Ellie arrived, fully dressed and obviously ready for her day out.

'Hi, boys, what are you up to? Is any of that French toast for me? Yes? Then I will have that small piece over there, thank you.' She kissed all three of them on the forehead in turn and then drank some tea and quickly ate the piece of toast. 'I'm sorry to be in a rush but Amanda has some timed tickets for the big show at the V&A so I must be on my way in the next few minutes. Will you both be OK with Daddy today?'

The boys nodded assent, still busy with their cooking attempts. Ellie turned to Jonathan. 'No work today, honey, just concentrate on the boys, OK? What have you planned?'

'Nothing so far but I thought we might go to the London Aquarium. It's been a while since we went there and then we can go out for lunch somewhere on the South Bank.'

'Lovely. You've remembered I won't be back until very late tonight? Amanda and I are going to this art installation and party in Hackney so it will probably be midnight before I'm home. There's plenty of stuff in the fridge for you but if you are too lazy just get a take-away. Don't forget to clean the kitchen, there's no cleaner until Monday. Bye, you all. I must go.'

Jonathan had a great day out with the boys and when they eventually returned home in the late afternoon, full of pizza and the normally banned fizzy drinks, George and Albee collapsed in front of the TV and Jonathan was able to concentrate upon the emails that had been arriving with a monotonous regularity throughout the day. Amongst the usual array of panics, problems, legal threats and cleverly-disguised spam, there was an email from Khalila with the background information on DVBR.

To: Jonathan Lomax
From: Khalila Hamez
Subject: DVBR

Jonathan
Here's the background search on DVBR you asked me for. Do let me know if there's more you need.

DVBR Pty Ltd.
Major shareholders are listed as D.V. DeBuss, A.S. DeBuss and J.G. Johnson.
Established 1984. Type of business: energy extraction management, oil, gas and minerals.
Employees: not listed
Financials: Last filed in 2016. Profit of US$4M on turnover of $49M.
Major business locations (from the website) Nigeria, South Africa, Mozambique, Mali, Zimbabwe.

The company provides drilling teams, management teams and complete turnkey operations for energy companies across Africa. Alistair DeBuss is the key player and CEO (D.V. is his brother who isn't mentioned anywhere that I can see so might be a non-exec shareholder?). Business started by their father, confusingly also called D.V. DeBuss. ADB crops up on some SA society websites (he has a former Miss South Africa as a long-term girlfriend), but has a relatively low profile. Seems to be involved in local re-development in Johannesburg where he lives in some splendour *link here* but nothing else notable from a search of SA press archives. Brother Dieter VB is an aspiring politician with the Freedom Front Plus - an Afrikaner rights party which has a long term aim of a separate Volkstaat. It describes its aims as Afrikaner Nationalism, Economic Liberalism, Social Conservatism and Christian Democracy. *Site link here*. They have 4 MPs in the assembly and are most popular with white farmers and the poorest whites in the country. DVB is seen to be on the extreme wing of the party and has not been successful in three local elections so far even after spending large sums of money on electioneering.

DVBR has been successfully prosecuted in Tanzania (where it no longer has operations) for safety violations that resulted in an explosion on site where eleven Tanzanian workers died, but apart from that the company has a good safety record. A bribery scandal in Tanzania involving a senior minister caused their withdrawal from that country rather than the safety issue. Website full of pictures of ADB outside of company built community centres etc. built near to their operational plants. The company has doubled in size since 2006 and has just won a major contract in Zimbabwe which will go on stream next year.

KH

So no great revelations there, thought Jonathan. The usual African mix of white Afrikaners with extreme views working in other African states where everyone conveniently turns a blind eye to their domestic political ambitions and prejudices. It was unlikely he could find out much more by further top-line research, and if they were involved in the arms shipments he would need do a lot more digging than he had the capacity for right now.

After putting the boys to bed and tidying up the kitchen, he slumped in front of the TV but failed to find anything to watch. This included his own channel which had a rather dreary repeat of an insight into the Thatcher revolution, a pre-recorded library filler originally from the History Channel. Shows such as this helped fill some of the hours on the channel when they were unable to successfully compete for audiences. Saturday peak time was one such graveyard. Television audiences were either watching talent shows or binge-watching Netflix dramas and there was nowhere for channels like his to make a mark. There must be something I can do here, he thought. He mused upon this scheduling problem whilst enjoying a vodka tonic. He later opened a rather expensive bottle of Burgundy, thinking it would make up for the thin fare of yesterday evening but then realised he was rather wasting it with the green chicken curry he had just ordered from the Thai takeaway down the road. He started drinking it anyway and was halfway through it before the curry arrived. He found an action film he had wanted to see on Amazon Prime and stretched out on the sofa, occasionally shouting encouragement or plot-lines to the characters but generally enjoying the escapism and mindless violence. It was quite a while since he last watched a film from beginning to end. He channel surfed for a while after the film finished and noted with dismay that he had managed to drink the whole bottle of Burgundy. He fell asleep still thinking he must tidy up his mess before Ellie came home.

He awoke in the early hours of the morning still stretched out on the sofa but covered in one of Ellie's luxurious cashmere throws. He checked his watch and saw it was two-thirty five am. He wondered if the throw was a peace offering from Ellie, who had also switched off the lights. He felt warm and comfortable and somewhat drunk so rolled over and went straight back to sleep.

It was almost ten when Ellie woke him with a cup of tea.

'Hello, sleepyhead, do you realise the time?' She kissed the top of his head and then pulled the throw off him. 'Come on. Up you get and off to the swimming pool to clear that thick head of yours. I will have a surprise waiting for you when you're back; make sure it's by 12.30. No later.'

She swept out of the room and he could hear the boys fighting at the other end of the house. He made his escape as quickly as he could. The swim did him a power of good and a large flat white in the club cafe seemed to clear the remains of his hangover. It also delayed his return until the appointed hour. In his fragile state he wasn't sure he could cope with the boys' noise and energy and the Sunday newspapers offered some alternative amusement. When he flicked through GBN's flagship Sunday paper he idly wondered how the mass pulping operation in Ireland was going and whether they would be found out. He hoped not; any scandal in a media company caused ripples right through the advertising sales world and he had enough revenue issues to deal with without the whiff of corporate misdemeanours.

He arrived back to a silent house at 12.30 precisely to find Ellie finishing mixing a jug of bloody Mary.

'I thought this might be the perfect aperitif for you,' she said, 'Vanessa has taken the boys out and will make them lunch and I'm taking you out for lunch at your favourite place in Kew. Just the two of us.' She handed him the glass, 'Drink up. Eddie will be here in fifteen minutes and you probably want to change.'

Changed and refreshed, they sat down in the restaurant and ordered the Sunday lunch option they had previously enjoyed there along with a bottle of good claret. Jonathan sensed that all would be well with Ellie and him and he wanted that very much; there was too much going on in his life at the moment to be at war with his wife over something as stupid as politics. After some catch-up chat about their respective Saturdays and talk about the boys and the quality of their lunch, conversation inevitably turned to the events of Friday night.

'I'm really sorry you had to find out about me joining the Labour Party in the way you did,' said Ellie hesitantly, 'Howie can be a bit of an idiot at times, I suspect he knew just what he was doing when he blurted that out.'

'It's OK, darling,' said Jonathan, 'It was not the best way to find out about something like that but I guess you had your reasons for not telling me sooner.'

'I tried, honestly. But you are so much better at political arguments than I am and to be honest I was scared to tell you. I'm glad I've joined and I feel good about the decision but I know it is a long way from your political thinking and won't sit well with the very people you are trying to influence.'

'I'm sure I can cope with that. It might be more difficult if you were thinking of standing for election. You are not thinking of standing, are you?'

'No, I'm not, although it has been mentioned. There's no point standing in Richmond, it's a blue versus yellow constituency and you know I have no time for tokenism.'

'Well, I have no problem with you being an active member of the Labour Party. I guess there will be things I shouldn't mention to you if I hear them from time to time but you know I rarely get the inside track on much anyway.'

'I wouldn't say that, darling. You are shaping up to be a key influencer in the Tory party and that's great because I know that you are a thoroughly decent man, and although we might be on different sides of the political divide, when it comes down to it you will always do the right thing.'

'Just watch out for Howie, that's my final word on the subject. There's something about him that doesn't ring true to me.'

'He's not so bad. He's as bright as they come and he works really hard for the homeless we are there to help. He's been a real shot in the arm for the organisation. Like all reformed sinners, he's bit over the top in his politics but he is a good man who really cares. He will probably put himself forward for election to the council.'

'You sound like you admire him, maybe fancy him a bit?'

'Now I know you are joking, you bastard.' She smiled at him in the way that had always melted his heart. 'You know that despite your no-good Tory politics you are the only man for me.'

'I know how lucky I am. So what's the story about Bathandwa and Howie? She's way out of his league.'

'The gossip in the office is that she's Howie's trophy asset. If you are trying to prove your socialist credentials then a flamboyantly dressed Xhosa radical human rights lawyer on your arm is about as good as it can possibly be. No-one knows much about their relationship – she is on a six month secondment to Lambeth Council working in legal affairs and lives in Vauxhall somewhere. I like her but she's hard work. It's unfortunate you ended up sitting next to her. She's pretty full on.'

'Luckily, she was content to do all the talking so all I had to do was mumble something occasionally.' He held her smile, reached his hand across the table to her and asked, 'Friends again?'

'Of course. Always.'

'What time will the boys be back..?'

She smiled again. 'You are hopeless Jonathan – there's no time for anything like that. I told you Vanessa is feeding them at home. They have been there for the last hour. Shall we finish up this rather good bottle of wine instead? I'm beginning to get a taste for fine red wine.'

'As long as you promise to be awake when I get back from the office tonight.'

'One minute past ten and my light goes off – so there's your challenge.'

Eddie drove them home and agreed to pick up Jonathan at six-thirty for his Sunday evening shift at the studio. He spent his free time asleep in front of the fire, pleasantly full of good food and wine and oblivious to the noise of the boys running around the house. He felt somewhat dragged into the office when Eddie arrived and left home reluctantly. He whizzed through his editorial meetings and unusually left the studio before the Sunday night flagship show aired. He was home before nine and spent the night in the welcoming arms of his wife.

Chapter 16

Over their usual Monday morning breakfast briefing session, Jonathan and Lottie discussed the stalled progress on the Mali investigation.

'Have you managed to get anywhere checking out on this Donald Brown character?'

'No, I haven't made much progress there beyond his profile on LinkedIn. I will get on to it today. How about DVBR and Andrew Gilmour?'

'I've half an idea about DVBR and I've sent an email off to Gilmour over the weekend requesting a meeting. We'll see what comes back. I've also got this Pioneer Group social this evening so I will do some more careful digging there.'

'I have made contact with a stringer in Mali. He does work for the BBC and for CNN there. He sees us as new money in the area and he's keen to work for us. Do you want me to ask him to do some follow-up work on the original *Sunday Times* story and see what he comes up with?'

'There's no downside to it. I doubt there's more than the *Times* have already discovered but yes, put him on to it. Send me the paperwork and I will sign the authorisation. I think the next thing we should be doing is tracking down the company that actually made these cluster bombs. I want to have everything ready to confront them as soon as we have any proof that it was the Government who authorised their export to Mali.'

As he walked into his office he called out to Carol, 'Carol, hi, good morning. Could you find an email address for me? Only got a first name – Bathandwa.' He spelt it out for her. 'Works at Lambeth Council Legal affairs in Vauxhall. On secondment from South Africa. There shouldn't be too many people there with a name like that.'

By the time his first meeting was over, Carol had emailed him Bathandwa's email address and he immediately emailed her asking if they could meet up for coffee in Vauxhall, maybe even that afternoon. Within ten minutes he had a reply.

From: Bathandwa Ngosi
To: Jonathan Lomax
Subject: Re: Coffee

Well, there's a Monday morning email I didn't expect. My curiosity is piqued. 3pm at the place you suggested will be fine. See you there.
B

Shortly after Bathandwa's email arrived, there was a reply from Andrew Gilmour saying he was in town on Tuesday and could meet Jonathan at eleven-thirty at his club on Pall Mall. Jonathan replied in the affirmative. Perhaps things would really move forwards this week after all. He asked Carol to shuffle his afternoon meetings around so that he could squeeze in meeting Bathandwa and turned his mind away from Mali to the many other pressing matters of the morning.

Bathandwa arrived in the hidden-away cafe shortly after three. She was wearing a dark business suit and carrying a heavy briefcase and looked very different from Friday night. Her piled up hairstyle still added several inches to her already tall figure but she looked every inch the dynamic young lawyer.

'Well, I certainly didn't begin my day expecting this meeting,' she began, ordering a peppermint tea as she sat down opposite him.

'Thank you for meeting with me at such short notice, Bathandwa, I really appreciate it.'

'As I said in my email, I'm intrigued. Call me Batt, everyone does.'

'Well, Batt, you are certainly looking very different today from your striking appearance on Friday night.'

'Howie asked me to wear my tribal dress, I think it turns him on and to be honest I love doing it. Even here in London it makes everyone look at you twice. Anyway, what can I do for you?' She hesitated and smiled, 'I presume this is not just a social meeting?'

'No, I'm following up on a story that could be real dynamite and have stumbled across a South African connection. I was hoping you might be able to help me fill in some of the gaps.'

'Go on.'

'It's about an outfit called DVBR and the two brothers who run it, Alistair and Dieter DeBuss, do you know of them?'

'Oh, yes, I know quite a lot about the DeBuss brothers. What do you want to know?'

'Well, I know something about their business but the politics intrigues me. What can you tell me there?'

'Alistair runs the business whilst twin brother Dieter plays politics. But the story I hear is that profits from DVBR are directly funnelled into Dieter's political ambitions and it's difficult to draw a line where business ends and politics begins. They are in it together. DVBR is pretty big in oil and gas as you probably know and is rumoured to have bribed its way around the continent to win contracts and smooth over operational problems.'

'Is that uncommon in the oil business in Africa?'

'Unfortunately not. Bribery started in colonial times when your Empire builders set tribe against tribe and bought what they could not win. It's a curse on our society and people like the DeBuss's use it to weaken democratic governments and sow discord. People like them are a curse on Africa.' Her eyes flashed with anger as she continued. 'Dieter is on the extreme wing of the Freedom Plus party. They supposedly stand up for minority white Afrikaner rights and have four MPs but the real agenda is a white homeland, stripping away some of the best mineral rights and farmland as a breakaway republic. The FP have enjoyed an upsurge in recent years but they are still just a vocal minority, a bit like UKIP here, I guess, in that they punch above their real weight.'

'Do they have a political agenda outside South Africa?'

'I don't know but I don't think so. DVBR works in some places where the oil majors would hesitate to deploy so they can charge a premium on their work. I don't know about any involvement in politics though. I suspect there is a lot of cash flowing around that never gets accounted for in their work around the continent. There have been suggestions that they have done some deals so that oil has flowed into places where the UN have agreed sanctions on oil imports. But no-one knows if that is really true. They have glamorous lifestyles and certainly Dieter's campaigns have been very well funded and no-one can be sure where all the money comes from. DVBR's official campaign donations are very modest.'

'But he's still failed to get himself elected?'

'So far, but I hear he is close to securing the nomination for a seat in the next general election and he will probably win that one. His glamour will play well on the national stage and he could end up as the next leader of the party the way things are going there. Why do they interest you so much? Surely they are outside of your area of political interest?'

'As I said, I'm digging through a complex international story that could be big. They are just one small part of it and I'm not sure how a big a role they might eventually play.'

'Dieter is here in London pretty frequently, I hear. He has some links with your Conservative Party friends, presumably those on the extreme right wing of the party.'

'It's not my party but that's interesting. I will do some more digging there. Thank you.'

'Well, Mr Lomax, this has been a most interesting chat. Perhaps I misjudged you at our first meeting or maybe you just make a point of meeting up with young women you bump into at dinner parties?'

'No, Batt, really I don't. But thank you for your insight, it's really very helpful. I would obviously appreciate it if you could keep all of this confidential. It may not lead anywhere at all and could just lead to difficulties...'

'Of course. It's our secret. I will email a friend of mine back in Jo'burg who will know a lot more about the DeBuss brothers than I do and I will send on anything that's interesting. We should aim to meet again and talk further before I go back in a few weeks.'

'That would be good. I will ask Ellie to fix a date with Howie...'

'Oh, we don't have to involve Howie; we are only ships passing in the night. I let him warm my bed sometimes to keep out this cold London chill but there's no future there; anyway, he's much too old for me.' She holds Jonathan's gaze for a long time and then smiles broadly and extends her hand to say goodbye. 'I look forward to seeing you again in the near future, Jonathan. Take good care.' She stands up and theatrically blows him a kiss, smiles broadly, winks at him and is gone, leaving him alone with his thoughts.

The Pioneer Group meeting that evening failed to provide any more useful information to add to Jonathan's investigation. He talked to a couple of Tories known for their interest in African affairs but his circumspect questioning didn't add anything interesting. Sir John Cressley was there, locked deep in conversation in another part of the room, but eventually Jonathan managed to get himself introduced through a third party.

'Sir John, I'm very pleased to meet you, I've been looking forward to saying hello.'

'Well, Lomax, I can't say I have a lot of time for your TV channel and what you are trying to do but at least you're on our side I suppose, so what can I do for you?'

His tone was brusque and unfriendly but Jonathan ploughed on,'You are one of the few key parliamentarians who hasn't responded to us and agreed to appear. Is there something I can do to try and change your mind?'

'I don't think of myself as more than a humble back-bencher and I wouldn't presume to tell the Government how to do things so I don't think there's much chance of me being on your channel. You've probably more chance with my son-in-law, he loves all of that stuff and he tells me you two are as thick as thieves.'

'We are looking at doing something with John but is there nothing I can do to persuade you to take part?

'No, I really don't think there is and, if you will excuse me, there's a man over there I really must speak with.'

He turned in the direction of his waved hand and walked quickly off to the other side of the room. At least he knows who I am now, thought Jonathan, even if he has no time for me.

The next morning, he arrived precisely on time for his meeting with Andrew Gilmour. He had checked out his picture on LinkedIn but had to wait several minutes for Andrew, or Andy as he preferred to be called, to appear from within the bowels of the club.

'Jonathan, I'm very sorry to keep you waiting. Come with me, I've organised coffee and somewhere we can talk in private.'

Andy was a tall, sandy-haired individual with an obviously military manner, used to being listened to. Jonathan followed him through a number of interlinked meeting rooms with variously overblown drapes, faded carpets and shabby furniture and eventually arrived at a small anteroom that had obviously only recently been converted into a small meeting room. The decor was pure warehouse office catalogue and although almost new was already starting to show its rough edges. The proffered coffee was indescribably awful. He studied Andy's face and noticed a slight nervous tick below his right eye and a small tremor in his right hand as he held the coffee cup. Nerves, past problems, or concerns over the current meeting? Jonathan couldn't be sure but sipped his terrible coffee silently as he waited for Andy to begin.

'I hope you didn't mind meeting here rather than at our offices but I sensed that it might be better to keep this meeting strictly private. Was I right?'

Jonathan agreed and asked Andy to give him some more background on him and his company Secure Alliance. Like most businessmen, Andy was only too pleased to talk about himself.

'Usual start to such a career, I suppose: British army commission, special forces, early retirement after the first Iraq war when I picked up some shrapnel in my back. No big deal but I had had enough of being ordered about by some bloody stupid politician so I let myself be invalided out. Wanted to put the skills of my chaps to a better use than they would have found in civilian life. We set up Secure Alliance as a bodyguard and hostage recovery firm and we've been going for a fair while. Still just twelve of us as partners in the business but we recruit others as we need to cope with demand and that's been booming over the last five years, especially in the Middle East and Africa. They are our two specialist areas.

'We work for a variety of customers: Governments, corporations and rich individuals. Most of our work is under the radar and to be honest that's another reason I didn't want you popping up at our offices, we try to keep a very low profile and media interest is strictly discouraged.'

'I'd like to talk about your evidence to the Foreign Affairs Committee on West Africa. You made an interesting claim there about Western Governments turning a blind eye to weapons sales to the Mali Government. Do you have any proof to substantiate your claim?'

'Of course I do. I saw cargo manifests that clearly showed weapons' shipments from Germany and the UK. More importantly there were the sorts of weapons we said we would never ship to such regimes.'

'Anti-personnel weapons?'

'Mortars, grenades, cluster bombs, the whole nine yards. The problem is, once you've sold them to countries like Mali you've no idea who will end up using them and against whom they will be used. I suppose there's some big idea that they will only be used against Islamic militants, but with every General there a law unto himself they could be used for localised tribal warfare as much as the great war on terror. They could also be sold on to other even less friendly regimes or even to the jihadists themselves.'

'But all this is private arms dealers selling these weapons without our Government's knowledge?'

'Not from the UK. It's just not possible for arms dealers to get hold of this sort of stuff in the UK. Sure, you can buy Chinese and Russian arms pretty easily but some of the stuff we see in West Africa is the same materiel we are supplying to our own Army and only the Government or the Army top brass could sanction those sort of exports.'

'Do you have any concrete proof to back this up?'

'I can't categorically prove anything. I took some photographs of one of the manifests but there's nothing on there that conclusively proves UK Government involvement. If pressed, they will hide behind the defence of rogue arms dealers and, as you know, the PM has launched a crackdown on them since the *Sunday Times* story hinted otherwise. You are the first person to ask me about this since I gave my evidence.'

'Why did you stand up and go public on this? I thought you said that your company valued discretion above all else.'

'We do, but one of my best men out there was blown up by what I know was a British-made bomb. I think the PM has lied to the country about it. You can't keep quiet about that sort of thing, even if it is bad for business.'

'Will you go on the record, on camera, and talk about this?'

'With no concrete evidence? You must be joking. This is not politics as usual where the *Daily Mail* will dig up some dirt about me, describe me as a mercenary and try and discredit my evidence. Doing something like that would get me killed, there's no doubt in my mind. If you are not ready for that sort of response you are dangerously naive and I shouldn't be talking to you at all.'

'Why then did you open this up at the Select Committee?'

'I chose my words very carefully, always hinting, never accusing. Even that got me a rebuke from one of my former senior officers. He's a General now and made no bones about the fact that I should keep my mouth shut if I want more work or any recommendations from HMG.'

'OK, I hear you. If I can get firm proof from another source will you then go on camera and add to it so that we have multiple sources for the story?'

'Only if your evidence is strong enough. I would have to see it firsthand and then decide. No promises. It must be conclusive.'

'I will get it, I think I'm close.'

'Bring it to me when you have it but don't email me anything. Just call me to request a meeting; I'm sure my email and phone are under surveillance. Yours may be too. You should go now and I will wait here a while before leaving. I don't think we should be seen together any more. Just call me on this number.' He gave Jonathan a business card, 'I will call you back from a clean phone to set something up.'

'OK. I will be in touch when I have something. Thank you.'

He left the room feeling more puzzled than ever and strolled out through the club common rooms where, for the first time ever, he thought everyone might be looking at him suspiciously. Andy Gilmour had certainly made him feel nervous and his use of language had raised the risk stakes in Jonathan's mind. More than ever, he felt he was on to something big here – even if he was making no real progress in discovering the truth. With one more furtive glance around the lobby, he left the building into the grey London morning.

Chapter 17

Once safely away from the building, Jonathan rang Lottie, who had left a voicemail asking him to call back.

'Hi, you called...'

'Yes, we might have something on Donald Brown. Are you coming back to the office? How was your man Gilmour?'

'I don't know what to make of him. He has nothing incontrovertible but is genuinely worried about surveillance and fears for his life if he gives us what little he has. Either he's paranoid or a conspiracy theorist or he knows more than he is letting on. I don't know which of the three but he's not the solid and dependable witness I was hoping for. I don't know how well he would stand up to difficult questioning. I would guess there's stuff in his backstory that he doesn't want to come out. I'm on my way back to the office right now so you can tell me about Donald Brown when I get in.'

Arriving at the River Factory half an hour later, he called Lottie into his office to continue the discussion.

'So, what's the story of Donald Brown?'

'He's only got a criminal record for insider dealing in the City in a former life. I think we can show a complete lack of ethical responsibility at Cavendale.'

'Good, well done – but I'm afraid it's just more circumstantial evidence.'

'He was done for tipping off a major BP shareholder that they should reduce their position as he had inside information on the company that would see their share price move sharply down. The investor did this too obviously and the watchdog investigation proved the information came from Brown. Brown was a big deal at one of the large merchant banks and he was paid a bonus by his own firm and the investor for his troubles. He had to pay both back and has never worked in the City again. More importantly, I've got some other good news. You remember authorising me to employ that stringer in Mali? He's emailed to say he's on to something already and will have something for us before the end of the week.'

'Great. Let's hope it's something we can actually use in evidence.'

'Do you think there's really any point in us investigating the UK manufacturer of these cluster bombs?'

'Given that the Government says they don't use them or stockpile them, I think any approach there will bring the security services right down on us and get everyone else to clam up. I can't think how we could make an approach there that wouldn't tip our hand, can you? I still want to know everything I can about the company though, so keep working on that. We know the cluster bombs ended up in Mali and we can probably make a case that Cavendale supplied them but what we are trying to prove is that HMG knew and condoned the shipment and then lied about their involvement to Parliament. I'm not interested in bringing down Sir John Cressley et al, dislikable bloke though he is. I want to rock the Government and expose all of their lies and cover-up.'

'I know; you are right. I will keep investigating. Let's wait and see what the stringer comes up with.'

'Leave me the notes on Donald Brown and I will look through them, but for now I can't think of any way forward there that makes any sense. Let's come back to it later in the week.'

Jonathan turned his attention back to his day job and was soon immersed in the daily routine. His key team all seemed to be pretty much on top of their respective jobs and normally only big problems landed on his desk. He reckoned there were probably seven issues he needed to concentrate on and called in Angie to deal with the biggest of them.

'Angie, hi. Thanks for making time for me. I'm sorry but it's bloody Melissa again. She's emailing me saying we – I think she means you –are not giving her enough support and she's left going on air without all the facts. What is going on there?'

'Boss, I'm sorry you've been dragged into it but you know how high maintenance she is. Ever since that fuss over her husband some weeks ago she's been in a bad mood with the team – as if it's their fault that her husband is a tax dodger – sorry, alleged tax dodger. She's at war with Amber and ignores all of her researchers and you can see the lack of preparation in her performances; her mind is elsewhere.'

'What do you want me to do?'

'Can you take her to one side and show her some affection? You know how much she likes to be charmed by the management and our relationship is too confrontational for me to do it. And anyway she likes to be fawned over by men, you know how she is.'

'OK. I will take her for lunch and show her the love. We really can't afford for her to be off song, she is so important to the publicity the channel gets in other media.'

'And she knows it and that only makes things worse. She swans about as if she was making the only show that matters and that gets everyone's backs up.'

'How about if we start giving her a producer credit for the show? I know it's against everything we've said before but it might just play to her vanity. What do you think? You wouldn't mind not being credited, would you?'

'I couldn't care less. If you think she's that shallow let's go for it. Anything to get her back on form again.'

He worked his way through the other six issues which were more complex and drawn out but as the days progressed he slowly bought the channel under full control again, although he knew full well that it would lurch from minor to major to multiple crisis on a weekly basis throughout its life, however long that might be. That was the inevitable given the type of television channel they had created.

On Thursday morning, Lottie was late for their breakfast meeting which was most unusual. He eventually saw her, walking slowly towards the cafe with her mobile pressed against her ear, engrossed in the conversation she was having. When she arrived outside at the window she waved her free hand towards him but then turned her back and continued talking on the phone. He sat there for several minutes wondering what could be so important that Lottie would give up her precious face time with him. When she finally walked in through the door she looked triumphant and ushered him quickly out of the cafe.

'This really can't be talked about in here.' She gestured to Mario, the owner, to put Jonathan's breakfast on the company account and, grasping his arm, said, 'The stringer's come up with something, it sounds conclusive at long last.'

'Tell me.'

'Let's get back into your office where we can talk privately.'

They walked into the River Factory, acknowledged greetings from staff they met on the way and only when they were safely in Jonathan's office and the door closed, did Lottie finally give him the news.

'Joe, the stringer in Mali, has got hold of some paperwork – don't ask how, it's probably best if we don't know – that shows that the price Mali wanted for the gas development rights in Northern Mali was advanced weaponry and that Cavendale agreed to do the deal on this basis. He is sending a pdf of the paperwork through to me at any moment. This is the smoking gun we've been waiting for.'

At that moment, Lottie's phone beeped. Looking in her inbox, she opened an attachment and together they looked at the fuzzy document. It appeared to be a Mali Government memorandum detailing the transaction, the basis for it and a shopping list of the weaponry previously demanded for the deal to be closed with Cavendale. On a second page was a further note saying that delivery would be handled by a company called THY Logistics of Johannesburg direct to a Ministry of Defence warehouse in the capital Bamako.

'This is just what we needed,' said Lottie, giving Jonathan her broadest smile and squeezing his arm.

'Well, it puts Cavendale squarely in the frame and gives them no wiggle room but there's nothing here that incriminates the UK Government. It's a big step forward but it's still not the full story.'

'Now we've got this we could look at confronting the Cressleys..'

'And we can probably destroy or at least seriously damage them. I just think Sir John will cover for the Government and end up in the Lords with a serious wedge of cash and several tame directorships and, as I said, he's not the target here, he's just the fixer.'

'Shall I get Joe to keep digging?'

'Yes. Tell him what we need and see if he can come up with more. Let's hope there is more or we are sunk.'

Jonathan started his work day but his heart was not really in it. He knew that the Mali investigation was slipping away from him and really there was no point bringing Cavendale down; apart from his dislike of Sir John, there was no great gain. It was a dull story – a company you've never heard of indulges in a weapons for gas-field exchange in Mali. It was good *Financial Times* stuff but wasn't going to shake the foundations of the Government and would be quickly forgotten.

He was at his charming best for lunch with Melissa that day and, by granting her a few productions wishes, an exec producer credit, pulling Angie back a bit from the producer role and lavishing praise on her looks and charm, Jonathan felt he had just about turned around his most problematic presenter. Melissa had just ordered her customary hot water, fresh coriander and ginger digestif to throw the restaurant staff into confusion and draw attention to herself, so he felt able to check his mail on his phone. There was a text from a number he didn't recognise. He opened it.

Jonathan. Just back from Africa. Drinks tonight??? 6pm Lord North St? Anna

Melissa was still explaining loudly to the poor waiter how the coriander must be torn and not chopped so he felt able to reply quickly.

*I will be there. Looking forward to seeing you again.
J*

Curious. What was her agenda?

'Darling, I do hope you are not texting other women when I'm meant to have your full attention this lunchtime. I don't ask for a lot.'

'As if, Melissa. Just the office intruding, I can't get away for too long.'

'Well, we must do this again, dinner on one of the nights when I don't have a show and we can drink lots and lots. How about next week? Maybe Tuesday?'

'That would be great but I will have to come back to you. You know my diary is full of boring meetings with politicians and advisors. Let me see if I can get free and you are definitely on. Have you tried the place at the top of the Shard?'

'Dreary, darling, dreary. Promises a lot and doesn't deliver. Leave it me and I will come up with somewhere much more exciting. I will get Carol to free up some space in your diary.'

Melissa left Jonathan to pick up the bill as she hurried off to a production meeting in Westminster and his thoughts returned to Anna. What was her game? He had a number of external meetings that afternoon and he ploughed through them without taking too much notice of what was actually going on. He spent most of them thinking about Anna's motives. He didn't know if he should confront Anna with the evidence he had or whether he should dig for more information. No matter how many time he game-played the possible conversations in his head, he couldn't pull together a coherent strategy. Why did she want to see him? He arrived at the Lord North Street house shortly after six and was shown into one of the downstairs drawing rooms by the butler. He still had no real plan: he would have to play it by ear.

'I will ask Miss Anna to join you, sir. She asked me to make cocktails and I have made Martinis. Would that be acceptable?'

Jonathan confirmed a Martini would be fine and sat on the sofa to await Anna's entrance. Really, who had uniformed butlers these days? Anna swept into the room, followed by the butler carrying a silver tray. He began to pour martinis from the shaker. Anna was resplendent in a long green velvet gown, sleeveless and with a plunging neckline that again elegantly displayed her considerable cleavage. Her dark hair was pinned up showing off a long and slender neck. She and Jonathan air kissed and she sat on the sofa next to him.

'I'm so glad you were able to make this evening. It's my only free time. I have a dinner with a couple of African potentates tonight, hence this get-up.' She gestured to her dress.

'They are very lucky men to have a dinner date with a woman who looks quite so wonderful.'

'Well, a little bit of couture does help a deal go down sometimes, you know. It's always fun to look glamorous. Here's to friendship.' She lifted her glass and drained its contents in a single gulp. 'It's the only way to drink Martinis I always think. At least, the only way to drink the first one.' She put the martini glass down carefully and looked closely at him whilst he sipped his drink. 'I'm sorry about the whole butler thing, it's one of Daddy's foibles; he does make a mean Martini though.'

Jonathan sat back and returned her stare. 'It's certainly a fine cocktail.'

'I'm so sorry I had to cancel lunch last week. We had something of a problem on the morning and it was all hands to the pumps I'm afraid.' She reached over and put her hand gently upon his knee. 'And tonight I have less than half an hour, I apologise that this is all so rushed but I did want to see you.'

'It's very much my pleasure.'

'Good. That's so sweet of you. Now, I've lots to talk about. I know that you've been doing a little digging into the Cressleys and our business and I'm intrigued to know why; it's not as if we are very interesting.'

Jonathan hesitated. Where had this come from? John, Ben, maybe Paul, maybe even Lottie?

'Anna, you know that's not true. Part of what I do is identify future stars of the Conservative Party and I think John could be one of them. With backers like you and Sir John he could go a long way. I just wanted to make sure there were no skeletons in his closet.'

'I'm not sure John really has the intellect to achieve greatness...'

'Since when has intellect been the key ingredient? He has the drive, the ambition and the contacts. He could be a serious contender.'

'Sweet of you to say so. It's true that Daddy does have a safe seat lined up for him. You mustn't let him know though, darling, it's Daddy's secret and he wants John to go through some selection disappointment before he gets it.'

'I understand and your secret is safe with me. You will want him in Parliament at the next General Election, I presume?'

'Oh yes, everything is mapped out for that. I just hope John doesn't disappoint us.'

'When I met him last week I got the sense of real hunger to succeed as an MP...'

'You mean instead of a failed merchant banker? Yes, he's keen but he has a couple of secrets we need firmly hidden away if he is make it happen.'

'I'm sure the problems he has at the bank can be smoothed out...'

'Oh, yes, that's no problem, we can airbrush that out of his CV. I assume when you dined with him last week he introduced you to his little Turkish delight?' Jonathan made no reply and Anna continued. 'Don't worry, darling, I know all about Esma.

She's a charming girl under all of that make-up. I stopped wanting to have sex with John ages ago so it's only fair that he should find comfort elsewhere and I'm pleased with Esma, she's good for him. Would you believe it, she's training to be an accountant in her spare time. I suspect I might have to help her find a position if John ever tires of her. She can't belly dance for ever, I suppose. She tried to teach me once but,' she laid the palm of her hand flat on her stomach, 'I just didn't have the tummy muscles for it. Shame. It would have been a great party trick.'

'Can you ensure her discretion? It could be a problem for an aspiring MP.'

'I think so. Esma and I have an arrangement and she does very well out of the two of us. Money often helps problems to go away, you know. Sometimes difficult things come out regardless but I don't worry about Esma. Now, back to your investigations of us, I presume they are now over and we don't have any issues we need to discuss?' She looked hard at Jonathan, her fixed smile at odds with the expression on the rest of her face.

'Yes, I've done my background checks on you all and there's nothing for you to be alarmed at.'

'I'm so glad, darling. It would have been tiresome if such things got in the way of what I hope will become a beautiful friendship.' This time her smile radiated real warmth in his direction. 'I'm hoping that we can get to know each other a whole lot better. I do hate these long dreary English winters and I'm hoping that some long cosy afternoons discussing politics interspersed with some fun might help get me through to the spring. What do you think?'

'It sounds delightful.'

'Don't let me interrupt your relationship with John, by the way. Although I think it would probably be best if he remained in the dark about our friendship, don't you think?'

'I think him knowing would probably complicate things quite a bit.'

'John can get jealous. It's a charming side of him.'

'Anna, let me ask the obvious question. Why is it that you are not standing for Parliament? I would certainly put my money on you to go far.'

'Thank you, darling, that's very kind of you. But I've learnt firsthand, whilst watching my father operate, that real power often lies out of sight, behind the curtain rather than on the stage, if you like. I think that's my best position, pulling the strings and watching the world dance. And anyway, can you really imagine me swapping brownie recipes with the Tory party wives and running weekly surgeries? It would drive me insane.'

'You are right. I can't see you in sensible shoes discussing cycleways.'

'Can you think of anything worse! I would probably go mad and stab them all. Slowly and with great enjoyment.'

At that moment, the butler knocked and entered the room.

'Miss Anna, your car is waiting and you are behind your scheduled departure time.'

'Thank you, James, I will be right out. Give me a minute.' Turning back to Jonathan, 'I'm sorry, darling, I do have to go. I can't keep my potential business partners waiting. Do you think this haughty, slightly sexy, English rose get-up will help get them over the line? I do hope so, this is a big deal for us. Remember what I said, and I will call you to organise a more leisurely get-together very soon. Please, stay here and finish your drink. I will call. Bye.'

With a swish of skirts and a haze of expensive perfume she left, leaving Jonathan alone in the room with the dregs of a now-warm Martini and even more to puzzle over. He sat there for a few minutes to give Anna a chance to exit the building and then stood up, placing his unfinished drink on a small side table. He opened the drawing room door but there was no sign of the butler in the hallway. He looked around, expecting his arrival but there was no sign of anyone. He let himself out of the main door, shutting it loudly behind him to mark his exit and wandered off towards Parliament Square. He really needed a large drink.

Sitting in the bar of St. Stephen's Tavern with a large gin and tonic, Jonathan texted Eddie and asked for a ride home in twenty minutes. He then rang Lottie and organised to meet early on Friday morning to review their progress and next steps.

'Lottie, I'm becoming as paranoid as Andy Gilmour but I don't think we can discuss this stuff in any sort of public place anymore. Your house for breakfast instead?'

'Jonathan, you know you never have to ask. I will be waiting.'

He drained the end of his gin and tonic and decided against another as he whiled away the time until Eddie arrived. Perhaps he could persuade Ellie to split a bottle with him over supper. He had texted her earlier to say that his dinner date had cancelled and he would be home to eat. If he couldn't work out Anna Cressley, he might as well have another drink and try to forget about her.

That evening over dinner, Ellie quizzed him over where the Mali investigation was heading but for the first time he found himself being less than honest with her about developments. He was truthful as far as telling her that progress was disappointing and he didn't have that much to add to what she already knew, but a mixture of concern about Ellie's new political allegiances and the mystery of Anna Cressley made him close down the conversation and move their conversation to talk about other matters. He hoped she didn't notice. Ellie updated him on the boy's activities, her work issues and the plumbing problems they were having at the country cottage.

'I really think we should get these central heating pipes fixed and sell the place. We hardly ever go there these days and we could do something else with the money. Perhaps we could buy a timeshare ski apartment and then we could go two or three times a year, even if only for long weekends. What do you think?'

He reached for his wine and took a long drink before he answered, 'It's an idea. I would hate to let the place go though. Perhaps we could hold onto it and rent it out for a few years and buy a ski place. One of those French timeshare apartments would be a good answer if we could get a place in one of the really good high resorts. I don't want to have to drive around to find snow and it will only get worse as climate change continues.'

'Leave it with me and let's see what I can up with. The idea of renting out the cottage hadn't occurred to me, are you sure we could afford it?'

'I think the rent would cover the mortgage so I don't see why not. The money is as safe there as anywhere else. Would you like another glass?'

'No, I'm fine thanks, you finish it. If nothing else it will ensure that you have a night off and don't skulk off to your study to get lost in emails for hours.'

'Woman encourages husband to drink more so he's too pissed to work. That's a new one.'

'You do need to take more time away from the office. Preferably not because you are pissed but simply because you will explode if you keep working at this intensity.'

'I know, I know. I think I can see light at the end of the tunnel, but, as the old joke goes, it might be a train coming the other way.'

'Let's sit down and cuddle on the big sofa and watch a film together.'

'You mean, behave like normal people?'

'Yes. Just for once, you know I don't ask that often.' She laughed, pleased to be having this conversation, their longest for several days.

'Let's. I might fall asleep though, especially if you choose a weepy.' He smiled back, pleased to be lost in the domesticity of their conversation.

'You are allowed. As long as I don't have to physically carry you to bed.'

She led him through to the sitting room and switched the TV on. After a while scanning through endless Netflix menus she found a film she wanted to watch and Jonathan grunted his approval. They stretched out together and started to watch the film. Ellie looked over as Jonathan's head bumped against her shoulder; twenty minutes in and he was already asleep. She smiled and let her fingers caress his face for a while. I must keep an eye on his drinking, she thought, and then turned her attention back to her film. He slept contentedly by her side for the next ninety minutes and then she helped him up to bed.

Chapter 18

On Friday morning, Jonathan arrived early at Lottie's house as arranged. Lottie had organised breakfast and as he ate, he briefed her on the previous evening's events.

'So, you still don't know what game Anna Cressley is playing? Apart from flirting madly with you, that is.'

'I'm not even sure that is the game. The trouble is, I still don't know what she is playing and that makes me feel like a chump.'

'Perhaps you've just got to go to bed with her..'

'I don't think that would help our investigation get evidence we can use, do you?'

'No, probably not. I was joking. I've been thinking about it all and I think we may both have missed a trick. We know that THY Logistics moved the arms to Mali but who moved them out of the UK? THY don't have any presence here so they either sub-contracted someone here or, I think more likely, were themselves sub-contractors to do the final leg of the delivery. If we can find out the UK and international agents we can explore all of the issues around export licences and legality and see if we can find some real evidence. What do you think?'

'Genius. Let's get on it straight away. Any more news back from your Mali stringer?'

'Not so far, but I know he's still plugging away over there.'

'Well, let's keep tabs on that too. Do you want to pick up on the shipping? You could take a few days out of the office and leave everything at Amber's door and really concentrate. What do you think?'

'I can leave everything except Melissa's show. She and Amber are at war so I've said I will deal with Melissa exclusively for a while. It's all Mel's fault, of course, it's just that Amber has been painted into a corner ever since that business about Mel's no-good husband and his tax fraud.'

'OK, well, if you can handle both things why don't you start work today on trying to uncover the shipping secrets and I will try and find out who on our team has been leaking our investigation to Anna Cressley.'

'My money is on Paul. You know he's got quite a back-channel going with Adam Robinson. They talk a couple of times a week. You didn't know? Well, I think Adam's as close to the party hierarchy as you can get and I think he has the ear of the PM too. Ben tells Paul most of the stuff he's up to so that's my guess. It won't be Ben, you know it's not me and I don't think anyone else has access to enough information.'

'Khalila?'

'No, I'm sure not. You carefully asked her to concentrate on Mali so she's no idea that we are looking at the Cressleys. It has to be Paul or Ben.'

'OK. Changing the subject, is everything in order for next week's conference trip to Budapest?'

'Yes, everything is fine. You are speaking at the opening gala dinner on Thursday night and on a panel on Friday morning. We fly back on the Sunday afternoon. I thought we could go out together first thing on Thursday and then we would have time to do any fine tuning to your speech in the afternoon. You can spend Friday and Saturday at the conference doing your meetings. Drew will be there hosting some event for European publishers on the Friday evening so we may get an invitation to appear there, and as you know Tom Schalke is organising a couple of meetings with a view to starting discussions on the European rollout of Catalyst. It should be quite a full-on weekend.'

'That all sounds great. Are we staying somewhere good?'

"Yes, the conference hotel's great. How's the speech coming along?'

'That's the other thing on my to-do list. I'm planning on getting it done this weekend. I will send you a draft to look at on Sunday afternoon.'

'That's fine. I will stay here and start working on the shipping stuff and let you know if I come up with anything.'

'OK, Lottie, thank you. What would I do without you? We will talk at the end of the day.'

Jonathan left Lottie's house and walked to the River Factory thinking about how he would approach talking to Paul; should he confront him and see what happens or should he try and do some digging and maybe find out more? He decided on the former course and once in his office asked Carol to invite Paul down to meet with him.

'Jonathan, sorry, he's not in yet. He's at a breakfast meeting somewhere. Shall I get him to come and see you as soon as he arrives?'

'Thanks Carol. Yes please. In the meantime ask Ben to come down will you.'

Ben entered the office in his usual good humour and bounced down on Jonathan's sofa, almost spilling the giant Starbucks take-out cup he carried everywhere with him at this time of the day.

'Hi, boss. What's happening? Have you heard about Lord Wincross? Only caught in flagrante delicto with his young researcher in a Lords ante room by his wife who kicked up a huge fuss and shouted the place down. Parliament is buzzing with the story. No-one likes him so it serves the old sod right.'

'Ben. It's a good story but I want to talk to you about something quite different. You remember I asked you to do some private research for me into the Cressleys?'

'Sure. Was there anything I missed?'

'I don't know. But I was shocked last night that Anna Cressley knows we have been looking into them. Any idea where that could have come from?'

'No. I don't know how that could have got out. I've told no-one about it. It wasn't that interesting, to be honest, so I'd almost forgotten about it.'

'Think carefully. You must have told someone.'

'No. The only person who would have known was Paul, who likes to keep a check on me. You don't think it could be him?'

'Yes, I probably do. Leave it with me for a while and don't say anything to anyone, especially Paul. I will come back to you later today. Thanks.'

Brusquely dismissed, Ben left the office and Jonathan waited for Paul to arrive in from his breakfast meeting. He flipped through his inbox and dealt with pressing matters until Paul knocked at his open office door and entered the room.

'Close the door and sit down Paul,' said Jonathan. 'I will just finish this email.'

He typed for a minute or so and then stood up and walked over to the sofa where Paul was sitting. He remained standing, looking down at Paul.

'I think you spilled information we were collecting on the Cressleys from this place to Adam Robinson or the Tory party hierarchy. What I want to know is why you did that and is it the only time it's happened?'

'I did tell Adam that you were looking into the Cressleys. I found out from Ben and I thought it was odd that you didn't confide in me, Jonathan. I just mentioned it in passing and Adam picked up on it. He thought it was more significant than I did, to be honest. He's quizzed me on it several times since then but I haven't told him anything because I don't know anything.'

'You know the dangers for a journalist of a story going off half-cocked. Why did you do it? You must know Adam has a direct line to the party bosses.'

'Honestly, I thought it was a nothing story. Adam asked me to keep him in the loop on anything he might need to know and

I imagined this was you just following a wild goose chase. Or maybe,' he smiled, 'just checking out Anna Cressley...'

Jonathan exploded at him. 'God damn you Paul! You might have fucked up something important and all you can think of is that I might want to screw Anna Cressley! You are finished here. We can't work together if we can't trust one another and I don't trust you anymore. Please clear your desk and get out of my sight before I say something I might regret. HR will sort out your settlement package. I'm sure Adam will sort you out a job somewhere. I will ask security to show you out.' He spun around and hitting the intercom barked, 'Carol, bring security around now to show Paul Kafferos out of the building. Take his passes from him and make sure nothing leaves the building with him apart from his own stuff.' Without waiting for a response he turned back to Paul. 'Still here? You can wait outside for security. I've got things to do.'

'Jonathan, I'm sorry. Adam has been a great source of leads for us and feeding him with some small stuff just seemed to keep the wheels turning. I don't think you know just important he is. It was Adam who persuaded the board to hire you and launch this channel and he sees it as a public lightning rod for the future of the party. He has the blessing of the PM too he tells me...'

'You really don't understand, do you? We are not the lapdogs of the Tory Party. As long as there's no viable opposition we are the closest thing they have to real scrutiny. You can't feed our information back allowing them to close ranks and freeze us out. I thought you were smart enough to understand this stuff but it seems I made a mistake. Goodbye, Paul, and close the door behind you.'

He turned back to his computer and ignored Paul's departure. He emailed Angie, Ben, Lottie and HR telling them all that Paul had left with immediate effect and that his responsibilities would be taken over by Ben. He then called Adam Robinson.

'Adam, hi. Jonathan here. It's been a while, how are things?'

'Jonathan, hi. All good here. What can I do for you?'

'I just wanted to let you know that I have terminated Paul Kafferos's contract today. I can't have my key managers providing a backchannel to the Conservative party behind my back. I'm sure you understand?'

'I know your independence is a big thing for you Jonathan, but Paul is a good guy.'

'Find him a new job, then, that's what you do. When you've done that stay away from my channel.'

'OK, point taken. I will stay away from your team. But make sure you don't lose all of your friends. You might want to call in a favour someday.'

'I am sure that day will come, Adam. But stay out of my business. We've crossed lines here, you and me. Let's stick to the headhunter and executive relationship and keep politics right out of it. We will both know where we stand then. OK?'

'Of course, if that's what you want, then that is how it will be. I must go now, Jonathan, I have a client waiting. Goodbye.'

Jonathan called Lottie, 'Lottie, hi. I've just warned Adam Robinson off so it will be interesting to see if any abuse and flak comes our way in the next twenty four hours. Will you keep a special watch on social media and let me know if anything happens? How are you getting on with the other project?'

'I'm making some progress but it feels like wading through treacle. Hopefully I might have some more for you by Monday. How did Paul take it?'

'Shocked, upset, but no-one lost their cool. He's a loss to us but I think Ben can step up and at least we know he's an unguided missile so we can protect against that. Angie has already emailed in to say she's pleased he's gone so there's one internal battle ended I didn't even know about.'

'She's never had any time for him. She thinks he's too stiff and formal and doesn't have the killer instinct about him. I guess we will never know now.'

At the regular Friday meeting with the Chief Executive, Drew showed no further sign of the problems he was facing from the Company's largest shareholder. He was very focused on the next week's conference in Budapest, where, outside the conference floor, he would be a major figure and he wanted to make sure that Jonathan's contribution to the conference would not embarrass him in any way.

'So let me get this straight, Jonathan, you still don't have the basis for the speech you are about to make, never mind the script?'

'I have a theme as I told you, Drew, but I will spend this weekend actually writing the speech. I can email you a first draft by Sunday evening and if you've got any objections we can deal with them on Monday. I'm not planning on saying anything that's too contentious so you don't have to worry.'

'OK. But this conference is a big deal for us. There are some big opportunities here with European publishers and there's so much mergers and acquisitions talk going on at the moment that I don't want anything to intrude into possible deal-making.'

'I will be suitably anodyne.'

'You know I don't want that. I want to you to impress. This is your first really big speech since you took over here and your operation might just be the jewel in our crown. I want everyone to leave that hall full of admiration and wishing they were as dynamic. Can you manage that?'

'I will try to excite without upsetting too many people. I know Tom Schalke is going to be there running a panel session on private equity in media and he's setting up some broadcaster meetings to discuss rolling out Catalyst to Europe. Hungary was top of his list, I think, heaven help us. How do you want me to play him?'

'Just go for growth and do what seems right. Remember that he forgets nothing and is an all round evil bastard. As long as you remember that he would kill his grandmother for a buck you can't go wrong with Tom.'

'OK. Is there anything more I should know before we finish?'

'Not really, newspaper sales are in the toilet again this week. What we need is a good juicy and long-running scandal, preferably with some kinky sex involved. If you know of anything, our editors will be your friends forever. Apart from that, all is fine. I did have one call today you might be interested in though; your friend Adam Robinson called and asked to be removed from a shortlist of head hunters we are talking to about a new Managing Editor post. He says he is conflicted and can't work with us on this one. Any idea what that is all about?'

'No idea at all, Drew. He must have too much work on. It's not like him to turn down business.'

Jonathan spent Saturday writing his speech, locked away in his study with the boys under strict instruction not to intrude. Ellie had organised a dinner party on Saturday evening so Vanessa had taken the boys to the cinema in the afternoon, leaving the house mostly silent; the occasional whizzes and whirs from kitchen appliances the only sounds of Ellie's presence as they both worked away on their individual projects. In truth, Jonathan would have preferred to have cancelled Saturday night's dinner, but knowing how anti-social he had been of late and remembering he would be in Budapest next weekend he had encouraged Ellie to go ahead. She had plunged into complex menus and exotic wine choices and invited eight people to dinner. Their table only just seated ten so the house would be fit to burst. Earlier in the week, he had stipulated no work guests and so the invite list was a mixture of friends new and old and should, she said, make for easy company. As was usual with Ellie, there were some husbands invited he hadn't met before but Ellie was convinced that as they were married to such lovely women they would be fine too. The break from work would do him good and he enjoyed entertaining at home, especially when, as tonight, Ellie went flat out to impress with her cooking.

The dinner party was a lively and drunken affair with much good humour around the table. Even the two unknown husbands were engaging and Jonathan warmed to them both. Everyone avoided talk of work and politics and that suited him fine. Ellie had produced a great menu and the guests were deeply appreciative and at their ease. Ellie was the perfect hostess and always managed her events perfectly without seeming to try too hard. Jonathan also noted approvingly her new little green dress, silk, he presumed, and thought to himself how good it looked upon her. It was just before one when they finally shut the door on the last guests to depart and they returned to the chaos of their kitchen hand in hand, their mood euphoric from too much food, wine and conversation. They decided they really couldn't face clearing up properly before the morning and as Ellie stood in front of the fridge about to put the remnants of the cheese away, Jonathan nuzzled his face into her neck and unzipped the back of her dress. Still facing away from him, and carefully putting the cheeses down, she shook the dress free and let it fall to the floor. He rubbed his groin against her bottom approvingly and then released her as she turned to kiss him deeply. He lowered his head to kiss her neck and breasts. They made love there, upright against the fridge with Ellie's long legs wrapped around his waist.

Afterwards, as they sat at the table amongst the debris of a successful dinner party with a final glass of wine each, he reached out and they held hands and smiled together. It was a long time since they had sealed a successful evening with passionate sex and they both went to bed tired, a little drunk, and happy.

Sunday morning was a tougher start. He swam despite his hangover but found inspiration hard to come by as he sat at his desk. The boys wanted him to play and as the writing got harder he indulged them, playing touch rugby and other games their mother chose not to understand. Boy's rough stuff she called it and made herself scarce. After lunch, he returned to his desk and ploughed on and on and it took the rest of the day with multiple re-writes and several more interruptions from the boys before he had something he was happy to send to Lottie. He wanted her to review it before it went off to Drew.

As usual, Lottie was frighteningly efficient and within two hours she had re-ordered his paragraphs, re-shaped his arguments and turned an average script into something he could imagine getting good reviews. He thanked her profusely and sent the revised draft off to Drew for his additional comments. He went to bed tired and satisfied and he realised as he fell asleep that for the first time in a while he hadn't thought about Mali all day.

Chapter 19

On Monday morning, he swam as usual but breakfasted in the cafe alone as Lottie was working on her logistics company investigation. She did text him to say she was making some progress and would be in to see him with her findings before the end of the day. He spent the morning dealing with the problems caused by Paul's exit and re-organised his team to deal with the changes he had made. He lunched with a junior minister in the Government who was rumoured to be on a fast-track to cabinet status, but try as hard as he might, Jonathan could detect nothing of interest behind the smooth PR veneer of this latest product from the Tory sausage factory: the right schools, the right special advisor status and the right manners, no glimpse of any personality or individualism. Just what the Prime Minister liked, he thought grimly to himself. Lunch over, he returned to the office and took a call from John Andrews, agreeing to a drink that evening. He remained sceptical that John could offer up anything that would constitute hard evidence but at least it gave him another chance to try and untangle where Anna was coming from. Lottie texted again to say it would be the morning before she had anything to share with him.

He met John at a Chelsea wine bar that was new to Jonathan and it was dark and almost empty on a Monday evening at 6.30. John was already there when he arrived and had bought a bottle of white wine and some tapas. He motioned Jonathan over and pumped his hand in a vigorous handshake of welcome.

'Jonathan, great to see you again. How the hell are you?'

'John, I'm good, thank you. You?'

'Bloody awful weekend. But apart from that OK. My wife is driving me mad.'

'Why is that? Thanks.' He signalled approval as John filled his wine glass.

'Beats me. She's normally busy with friends and socialising but this weekend was empty of all of that and seemed to stretch on forever. She's uptight about something at work. I don't know what, she wouldn't tell me. It must be pretty serious because she's usually pretty good at switching off.'

'So you spent the weekend getting it in the neck.'

'Yesterday all I really wanted to do was to run over to Esma's and spend the day wrapped up with her but Anna was refusing to budge and I couldn't find a suitable excuse.'

'Does she know about Esma?'

'She knows or suspects I have someone else but not who. Anna and I, we, we don't have a normal relationship in that way, haven't had for a long time. I think she might be involved with some young chap in Africa, a Major in the army in Mali, I think. But maybe that's all flirting too, it's difficult for me to tell with Anna. We don't talk about these things and it's always difficult to tell with her where business ends and her personal life takes over.'

'But she will play the role of the dutiful wife in your campaigning?'

'Of course. She will charm them all when she turns up. You've seen her in action. I think she knew I wouldn't win that last selection meeting so she chose not to even bother showing up. She's too smart for me and maybe too smart for herself, she will catch herself out one day.'

'How does she get on with Sir John?'

'They are as thick as thieves those two. Sure, they argue as well but they are always off in corridors whispering to each other and controlling the board meetings with everything pre-agreed between them before the rest of us sit down.'

'But Anna gets a free hand in running the oil and gas side of the business?'

'No, not at all. The old man is all over the politics of the deals and the money. It's just that he doesn't want to get involved in the technical side of exploration, drilling and all that. There's a guy called Donald Brown who does all that stuff for Anna and she and the old man do the deals.'

As John seemed happy to talk about the business Jonathan ploughed on. 'You said last time that doing business in Africa is tricky with bribes and all that sort of thing. That must drive you all insane.'

'Well, it doesn't make life any easier, that's for sure. That's where the old man is so good. He has his fingers in all of the markets we work in and knows whose palms to cross with silver and whose to ignore. Anna's pretty good at that too and I suppose she will do it all when the old man decides he's had enough and wants to retire to his shooting and his arboretum.'

'But that's a way off yet?'

'I will be the last to know but he doesn't look like he's going anytime soon. I think he's keen to take the property company public or merge it with a public company. That would give him a way out and he can't go public with the energy business because it wouldn't survive the scrutiny of a flotation or a trade sale.'

'Because of the under-the-counter stuff?'

'Partly. Admitting in formal documents that you bribe government ministers and officials to win business is a tricky sell – even using the euphemisms for which the finance world is so famous. But also because of its tax structure. Profits from that business go through some extreme international money washing, if you get my drift. There's no way that could be exposed to daylight. It makes loads of money but none of it gets taxed here.'

'I guess it's a good retirement income for him.'

'And it will fund my lifestyle if and when I do become an MP and have to live on a backbencher's pitiful salary, so I can't complain. One board meeting a year in the BVI is a small price to pay for a tax-free income stream.'

Jonathan thought it was time to move the conversation on. John hadn't drunk enough to miss Jonathan's line of questioning and he might be able to return to Cavendale later after another bottle of wine.

'Maybe, if I can make you a fully fledged television pundit, you will have an entirely new income stream to call your own.'

'Wouldn't that be fantastic. I'm really thinking, however, that television could help me climb the greasy pole of ministerial promotion and that would open up hundreds of possibilities.'

The man is shameless, thought Johnathan. His only objective in holding office is to make more money and wield more influence. 'Why did Sir John never accept a Government position? My spies tell me he's been offered a number of roles?'

'He's always liked pulling the strings from the sidelines, building alliances and influencing events. I don't think he would have made a good junior minister of fish farming or whatever; he would have pissed off everyone: civil servants, our former EU partners and industry itself. He's very good at putting people's backs up.'

'He certainly didn't make an effort when we were recently introduced.'

'Yes, he has a special place in hell reserved for journalists, so you are not alone there. Also, he would not be keen on the sort of channel you are running. He thinks policy should be drawn up away from prying eyes, in a darkened room, and with no scrutiny – much like his businesses – and then imposed from above. He lectures the PM on the subject I believe.'

'Really? Does he get much face time with the PM?'

'They are really close. The PM uses old Sir John when he has a dirty problem that needs cleaning up with no fuss. That skill gives him access and the PM's ear. You have no idea how influential he is in the corridors of power.'

'I didn't know any of this. Fascinating.'

Warming to his theme, John went on, 'Sometimes it works brilliantly for us. Recently we had a problem in Mali, I think I told you what a hell hole that is, and the Government had a problem there too that it needed help to solve without any publicity or comeback. The old man saw the opportunity and using the Government's money he solved our problem too and everyone went away happy with only the poor old British taxpayer the loser. It was pure genius.'

'That sounds incredible. Are you able to pull off deals like that often?'

'Only a few times I know about. It's unusual to have all the pieces in the right place at the right time. In Mali it worked well because the Government couldn't be seen to be doing business with them after the French turned them down and we were able to give the Malians what they needed and secure the gas deal that was out to tender.'

'So it was arms the Government wanted to sell to Mali..'

'Yes, as usual HMG wanted to sell weapons to Mali to help them fight the Islamic insurgents but couldn't be seen to be doing it. A little paperwork doctoring and we managed to get the arms out there and use them to win the contract. A very sweet deal and everyone went away happy.'

'I can see why you wouldn't want this sort of stuff to come out.'

'Us doing the Government's dirty business in Africa? It would finish us both off. Mum's the word, very few people know about this.'

'Of course.' Time to move the conversation on, Jonathan thought. He paused theatrically. 'So, how do you want to approach your screen test? Would you like to do it solo or shall we setup a panel session for you or both?'

'Perhaps both if it's not too much trouble,' John reached across the table and emptied the last of the bottle of wine into his glass, 'I'm not sure I'm going to be a natural at this, you know.'

'Honestly, you will be fine, I've asked Lottie, my PR Director, to look after you and she knows all there is to know about appearing successfully on TV, I promise you.'

'Good-ho. Do we have time for another bottle? I've got to go on to dinner but I have another half an hour.'

'I'm afraid I'm on a tighter schedule, John. I'm meant to be at a launch party in central London right now and I must show my face before it ends. Maybe we can do dinner next week after your screen test and go through the results?'

'I'd like that. Let's go somewhere smart. I will sort it out. I rather think I will have another glass here and catch up on my emails. See you next week, Jonathan. Bye.'

They shook hands and John reached forward for an awkward man-hug at the same time. Jonathan responded and they briefly hugged before he walked out of the wine bar.

Eddie was waiting with the car across the street. Jonathan climbed into the car and called Lottie even before they pulled away.

'Lottie, hi. I've got it. John only fessed up the whole thing and I recorded it on my phone...'

'Jonathan, don't say any more. Please.'

'What's wrong?'

'I had a visitor this evening. This thing is blowing up. I don't think we should talk on the phone. Do you remember that place by the river where you bought me dinner years ago and persuaded me to come and work for you?'

'Of course, you mean the...'

'Don't say it, you fool. Meet me there in fifteen minutes and we can talk. Bye.' She hung up and Jonathan was left staring at his phone for a moment. He then leant forward and said, 'Eddie, change of plan, I'm afraid. We're off to Fulham. Do you know the Crabtree by the river?'

Eddie acknowledged the request and swung the car around. Jonathan continued to stare at his phone and then sat back to think through developments.

Lottie was sitting at a corner table with a gin and tonic for him and a glass of wine for herself when he arrived. It was the most private table in an already busy and noisy pub.

'Thanks for the drink, Lottie. Do you want to eat?'

'Maybe later.' She lowered her voice so that only he could hear her. 'What did you actually get from Andrews?'

'He told me that Cavendale helped out the Government by supplying arms to the Mali Government and using the arms, which were paid for by British taxpayers, to sweeten the bid they were in to win the gas fields contract.'

'And you've got all of that on your phone?'

'Yeah. It may not be the best quality recording but it will be good enough to use even if not for broadcast.'

'I had a visit this afternoon from a man who I presume is MI5.'

'What?'

'I think my digging into the arms transportation has set off alarm bells somewhere. That's why I didn't want to talk on the phone. We should assume from now on that all of our communications are being listened in to. Give me your phone.'

Jonathan handed over the phone, 'What are you doing?'

'I'm going to upload the audio file to iCloud.' She tapped a few buttons and put the phone down on the table. 'That will take a few minutes to upload. It will be safer there; we know how Apple aren't keen at sharing data with Governments, even their own. When you get home tonight go to iCloud on your laptop and download four copies onto thumb drives. Give one to me, one to the company legal director, mail one to someone in the US you can trust and keep one to transcribe. Do you have someone in the US you can trust with a secret?'

'Sure. I can mail it to Andrew in New York. He's an attorney as well so that will add another layer of defence. What did this spook say to you?'

'He made it clear that we should stop our digging immediately and that unspecified bad things might happen if we don't.'

'You're not serious? He threatened you?'

'In a very roundabout way, yes.' She paused and picked up the phone, looking at its upload status. 'Nearly finished. Now, when you give the thumb drive to the legal director and in your note to Andrew, make sure you say the information is privileged and they shouldn't try and open it. Ask Eddie to put the New York letter in the post. They are bound to be watching your house and if they see you at a postbox they will put two and two together.'

'You really think we are under surveillance?'

'Probably even now. I don't think I was followed but I'm an amateur at this stuff.' She picked up his phone again and checked the upload was complete. She powered the phone down and, using a paperclip from her bag, extracted the sim card. She gave the sim to Jonathan. 'Put this into another phone you have but remember everything you say on it will be listened to. The same will go for all of your emails. I will pick up a couple of pay as you go phones in the morning so we can talk on those. Hide this phone somewhere safe too.'

'I think they call them burner phones.'

'Jonathan, we are not in some drug-dealing B movie. This is serious. I am scared. I'm also close to getting the information we need from the shipping company Abacus Logistics. I'm meeting the marketing director tomorrow morning at ten-thirty in Covent Garden. I think you should be there too.'

'What have you found out?'

'I frightened this guy Richard Smith. I said I had proof, which is stretching the truth a little, that THY re-shipped the arms from Cape Town to Mali and proof they picked up the shipment from an Abacus Delivery point. There are no records of approval from the South Africans and no export licence from the UK so I challenged him that this was an illegal shipment and they had broken the law.'

'And what did he say?'

'He said there was no export licence but he has documentation that proves the shipment was legal and it's that he has promised to show me tomorrow. He let slip this shipment was codenamed RedFox.'

'And it was after this conversation that MI5 showed up at your door?'

'I know, I've thought the same. But what do we have to lose? If we get a copy of the authorisation of this RedFox shipment plus your recording we have the whole thing completely wrapped up.'

'But don't you think MI5 will step in as soon as they see we are meeting this Richard chap? Even if he shows up that is. Do you even know what he looks like?'

Lottie nods and shows him a picture on her phone. 'This is from the company website. I think he does want to keep the media away from his company but he was probably also the one who talked to MI5 – unless they were already bugging my calls. I can't think who else it could have been.'

'So, if we meet him tomorrow morning we should assume we will be overheard at the very least and maybe re-directed onto some wild goose chase to throw us off the scent. How should we play it?'

'I don't know. Shall we sleep on it and meet for breakfast at my house and come up with a plan?'

'OK. Do you want to eat?' Lottie shook her head. 'In that case, let me give you a lift home and as you say we can mull over this until the morning.'

After dropping Lottie off outside her front door, Jonathan sat in silence in the back of his car. In his pocket, his sim-less phone weighed heavily upon him. When they arrived back at his house in Richmond he leaned in towards his driver. 'Eddie, will you do me a favour. I have some data on this phone that's going to cause a stink when it comes out. I need to hide it. Will you look after it for me for a couple of days? There's no sim in it so it won't ring and disturb you.'

'Of course, boss, no problem. I will keep it with my valuables for you. Just yell when you want it back. Will you be on the same phone number for the morning? If you remember, I'm doing early as well for a few days to cover for holidays in the driver team.'

'Yes, I've got an old iPhone and I will put this sim into it. Same time as usual in the morning for my pick up. See you then. Thanks Eddie. Cheers.'

Ellie was waiting for him as he let himself in through the front door. 'How are you, darling? You look worn out.'

'It's been a busy day and I know it's late but I'm ready for some food if there is some.' He leaned in for a welcome home kiss.

'You know I don't expect you for dinner in the week and I ate with the boys – but how about an omelette and a glass of wine?'

'I think I should pass on the wine but an omelette would be lovely.' They walked through to the kitchen together.

'Have you made any progress on the Mali arms deal front?' She said, pouring herself a glass of wine and offering him one too.

He nodded acceptance but hesitated for a moment before replying. 'No, not really. I'm not sure we will be able to get that one to stand up.' There was no point worrying her with today's news, he thought. Let's see how tomorrow goes.

Chapter 20

The next morning, Eddie was waiting outside the house to drive him to the pool but swimming gave him no release. As he ploughed up and down the marked-off lanes with the other serious early-morning swimmers, he puzzled through his options but couldn't think his way through how he should handle the day ahead. Every way forward seemed difficult and there was no way of knowing if this Richard character would even show up.

He had put his sim card into an older model iPhone and copied the iCloud file onto thumb drives as Lottie had advised, and when Eddie dropped him off at Lottie's house he asked him if he would go to the post office and mail the New York-addressed envelope for him. Eddie took the envelope and said he would also go and find breakfast, and for Jonathan to call him when he was five minutes away from needing the car. Jonathan walked up to Lottie's front door and could not but help looking around for snoopers whilst he waited for Lottie to answer.

'Jonathan. Hi. Come in quickly.'

'Morning.' He followed her into the kitchen where a pot of coffee was waiting. She looked agitated and in need of sleep. 'What's happened? You look dreadful.'

'Joe, our stringer in Mali, has been arrested. His wife emailed me overnight. She can't get any information on what's happening to him but she's convinced it was because of the work he was doing for us.'

'He's a Mali national?'

'Yes, but on our payroll. What can we do?'

'I don't know. I will pick it up with the legal guys as soon as they get in, which shouldn't be long now. Don't worry. Have you had a chance to work out how we play this Richard guy this morning?'

He poured himself coffee and offered one to Lottie. She declined with a brief shake of her head.

'I think we have to lean on him quite hard. It's a family business and he's the son of the owner. He will be very concerned that this could explode in their faces and trash their business so he will want to dampen down any fires and see his company kept out of it. Let me do the talking as I have already spoken to him and then let's plan out a course of action from where that meeting takes us.'

'OK. I've asked Eddie to mail a thumb-drive to New York and I've got three more here. There's one here for you to keep somewhere safe.'

He handed her a thumb-drive and she walked over to the kitchen cupboard and carefully placed it inside a metal tea container.

'That will have to do for now. I will find somewhere better later on. Now, can we get back to Joe?'

Jonathan called Legal Affairs and explained the problem to them. 'I will ask Lottie to email you all of his contact details and everything else. We need a switched-on lawyer on the ground in Bamako.' Pause. 'Yes, I know that's not a request you get every day but can you get onto it with some urgency.' Pause. 'No, I can't tell you on the phone what he was working on but it concerns the UK every bit as much as Mali. I'm happy to brief you face to face later today but for now you've just got to get a local lawyer we can trust.' Pause. 'OK. Thanks. Call me when you get some news.' He turned to Lottie, 'They are on the case. Will you email them with all the details? Apart from that, there's nothing more we can do – we will have to be patient.'

Lottie emailed Legal Affairs with Joe and his wife's contact details and the freelance agreement Joe had signed with the company. 'I'm sorry, I haven't even offered you breakfast, there's only some muesli here, will that be OK?'

He nodded and the two of them sat silently munching the muesli for a few moments. When they had finished their meagre breakfast, Jonathan called Eddie to say they were ready to be picked up. He arrived in the allotted five minutes and on the short drive into the office Lottie asked to be dropped off on the high street.

'I will pick up a couple of new phones and see you in the office. I've got loads to do before we leave. Shall we head out at about nine forty-five so we can be there in plenty of time?'

Jonathan agreed and confirmed the time and destination to Eddie. Once in the office, he worked through his inbox and cancelled most of his meetings for the day, including a lunch date with a cabinet minister.

'Carol, tell him I'm sick and infectious and don't want to bring him down with it. Major apologies and all that. Re-book when you can but not in the next seven days, even if there's space.'

At nine forty-five, Lottie walked into his office with two simple, somewhat retro, Nokia phones. She gave Jonathan the black phone. 'I've put my number into that black one and yours into this blue one. We should be fine talking on these but don't give the number to anyone else, not even Eddie or Ellie.'

'Do you think we are taking this a bit too seriously?'

'Maybe we are, but at least we can talk and text securely now without worrying as to who might be listening in.'

They walked out together to the car and Eddie drove them through a myriad of backstreets until they reached Covent Garden. They were meeting Richard in the piazza itself – he had said he wanted the meeting to be in a very public place and had chosen the venue himself. They walked through the pedestrianised area which was thronged as usual with international tourists gawping at the sights whilst working Londoners urgently pushed their way through the slowly drifting crowd of visitors. They make their way to the chain cafe Richard had specified in the middle of the piazza, ordered coffee and sat down at a table for four. The coffee, when it finally arrived, was mediocre and lukewarm but at least the delay gave them an extended occupancy at the busy cafe. They both found themselves looking around at their neighbours and passers-by but it was impossible to see if they were being watched: it was the sort of place where everyone was watching someone else.

Time passed by and they were beginning to think they had been stood up. They ordered more unwanted coffee from an aggressively shaven headed, heavily tattooed and unfriendly waitress to keep their hold on the table and waited. Both of their work phones rang frequently and they both tried to terminate calls as briskly as they could without rudeness.

Eventually, Richard Smith arrived at their table. 'Lottie?' he said, and upon her nod he sat down heavily. Richard was a forty-something balding guy in a badly fitting overcoat who carried more spare pounds than his company photograph had indicated. Lottie nodded. 'And who is this? You didn't say there would be anyone else here.'

'Richard, this is Jonathan, my boss, the MD of the business. He's leading the investigation so I thought it would be good if you could meet him too.'

'That's fine, I suppose. I don't want this conversation recorded or filmed. Will you give me your word you two are not doing either?'

Jonathan said, 'Richard, hello. Yes, you have my word. There's no recording of this meeting taking place so you don't have to have any concerns.'

'Tell us your side of the story, Richard. Give us your version of RedFox,' Lottie urged.

'Well, where to start? We are a family firm and we specialise in complex logistics, moving difficult things around the world. That could be sending very large turbines that can't be containerised through to shipping across multiple borders with different technical or regulatory issues. If it's complex, we claim we can sort it out and if it's not difficult to do there's one of the big guys that can do it cheaper than us. We have a niche in the market, that's what makes our business work.'

'OK, we get the picture. Tell us about Cavendale,' said Lottie, interrupting his flow, which she sensed could go on indefinitely.

'Sure. They are one of our bigger customers. We mainly move sensitive oil and gas components for them. Most of their stuff goes to Africa and we are pretty good at all of the customs idiosyncrasies you see there.'

'And RedFox?'

'Well, we move some pretty sensitive stuff for them from time to time and this shipment was obviously one of those. I guessed it was armaments from the pick-up location and their secrecy about the project. They normally get us to pitch for business but this one was given to us on a plate. I asked for their export licence for the stuff – I still don't know what was in the RedFox shipment – but they told me there wasn't one but it would all be OK. Well, obviously I didn't accept that and asked for documentation before we picked anything up. That's when I got a letter that confirmed everything was in order and we could go ahead.'

'Who was the letter from?'

'The Cabinet Office. It said that for reasons of national security there would be no export licence but HMG wanted to approve Cavendale's shipment to Mali. It said everything about the shipment had to remain confidential, including the letter itself.'

Lottie looked around her again and asked, 'Do you have a copy of the letter for me?'

'No. I have it in a secure place but I'm not going to breach confidentiality by sharing it with you. I'm just telling you that it was all approved at the highest level to get you off my back. I don't want to be dragged through the mud by you lot so I'm telling you the letter exists, it's in a safe place, and if I need to I will release it to stop you making insinuations against my business.'

'Why did you sub-contract THY to ship it from South Africa?'

'We don't have the relationships in Francophone Africa they do. It's what we always do when we ship sensitive stuff to one of those countries. South Africa is a good staging post for a handover of that sort.'

'Did they know what was in the RedFox shipment?'

'They knew it was secret. Those guys don't ask too many questions.'

'Who is your contact at Cavendale?'

'For this project it was Donald Brown. He's the COO. That's how I knew it was sensitive. It's pretty unusual to have someone like him give me direct instructions.'

'Are you sure we can't have a copy of the letter from the Cabinet Office?' asked Jonathan.

'I said no before and I meant it.'

'Did you brief MI5 about our call yesterday?' asked Lottie.

'No. Why, have they been in touch?' He looked around, panicked. 'I don't want to be part of anything, you know. I didn't tell anyone about your call, honest.'

'Then either your phone or mine is being listened to,' said Lottie coolly. 'I suspect it's yours so be careful what you say on it.'

'In that case, I don't think I want to say any more.' Visibly rattled, Richard started up from the table, dragging money from his trouser pocket.

'It's OK, the coffee is on us,' said Jonathan, trying to soothe.

'No. I don't want anything from you, not even a cup of coffee.' He threw several coins down onto the table. 'Please do not contact me. I don't want to see you ever again.' He gathered his over-stuffed brief case to his chest and hurried off, soon to be lost in the crowd of tourists that thronged the piazza.

After a pause, Jonathan asked, 'Well?'

'More frustration. Without the Cabinet Office letter we don't have the proof we need.'

'But we know some more. We now know that Donald Brown is the guy we need to investigate and we have the first real insight that solid evidence does exist that the Government authorised the shipment. If the letter is from the Cabinet Office then the PM must have known all about it and then later lied to Parliament. We do have something even if it's not everything we need. In the last twenty four hours we've made real progress.'

'Where does MI5 fit in to all of this?'

'That I don't know. If Richard is to be believed, and I don't know why we wouldn't believe him, the tip-off must have come from someone else. Cavendale?'

'But why yesterday? It can't have been your meeting with John Andrews. Who else could have tipped them off that we were close?'

'I don't know. Or maybe I do. What exactly was the stringer working on when he was picked up?'

'He was working on getting hold of documents from the South African shipper THY.'

'That must be it. The timing is right. So we can safely assume that the Mali Government has a direct line to our own. Joe gets caught out and we get a visit from a spook. It must be the connection.'

'But Joe doesn't know that much.'

'He knows enough. Any attempt to get information and evidence on the RedFox shipment will have set off alarm bells in Bamako and in London. As soon as he admits he's working directly for you there's a visit to you from MI5. It's been puzzling me, why you and not me? It's Joe who is the link.'

They made their way back to where Eddie was waiting for them and sat back into the car for the journey to the River Factory.

'Let's see if we can get in front of Donald Brown and see if we can push him into saying something that backs up John Andrew's version of events,' said Jonathan.

'Will you try and record the conversation?'

'I can try but I really need to get some documentation. I especially need to get hold of that letter from the Cabinet Office. If we get that then the whole thing blows wide open.'

The traffic slows down their progress to a crawl. Lottie decides she will bail out from the journey as she has a meeting with journalists off site and is now running late. She hops out and tells Jonathan she will see him back at his office after lunch. He sits back in the seat and scrolls through his emails. Eddie is patiently working his way through the traffic, but as they leave the Strand to make their way around Trafalgar Square, blue flashing lights behind them cause further chaos. Cars are moving over onto the pavement to let the police car through. Waiting until it is directly behind them, Eddie does the same but the police car pulls sharply towards the pavement in front of them and a uniformed officer and a very tall man in a dark suit get out of the car and motion to Eddie to switch the engine off. He does so and winds the passenger window down. 'What's wrong, officer?'

Looking directly into the back seat where Jonathan is sitting on the driver's side, the tall man in the dark suit asks, 'Are you Mr Lomax?'

Jonathan lowers his window before answering. 'Yes. I am.'

'Then I must ask you to come with us, sir.'

'And why exactly should I do that?'

'The police officer can arrest you here and now and create further traffic chaos or you can agree to come with us. It's entirely your choice but we presume you don't want to make this any more public than it already is.'

Jonathan takes off his seat-belt and says to Eddie, 'If I'm not back at the office in a couple of hours tell everyone I have been arrested.' He turns back to the tall man. 'Where exactly are you planning to take me?'

'I'm afraid that I can't answer that question, sir.' He tries to open the car door but the central locking is on. He turns to Eddie. 'Please release the central locking and hand over your phone. You must not make any calls or talk to anyone about this matter or you will be under arrest too.' Eddie unlocks the doors and hands over his phone from the dashboard cradle.

'Will I get my phone back?' he asks.

'Mr Lomax will return with it after we've had the chance to ask him some questions.' Turning again to Jonathan, he opens the door. 'Now, sir, if you would come with us.'

Jonathan gets out of the car and makes his way with the tall detective slowly to the police car in front, blue lights still flashing. This encourages a sizeable crowd of pedestrians to gawp and chatter. Some take photos on their phones. The uniformed officer, who had followed behind the two of them, opens the rear door and places his hand over Jonathan's head to protect it as he moves to sit in the rear seat. The policeman then gets in behind the wheel and starts the engine. Finally, the tall man sits down in the front passenger seat. Once the three of them are inside the car, the blue lights are extinguished and the car moves smartly away. The traffic congestion ahead has eased and Jonathan looks out of the window as they drive down Whitehall towards the river. No-one speaks. The car reaches Downing Street and is briefly caught up in traffic but turns left onto Richmond Terrace where the traffic is once more at a standstill.

'Where are we going?'

'We will be there shortly, sir,' replies the tall man without looking around.

As he says this, the traffic moves forward and before long the car turns left again into the Ministry of Defence entrance and then swings around to park outside a small undistinguished doorway at the back of the building. The tall man indicates for Jonathan get out of the car. He does so and the tall man gets out too and together they make their way to the doorway where an armed Army guard gives them access without a word. They walk in silence to a bank of lifts and make their way to the fifth floor. They arrive outside a meeting room that appears to be exactly the same as several others on the same corridor. They enter. The room is empty except for a large glass meeting table around which are six blue office chairs. There is a pot of coffee, cups, glasses and three plastic bottles of water on the table. The man indicates that Jonathan should sit down. He does so. Apart from a large oil painting of a long vanished regiment fighting in red uniforms in a desert somewhere, the room is anonymous and cheaply furnished.

'Help yourself to coffee or water. Your host should not be long. I would be obliged if you would give me your phone for safekeeping. Your phone and your driver's phone will be returned to you when you leave.'

Jonathan hands over his iPhone and the phone Lottie had given him that morning and helps himself to a bottle of water. He unscrews the top and drinks from the bottle. The detective places the two phones into a small plastic bag and then into his jacket pocket.

He continues, 'I shall be just outside the door, sir. As I said, you should not have to wait for too long.'

He leaves the room and shuts the door behind him. Jonathan waits. He looks at his watch: it is ten past twelve. Ten minutes pass before the door opens.

The first person into the room is a dark suited and serious looking young man carrying a large stack of files. He places these down on the table and looks hard at Jonathan.

'Mr Lomax, I'm Ben from the security services. I'm sorry we will have to wait a few minutes more, the man you are meeting today is just finishing off a phone call, I believe.'

He sits down on the other side of the table, takes out a pen and extracts a yellow legal pad from amongst his files. He turns over the pages until he comes to a blank one where he makes a few notes and then looks back at Jonathan.

'You are probably wise to avoid the coffee.'

'What am I doing here? What's going on?'

'If you can be patient for just a few more minutes, Mr Lomax, all will become clear. Just a few more minutes, I promise.'

Five more minutes pass and Jonathan makes a show of looking at his watch and catching the eye of the other man but gets nothing in response. The door finally opens and Jonathan is very surprised to see the Prime Minister walking into the office. Tall, patrician and as usual dressed in an immaculate dark-blue suit, he greets Jonathan warmly, stretching out his hand in greeting.

'Jonathan, it's been a while. How are you?' Without waiting for a response, he continues, 'I'm sorry for all of this cloak and dagger stuff and whisking you here but I wanted to talk with you urgently and the front door at Downing Street is a bit public for some meetings, I do hope you don't mind?'

'Good afternoon, Prime Minister.' Jonathan's response is guarded and noncommittal.

'Oh, come on now, Andrew, please.'

'Prime Minister, what is it you think I can do for you?'

'Well, let's sit down and discuss it, shall we.' He sits down opposite Jonathan and helps himself to a black coffee. He tastes it and screws up his face. To Ben he says, 'We must do something about the coffee in this place, Ben, perhaps there's a case for privatisation?'

'I think the security issues may be problematic, sir,'

'Of course, of course, everything I want to do has unintended consequences.' He looks at Jonathan again, 'You are certainly safer with the water than MOD coffee, Jonathan.'

He reaches for a bottle of water and slowly unscrews the top. He plays with the top between his fingers but does not drink from the bottle. There is an uncomfortable silence that drags on.

'Jonathan, we seem to have got ourselves into something of a pickle.' He pauses. 'I know you are very busy investigating Cavendale and the Cressleys, looking into their deals in Africa and it's really not very helpful to us. There are things that sometimes go on in Government that are not helped by having the glare of publicity shone upon them and this is one I'm afraid. Sir John Cressley has played a very significant role for this Government, and earlier ones; helping us achieve things that are in the national interest but cannot be seen to have been done by HMG. He's not the only such person, but his role in helping us achieve our objectives in Africa has been considerable.' He pauses again and looks hard at Jonathan. 'And now all of that good work could be undone by you, playing investigative journalist rather than running that interesting TV channel of yours.'

'I can show that Cavendale supplied British anti-personnel weapons to the Mali military and that some of these weapons were used to put down tribal disturbances that had nothing to do with any war on Islamic fundamentalists.'

'Oh, please, spare me your moralising. We both know that this is a convenient stick for you to beat me and the Government with and the material facts of the matter at hand are completely beside the point.'

'You condoned the sale of hideous weapons to a regime outlawed for such sales and then you, and a large chunk of your cabinet, lied to Parliament about the sale. Not just once but on multiple occasions.'

'And I may have to again. That's what realpolitik means, Jonathan. Doing things you don't really want to do for the sake of a greater good. In this case, propping up the Mali Government and helping the fight against the Islamic insurgency there. It's a huge problem right across swathes of Africa and we can't sit back and wring our hands and do nothing to help. I'm sorry there was some regrettable collateral damage, as our American friends say, but I do not regret my actions and would do the same again, if the need arose.'

'But you would regret them becoming public.'

'Indeed I would. It would be very embarrassing for me and for other members of the cabinet. I would certainly have to resign. I've shouted about the value of personal integrity long enough and it would be impossible for me to carry on. The Defence Secretary would have to follow me through the door and it would be touch and go for the Chancellor and Home Secretary too. They would probably survive but both would be tarnished and would not have much support in any leadership election. So, the political brains of the Government would be exiled to the back benches and my dear party would be forced to choose a new leader from the bunch of intellectual pygmies who would then put themselves up to be my successor. You can imagine the candidates. There may have to be an election and although we are well placed in the polls, this sort of difficulty could let Labour into Number 10 for a final swan-song before they bankrupt the country. The whole country would be set back by the loony bloody lefties running Labour today. You can give them, literally on a plate, their only chance in hell to win a bloody election. Is that what you want to do?'

'I don't think we can have a viable democracy where the Prime Minister lies repeatedly to Parliament.'

'My arse. You are trying to take me down because we had some difficulties in the past...'

'Our former relationship has nothing to do with it.'

'Well, let's park that one for now.' The PM hesitates theatrically. 'Let's look at moving forward instead.' He pauses again. The room is silent except for the noise of the lifts whirring across the corridor. 'Let's look at what we have got. You really have some evidence against Cavendale and the Cressleys and some circumstantial evidence against me. You really need that document from the Cabinet Office to prove your case and I'm pretty sure you don't have that or you would be waving it in my face. Am I right?'

'I know it exists and what it says, but no, I don't have a copy.'

'I thought so. So what you do have against me is a recording of that idiot John Andrews telling you that HMG knew everything about the arms shipment to Mali and actively encouraged it. Yes?'

'In other words: the truth.'

'Hmm.' He turned to Ben, 'have you got the phone?' Ben takes an iPhone out of his pocket and hands it to the Prime Minister. Jonathan realises it is not one of the two phones he gave to the tall man but another, newer phone.

'Yours, I believe.' The Prime Minister hands the phone across the table to Jonathan. He sees from the case that it is his phone, the one he gave to Eddie for safekeeping. 'Don't blame your driver by the way. He's been working for Ben for a couple of weeks now. It's always useful to have ex-servicemen to call on in one's hour of need, especially if they've already signed the Official Secrets Act. He's been very useful at helping us keep tabs on you. Anyway, your conversation with Andrews was very interesting – now deleted, of course. For one thing, it showed what a cretin he really is and secondly how close you were to getting the full story.'

'You broke into my phone? Into my iCloud account?'

'Yes,' this time it was Ben who replies. 'Our friends in Cheltenham have been working on this problem for a while. Apple are most unhelpful. Yours is the first one we have broken into without American help.'

'You know I have other copies.'

'I'm sure you do. That's the nature of these digital devices today. We have to learn to live with it.'

It was not at all clear to Jonathan if the Prime Minister was referring to the problem with a digital society or Jonathan's multiple copies of the audio file, two of which were currently lying in his jacket pocket.

The PM continues. 'Your driver of course gave us the one heading for New York but we aren't stupid enough to believe we can capture them all. We will have to cope with that problem. So, Jonathan, I have a proposition for you and it's one I believe you need to think very carefully about.' Turning to Ben, he said, 'Ben, could you give us the room please?' He waited for Ben to leave the room and close the door behind him. 'That's better. Jonathan, we all know that you are enjoying the novelty and the power of your new television station, influencing policy and mixing with the movers and shakers. Well, I can stop all of that obviously. It would not be hard to phone up Tom Schalke and have you removed. You look surprised? Tom and I go way back and if I tell him the whole Party will reject any involvement in your channel if you remain in charge I think we would see movement fairly quickly. But I don't want to do that, Jonathan, that's not the proposition I have for you. You may not be surprised to hear that Sir John Cressley will have to step down from Parliament; I feel some health issues might be coming on and a by-election in a safe Tory seat offers exciting opportunities for a young go-ahead man like yourself.'

'You would put me forward for his seat? What about the selection committee?'

'I think we can safely assume that I can pull in the necessary votes for you there. Once elected, you have a seat there for life. As long as you go back to Northamptonshire once in a while and open a few fetes you are rock solid. I will promise you a senior cabinet post within the year. God knows we need some smart young people around the table, there aren't too many on the back benches these days. From there the sky is the limit. We can do great things together. Despite our difficulties, I have always rated your brain and your drive...'

'And if I were to accept this offer, how do I know that you would keep your word?'

'I'm a man of my word, you know that. Also, you will still have the recording so you will have me over the proverbial barrel. As I said, it's something I will have to get used to.'

'So you see me resigning my career and joining you in Government? Why should I want to do that?'

'Because I know you really want to be in the team that changes things, Jonathan. I know that from our earlier relationship. Your passion was one of the things we fell out about and I regret that, honestly I do. I'm giving you the chance to help make change happen. When Adam came to me and told me of your plans to develop Catalyst, I was very keen to be of real help in making it happen. We need to re-vitalise our political thinking and challenge the status quo.'

'And so you helped me land the job?'

'I only had a brief chat with Drew and Tom to help their decision along. Drew was worried about the risks and I told him not to worry and that you were a good man to back. I'd like to think my support helped him make his mind up. Now, we will have to find a way of bridging your salary drop for a year or two but a few non-executive directorships will do that and I can make those happen too. On the opposite side of the coin, I, of course, would want your word that you will drop the investigation and remain forever silent about arms deals and Mali etc. etc. You would have to square off that rather good looking publicity woman..?' He hesitated, searching for a name.

'Charlotte Edwards,' said Jonathan.

'That's it, Charlotte, everyone calls her Lottie, I believe. Quite striking in a somewhat boyish way.' He holds Jonathan's glare and then continues effortlessly. 'There may be some other loose ends too but once they are tidied up we can move forward together. What do you think?'

'I think you under-estimate me if you think you can buy me off with a seat at cabinet.'

'Well, what I want you to do is to think about my proposition for a few days and then come back to me. I would of course need your word that you will suspend any further investigations for that period and also agree not to publish anything in that interim. Will you at least do that for me, Jonathan?'

'I will do as you say, three days. I agree to think through your offer for that time. And agree not to do anything in that period. I'm going to be in Budapest anyway, I'm speaking at a media conference.'

'Excellent city. I've enjoyed surprisingly good food there on my visits. Travel is good for thinking things through, so do so. I will get Ben to text you a secure number you can call me on to give me your answer. I do genuinely hope we will be able to do business together. Now', he looked at his watch, 'I really must be off. I have the Irish Premier in two minutes and I have to be back at Downing Street to greet her or she will be grumpy for the whole meeting. You know how touchy the Irish can be if they perceive a British slight.' He stands up and Jonathan does the same. Stretching his hand across the table to shake hands, the PM continues, 'Jonathan, once again, I do hope we can work together. John, one of my personal detectives outside, will show you back to the car and take you to wherever you want to go...'

'I think I would rather walk,' said Jonathan, declining to shake the outstretched hand of the Prime Minister, who withdraws it, a flash of annoyance crossing his face.

'Well it's a lovely day for it. Enjoy the sunshine.' He smiles broadly and then turns on his heel and walks quickly out of the door. Ben appears in the doorway and returns to his papers and notepad on the table. Neither speak.

A moment or two passes. John comes in and hands Jonathan the plastic bag containing his two phones and Eddie's phone. He now has four phones and barely enough pockets to accommodate them. Ben gathers his bundle of papers together and then, realising he could not shake Jonathan's hand, puts them down again.

'Mr Lomax, thank you for this meeting. I am sure we will meet again sometime soon.'

He holds out a hand but Jonathan again ignores it and walks out of the room with John following close behind. How bloody dare he? How did he think he could get away with it?

He strides to the lift and presses the down button. It doesn't light and John behind him says, 'I'm sorry, sir, it needs a pass to operate.' He waves his pass in front of the sensor, the lift audibly responds and they make their way together in silence to the ground floor. Jonathan is escorted to the front door and once outside walks off rapidly towards the river. He is furious.

Part Three

Chapter 21

'Where have you been?' Lottie rushes into his office. 'I've haven't been able to reach you. What is going on?'

'Sorry, Lottie. I've been wrestling with a problem. I walked back from the river. The traffic was terrible and I've got a problem to sort out with GBN. I can't tell you what it's about; Drew has sworn me to secrecy.'

'Can I help?'

'No. I have to do some serious thinking to see if I can help him out. I hope to get it sorted before we go off to Budapest.'

'Do I need to warn the organisers of a problem with your speech?'

'No. I will be there and giving the speech you have seen. You know how much I am looking forward to it.'

'Me too.'

'Just give me some time. I have some production issues to deal with this afternoon and this new problem with Drew will take me out of the office for most of the day tomorrow. Let's put Mali on the back burner until we've got the Budapest speech out of the way and then I can give it my full attention.'

'What about Joe?'

'We've got the lawyers on it. We can't do anymore. Let's be patient and see what they come up with.'

'OK. I suppose so. Do you want me to do some more digging around Donald Brown?'

'No. Let's stop everything until we re-group in a few days. There's no point starting fires when we can't give them our full attention.'

'I hear you – but I can't help thinking we shouldn't be wasting this time...'

'Trust me, Lottie, give me a couple of days. Now, you need to let me go. I've got Angie waiting in the conference room with a team of producers ready to present their ideas.'

Jonathan did have his usual full afternoon of meetings that Tuesday afternoon, but he also wants to lose himself in work and get his meeting with the Prime Minister out of his head. He had been completely sideswiped by the direct approach the PM had taken with him and he had to put that meeting into a box until he had time to think about it and deal with it properly. He would get Carol to free up his diary for most of the day on Wednesday and he would give himself time to work everything out. Once he had resolved his own mind he could talk to Lottie, but until then, he wants to keep his thoughts very much to himself. This was a decision he had to make on his own.

He moves from meeting to meeting in the building until it is time to leave to go to a drinks party for the launch of yet another new Sky channel. It would be a good opportunity to network and see some old friends. He leaves the building and his car is waiting outside.

'Hi, Eddie. We are off to Mayfair please.'

'Yes, boss. I've got the address here.'

'Did Carol give you your phone back?'

'Yes, thanks.'

'Eddie. I'm off to Budapest on Thursday and after you've taken me to the airport then, I've asked to be assigned another driver. You will go back to the Director's pool at GBN.'

'Boss. You have to understand what I did...it was only because the security spooks told me I had to...'

'I know. I might have done just the same. But you must realise that I can't have you as my driver any more, Eddie. I have to be able to trust you completely and we can't carry on pretending that nothing has happened. I'm certain it's for the best.'

'But, boss...'

'No buts, Eddie. I have already spoken to the Fleet Manager and organised it. Of course, I haven't told him the real reason. I just said I needed a change and that you were a great driver, just not the right guy for me anymore. There's no black mark against your name or anything like that. It's just over.'

They drive on to Mayfair in silence. When they arrive, Jonathan gives Eddie the night off and says he will find his own way home. He picks up a glass of champagne and moves into his party persona, greeting old friends and new acquaintances with equal courtesy and interest and then he works the room to ensure he didn't miss anyone important. Within an hour he is done and ready to leave. He just needs to exit quietly before the main presentation starts and then no-one would remember him leaving early. He is almost out of the door when Sky's Political Editor grabs his arm and turns him gently around.

'Jonathan, hello, how are you? It's been a while. How's that fledging channel of yours shaping up? Still fighting the good fight and scaring the establishment?'

Alison Wright is the doyenne of London's political hacks. She has seen it all, heard it all and, if rumours were true, made up most of the rest. She and Jonathan had worked together briefly at Sky after she was joined from the BBC and had enjoyed a good working relationship. Although he was one of the corporate bosses by then, she still saw the journalist in him and this gave them a common bond and an easy friendship.

'Alison. How lovely to see you. I was hoping you would be here tonight.' They air kissed and smiled at each other. 'You are looking great, what's the secret?'

'Jonathan, you old flatterer. I have been trying to lose a few pounds and I've given up the booze and I'm trying the green tea diet. I don't want to get too old and too fat to be on TV. You know what the channel bosses are like with older women these days.'

'Well, darling, you can come and star on my channel anytime Sky says anything unkind to you.'

'Melissa and I on the same channel. You must be a sucker for punishment.'

'You know you were my first choice, but I knew there was no way I could prise you out of Sky.'

'You really do say the nicest things, sweetheart. Even when I know you don't mean them.' She pauses and looks directly at him. 'Now, down to serious stuff for a moment. My impeccable sources tell me that you are irritating our illustrious PM somewhat these days. Now why would that be?'

'You know we were never that close, even when I was advising him a while back. I don't think he's that keen on policy ideas coming from the media; although you would think a lifetime of dealing with the *Daily Mail* would have prepared him for that sort of thing.'

'And that's all? There's nothing more?'

'I'm pleased to know I'm irritating him. It means we must be doing something useful. But nothing else. No gossip there, I'm afraid. Now how's that lovely wife of yours?'

'She's tip-top thank you. How's Ellie?'

'Well, do send her my love. Ellie is fighting fit, thank you. It must be time for a get-together. I will ask Carol to organise something for the four of us. Now, if you can excuse me, I was just trying to sneak off early to see Ellie and miss the big corporate speech everyone is not waiting for.'

'Of course, I won't tell a soul. Dinner would be lovely. Sometime very soon, it's my treat.'

'You are on. Leave it to me. Bye, Alison.'

Once out of the venue, Jonathan walks along the street for a little way. Several cabs with yellow lights illuminated pass by and one even slows down anticipating a fare, but he waves it away and continues to walk through the lightly drizzling evening. He walks on aimlessly, occasionally looking in shop windows, and eventually finds himself at Green Park station.

On a whim, he enters and gets on a westbound Piccadilly tube. It must be a couple of years since I was last on a tube train, he thinks to himself, and he watches his fellow passengers lost in their own electronic worlds as the train shakes, rattles and bangs through its long procession of stations. Most of them bring back memories for him; with drunken friends misbehaving at South Kensington, stuck overnight with a girlfriend at Gloucester Road waiting for the first train to carry them home on New Year's day, memorable youthful concerts at Earls Court, visiting his father in hospital at Barons Court and thinking it might be the last time he would see him. He changes trains at Hammersmith and, after waiting for several minutes, the right train arrives and the District Line tube slowly creaks its way towards Richmond. By the time he arrives there the rain is falling heavily and there are no taxis. He walks the fifteen minutes to his front door and is soaked through by the time he arrives. Ellie comes into the hallway and looks on, slightly puzzled, as he pulls off his jacket and shoes and wet socks and heads upstairs to change.

'Why don't you have a shower too? You must be drenched right through.'

'That's not a bad idea. I think I will.'

When he emerges downstairs ten minutes, later he is wearing jeans and a grey sweatshirt and his hair is unkempt from vigorous towelling.

'That's so much better. I had to walk from the station and it's raining pretty hard.'

'Where's Eddie?'

'I gave him the night off and I couldn't get a cab in town, you know what it's like when it's raining, so I thought I would get a tube instead. My suit will have to go to the cleaners so it was an expensive decision.'

'How was your day?'

'Yeah, OK. Nothing special.'

'Have you made any progress on your Mali investigation?'

'No. I'm not sure we are going to get anywhere. Every door seems tightly shut. I have deiced to put it all to one side until I get back from Budapest but I'm not sure even then I will be able to make any progress. It could all be over. Is there any food in the house? I'm famished.'

'I thought you were out socialising this evening.'

'Only the usual crappy canapés on offer. And somehow I missed out on lunch too so I would love something – anything – to eat.'

'That's two consecutive nights that you've come home and asked for food. I'm going to have to take shopping a bit more seriously if this is going to become a habit.'

The next morning after swimming he directs Eddie to take him to Paddington where he has an early morning breakfast meeting with Drew. Although he had not told Lottie the whole truth, his CEO had called him when he was walking back to the office from the Ministry of Defence and asked for an early morning meeting. Jonathan presumed this was all to do with Tom Schalke rather than any sudden concern for the television business.

'Jonathan, thanks for coming over so early. I know you are an early-bird but I appreciate you moving things around for me.'

'Drew, it's not a problem. What can I do for you?'

Jonathan accepts the cup of coffee from the uniformed waiter and picks up a croissant from the plate on the meeting table. He breaks up the croissant with his long fingers as he waits for Drew to begin.

'As you know, I'm having a tough time with Tom Schalke.'

'He only ever talks to me about TV.'

'Well, he sings your praises whenever he gets the chance but he's a real git when he doesn't get what he wants and currently I'm in his crosshairs.'

'What have you done to upset him?'

'Not doing things as fast and as furiously as he would like. He wants to see massive cost-savings across the board and whilst I want to achieve the same result I also want a functioning business left at the end of it. At the same time, the new fund-raising is proving tricky and we are getting close to breaching our banking covenants. As a public company that would destroy the share price. I suspect he is trying to screw us down so we don't have any choice but to accept harsher terms and he probably wants my head too.'

'He hasn't spoken to me about the wider business at all. He called last week out of the blue and talked television and politics but that was all. He's also set up a meeting in Budapest to meet some Hungarian TV executives about possibly rolling out Catalyst there but apart from that we haven't discussed anything.'

'Well, he hasn't replied to my invitation to our drinks party in Budapest as yet and I take that as a bad sign. You will be there, of course?'

'Yes. It's in the diary. It looks like a busy trip. There are lots of meetings set up already.'

'I'm looking forward to hearing you deliver your speech; it will really set the tone for the sort of business we want to become.'

'Thank you. I'm sure the speech and the dinner afterwards will throw up some interesting responses.'

'I want to use your moment in the spotlight to announce that you will be joining the PLC board. I think it's time. What do you think?'

'More to the point: what does Tom think?'

'Jonathan, I'm still capable of independent action, you know. He actually thinks it's a good idea. He wants you to have some PLC board experience; I think he sees you as my long-term successor.'

'Well, in that case I guess I would be honoured. But I've no interest in your job. From where I'm sitting it looks to be nightmare and I know nothing about the business of running newspapers. My only concern is that I still want to be single-minded about growing and improving the TV business.'

'Of course. I don't want you enmeshed in all of the problems of the newspaper business either. It goes without saying that it also means a salary bump and more share options so there's a personal upside for you too.'

'Drew, thanks, I'm delighted to accept. It's a great honour.'

'My only proviso, Jonathan, is that you remember whose team you are on. We will have a big tussle with Schalke before long and we need to stop him trashing the business for short-term gain. His horizon is based around a profitable sale in three years' time and my horizon is making the business fit for the future, and your division is central to that success.'

'I will remember, boss.'

'Good. I will have corporate PR work with your woman and set it all up for announcing after your speech. That should give you an extra fillip in the press. Now, as we won't be having our usual Friday briefing, how's the business looking?'

'Good. This week's numbers, especially online, are our best ever and ad revenues, although still below target, are picking up. I'm still worried about some of the editorial content but that's always going to be a challenge working on the budgets we have to manage with. I'm going to spend a few hours today working on some alternative show ideas that we will start feeding into the schedule over the coming month or two. I think it's really important that we don't stand still and we keep re-inventing ourselves.'

'Have you done anything about international expansion or is that just Tom's pipe-dream?'

'I've done nothing at all. This weekend and my speech is really the start of the campaign. I'm not at all sure that Hungary, given the politics there, is the right market for our first rollout but let's have the meeting and see how things go. I will push back against Tom if I feel it's the wrong place; it is critical that the first rollout sets the model for future expansion. I've extended my stay until Sunday morning so I can fit in any extra meetings on the Saturday if I need to.'

'Good idea. I'm afraid I'm flying back first thing on Saturday. Probably with a hangover from hell after our party on Friday. You know how newspaper men can drink. These days it is probably worse as we all drown our sorrows and tell each other endless stories about the glory days.'

Jonathan leaves the Paddington meeting in a downbeat mood. He is vaguely enthused by the promotion to the PLC board but still weighed down by the Prime Minister's ultimatum. He emails Lottie to tell her of the promotion and to get her working on the press release but didn't reply to her response asking when he would be in the office. He needs some time to think and sits in a smart but soulless coffee bar in the Paddington basin nursing a flat white for an hour and playing the options around in his head. With nothing resolved, he wanders off along the canal in the brilliant winter sunshine. The walk brings back memories of the day he accepted the job with GBN. However, today nothing is clear; the more he works through different scenarios in his head, the more confused he becomes.

He lunches alone at a small Italian cafe and then makes his way to the studios. Lottie is waiting for him outside his office, having been notified by him of his imminent arrival. 'There's been no movement with Joe in Mali,' she says. 'Our lawyers haven't been able to talk to him directly and say there's no sign of when they might be allowed access. I'm really worried for him, anything could happen.' She looks on the verge of tears.

'Lottie, it's not the UK. You must accept these things take more time out there. We've got good people on it, you must be patient.'

'But we've put him in this position. He could be kept in jail without trial for weeks, even months. He might just be disappeared.'

'There is no more we can do.'

'That's easy for you to say but you don't have his distraught wife emailing you every few hours.'

'I know that but honestly we just have to sit tight. He's a Mali citizen and there's nothing more we can do from here.' He changes the subject to break out of this spiralling conversation. 'Have you sorted out the PLC stuff with corporate?'

'Yeah, that only took a few minutes. Congratulations, by the way.'

Lottie is unusually unenthusiastic in her praise. Usually his career advancements meant more to her than they do to him but Joe's predicament in Bamako is dominating her thoughts and everything else seems less important.

'I'm tied up all afternoon with meetings, mostly commercial stuff with the ad sales guys, but let's talk again at the end of the day and if there's still no progress I will chivvy up the lawyers. How's that?'

'Thanks, Jonathan, I appreciate it. I did mean well done on the PLC thing, you know how proud I am of you. Are you all set for the trip tomorrow?'

'Yes, I think so. If we aim to leave here at ten we should have plenty of time. That means I can get my swim in and have an early meeting with Angie before we need to leave.' He holds Lottie's gaze, 'I'm really looking forward to the trip. Now go and get some work done!'

He leaves the office before seven for his dinner date with Ellie. He had organised this a week before as he is spending nearly the whole weekend in Hungary. Eddie drives him to a small but favourite restaurant outside Kew where he has organised to meet Ellie. He is the first to arrive. He orders a vodka tonic and sits back to wait for Ellie's arrival. She arrives, late and flustered, ten minutes later.

'Sorry, had a devil's game with the traffic. I was stuck in the back of an Uber for what seemed like hours...'

'Don't worry. Let me get you a glass of Champagne. I will have one too. We've something to celebrate.'

'What?'

'Drew's putting me up for PLC board membership.'

'That's great, darling, well done.'

'You might say that with a bit more enthusiasm.'

'I'm sorry, it's been one hell of a day and you know how I feel about GBN's newspapers.'

'I'm not planning to have any more to do with them but it will mean a pay rise and new share options and all that stuff so the ski chalet is now a definite option if you still want to do it.'

'You know it would be fabulous for the boys,' she says, taking a deep gulp of Champagne. 'I'm sorry, it's selfish of me to be churlish. You must be delighted.'

'Well, it's complicated by politics. Drew is fighting for his life with the hedge funds and he needs some more backing on the board. That's the subtext. Although I owe him for the job and giving me a free hand at Catalyst, I'm not sure that allying myself to him is the best long-term strategy for me.'

'But once you are on the board you can play it the way you need to. You will only have to ensure you are acting in shareholder interests.'

'Sounding like a lawyer there, my darling. You are right but keeping the peace between shareholders that may not be so easy. What shall we eat?'

They choose from the menu and then return to their earlier conversation. Ellie asks, 'When will the news go public?'

'They plan to announce on Friday evening after I make my big speech in Budapest. That way they maximise the newsworthiness of the speech and make the biggest impact.'

'I'm so sorry that I won't be there to share your success with you.'

'You know how these conferences are: all back-slapping and networking. I don't suppose I will have any time to see the city which I hear is very lovely. You would be terribly bored. Perhaps we can go back there sometime, just the two of us and explore it at our leisure.'

'That would be great, I would really like that.'

'Now, tell me about your week. I feel I am completely out of date with your news. Tell me all.'

Ellie tells him of her struggles with Hounslow Council and the legal fights she and Howie are having with a Richmond Housing Association. He listens quietly, pleased to be talking about something that is not to do with politics or media and admiring his wife's passion and eloquence whilst she talks. He nods encouragingly at the appropriate points in her monologue but makes little contribution to the conversation through dinner.

'I'm sorry, now I'm going on and on. You've made a really good show of looking interested but that's more than enough about my charity work. Have you got everything ready for your Budapest speech?' She finishes off her glass of wine and sits back waiting to hear his response.

'Yes, I think so. I wish I wasn't away for so long though.'

'It will do you good. You need a break from the office and you know you enjoy meeting all of your work cronies and doing that luvvie thing you claim to dislike so much.'

'I guess so. It's just that I already spend so much time away from you and the boys and here's another weekend given over entirely to work. By the time I'm back on Sunday afternoon it will be turnaround time for it all to start again on Monday morning.'

'Well, why don't you grab the bill and let's go home and make the most of what remains of the night. I will Uber a ride whilst you are doing that. I can't believe how much time off you've given to Eddie recently.'

Chapter 22

'I cannot believe you are going to let him off the hook.'

'Lottie, I've thought it all through and there's no alternative. If we go public on this the Government will fall, there will have to be an election and there's every chance the lunatic left will get into power. It's too awful to contemplate. I have no choice.'

'But he is guilty of bare-faced lying to Parliament – never mind selling arms to a dodgy regime that used the weapons on innocent people.'

'All true, I know. But there's no other way. We will just have to bury the story and move on.'

'Move on. What about Joe? How is he meant to move on from a Mali jail?'

'We will get Joe out, I promise. I will lean on the PM to ensure he does that for me.'

'And what else has he promised to do for you?'

'We've talked about a future in his government. Cressley's going to have to step down and the PM reckons I will get his seat and a senior cabinet post in next to no time. But I only want to do it if you are onside with the idea. You know we are a team and I won't be able to manage it without you. You would be my Director of Communication or special adviser or whatever you might want to call the post but you are essential if we are to make this work.'

Lottie sits up in bed, the sheet falling down from around her small pointed breasts. She reaches for a cigarette from the bedside table and lights it, drawing the smoke deeply into herself. There is silence in the room.

'So, you thought you would enjoy your evening of speech making, your job promotion, and then, after a night fucking me, you would finally get around to telling me about your decision?'

'Lottie, it's not like that. I only made my mind up in the early hours of this morning. It's been a really tough decision.'

Lottie gathers the sheet around her and walks off to the bathroom. Over her shoulder she calls out, 'When you've finished dressing, leave me alone here. I need to think. Go and have breakfast.' Jonathan does as he is told, pulling on his shoes and his jacket and taking the key card as he leaves the room.

Today, Friday, is a day full of meetings in and outside of the conference sessions and ending with the GBN drinks and a conference dinner. They had planned to spend Saturday as tourists, ducking out of the conference apart from Tom Schalke's lunchtime meeting with the Hungarian TV executives and they had organised to dine alone. He had struggled a couple of weeks ago to reserve a table at the famously overbooked Onyx restaurant. They would then spend Sunday morning further exploring Budapest before flying home together after lunch. Now all of that careful planning and organisation was flying out of the window: if Lottie was as angry with him as she seemed to be, the whole weekend might go up in smoke. It had been months since they were last able to organise a weekend away together and he had been excited about the opportunity. Keeping a low profile in a conference hotel was important to both of them but he had upgraded their two rooms at the Boscolo into an executive suite without any fuss and they had spent the late evening drinking too much champagne and revelling in the baroque Austrian style of the enormous bedroom. Lottie was ecstatic at the reception his speech had received and had been working her press contacts to make sure it got the coverage she felt it deserved. Once she had finished with work she turned her full attention on him. As usual with Lottie, their lovemaking had been fierce and passionate and had kept them awake much of the night. It was only as he watched her sleep, spread over the enormous bed in complete abandonment, that he finally made his mind up about his reply to the Prime Minister. Once he had made the decision, he could see that he had really no alternative and had told Lottie as soon as their morning sex was over and she was snuggled deep into his arms. He has struggled to understand why Lottie couldn't see the logic of his arguments, surely it was obvious?

As he leaves the room heading towards breakfast, he realises he is also slightly hungover. He really does need some breakfast, especially as he has the first of his scheduled meetings with two German journalists at nine am and is then on a bloody panel session about helping disadvantaged young people break into traditional media. More bloody liberal hand-wringing, no doubt. He makes his way down the corridor, greeting a couple of fellow executives in the lift and finds a table for two in the corner of the breakfast restaurant. Maybe Lottie will join him after a few moments of reflection. She must see that his decision is the only logical course of action open to them. He takes out his phone and after looking up the number he had been given to reply to the Prime Minister, he texts,

You have a deal. Jonathan Lomax

Within a couple of minutes, the response comes back.

I knew I could count on you. Welcome to my team. Will talk on your return. Enjoy Budapest and all of her delights

The deed is done. There is no going back now. He looks up to see the two German journalists waving from the other side of the room as they make their way towards him.

Lottie was just as hungry as Jonathan. The combination of too much champagne, sex and bad news had made her ravenous. She orders some room service and sits on the sofa in her voluminous hotel bathrobe, waiting for it to arrive. Damn Jonathan. He always thought he knew best and he always made big decisions without ever consulting her.

How had she let it get this far, she wondered. She had fallen for Jonathan soon after she started working for him. She prided herself on being a hard-bitten, no-nonsense career-girl and was proud of her reputation for efficiency and brains within the industry. Her private life had featured several smart and intelligent guys but somehow none of them had ever really set her on fire. With Jonathan it was different. She liked everything about him, his physique, his smile, his self-confidence, his smell, his style and, most of all, his mind. Of course, she had promised herself that nothing would ever happen – he was a married man and she had no intention of becoming the other woman. She had made a point of keeping her distance even though she sometimes fantasised about him when she was alone. But when, three years ago, at a conference in Paris, he had kissed her in an elevator, she had no misgivings about responding to his advances. She had taken him to her bed where they remained for the rest of the trip apart from a brief interlude when Jonathan had to get up and make his presentation. He completed her and when they were together she was as happy as she could be. It really was that simple. When he was with her it was good and when he was away there was just a gap in her life that only he could fill.

Much of her life was spent waiting for him. That was the fate of the mistress, she told herself. The wife was always there in the background and Lottie was under no misapprehensions that Jonathan would ever leave his lovely wife for her. She knew her place. They had occasional sex late at night in the office but mostly it was at her house in Wandsworth when they could find the time and the excuses to get away with it. Conferences and foreign trips were infrequent delights and it was rare to have him for a whole night. When they had extended time together, Lottie was always keen to show him her inventiveness as a lover. Jonathan was demanding in bed with a long list of sexual fantasies. She set out to fulfil them as best she could, wanting to please him and do things for him that she thought his wife could or would not do. He loved her dressed in tight leather and she slowly found herself responding to the role of a dominatrix and it was perhaps only at these times that she thought she might actually have some control over him. She even reluctantly engaged in a threesome at his request, but felt herself inadequate alongside the pneumatic and statuesque Ukrainian escort he had booked for the night. Despite his frequent entreaties, she had refused to repeat that experiment. Mostly, though, she was keen to show herself to be a flexible and adventurous lover, always happy to respond to his wants and desires. She indulged his cocaine habit and occasionally took some herself but never found the drug rush as enthralling as he so obviously did.

She also knew that Jonathan was serially unfaithful to her. It seemed easy for him to admit his adventures to his mistress and she knew she was powerless to stop him straying. She tried to project an indifferent attitude but they both knew his dalliances upset her. Women didn't actually throw themselves at him but he was courteous and charming and good-looking and if he put any real effort into seduction he would usually stand a good chance of bedding his target. He told her that he couldn't help himself: attractive new women were like a drug to him and seducing them into bed was the greatest pleasure he knew. He would say that having won the seduction battle, the actual fulfilment was less interesting to him but Lottie often wondered if he made this part up for her benefit. She had warned him never to bed any of the women working for her but had watched on helplessly as attractive young interns were enticed into his lair, only to be discarded shortly afterwards. Lottie prided herself that at least he kept coming back to her and she was determined that she would not lose him to another woman. She liked to think that Jonathan saw their relationship as one of equals. It was true she worked for him but they both knew that she was the real power in this new age of social media, driving his reputation forwards through a series of witty and insightful tweets, articles and interventions. Lottie had built his career and she made sure, without labouring the point, that he understood he couldn't sustain his upwards trajectory without her tireless promotion.

Did he love her? She had pondered this question many times whilst sitting alone late at night nursing a bottle of wine. He often said that he did when they were alone together, but what did that really mean? She rather thought he might love her, but in his own, somewhat unsatisfactory way. He was caring and considerate. He respected her views and often asked her for advice. He bought her expensive gifts and frequently apologised when leaving her to return to the family home. At work, they were business-like and on-message; neither of them wanted to be outed as lovers: it would have created real problems in the office. She was sure no-one knew about their relationship. Jonathan's dalliances with interns were, of course, well-known around the building and several women confided in her that he was a rat to treat his wife so badly. Some also shared with her that they would like to be next on his list, maybe assuming that the message would get back to him via her. She was sure she would not have heard such comments if their own relationship was a matter of office gossip.

Her thoughts are interrupted by the arrival of room service and for a while she sits back enjoying her food and tea and letting her mind wander aimlessly. When she finishes her breakfast, she quickly showers and dresses. She has made something of a decision. She picks up Jonathan's private credit card from out of his briefcase where she knows he keeps it and sends him a text.

I will be out all day today with phone off. Back for GBN drinks. Lottie

Having sent this message, she switches off her phone and leaves the hotel, heading for the most expensive shops in the city. The least she can do, she thinks, is to behave like a mistress for once. Other, more important, decisions can wait.

Chapter 23

Jonathan picks up Lottie's text in the middle of his meeting with the dull German journalist and his photographer. He isn't sure what to make of it. It is probably a good thing that Lottie wants some time on her own but it was highly unusual for her to switch her phone off for anything and it is pretty obvious that she is doing so to avoid him calling her back. He also notes the formal signature of the message and the absence of the usual innocent xx. He is brought back to the present by another apologetic question from the patiently waiting German interviewer. He answers that and the remaining questions and smiles whilst the photographer takes photographs of him for their publication. When he is finally free from posing, he looks at his watch and sees he is already due for his panel session. He makes his excuses and hurries away. The panel session is every bit as dull and useless as he knew it would be and the audience hopeless in their questioning and grandstanding. This unfortunately sets the pattern for the day. He is much in demand following his successful speech the night before but is distracted and inconclusive in his meetings with fellow executives. He falls behind in his schedule and keeps most of his appointments waiting. He is late for lunch with a US executive and this poor start sets the tone for the formal and clipped nature of that meeting.

By four thirty, he is done with meeting people and, although he had scheduled himself to attend the late afternoon conference session, he returns back to the hotel suite, where, finding it empty as he had expected, he lies on the bed and quickly falls asleep.

Lottie returns to the suite at about five-thirty and finds Jonathan asleep on the bed. She sets down her many packages and takes herself off for a beauty session at the hotel spa. When

Jonathan wakes a little later, he is surprised to see a collection of expensive shopping bags on one of the sofas and in Lottie's continued absence takes himself off to shower and change for the GBN drinks party. The conference dinner is a black tie affair, so he changes into his dinner jacket and waits for Lottie to return. Time passes and Lottie does not re-appear. He needs to be at the drinks party on time to show support for Drew so, leaving her a note to say where he is, he exits the room and makes his way down to the event.

Although he is only ten minutes later than the advertised start time, the room is already quite full of newspaper executives when he arrives. Drew hurries over and asks if he has heard anything from Tom Schalke.

'I haven't spoken to him. I don't even know if he is in town.' says Jonathan truthfully.

'Well, come and meet some newspaper people. Everyone is keen to talk to you after last night's triumphant speech.'

He circulates in his well-practised fashion, never staying too long but never leaving his companions feeling short-changed by his departure. Working the room, he sees out of the corner of his eye an elegant woman stride into the room wearing a very low cut and figure-hugging long red velvet dress. She looks stunning and is drawing admiring glances from the mainly male audience in the room. He realises with a start that it is Lottie; he has never seen her dressed like this before for a work party. Normally, he would have expected to see her in a black dinner jacket and trousers, looking elegant and business-like, sexy in an understated way. There is nothing understated about her tonight. She turns to take a glass of Champagne from a passing waiter and he sees her dress is backless too. Her tanned back is certainly a different colour from how he remembered it from that morning. Even her short hair looks changed: to his untrained eye, it looks as if the extreme tips have been dyed silver. It's as if her hair has picked up a Budapest frost. Their eyes meet and she smiles broadly at him and walks directly across the room, her small hips swinging gently in the close-fitting red dress and high heels.

'Don't you look fabulous tonight,' he starts and leans in for a customary air kiss. But as they move close Lottie turns her face and kisses him full on the lips. Surprised by this, he is slow to withdraw and he is aware that a small number of fellow guests have witnessed their intimate contact.

'Darling, don't worry. This dress is just the first of many changes. You wait until you see what else you bought me today.' She gulps back some of her Champagne and holds her glass out to a waitress for a refill. Re-armed, she continues, 'Relax, I'm not here to show you up. Just don't want to be your dirty little secret anymore.' She turns as Drew walked by, 'Drew, is there anything I can do to help this evening?'

Drew looks approvingly at her. 'Charlotte, relax. You should just celebrate last night's success. Enjoy yourself and leave the work to others for once. You look wonderful, by the way.'

'Well, thank you. I don't usually get the night off at these events so tonight I aim to have some fun.'

Jonathan continues to network the invited group and Lottie is at his side for the whole evening. Whilst he introduces her to all as 'Charlotte Edwards, my Publicity Director', he is under no illusion that everyone sees a very different role for Lottie whilst she wears that dress and stands so closely beside him. Eventually, the drinks party comes to a close and the invited guests start to make their way through to the conference dinner. Lottie leans in to him and says. 'Do we really have to go to the dull conference dinner?'

'Well, I have to. I'm hosting one of the tables so it would look pretty strange if I wasn't there.'

'Can we make a swift exit and go on and party?'

'Of course. As soon as we can make our escape quietly we will. Have you found somewhere for us to go?'

'I was recommended somewhere very cool whilst I was shopping today. It sounds just the place. I want to put all of the stress of this week to one side and just have some fun whilst we are here.'

Jonathan smiles to himself. It was going to be OK with Lottie: she was making her peace with him. He was going to have to be more careful about bringing her on business trips if she wanted to flaunt her mistress status but probably tonight was a one-off, all about revenge for not telling her about the PM's offer. After the rest of the weekend together, it would all be fine again. He might even have enhanced his business status with such a pretty girl so evidently on his arm. He starts to engage in an introductory conversation with the dinner guests on either side of him and occasionally glances across the table at Lottie, who is deep in conversation with a bearded Scandinavian-looking guy, old enough to be her father.

The dinner passes off without event and the food and drink are unexpectedly good. The company around the table is adequate if unexciting, thinks Jonathan, and he is more than ready to leave when Lottie comes over and stands behind him.

'Can we sneak out now? I feel like that old guy next to me has spent the evening mentally undressing me.'

'I can see why, but tell him hands off. I'm planning on doing that later,' he says quietly to her. 'Yes, let's head off. If you go and get your coat from the room I will meet you in the lobby.'

'No. Let's leave together. I want to be seen on your arm and I don't have too many chances of that.'

Jonathan says his goodbyes to those around him and they walk towards the lobby together. Lottie puts her hand into his and they leave the room hand in hand.

'Thank you. Now, wait here whilst I get my coat. If I go out like this I will freeze to death.'

Jonathan waits for Lottie to return, occasionally nodding and greeting fellow conference delegates as they cross the lobby. Lottie eventually returns, dressed in an elegant long grey woollen coat. She twirls in front of him. 'Do you like?'

'I like it a lot. You look great.'

'Thank you. You had better prepare for your next Amex bill. I hit it pretty hard today.'

'No more than I deserve. Let's get a taxi. Where are we going?'

The club in Buda is every bit as smart and sophisticated as Lottie had suggested. It was obviously where rich and beautiful residents and tourists alike came to play. Everything is loud, glamorous and expensive. Lottie orders a bottle of Champagne and they drink half of it before venturing out onto the dance floor. They dance until Lottie declares her feet are falling off and, stopping only to drink the rest of their Champagne, they find themselves outside on a dark and bitter night without a taxi in sight.

'Let's walk down to the Danube. There are bound to be taxis on the riverfront,' says Jonathan, and so, arm in arm, they walk along to the river. They eventually find a cycle rickshaw willing to take them back to their hotel and they snuggle up together upon the small rear bench under a cover whilst their cyclist puffs away in front of them.

'Thank you for a brilliant evening, Jonathan,' says Lottie leaning into him. 'This is so romantic.'

Back in the hotel, they make their way back to their suite where they fall upon one another with a renewed passion that leaves them exhausted. They both sleep late in the morning and are only woken by Lottie's phone, with one of her journalist contacts trying to get a story from her. Lottie batts her questions away quickly and then climbs on top of her horizontal lover. 'Time for a quick one before breakfast?'

They spend the day as happy tourists in the city. Tom Schalke has cancelled their lunchtime meeting via text. He was caught up in some problem and wanted to be at the first meeting with the Hungarians so he had re-arranged it to London in a couple of weeks' time. That suits the two of them just fine and they trip from coffee house to art gallery to exclusive shop to museum through the day. Jonathan buys

Lottie some large silver jewelled earrings and she buys him an expensive new wallet that he supposes he will have to hide from Ellie until he comes up with a reason for ditching the one his wife had bought for him at Christmas. They walk arm in arm through the city streets and laugh and relax in each other's company.

Eventually, tired and cold, they return to the hotel where Jonathan lies on the bed and Lottie takes a bath. Tempted as he is to join her, he resists the urge and instead turns to his emails that he has ignored through the day. He is pleased to see there is nothing too serious and by the time he had finished dealing with the important ones, Lottie is out of the bath and wrapped up in the hotel dressing gown standing in front of him.

'Do you want to see what else I bought with your money yesterday?'

'You mean apart from the red dress, the new coat and the leather trousers you had on today?'

'Yes, there's more. Let me show you.' She pulls out some more very high heeled shoes, ivory satin lingerie and a short green dress that was obviously going to fit very snugly. 'This is for tonight. I think it's about time I started dressing up for you.'

Wondering, but not daring to ask, how much yesterday's spend had actually cost, he thought Budapest was shaping up to be one of his most expensive weekends away. It was a good thing the company was picking up the hotel and flight tab.

Lottie looks sensational in her new dress and shoes, and dinner is every bit as good as the reviews had suggested. Their talk together is light and amusing and full of the obvious affection they have for each other. They avoid any mention of work all evening. After a long day's sightseeing, they are much too tired for any late night dancing and return to their hotel for a nightcap and then to bed. He carefully takes off her expensive new dress and they make slow and passionate love.

They lie in each other's arms for a long while before Lottie stirs herself and walks naked over to the fridge. She comes back with two mini-bottles of Champagne and, wrestling the top of one, she hands it to Jonathan. Whilst sitting upright in bed and struggling with the top of the second bottle, she says, 'Jonathan. I've something serious to say. That might be the very last time we make love. I'm glad it was so lovely. If we are to continue I have some very serious proposals as to how everything will have to work from now on.' She pauses, looks hard at him and without waiting for a response continues, 'First of all, there are to be no others. If I am to be your mistress going forwards, then you have to stop bedding other women. That's non-negotiable and if I discover you have let me down I will walk. Second, you have to show me more respect, both in public and in private. I know what you and I have will always be a secret, that's understood, but when we are working together then it has to be a relationship of equals. If I am to run your political career then that's no more than I deserve. I want everyone to see and understand my role as an adviser. Only when we have time alone together does the other us come out to play. Finally, my third demand is that we have to look to make a positive change in the world. You have found yourself being promised a key role in shaping the future of our country. Let's not waste it with petty politics and point-scoring and willy-waving. Let's go balls-out for really doing something that improves people's lives and makes a difference and changes things. Let's not waste this opportunity. That's it, my three point manifesto. It's non-negotiable and I'm deadly serious.'

Jonathan takes a slug from his Champagne bottle and after a short pause replies, 'Lottie, of course I understand that things have to change and I'm honestly really happy to accept all three of your demands. They make a lot of sense to me and I really don't want to lose you, either professionally or personally. If we can't do something great together then there's really no point in doing it at all.'

'I know asking you to be faithful to me is ludicrous when you are being unfaithful to Ellie by sleeping with me but I can't take your casual infidelities any more...'

'Darling, don't say another word. Really, that is the easiest of the three promises to keep. I'm glad you want me that much.'

'I love you, Jonathan.'

'I know and you know that I love you too.' They hold each other tightly and Jonathan strokes her hair. 'Really, my darling, you are a fool to worry so much about things. I'm completely signed up to your manifesto so there's absolutely no problem. I believe we can do something really meaningful together.'

'Thank you.' She reaches up and kisses him hard. 'Don't worry about me. I will only demand one or two weekends a year like this where I can parade on your arm as your mistress and dress like one. No-one in the Tory party will ever know. The rest of the year I shall be back to black power suits and inscrutability. Only you will know about the passion and the lacy lingerie that lurks underneath.'

He smiles at the thought, caresses her small breasts and whispers, 'now what was that about the last time we make love...'

They stay in bed on Sunday morning and have late room service.

Chapter 24

'So, how was it?'

'Hi, darling. It was hard work, but as I told you on the phone, the speech went down well and I made some useful contacts.' He drops his bags and leans in to kiss her hello.

'And how was Budapest?'

'It looked lovely at night across the Danube but you know how it is, I hardly left the hotel for the duration. This morning it was very grey and trying to snow as I left for the airport. How are the boys?'

'They are good. They are watching cartoons together upstairs so perhaps leave them for another ten minutes or so and we can talk.'

'OK. I have presents for them, the pick of Budapest Airport. I bought you something too.' He digs in his briefcase and hands her a very small green box. 'Only the airport again I'm afraid but I hope you will like them.'

Ellie opens the box and finds a pair of silver earrings inside. They are small and delicate and very pretty.

'Jonathan, they are lovely. What a clever choice. You really didn't need to buy me anything.'

'Well, I have something to celebrate with you so I thought a present would be a good start.'

'Come on then, tell me, what's the celebration?'

'The PM has asked me to stand for Parliament.'

'What?' Ellie's face is frozen in fear.

'He called me and told me that he wants me to stand and be fast-tracked into the cabinet.'

'Is this to do with Mali and the arms deal?'

'No. He doesn't know I was working on that. I think I told you that I can't prove anything there anyway. No. He told me that I had researched well on some focus group thing and he wants new blood in the cabinet bringing in some new ideas to revive the Government. The channel has really projected my image in the party it seems and several others have put my name forwards. The clincher is that Sir John Cressley himself is about to announce he is quitting Parliament, dicky heart or something, and the PM is going to wangle me onto the shortlist. Safe Tory seat and all that. From there of course it's up to me but he has promised me a cabinet seat in double quick time.'

'Do you really want to do it?'

'Ellie, I've been thinking a lot in the last few weeks that I really want to do something to make a difference. I've been very lucky,' he waves his arm around, indicating their house, 'we've been very lucky. I know we have worked hard to achieve all of this. But I was looking for a chance to make something good happen and when I got the call I realised it was what I had been waiting for. I know Parliament is just a talking shop and backbench MPs don't have any power but if I get a cabinet post then I can do something to make this country a better place for everyone to live in. I know our politics are not the same but I know how much you share the commitment to make a difference. So, yes, surprisingly, I do want to do it.'

'And how about GBN? You've only just been promoted to the Board.'

'I know. I need to talk to Drew tomorrow. If I don't get selected then there's nothing to worry about. If I do and win the seat then I can carry on as a PLC board member for a while and help Angie take over running the channel. I can probably become a non-executive if they need me to. Once a cabinet post comes along I don't think I will be able to stay on board but I can pick up some other non-executive directorships along the way to keep the family finances steady. Adam Robinson will only be too happy to help, I've turned down a couple already.'

'So the ski chalet is off?'

'No. Let's do it. We might have to let the cottage go though. If I get selected we will have to buy somewhere in Northamptonshire to keep the constituents happy.'

'I don't get this, Jonathan. It seems only yesterday that you were telling me that MPs had had their day and social media and television were the new way to change society and make things happen. And now here you are joining the old guard as if we were living in 1997.'

'And if it weren't for the promise of the cabinet job then I would agree with you. I don't think I can do a lot more in TV. I've never been corporate enough for the US networks, as you know, and I was never on the inside with the Murdoch family so that route isn't open to me either. Catalyst has been great fun and I'm proud of it but it can't grow in the UK and GBN themselves are under the cosh from declining ad revenues and the sharks who run the hedge funds, so God knows if they will stay the course anyway.'

'And do you think you can trust the PM? You never had much time for him when you were advising him.'

'Yes. I think I can. He is a man of his word. We don't have to be friends but I recognise his strengths and I guess he must value mine. I suppose if we fall out irrevocably down the track all bets might be off but hopefully by then I will have built a power base of my own. As you can see, I'm really excited about this now that I've got my head around it.'

'I can see that. I'm a couple of days behind you. Have you talked to anyone else?'

'No. I wanted to talk to you first. I will talk to Adam and get his blessing – even though I suspect he may have had something to do with the offer beforehand: he and the PM are very close. I will also talk to Lottie. It's a slam dunk that she should join me and keep pushing my image and profile. It will be needed now more than ever.'

'Yes. I guess it will. Will you be able to afford that?'

'I will make sure I can. Don't worry about the money.'

'Of course, I could always come and run your private office. It's quite common in Parliament...'

'But you have the boys to look after - and your charitable work here. That will be a big positive for me, I can assure you. Also, if I'm honest, I don't know how successful it would be if you were to work for me. You know some of my people think I'm a real bastard.'

'I suppose you are right. But I will get to see even less of you if you are at the House and then shooting up to Northamptonshire at the weekends, and you know how busy the boys are becoming now they are growing up. I refuse to relocate them up there. They are both doing really well at day school and then there's my work...'

'Don't worry, the last thing I want to do is live in the middle of the bloody countryside and commute to London most days. We will manage. It won't be every weekend, I promise. And we can afford to buy somewhere nice up there that the boys would probably enjoy in the holidays.'

'If you really want to do it then of course I will support you. It seems a strange choice to me but I think I can understand why you want to try something new. You must promise me though that you won't become a career Tory minister living only for the machinations of power. If you become that person then I don't think I would want to be your wife...'

'Darling, I'm doing this because I think I can make a difference to people's lives. The prospect of socialising with Tory High Command fills me with dread. I'm going into this to achieve something good – if I didn't think I could then I wouldn't be doing this – staying in TV would be much the safer choice.'

'I'm only saying what I fear, darling. I know the lure of power has always fascinated you and I don't want to see you corrupted by it.'

'Let's talk more over supper. Is there anything to eat? I had brunch today but missed lunch. Shall I open a bottle of

Champagne? Let me go and say hello to the boys. I will be straight back.'

Ellie is left alone in the hall wondering just how things had come to this surprising turn. She thought how little she really knew Jonathan when he could amaze her with such a plan. He would be a terrible constituency MP, she thought, it's a good job he's fighting for a safe seat. The only way he will impress his constituents is by successfully climbing the greasy pole to power and glory; he will never be the guy to sort out their social security or local school issues or whatever. At the same time, she knew he would succeed; he was the sort of man who could make things happen when he put his mind to it and his determination was one of the things that had first attracted her to him when they met. She moves through to the kitchen and starts pulling out the tapas she had previously prepared so they could enjoy a stress-free family supper with the children. Jonathan comes downstairs with two noisy and excited boys and gives them their airport gift shop presents before bringing them through to the kitchen. She stands back and watches them play together and thinks how lucky she is to have such a warm-hearted and happy family and she must always remember that.

Later that night, when she is lying in his arms, she murmurs, 'Jonathan Lomax MP. You know, it has quite ring to it.'

'Don't count your chickens, my love. There's no way this is a done deal yet.'

***

'I just don't believe you.' Drew is visibly angry behind his desk when Jonathan breaks his news to him first thing on Monday morning. 'I've only just promoted you to the PLC board and you're now saying you want to become a bloody MP. What the hell is going on?'

'Drew, I know the timing is terrible and that's not of my choosing. It was the PM himself who asked me to do this and it's always been something I wanted to do if the right opportunity came along. I may not even get the nomination from the local Tories, in which case it will be just a few days wasted traipsing up to Northamptonshire, and even if I do win then I can carry on here for at least a year until a cabinet position becomes available. It really won't make a huge difference and I can carry on training Angie and Ben to run the show and make some more room for them so they don't get poached. I thought I could become – let's say, executive chairman of Catalyst for the interim period – and if I ever make a cabinet job then we can make other arrangements.'

'Other arrangements? You can't seriously expect to carry on as a board director of a media company if you are in the cabinet.'

'No, I don't mean that, clearly that would be impossible. What I meant was that I could become a non-exec director and continue to provide support to you and the TV team...'

'If you do make the cabinet, your position here would have to be over. You must see that. Leave me to think this through. We will talk again in a few days.'

Jonathan leaves Drew's office and quickly walks out of the glass and steel building. It hadn't gone as badly as he feared: Drew is pissed off with him but he would see that Jonathan's solution was the only one in town and he didn't have any other choices. As he walks towards his car, his phone rings.

'Jonathan. It's Adam. This is a bloody turn-up for the books.'

'I thought you were probably behind it all.'

'No. It never crossed my mind that you might hanker after a career in politics. The PM only told me the news yesterday evening. Sir John will be gone tonight. The PM has asked me to shepherd you through the selection process. He thought you might prefer to have someone by your side whom you know and trust. What do you think? Can we put the Paul episode behind us?'

'Adam, I would be delighted. Paul is forgotten already. Can we meet this morning to talk it through?'

'Not today, I'm afraid, but I could do tomorrow afternoon. Why don't we meet at lunchtime and take a drive up there so you can get a better sense of the place? Have you told Drew yet?'

'I've just been with him. The news went down pretty badly but he will get his head around it and see the route I've offered is the only way forward for him.'

'You are sounding like a bloody cabinet minister already. I think you will be great by the way – it's just what the Party needs.'

'Thanks, I really appreciate your support. It all seems quite scary suddenly.'

'Don't worry, just keep your head down until we meet tomorrow and then we can work things out.'

Well there's my minder sorted out, thinks Jonathan. The PM obviously wants to continue to keep a close eye on me and make sure I don't go off-piste anytime soon.

***

Jonathan is deep into a busy Monday afternoon when Lottie comes into his office and closes the door behind her.

'Hello, you, how are you today?'

'I'm really good, thanks. I so enjoyed our time together in Budapest. I have lots to do today but I wondered if you might be able to come round to my place for an hour or two after work tonight. I could get some sushi in.'

'Lottie, I'm sorry, I can't. I've promised Ellie I will go to school for George's parents' night so I've got to get through this and leave early. I'm sorry. I would have really liked to. Perhaps we could do breakfast tomorrow instead? If I miss my swimming I could be with you really early and then we could have some time together?'

'That would be great. I will make sure I have something in to eat.' She smiles broadly and continues, 'There's still no update on Joe. I've chased the lawyers again but nothing seems to move quickly in Mali.'

'Let's not worry until we have to. Just keep pushing them along.'

'Will do. What's the latest on your political ambitions?'

'Adam called me this morning and told me that Sir John will announce he's stepping down with immediate effect this evening so we will be in the starting blocks very soon. I'm going up there with Adam tomorrow afternoon for a look around and to get his spin on things. I will feed everything back to you, of course – in fact, why don't you come with us? We will be staying overnight.'

'I'd love to, and even creepy Adam couldn't keep me from tiptoeing into your bedroom, but we've got the Press awards dinner tomorrow night and we are up for two awards. I can't leave Amber and the others to manage without me.'

'Of course, I'd completely forgotten. No, you must be there. It's really your award after all and great for the channel too.'

'When will you announce your candidacy?'

'Let me find out from Adam tomorrow. I don't suppose much will happen in the next few days.'

'How did Drew take the news this morning?'

'It went OK. Not great, but he didn't throw me out.'

'When will we tell the staff?'

'Let me get through tomorrow and then we can draw up a plan together on Wednesday. How's that?'

'Fine. I'd better let you get on. I will be waiting for you in the morning. Come as early as you can.'

***

Jonathan's new driver drops him at Lottie's house just after 6.15 on Tuesday morning and, as she had said, she was ready and waiting for him. Later, when they are lying in bed, drinking tea and listening to the Today programme, the news about Sir John has a surprising twist.

'Last night, Sir John Cressley announced he was stepping down from Parliament with immediate effect due to poor health. Sir John is one of the most influential MPs you've probably never heard of. He's been a major influence in the Tory party for over twenty years and combines running a successful property and energy company with his political duties. He's seen as a fixer with a strong contact book. His seat, Northamptonshire South, is a Tory stronghold and the Government will probably want a snap by-election before opposition parties get their act together. Rumoured candidates include Sir John's son-in-law, John Andrews, and the head of the right wing TV news channel, Jonathan Lomax. There will be lots of potential candidates for the local party to choose from as this is one of the safest Tory seats in the country. Sir John had a majority of almost eleven thousand at the last election and although no Government wants a by-election when they have such a slim majority, this one looks pretty straight-forward for them...'

'How the hell did that happen?'

'That's the Tory party machine in overdrive. They've planted that story to put others off. Two external candidates, no need for further applications. I had better get up and on to this. Your Twitter feed will go mental. I'm guessing no confirmation, no comment, no denial?' He nods. 'In that case, darling, leave it all to me. You know this is what I do really well. Help yourself to the shower.'

She hurriedly pulls on a bathrobe and trainers and heads downstairs to her laptop. He watches her go downstairs and thinks how much he loves her snap transformation from lover to powerful executive. His phone buzzes and he looks at the caller ID. Best to ignore them all, he thinks; let it all begin and let's control as much as we can. He wanders naked into Lottie's shower and enjoys the escape provided by its powerful stream of hot water. He finds the spare towels and when he makes his way downstairs he sees Lottie typing away furiously, oblivious to his presence.

'How is it?'

'OK so far. This story can only grow though. I've had three requests for interviews from national newspapers already. Look, we need to be careful. I will pull on some clothes and check the street before you leave. The last thing we need is some picture of you leaving my house at this time in the morning. We can explain stuff later but I want to be in control, not reacting to others.'

She hurries upstairs, and whilst she is dressing, Jonathan helps himself to a bowl of muesli. Lottie returns dressed for her normal morning run.

'I will go outside as if for my run and then realise I don't have my phone and come back in. I can look both ways down the street and see if all is clear.'

'I think you are over-reacting, but you are the boss. Come here first.' He pulls her to him and they kiss long and passionately. She eventually pulls back. 'I will see you in the office in an hour or so. We need to break the news to the team as well. They will have heard the story so let's not deny anything. Wait here.' She steps outside and closes the front door behind her. In a few moments, she returns. 'It's OK. Go now before it changes. There may be someone outside your house, so you should warn Ellie. Luckily, there's lots of other news today so we are probably safe.' She pulls his head to hers and they kiss again. 'Now, get out of here before I drag you back into my bed. Remember, no comment.'

He walks to the office, calling Ellie on the way. She too had heard the Today story but had not heard from any journalists. She tells him her friend Howie had called and asked if the story was true.

'What did you tell him?'

'I told him the truth. I'm not going to lie to my friends. I said you had been approached and you were considering it.'

'That's OK, but please, don't say more than that to anyone.'

'Don't worry, having a Tory MP for a husband is not good for my image either you know.'

'Please, Ellie, it's not funny.'

'Who is laughing? Where are you?'

'I'm just walking into the office. I needed some fresh air to think before I get into work and the world goes mad. I will call you later when I know more.'

Even though it was still early, the early starters in the office are clearly gossiping as Jonathan arrives and greets them. No one asks him any questions. Lottie had drafted a release and it is waiting for him when he sits down at his computer.

Catalyst Press Release

Jonathan Lomax, Managing Director of the new television channel Catalyst, confirms that he has been approached about putting his name forward to become the Conservative candidate for the Parliamentary seat of Northamptonshire South. This seat has become vacant as the incumbent, Sir James Cressley, has announced that he is stepping down with immediate effect.

Lomax says, 'I have made no decisions about letting my name go forward at this point. I am flattered to have been approached and will give the idea serious consideration. I will not be making any further comments at this stage.'

Lottie's covering note explained that her release was the closest she could get to killing the story without killing the story. She had already released it to staff and media outlets alike and hoped he is happy with that.

Calls to his phone are now coming in thick and fast, and he checks the caller ID on every one but allows them all to go through to voicemail. The first call he actually takes is from Adam.

'Adam, how the bloody hell did this happen?'

'Calm down, Jonathan. It's come from Central Office. They want to head off the usual carpetbaggers and give you a clear run. You had better get used to them doing things without telling anyone first, it's very much their modus operandi. It was a shock for me too but now it's out we can use it to our advantage. It has set down a marker and your name is now squarely in the frame.'

'Shall we still go up there today?'

'Yes. Now the cat is out of the bag there's no point in pretending. It doesn't matter if we go today or next week. I will come and pick you up at three as arranged. I've booked the only good hotel up there and organised to meet Sir John's agent for dinner. Nothing promised to him but good to have a man who knows where the local bodies are buried and who is who on the local committee. I want to get first shot at him.'

'OK. As long as you are sure we are not adding more fuel to this story. See you at three.'

Amongst the long list of incoming calls displayed on his phone he sees one from John Andrews and one from Tom Schalke. He puts his phone down and asks Carol to call the entire management team into his office in ten minutes. He then calls Tom. This was not going to be good.

'Tom, hi, sorry to have missed your call it's been crazy this morning...'

'Jonathan, what the fuck is going on?'

'You mean with the Today story?'

'Of course I mean the fucking Today story. How could you do this to me?'

'Tom, it's not aimed at you.'

'I had you lined up as Drew's successor and now you've blown it.'

'Tom, you know I have no interest in newspapers. Slowing down their rate of decline and cutting costs is not a job for me. I wouldn't be any good at it. I've spoken with Drew and we've worked out a plan so everything is taken care of. I haven't even got the nomination yet, never mind the seat.'

'I've no doubt your path has been smoothed for you. Let's not pretend otherwise. Your old pal the PM has obviously put you up for this.'

'I think he wants new blood in the Government.'

'Well, he's made an enemy out of me. Didn't even ask. What's more he owes me. Fucking cheek. It was him who persuaded me of the merits of your channel idea in the first place. As for you, you're off my Christmas card list too. It's hard enough running a business like mine without these sorts of distractions. The Hungarians are over on Friday, I want you to clear the afternoon for us. I want this first deal to happen quickly and then rapid rollout across Europe. If we can get four up and running by the end of this year we will float the business.'

'Is Drew onside with this?'

'I couldn't care less. He probably won't be in charge by then anyway.'

On this final news, Tom hangs up without bothering to say goodbye.

Adam's car picks up Jonathan at the appointed time and they then collect Adam himself on the way north. Adam has a whole sheaf of documents from Conservative Central Office detailing the constituency: social make-up, educational standards, age-profile, voting history, referendum voter breakdown, immigrant breakdown, local voter issues, major employers, education and health facilities. All shown by time and with future trends extrapolated.

'How the hell do we work out what's important in this great pile of stuff?'

'We don't. You just digest and learn all of this. The local party activists tell you what's important to the core Tory voters and the voters on the street tell you what's important to them. If you listen to Central Office you will never win. Listen to the local people and stand up for them. From my reading, the closure of the local minor injuries hospital is the main issue on the streets; there's real anger that everyone will have to go into Northampton even for day surgery. The hospital there is only average and typically the local hospital is rated as outstanding; it's those bean counters at the Department of Health who want to close it because it doesn't meet their efficiency standards. It's the only red flag I can see in this seat. We need to think carefully about how you handle this one.'

'Do you have an answer?'

'Not yet. We need to side with the people but can't piss off the Government. Let's leave it to one side for the moment. Declining public transport will be the second issue here as it's a rural constituency. That's even harder to deal with. Anyway, here's the other dossier.'

This second sheaf of paperwork contained a critical analysis on the other parties' local organisation, potential candidates and local strengths and weaknesses.

'This one will be updated weekly as the campaign moves forward. You can see the local UKIP leader is a prize nutter even by their standards and the local Labour party is a shambles so they could put anyone up for this. They don't see it as a winnable seat so they'll probably put up some twenty-something special adviser who they would like to get some experience in the firing line. The Greens don't have any local organisation so they are a sideshow. The Lib Dems don't seem to amount to much but they are always the ones to watch in a by-election so it looks like a fight against the libs and the kippers. Couldn't have planned it better if I had tried.'

'How about the local agent?'

'We are meeting him tonight. He doesn't want to be seen in public with us as yet so we are meeting him in my hotel room at seven. That gives us plenty of time to have a drive around and for you to get the feel of the place and then we can have some dinner afterwards. Nowhere too expensive, mind you: you need to be seen to be a man of the people now. The last thing you want to be seen as is a London swank. London is bad enough: do you remember the story about Peter Mandelson mistaking mushy peas for guacamole when he visited a Hartlepool fish and chip shop? He never lived it down.'

'I get the picture.'

'When the PM got wind of your idea for the TV channel from me and then asked me to help drive it through, he thought you were the ideal man to help bring about change in the Party. We both thought that your role would be outside the machine but now you are about to join the evil empire that is the Tory Party, remember that hypocrisy is your closest friend; even if you don't fit the bill as a man of the people you have to play the part as if it means something – at least when it suits you. That's mostly at election time in a place like this.'

The constituency is a patchwork of villages, market towns and rich farmland and they drive around trying to get a better sense of the geography. They walk along the local high streets and evaluate the shops and the passers-by. By six pm, they have had enough and check into their hotel. It is a fine old Georgian building that had recently been made over into a plush boutique hotel and restaurant. It shouts its 'weekend in the country' credentials a bit too loudly but is comfortable and discreet.

At seven o'clock, they wait in Adam's room for their visitor. He is a few minutes late. Bruce introduces himself and accepts the proffered scotch. His body language as he sits down is somewhat restrained and unfriendly. He is a small slight man around sixty years old, Jonathan thinks. His greying hair is cut very short but a natty goatee beard indicates a more flamboyant personality than first appearances suggest. A ladies' man, thinks Jonathan.

'So, Jonathan, you are the man Central Office wants us to pick?'

'Well, Bruce, I don't know that. We are all just exploring things at the moment...'

'Let's not beat around the bush. You wouldn't be here if you weren't gagging for it. I just need to decide if you have what it takes and if I can work with you.'

'I know from the notes I've seen that you have been a great agent for Sir John.'

'The old bugger just used me as his man on the ground so he didn't have to pay much attention to the place. I'll bet it doesn't say that in your notes. Bruce, do this, Bruce, do that. When he was up here he was far more interested in his bloody arboretum than any of the real issues on the streets. I used to do most of his surgeries. Good riddance, I say.'

'Have you thought of standing yourself?'

'It's not what I want or who I am.'

'Then tell me what you do want in a local MP and we can see if I fit your bill.'

'Well, the first thing I would want from someone like you, who is not going to spend a lot of time up here, is respect for what I do and what I achieve.'

'Understood.'

'I want honesty and transparency.'

'Accepted.'

'And I want to be recompensed fairly for the work I do up here.'

'I will make sure Jonathan understands how that works so you have no worries on that score,' interjects Adam. 'We will look after you.'

'Good. Well, Jonathan, it hasn't been hard to find out about you from our friend Mister Google but tell me the truth: why do you want to be the MP here? And don't give me any of that guff about giving something back to society etcetera, etcetera.'

'The honest answer to the question is that the Government has promised me a cabinet post. They want new blood to help run things and I want that too. I have no interest in being the local MP here – sitting on the back benches playing politics and attending fetes up here at the weekend.'

'Good. I like honesty. That's important to me. You must, of course, never repeat what you've just said to a living soul. If you had told me anything different I would have finished my scotch and left for good. That's the first point – honesty and transparency. But only to me, remember, and especially not to anyone else locally. We've got a battle on our hands to win over the local party: they won't take it well having a candidate imposed on them by London. Loyalty to the Conservative Party can only go so far up here. We will have at least one local rival. Megan Smith is well regarded locally and has made the 'save the local hospital' campaign her own. She's the woman to beat. John Andrews will have a go trying to run on the family ticket but you will knock the socks off him, I suspect. There may be another local candidate, Brian Appleton. He's a dark horse, fiercely independent and something of an outsider here, despite having lived locally all of his life. We need to watch him.'

'How big an issue is dissatisfaction with the Conservatives?'

'One step at a time, Jonathan. Once we've got the nomination we will worry about the other parties. The local Tory party here is a typical shire party: hard on immigration, hard on scroungers, soft on the elderly, pro-NHS, big on defence. Stick to those and we will win and then see off all-comers later on down the track without changing our stance at all.'

'What are the biggest mistakes I can avoid?'

'You are London elite. That's a problem but there's no sense in trying to hide it. You are smart, successful and ambitious. That's fine. Just don't be smug or patronising. The older women in the party will try to mother you but the old blokes will reject you. Accept the former and work on the latter. Pub time will be important. Just, for God's sake, don't come out with any nonsense about always having supported the local football team or any of that sort of shit. If you don't know about a local issue say you don't know and ask the public to brief you there and then. The people here may be provincial but they are far from stupid. Our pitch is simple - you are the best candidate for the job and we will teach you about the local issues and what you need to fight for.'

'What do we do about the hospital closure plan?'

'Don't worry. I have some ideas for that problem. It's important not to get fixated by anything at this early stage.'

'Bruce. Do we have you on board? We want you, but can you work with us?' asked Adam.

'Yes. I think we can win. So I'm in.'

'Come and join us for dinner downstairs then and we can carry on getting to know each other better.'

'We'll be going public as soon as we sit down and eat together.'

'We are fine with that if you are.'

'Let me just call my partner and say I won't be home for dinner.'

They wait whilst Bruce calls home. 'Andrew, I'm sorry I won't be home for dinner after all. I'm going to eat with Jonathan Lomax. Yes, it all went well. I won't be late. Love you, bye.'

Just goes to show, thought Jonathan, you should never judge a book by its cover. Dinner is a lighter affair as they talk in a public arena about families, the locality, sport and national politics. Bruce displays a liking for the expensive claret Adam chooses and they insist he leaves his car at the hotel and they call for a taxi to take him home.

'What do you think?' asks Adam as they return to their table to finish off the second bottle of wine. They are the only people left in the restaurant. It is 10.15.

'I think he's ideal. He knows the ropes and he tells it the way it is. I like him.'

'Good. Just remember never cross him. Good agents are worth their weight in gold and if you lose them on the journey they can make your life impossible. Now, let me sort out the bill. No, don't fight it. The PM told me to tell you that this one is on him. Quite when and how I get the money back from him is a different issue.' He smiles and waves a credit card at the patiently idling waiter.

Chapter 25

Whilst Jonathan and Adam are enjoying the company of Bruce, Lottie is at the Annual Media Publicity Awards at the Grosvenor House Hotel. She hates awards ceremonies but as the channel is up for two awards it is important to be there tonight. She has changed into her familiar black tuxedo and hosts the Catalyst table. She is joined by Angie, who always enjoys a good party, Ben, Amber, and a handful of guests the advertising sales director has brought along and clearly needs to impress. She finds herself sandwiched between two dull advertising bosses who are obviously on a mission to drink themselves into a stupor. She wouldn't have minded that so much if they had been more amusing company.

She looks around the table and notices that both Amber and Angie are also going for alcohol overdose. Angie would be fine but she would have to watch out for Amber. If they ended up making a trip to the stage to collect awards later that night she had better do all of the talking. She makes yet another conversational gambit to the idiot on her right and again it falls upon stony ground. How did these guys manage to tie their own shoelaces in the morning? She gives up and sits back to enjoy the start of the spectacle of award giving. No industry slapped itself on the back quite as passionately as the PR business and no other industry had a higher opinion of its own importance in the world. Many of these people actually thought they were doing something important. She watches as the usual suspects are nominated, winners announced and short emotional speeches made. It was a job application market and Lottie was smart enough to realise it was nothing more.

When the award for best media start-up is announced a hush of excitement descends upon their table. Their nomination is announced and when the winners' envelope is opened it is no great surprise to her that they are the winners. Accepting the congratulations of those around them, Lottie and Amber make their way to the stage together.

'Let me do the talking,' says Lottie as she helps Amber, in her long strapless dress and high heels, ascend the steps to the stage.

'Thanks. My mind is a complete blank,' replies her colleague, hitching up her dress when it threatens to slip down as she approaches the stage.

They accept the award from the host and Lottie steps forward to the microphone.

'Thank you all for this wonderful award. It's been a huge challenge launching an entirely different sort of television channel and really the PR has been the easy bit. Our real thanks have to go to everyone who has worked so hard to make it an editorial success. The whole team has lived for the last few months on adrenalin and excitement with a little bit of fear thrown in too. We have become a closely knit family and whilst I know that can sound clichéd, in our case it's true. This is the first award we have won since our launch and it really is for everyone who works at Catalyst. Thank you. It means a lot to us.'

They leave the stage to the usual muted applause and when they arrive back at their table she sees the two guests have bought large quantities of Champagne to celebrate. Even missing out on the second award they are nominated for doesn't slow them down and Lottie can see that Amber and Angie are beginning to look more than a little glazed. She also suspects that Amber is becoming less able to fend off the obviously unwanted attentions of one of their guests. As the evening begins to draw to a close, she scoops up the drunken Amber and tells the group that she will see her safely home. Once they had found a taxi on the street, she sits back with the award in her hand and relaxes. Amber doesn't look too great and Lottie texts Jonathan to tell him of their success. He texts back his congratulations. The noise of his reply seems to awaken Amber.

'Who was that?'

'Jonathan saying well done to us both.'

'I wish he was here now.'

'Yes, it's a great shame he couldn't make it. It would have been good to celebrate our first award.'

'I really, really wanted him to be here,' slurs the drunken Amber, 'I've really missed him.'

'What do you mean, Amber?'

'Lottie, you don't understand. I know it's wrong but I can't help it. I know he's married and I shouldn't but I can't resist him.'

Lottie can hardly believe what she is hearing. 'Do you mean you and Jonathan are screwing?'

'It started two weeks ago and I tried not to; I know how bad his reputation is but I couldn't stop myself and since then all I've thought about is him. He's come by my place a couple of times but it's difficult for him to find an excuse to get away from home. I'm mad about him. I'm so miserable. Oh, Lottie, do you hate me?' Amber starts to quietly cry, her shoulders heaving as she tries to suppress the tears.

'Of course not, Amber, don't be silly. I understand.' She holds Amber to her and the rest of the taxi ride passes in silence between them with Amber's head resting against her shoulder. When they arrive at Amber's flat, she asks the driver to wait whilst she sees the drunken Amber safely through her own front door. Once she is back in the taxi and on her way home she starts to compose her thoughts. How could he do this to her? She had told him no chasing any of my team and here he is screwing her deputy. How could she cope with this, especially after their weekend away together? For a while in Budapest she had really thought he loved her and now this. With the courage of too many glasses of champagne inside her, she decides she will confront him tomorrow and resolve things one way or another. She hates the fact that she ends up crying herself to sleep that night – still able to smell him on her sheets.

***

Jonathan is not back in the office until mid-morning on Tuesday and as soon as he returns he asks for Lottie and Amber to come to his office so he can personally congratulate them on last night's triumph. As soon as he sees Lottie's face he guesses what must have happened. Amber is hungover but happy and basks in his attention; Lottie just looks surly. When he has finished congratulating them he asks Lottie to remain as he has some social media stuff to talk about with her. As soon as the door is safely shut behind Amber, Lottie launches into him, her voice low but her anger only too obvious.

'How could you do this to me, you bastard? I told you, don't mess with my staff but no, you can't resist a pert redhead, can you? One eager smile and you are in there trying to score. I just can't believe that you would do this to me. Did the weekend mean nothing to you?'

'Lottie, I am so sorry. It is history. Honestly, it was just late one night in the office when you were off at some meeting somewhere. I knew I shouldn't but she came on to me and you know how hopeless I am in those circumstances. I'm not making excuses, it's all my fault. But it was only the once and, just as I promised you, you are the only one for me now.'

'She told me last night that you've been round to her flat.'

'I have. Late at night on two occasions. But only because she called me and sounded desperate both times. I really thought she might harm herself or do something really stupid. I promise you nothing happened on either of those visits, it was just a one-off office bunk up that seems to have got out of control. I don't want to hurt her, or you. I'm really sorry, honestly I am.'

'How are you going to resolve it with her?'

'I don't know. What do you think I should do?'

'Woah. Don't involve me for a start. But before the end of the day you need to have told her that she means nothing to you and it's all over. Don't leave her with one shred of doubt in her mind. Can you do that?'

'Yes. I will do it right now. Lottie, tell me you forgive me. I can't bear it if this comes between us.'

There is silence for a long twenty seconds before Lottie replies. 'You know I forgive you. I don't want to but I couldn't bear it if I couldn't have you.' She turns on her heel and marches out of his office.

Jonathan sits back in his chair and wonders how he got himself into this mess. He needs Lottie by his side if he is to make this new chapter of his life work and he really has to make sure she is onside. Why was he such a fool when it came to chasing women? It wasn't even for the sex: Lottie was as inventive as any man could wish for and Ellie was a wonderful wife. It was just a part of him that, try as hard as he might, he found it impossible to control.

Lottie hadn't been his first infidelity. In fact, it had started long before her. His first one night stand was at yet another conference where he was speaking – Lisbon, just before George was born. He had met up with an old girlfriend called Alicia who was at the conference as a media correspondent for a national newspaper and whilst sitting next to him at the conference dinner she reminded him of the great sex they had had a few years before. The promise of a night of rough sex with a little coke thrown in was enough to stir him into action and a second bottle of wine sealed the deal. They screwed for most of the night, and when he flew back the next afternoon, Jonathan spent the flight rationalising his disloyalty. Sure, he felt bad and part of him wished he hadn't done it but Ellie was heavily pregnant and sex was firmly off her agenda. It was just sex. He knew that lots of men were unfaithful to their wives in the latter stages of pregnancy and thought, I will just put this away as something I wish I hadn't done and move on. Ellie need never know and no-one need get hurt. When Alicia called a couple of days later looking for a re-match, he politely declined and suggested an expensive lunch together instead. It was always smart to stay on the right side of the press.

His second conquest followed shortly afterwards and was much easier. A provocatively attractive young intern whom he fucked across his desk late at night in the office. She knew he was married and she had no illusions about the future, he reasoned. It was meant to be just a one off and although they repeated the encounter a couple of times in the following weeks, they both knew it was no more than office sex and meant nothing. In fact, he realised then that he had re-discovered the thrill of the chase. The intern was the first in a long line of conquests. He knew he was attractive to women and had never held back from flirting with them to win his arguments and charm them to accept defeat in negotiations. Now, he began to use his charms and the privileges that came with power to lead some of them into bed. The more he succeeded, the more fascinated by the chase he became. He would normally have his eye upon at least one woman in the office and often he would carefully engineer opportunities just to see if he could still work his magic. The tougher the challenge, the more he liked it. He loved the single-minded purpose of it all and how thrilling he found it to win when a woman gave in to his charms and allowed him to take her to bed. Easy victories were also enjoyable but it was the seduction process that really appealed. It was like a drug to him and he always responded to any opportunity. It was not unusual for him to be turned down, but he usually left having at least charmed and flattered his target along with the guilty secret of a shared intimacy. It was not unusual for women who had rejected his sexual advances to become long-term friends. It was even more common for former lovers to remain close and Jonathan was careful to let them all down gently – just as he had done before he was married.

It was his temporary posting to New York that really gave him the freedom and the opportunity to play the field. A central Manhattan apartment, a generous expense account and an English accent, were used to seduce a continuous stream of younger women and alleviate the boring day job at Fox. When he came back to England, he continued in the same vein, always careful to move on and not get too emotionally involved.

When he first bedded Lottie, he had thought nothing very much about it, but as time went on and the experiment was repeated frequently, he realised that he had found someone very special to him and although he had tried to wriggle clear of her on several occasions, she accepted his straying and always took him back. She indulged his fantasies and even suggested several of her own. She was also indispensable to his business success and the holder of most of his secrets. This combination was deadly and although he never used the word 'mistress' to describe her, there was no doubt that she enjoyed that enhanced status in his mind. He began to confide in her and think of her in a very different light to his other women. Jonathan had always controlled his extra-marital relationships carefully and had never doubted his ability to do so. He didn't think of this as predatory behaviour: he never hid the fact he was married with children and consequently any woman who took him on had to play by his rules. He never let these women get too close and only Lottie had crossed the line to become essential to him. It was always Jonathan who ended his numerous little affairs and he knew he enjoyed being in charge. Only one woman had turned the tables on him so far.

He had met Julia at a Richmond Christmas party. She was recently divorced but had all of the glamour of the rich and beautiful. Julia had been abandoned by her banker husband for a newer, younger and shinier model and left with a very generous divorce settlement and two young children whilst he decamped to New York with his new lover. Julia was quite envied by all of her girlfriends for her independence – from men, from money worries – but all found her difficult to get close to. At the Christmas party, Julia pulled Jonathan to one side and asked him if he wanted some extra-marital sex – no strings, no emotions, just good old-fashioned fucking every once in a while. He found the offer irresistible and began a curious occasional relationship with her. They would meet up every few weeks, usually as Jonathan was on his way home from work, for athletic and sweaty sex for half an hour somewhere in Julia's house. He would then shower and leave. There were no side issues for Julia: once they were done, she very obviously wanted him gone until the next time. Consequently, this affair lasted for several months, much longer than his usual diversions.

The straightforward nature of their relationship was shattered one day when Julia announced, just after a particularly energetic session, that she was pregnant and they had just enjoyed sex together for the last time. Jonathan was appalled. He instantly knew he had been used and Julia's smile as she told him said it all; another child with a suitable donor had been her goal all along and Jonathan had been her victim. She told him she did not want anything from him. She didn't need emotional or financial support for the baby and she would tell everyone, including the child, that she had become pregnant via a sperm donor – which in a way she had.

Julia was good to her word. Her friends marvelled at her composure and independence – even Ellie told Jonathan how impressed she was by her distant friend's determination to do without anyone else in her life. Julia's baby daughter was christened Agatha and once the neighbourhood mothers had stopped cooing over the baby, a live-in nanny had been hired and a loft nursery added to the already impressive house, life returned to normal. Julia never contacted Jonathan about the baby and behaved distantly on the rare social occasions where they ran into each other. He began to consign the whole experience to history and even began to doubt the whole thing – had it really ever happened and was the child even his?

Eighteen months or so after the birth of the baby, Julia and her newly enlarged family moved to Notting Hill and he never heard from her again. He had to admire her style in getting exactly what she wanted.

Before the problems with Amber, only one woman had over-reacted to being let down and he had genuinely feared that she would spill the beans to Ellie. A former employee, she turned from a gentle and loving woman into a vengeful and bitter person and he had done his best to keep her sweet whilst working his contact book as hard as he could to find her a significant promotion somewhere else, anywhere else. Somewhere else ended up as a highly paid job in Dubai and he heard from other contacts that she was now thriving there and happy in a new relationship. After that episode, he had sworn never again, but before long he had picked up with a former lover and then yet another new intern caught his eye.

He had known that Amber was forbidden to him and he supposed that increased his desire. She was smart and pretty, his favourite combination, but no prettier than several women currently working in the office. It was clear that Amber was drawn to him and the seduction itself was ridiculously easy; she melted at the first kiss and had no hesitation in undressing in his office for enthusiastic sex on the long sofa. It was only afterwards when she asked if he would take her home and when in the back of his car she stroked his arm and rested her head on his shoulder that he realised he might have misread the signs after all. Amber didn't want the thrill of sex with the boss but wanted a real relationship with him. He had tried to shut things down there and then, talking about his wife and children. It hadn't worked. Amber had found excuses to wander into his office over the next few days and made it clear that she wanted to repeat the experience at the first opportunity. When he turned her down a few days later, she took to texting him and it was these despairing texts that had necessitated the two late night trips over to her apartment. He genuinely thought she might harm herself. Seriously worried now, he gently turned down her demands to climb into her bed and patiently explained to her over and over again that he was married and could not continue to see her. He told her it was all his fault and that she should have a relationship with someone her own age and, more importantly, single, but he could see that Amber wasn't listening to him as he talked her down. He had even considered telling Amber about Lottie to help push her away but realised that would be an even more foolish thing to do. In many ways, Lottie knowing about Amber was a relief. Lottie would get over her anger and she could help him navigate an escape route. Amber's intensity and anguish had made Lottie's demand for extra-marital fidelity seem a very attractive lifeboat to Jonathan when she talked about it in Budapest.

What a tangled web I have woven for myself, he thinks, and turns back to his desk to look through his long list of missed calls and messages. He sees two from Adam. He calls back and Adam confirms that Bruce is enthusiastic and on-board Team Lomax.

'I think you charmed him well enough last night, Jonathan. He also knows which side his bread is buttered on. With Tory High Command behind us, you have to be the clear favourite at this stage.'

'What more do we need to do today?'

'Nothing. Let's see how things settle down for a few days. Any more interest from journo's?'

'Not really. Lottie is putting them off for the time being.'

'Let's re-group in forty-eight hours and see where we are. It's a mistake to look too eager at this early stage of proceedings.'

Realising he can put off the issue of Amber no longer, he calls Carol to ask Amber to come down to his office. She comes almost immediately and shuts the normally open office door behind her. She sits down on the long sofa – the very sofa upon which these current difficulties had begun. She smiles sweetly and looks up at him expectantly.

'Amber. Look, I'm really sorry but we can't go on like this. It's all my fault, I should not have seduced you the other week and given you false expectations as to where things might go. I don't know why I did it. I mean...you are a very attractive woman and I was tempted but that's no excuse. I'm a married man and my marriage means everything to me. It can't happen again. I won't let it.' He pauses to draw breath.

Amber looks crushed by his statement and begins to speak, 'I thought...'

He interrupts her quickly. 'I'm so sorry that I let you think it was anything more than a casual late night encounter in the office. That was very wrong of me. Amber, this is all my fault.'

'I'm sorry too. Do you want me to leave?'

'Why don't you take the rest of the day off and then we can all turn over a new page tomorrow.'

'You, you don't want me to leave the company?'

'Heavens, no. Why would I? In fact, there's going to be a lot more for you to do shortly. I really need you to stay. But only if you think you can handle it.'

She looks doubtful. 'I can handle it,' she says.

'Amber, I'm so sorry.'

'No, it's me who should be sorry. How can I have been so stupid in the first place to think there was something more? Don't worry, I won't call you or embarrass you in any way. Can we keep this our secret? I am so ashamed of myself for thinking it could go anywhere...'

'Of course. Let's do just that. Again, I'm so sorry, this is all my fault and I can't apologise enough for my behaviour. Thank you, Amber.'

As he says these words, he thinks that the only other person who knows about tall of this is Eddie. He would need to think through the implications of that one very carefully. He looks back at Amber and smiles apologetically once more. She still looks as if tears are very close but she smiles bravely at him and then stands up and makes her way out of the office without another word.

Chapter 26

The next two days pass quietly in the office with no further developments on the selection process. Jonathan spends some time ploughing through Conservative Central Office policy documents so that he can start to understand the party line on various domestic affairs that really don't interest him. He does this as Adam has impressed upon him just how important it will be to appear fully briefed at the selection meetings. Whilst he is probably starting in the position of favourite and might have the votes he needs to secure the nomination, it is vital that he looks like the best candidate to everyone around. Especially as he is a 'blow-in' from London. Adam says that things will really start to hot up over the weekend and he should be ready to visit again in the early part of the next week.

Jonathan gets an email from John Andrews who says he is suspended from his bank and has heard that it is more than just a rumour that Jonathan is going to stand for Sir John' seat. Andrews makes it clear that he sees this as an act of betrayal from a man he considered a friend and wonders if Jonathan has always just pretended friendship to pump him for information. Jonathan decides not to reply to this email.

Things are running smoothly at Catalyst for once and he cries off a couple of functions to spend a little more time at home, mainly in the expectation that he would soon be away a lot more. Things do not go to plan, however. Ellie is deeply preoccupied in a legal battle she is involved in against Hounslow Council and is either reading documents or emailing or texting Howie until late at night. He ends up one night ordering a take away for them both and watching television alone whilst pretending to study Conservative plans on the development of the despised Universal Credit scheme. This was not his original plan. Ellie apologises frequently for her entanglement but is up against a battery of local authority lawyers and only has Howie to help her in her battle with them.

On Thursday morning, he gets an unexpected text.
Can you cancel everything and make lunch today? Anna x
He replies:
Of course. Where would like to meet?
Lord North Street house. I will get some lunch brought in. 1pm

He calls Carol to cancel his lunch date and reschedule a couple of early afternoon meetings and sits back and wonders what is on Anna's agenda: what does she want from him now?

He asks his new driver to drop him just around the corner from the house on Lord North Street and wanders around for five minutes enjoying the crisp sunny day. He flicks through his emails whilst he waits for the clock to run down until his 1pm deadline. He does not want to arrive early. Eventually, Big Ben around the corner rings out the hour and he slowly walks up to the front door and rings the oversized bell.

The familiar butler in full uniform opens the door and, obviously expecting Jonathan, ushers him without a word into the hallway. He waits there for two or three minutes until he hears the click-clack of high heeled shoes on the marble stairway above.

'Hello, darling, I do hope I haven't kept you waiting,' she calls out from the flight above.

'No, I'm just admiring your flower arrangements.'

'Not mine, I can assure you.'

She is now down on his level and dressed for work in a fashionable yet elegant pale-blue suit with her hair tightly pinned up around her head. In her heels, she is at least as tall as him and after they air-kiss their hellos she leads him through to the drawing room where an ice bucket and a bottle of champagne are waiting for therm.

'I do increasingly dislike restaurants where everyone seems to want to know your business,' she says with a smile. 'I've discovered a great Japanese place around the corner that is only too happy to deliver. You like sashimi, I presume?'

'I do. Very much.'

'That's just as well under the circumstances.' She laughs. 'Let's have a glass of Champagne whilst they sort out the table next door. Would you be a darling and pour?'

Jonathan walks to the ice bucket and, noting the expensive brand, opens the bottle and pours out two glasses of Champagne. Returning to the small sofa where Anna is now sitting, he passes her a glass and sits down closely beside her as the sofa is only just large enough for two people to share. She sips from her glass without taking her eyes from him. He does the same. She smells as delicious as the Champagne. After a few moments of silence, she moves the half-empty glass to a small table by her side and begins to talk.

'You are probably wondering why I contacted you out of the blue and invited you for lunch.'

'It did cross my mind...'

'Well, it's not just for your good looks and undoubted charm.'

'You surprise me.'

'Jonathan, let's be frank with each other, shall we? I know all about your investigation into us and our operations in Mali. I must admit I was, indeed I still am, flattered by your attention, but we both know that you have befriended John and managed to pull together some evidence that could be extremely embarrassing for all concerned. Well done by the way, we thought we had covered our tracks very well.' She smiles warmly at him and puts her hand gently upon his knee. 'I was never in doubt that you were dangerous but perhaps I underestimated just how tenacious you would be.'

'If you know all the details...'

'Yes, of course. The PM called daddy and briefed him before asking him to resign. I can tell you that shook him, having to fall on his sword on the very day he was outed.'

'And he bears me malice for that?'

'Of course he does. The same is not true of me, however. The PM told him that you would be standing in his seat. That sent him over the edge, naturally, adding to his very real sense of injury. He's retired off to his estate, hurt, and claims he wants to stand down from Cavendale too. I've wanted him out of the business for years so all of this suits me just fine. It's just that the manner of his leaving is – shall we say – a little bit sudden. The PM has told him that if he keeps his head down there's a seat in the Lords for him and that's about the only thing that is keeping him going. At the same time, poor John is making all sorts of plans to stand for election in a safe Tory seat and doesn't even realise the whole process is sewn up before it even begins.'

'And what do you want, Anna?'

'A refill first, darling, would you mind?' She offers up her empty glass and he walks over to the ice bucket and, having refilled both glasses, returns to sit beside her again. 'Thank you. Now, where were we?' She pauses for effect, sips her Champagne and continues. 'I think having you as our new local MP can only be a good thing. I think we can do business together, don't you?'

'I'm not at all sure what sort of business we might be able to do together, Anna.'

'Jonathan, let's not jump the gun and discuss specifics. What I mean is we can be friends. Friends help each other and look out for each other. You will be in Government soon and I will be running the business. It's quite obvious that you will be in cabinet in no time at all and we can help you to help us. We can work on details later.' Putting down her now empty glass, she stands up and continues, 'I think this is the third time you have been here and no-one has ever shown you around the house. It's really quite famous. Let me show you around. Shall we start upstairs?'

Without waiting for a response, she starts to walk towards the door. He follows her out of the room and up the ornate marble staircase. He looks admiringly at her long legs and her shapely bottom as she ascends the staircase, telling him of the great Victorian and Edwardian politicians who have owned the house over the years. Some of their portraits hang in heavy gilt frames on the walls around them.

On the first landing she says without turning around to look at him, 'My bedroom first, don't you think?' He follows her into a large bedroom with floor length windows and heavy nineteenth century furniture dominated by a large and ornate four poster bed.

'All a bit Victorian Gothic for my taste, but it's still impressive, don't you think?' She indicates the large portrait on the wall, 'Landseer, not one of his finest, but looks good in here.'

When he turns back to look at her, she is undoing the buttons on her suit jacket. She drops the jacket onto the bed and, without another word, moves forward and kisses him hard and long, sliding her tongue into his mouth and pulling his head towards her. He responds to her embrace and before long they are wrestling their clothes off across the bed. Her beauty and passion excite him and it is nearly three o'clock when she asks him if he would now like something to eat.

'It's a good job we are just having sashimi for lunch,' she says as she slips on a long ivory satin robe. 'Wait here and I will bring a tray upstairs. I'm not letting you out of my bed just yet.'

Whilst he waits for her return, he digs out his phone and notes the missed calls and messages. They can all wait, he thinks. He puts the phone to one side as he hears her returning footsteps and sees she has bought up a large tray of sushi and sashimi and a full bottle of white wine. She puts the tray down at the side of the bed and drops her robe onto the floor, once more revealing her wonderful naked body. She fills two long stemmed wine glasses and hands him one.

'Now, food or sex? I know which one I want first.'

When he eventually finds himself back onto the street, showered but still a little light-headed, it is almost half past four and by now his list of missed calls is intimidatingly long. He calls Carol first.

'Carol, I'm sorry, something unexpected happened and time escaped me. Who really needs to talk to me?'

'Jonathan. You mustn't do this to me. I've had everyone going mad trying to get hold of you. From the outside, Drew and Tom Schalke have each called twice and left voicemails for you. In here, Lottie desperately needs to talk to you and Adam Robinson says you really need to call him back today. Your 4 pm meeting has started without you. The rest will just have to wait. Are you on your way back now?'

'Yes, I'm just getting into a taxi. I will start calling now. And, Carol, thanks.'

His calls in the taxi are briefly interrupted by a text from Anna.

Wow. Sex with a capital S. Looking forward to the rematch. Weekend? Anna x

He smiles at this text and replies.

Wonderful. You are quite magnificent. Sunday pm?

He calls Lottie to find out that the company lawyers had at last been able to speak to Joe but there is still no information about when or indeed if he will be released by the Mali authorities. She also tells him that Tom Schalke has sold his stake in the company to another hedge fund and everyone in the office is trying to work out what this might mean for them. She asks him where he had been for much of the day and he lies, telling her he has been closeted with Conservative advisers helping him try to get to grips with the economic policies of the Government.

When he calls Drew, he has the sale news confirmed, although Drew is obviously also in the dark about the consequences. Drew is meeting the new shareholders that evening so promises to update Jonathan in the morning. Jonathan does not return Tom's calls; that could wait until he knows more about the new shareholders.

It's a late evening in the office catching up on the lost afternoon and by the time he gets home it is past eleven. Ellie is still working, papers and files spread across the entire dining table. She glances up.

'How was your day? You are back late – another dinner?'

'No, just lots to do and somehow the day got completely out of control. Would you like some tea? I'm thinking I may take some up to bed whilst I plough through these Tory selection documents.'

'That would be nice. I'm going to be here for another hour or two. We are in court tomorrow morning for a preliminary hearing and then for most of the week after and unless I can find something in this lot,' she waves her hand at the mass of documents, 'then the council are going to destroy us. They've got half a dozen lawyers working on this and all I have is Howie's help and advice for a couple of hours a day.'

'Is there anything I can do?'

'Thank you, darling. How kind of you. But no, not really. This is very technical legal stuff. I'm struggling to stay on top of it myself. I've organised for Vanessa to be here all of next week so I don't have to worry about the boys. I hope that's OK.'

She arches her neck and pouts for a kiss and he bends down over the table and obliges. He rubs her neck in the way she likes and she ostentatiously pretends to relax her shoulders. He leans in and kisses her just behind her ear.

'Of course. Peppermint or camomile?'

'Ginger, I think, please, I need some more energy.'

She smiles at him and takes off her newly acquired reading glasses to better look at him. She watches him walk away towards the kitchen and thinks to herself that she must try and spend some more quality time with him once she is through this dammed case.

He brings her the tea and goes up to bed, checking in on the sleeping boys as he goes by. He starts to read whilst drinking his camomile tea but dozes off pretty quickly. The next thing he knows is the alarm sounding and some farmer talking about sugar beet subsidies. It is the start of another day. Ellie is already up and working at the dining table when he goes downstairs.

As he is driven to the office from his Friday morning swim, his first call is from an agitated Adam Robinson.

'Jonathan, hi. Selection meeting next Tuesday evening. All nominations in by lunchtime today. I knew the PM wanted this wrapped quickly but this is double quick time. It means the by-election will be in just a few weeks' time. They will probably announce the date in Parliament in the next couple of days. Can you commit to all day Tuesday on the stump?'

'Sure. Do we need to spend more time up there?'

'Best not to. We don't want to be seen to be doing too much outside influencing. Bruce is busy behind the scenes and he's the man who can really make a difference for us.'

'Has he told you who else will be standing?'

'Yes. The three he mentioned will all be standing. Megan Smith remains the difficult one. Bruce is trying to wrest some support for her in your direction and obviously the committee will make it hard for her as you have been chosen by London and they want to be seen to toe the line.'

'What more should I do?'

'Let's get on top of the local hospital issue. It's important you know all the facts. I will get the info from the Department of Health and see where we go from there. I will talk to Lottie and see if we can get a puff piece in Monday's *Telegraph* – they are usually OK for a favour and perfect for the audience we are aiming at. Apart from that, we will have a run through of your speech on Tuesday morning – ten minutes maximum – I will send you some guidance as to what should be in it: usual hot buttons, family, society, honesty, public service, giving something back, etc. etc.'

'OK. I will work on a first draft over the weekend and get something to you to have a look at. The only issue I can think of is that Ellie is going to be in court next week and she won't be able to be there. Is that a problem?'

'I will let Bruce know. He can prepare the ground so it will not be an issue. Even Tory members understand the issues of working wives these days.'

He briefs Lottie over their breakfast meeting and tells her that Adam will call about a profile piece in Monday's *Telegraph*.

'With all of the ownership changes here do you think anyone will care that much about a profile on you?'

'Well, let's write the piece for them, Lottie. We can touch on that, the selection and the happy family man. You know the *Telegraph*: they are as lazy as can be, so if we do the work for them it can go straight out. As long as it's their own photographer they are cool.'

Lottie looks doubtful but agrees to draft the piece and set up the article. 'What do we need to say to the staff about the shareholder change?'

'Nothing. It's not about them, it's just a power-play by Tom Schalke. Business as usual. Back to the selection committee. Will you have a look at the first draft of my speech this weekend before I shoot it over to Adam?'

'Of course. Will I get to see you this weekend?'

'I don't think so, darling. Maybe we could squeeze in an hour this evening? I don't have to be back home early today.'

'That would be great.' She then whispers to him, 'I want you badly.' Pausing for effect to sip from her coffee, she then continues in a normal voice, 'I'm still worried about Amber. You did say she left the office happy?'

'Yes. It was a difficult meeting but I don't see any further problems. She understands how things really are. Will she be back in the office today?'

'I don't know. I've texted and called her but had no reply. It's not like her. I'm worried about her state of mind.'

'Well, let's wait to see what happens. I'm sure it will all be fine.'

'There's been no update from the lawyers on Joe so nothing more to report there.'

'Patience, Lottie. As I've said before, we are in the lawyers' hands on this one.'

'I seem to be the only one pushing this along. It's as if no-one else really cares. How much longer will this poor guy have to remain in jail? God knows what the conditions are like.'

'I will call the lawyers if you think it will help but I don't see how we hurry this along.'

Their conversation is interrupted by his phone: it is Tom Schalke.

'Jonathan. Sorry we didn't talk yesterday. I wanted to tell you our plans before the news hit the press.'

'Hi, Tom. I thought you told me you were long-term investors?'

'And so we were, Jonathan, but a deal is a deal. The new guys, Sympatico Capital, they made us an offer we couldn't refuse. Our investment has been under water almost from day one and this deal showed us a profit so I couldn't turn it down.'

'What will they want to do with the business?'

'You will need to talk to them. I haven't asked.'

Tom hangs up with a cheery goodbye and vague talk about lunch sometime that they both know will never happen. Jonathan and Lottie walk to the office together. Most of his day is taken up with editorial matters and Angie and Ben are in and out of his office as the three of them discuss changes to existing shows and new formats they want to develop. He feels reassured that the two of them are on top of the details and will be able to manage the company on a day-to-day basis when he pulls back. Lottie emails to say that Amber has not shown up and is still not picking up her calls or texts. He lunches with an important new financial backer of the Tories who obviously wants to increase his influence and is out to win new friends in the party. It is a turgid meeting and he is glad to be able to leave early with the legitimate excuse that he has to travel to Paddington to see the CEO.

Jonathan's usual one-on-one meeting is replaced by a gathering of senior executives and directors in Drew's office. The mood is sombre when Jonathan walks in some five minutes late.

'Jonathan, good. I think we are all here now so can someone shut the door and we can begin,' says Drew in place of a greeting. 'Now, as you all know, we today have a new major investor in the shape of Sympatico Capital. I met with their CEO this morning to hear his ideas and I have to tell you that not all of his thoughts are that positive. First of all, there's to be a freeze on all hirings and pay increases. They want to go through the books and see how much further we can reduce headcount and costs.' There are widespread groans across the room. 'Second, they want to halt all new developments until they've had a chance to review strategy. They promise they will be quick and they have a team from McKinsey starting here on Monday morning.' More, louder groans from the room. 'Of course, they promise to be supportive, hands-off investors but I think the two orders I've given you suggest otherwise. I know we've spent the last two years slashing and burning costs but I suspect there's yet more to come. I'm not going to take any questions today as I don't know any more than I have already told you. We will get together again on Monday morning to meet the McKinsey crew and set up further meetings from there. Can I ask all of you to be as helpful and open as you can be to them? Thank you. Let's get everything we can cleared from our diaries for next week in anticipation of some long days with the geniuses from Jermyn Street. Thank you all. Oh, Jonathan, before you go can I have a word in private?'

Jonathan and Drew walk over to a vacant corner of the room as the other executives start to exit the room.

'Jonathan, one more thing he told me. For your ears only. He hates the TV channel with a passion. He wants to meet you later next week to discuss major changes.'

'And do we have to go along with this?'

'He's now our biggest shareholder and his track record shows he is happier stripping assets than investing. You've got the devil of a game in trying to persuade him that more investment is required and I expect international rollout is off the table.'

'What do you want me to do?'

'At the moment, sit tight and let's get through next week and see where we end up. If he approaches you this weekend then play dumb. At least you won't have the McKinsey guys on your back next week – although that might be a bad sign too. I just don't know anymore. If I could find a way to cash in my share options today, I would be out of the door in a heartbeat.'

Jonathan travels back to the River Factory depressed by Drew's news. By the time he is back, the production team are in top gear for that night's shows and he walks quietly to the back of the gallery to watch this well-oiled machine in action. He is impressed by them and by everything they have achieved so far. It would be criminal to throw all of this away just because some American hedge funder doesn't like their channel.

Chapter 27

Jonathan arrives at Lottie's house just after eight and, finding the front door unlocked, enters without knocking. He takes off his coat and throws it over an armchair. He can hear Lottie moving about upstairs. He goes into her small galley kitchen and finding a half empty bottle of wine in the fridge, he pours out two glasses and calls up the stairs, 'Lottie, it's only me. I've poured you some wine. Shall I bring it up?'

'Yes please, darling. I'm ready for a drink.'

He walked upstairs and into Lottie's bedroom. She is stretched out across her bed wearing her black leather corset and long black boots.

'I thought you might like some discipline now you look like becoming a Tory MP,' she murmurs, smiling. 'Come over here big boy.'

He passes her the glass of wine and they kiss hard as he sinks down on to the bed next to her. She takes the wine glass from him and, putting hers down too, begins to undress him. Once he is quite naked, she pushes him back on the bed and climbs on top of him. Later, exhausted, they relax and finally drink their glasses of now warm wine. When Jonathan goes downstairs to get more, Lottie pulls off her long leather boots whilst she waits for him to return. They climb under the duvet together and cuddle whilst they slowly drink their wine.

'Is that the time,' says Jonathan, eventually looking at the bedside alarm clock. 'I really must get back home. Is it OK if I have a shower?'

'Of course, my love, help yourself.'

He takes himself off to the shower and she hears the water being turned on. She wonders for a moment about going to join him but she knows he has to get home and it is unfair of her to make too many demands upon him. Whilst she lies there, still wearing her corset and fantasising about shower sex with Jonathan, his phone buzzes on the side table next to her. Assuming it would be a text from the *Telegraph* journalist, she flicks to the messages screen using Jonathan's passcode to get there. The text is from Ellie asking him to pick up some Chinese food on the way home. She feels embarrassed to read this message and is just about to put the phone down when she notices an earlier text to him from Anna Cressley. What was all that about? She scrolls down to the message.

Wow. Sex with a capital S. Looking forward to the rematch. Weekend? Anna x

She looks at the date. Yesterday at 4.45pm. She looks at his response:

Wonderful. You are quite magnificent. Sunday pm?

Yesterday 4.47pm. The bastard. The utter, utter bastard. How could he do this to me? Carefully, she copies the messages and texts them to her own phone. She then deletes that outgoing text on Jonathan's phone. Climbing out of bed, she pulls off her now ridiculous-seeming corset and pulls on her everyday robe which is hanging on the back of her bedroom door.

By the time Jonathan emerges from the shower, Lottie is dressed and downstairs composing herself. Determined not to let on about her discovery or break down in front of him, she smiles and kisses him goodbye and ushers him quickly out of the flat. It is only when he is safely out of the door and gone that she curls up in her large armchair and sobs and sobs.

For Lottie, Friday night passes in a daze. How could she have been so stupid? Why did she ever think she could trust him? He had slept with Amber and now, even though she had only just given him an ultimatum on the subject, he had gone off and slept with the prime mover in the Mali arms scandal. Anna bloody Cressley. How could he have done this to her? She opens another bottle of wine and drinks half of it without noticing. Eventually, she decides to go to bed and takes the rest of the wine upstairs with her. The two empty wine glasses stand silently accusing her. She climbs into bed and then realises the bed linen still smells of him. She pulls off the sheet, pillowcases and duvet cover and, throwing them down the stairs, re-makes the bed with fresh linen. She then showers, rubbing herself vigorously as if to rid her skin of his imprint. She stays in the shower until the water starts to run cold and then, having dried herself on a fresh towel, she wraps herself up again in her bathrobe and climbs back into her bed. How could she have been so stupid? She repeats this to herself over and over. Why did she ever think he would change? How could he treat her so cruelly? The thoughts swirl around and around in her head as she sits in the bed, sometimes drinking, sometimes crying, always angry. She sleeps fitfully.

She wakes the next morning with an almighty hangover and an empty pain in her stomach. She stumbles downstairs, puts the kettle on and pours some muesli into a bowl. She makes and drinks her tea and stirs the cereal around her bowl before deciding she feels too ill to eat. Jonathan's deceit is churning around and around in her head and mixing very unhappily with the alcoholic metabolism going on there. Why is he doing this to her? Does he not care for her at all? Why does he need to look elsewhere for sex? Slowly, the logical side of her mind takes over from the emotional one. She must have been mad to have ever believed him. He had lied to his wife about her for over three years; why did she ever think he would be true to her?

She pulls on some clothes, takes some paracetamol for her throbbing head, and forces herself to eat some breakfast. Lottie then opens her iPad and checks her inbox and other messages. She is pleased to see an email from Amber apologising for her absence along with emails from the *Telegraph* approving her article and agreeing to use a photo she had supplied to them. The journalist wants to call Jonathan later in the day so she suggests a time and texts him to let him know to expect a call. She trawls his Twitter feed and sees nothing there that needs a response. Satisfied that she has acted professionally in all of these things, she texts Amber and suggests they meet in Wandsworth for lunch or tea if she is available. Amber texts back almost immediately suggesting a location for tea. Lottie needs to talk to someone about Jonathan and Amber is the only person she can think of apart from her sister Hannah. Hannah has been the only person Lottie has told about her affair with Jonathan and a close relationship almost came to an end as Hannah lectured her on the grim realities of life as the other woman. They eventually agreed not to fight and have since tried hard to avoid the subject, although Lottie knows that it bubbles below the surface in most of their telephone conversations and sours the relationship between the two sisters. Hannah lives in Leicester and they don't see much of each other, and Lottie doesn't want to hear the satisfaction in her older sister's voice when she tells her of the serial betrayal of her lover.

Lottie passes the rest of the morning in a mechanistic haze, washing her dirty bed linen and cleaning her kitchen, packing away a delivery from Waitrose and ploughing through some overdue administrative chores. She just wants to keep her head clear of Jonathan Lomax. At lunchtime, she pulls off her clothes, puts on her running gear and takes herself off for a long run. She comes home, showers and dresses to meet Amber for tea. The run has at last cleared her hangover and her mind.

'Amber, how are you? Are you better?'

Amber is already installed in the smart cafe when Lottie arrives.

'I'm OK, Lottie, thanks. I'm sorry about yesterday, I really am. I've ordered tea and cakes for both of us. My treat.'

'Excellent, I really need some cake,' says Lottie, sitting down opposite her. 'Look, Amber, don't worry. Remember, I know everything. There's nothing to be ashamed about. I've made the same mistake myself.'

'In the past?' began Amber.

'No, with Jonathan. He and I have been lovers for over three years.'

'Oh no. Lottie, I'm so sorry. That just makes everything even worse...'

'Amber, don't worry. It's not about you. I just wanted you to know that you are far from the only one taken in by Jonathan Lomax. Just last weekend, he was telling me how much he cared for me and then I find out about you and him and now I find he's also shagging someone else. The thing that hurts most right now is my own stupidity in ever believing him...'

'Lottie, I had no idea...'

'Of course not. Why should you. We were very discreet.' She waits whilst the tea and cakes are slowly laid out across their table by the charming but incompetent waiter. 'The fact is, he is the only man I have ever truly loved and I hid from myself all of the unpleasant facts about him. Starting with the very real issue that he is married and has two children.'

'And I assume his wife is lovely.'

'Quite lovely, although I have only met her a few times. I just closed off from the fact that I was involved in cheating on her too, and I also kept turning a blind eye to his occasional flings in the office. I thought if I made myself irresistible to him he would always come back to me and I guess a small part of me always thought he would eventually leave his wife for me. I have been so very, very stupid and that's what really hurts the most.'

'I don't know what to say. I thought I was the only fool who thought she was in love with him and now I see you suffering so. It seems all so wrong.'

'You don't know the half of it. There's another side to the charming exterior of Jonathan Lomax that you would never guess at.'

Lottie continues, telling Amber the complete story of the Mali investigation, the continued imprisonment of Joe, Jonathan being bought off by the PM, and then having an affair with Anna Cressley. Amber sits back in the chair, mouth open in amazement, eyes popping out of her head.

'So, the deal would be for you to go and run Jonathan's campaign and political office...'

'And leave you to run the PR for Catalyst, with him taking a back seat whilst he remains a backbencher. He would then exit completely when he joins the cabinet.'

'And you still have all of the proof to make the story of the Government's lies and cover-up stand?'

'Yes, I do. Jonathan thought he was being clever taking the thumb drive from my tea caddy yesterday on his way out without me noticing, but I had already copied it and hidden it online so I have all the evidence I need.'

'What will you do with it?'

'Not me, Amber – us. I am going to need your help next week. Jonathan may have been bought off but I'm not that easy and now I'm on my own again I intend to do the right thing.'

'I'm completely here to do anything you want me to do. You can count on me.'

'I know, Amber. I've always known I could count on you from the moment we started working together. I will brief you on Monday when I've sorted out some more stuff tomorrow afternoon. Until then, not a word to anyone. Bloody men. Why do we always fall for the crap ones?'

They head out of the cafe, and after hugging on the street, Lottie is walking home thinking through her next steps when her phone rings with the distinctive tone that signifies Jonathan calling. She answers, not sure she can trust her own voice.

'Hello, how did the *Telegraph* go?'

'Fine. Nothing difficult there. I think the piece will be good on Monday. Rising new star and all of that sort of stuff. I've written the first draft of my speech for Tuesday evening and I was wondering if I could email it over to you for your thoughts?'

'I'm not at home right now but I will look at it later and get back to you.'

'Lottie, is everything OK? You sound distracted.'

'It's just it's difficult to talk right now. Email it to me and I will look at it this evening. I've got to go now, bye.'

She hangs up, realising for the first time just how difficult it was going to be with him going forwards. They spent most days talking at least half a dozen times as well as the innumerable texts and emails that passed between them. Nearly all business, but often with a veneer of gentle banter and careful flirtation. By the time she reaches home, Jonathan's email is waiting for her and she carefully reviews it, making some small amendments but thinking to herself that he is really very good at this sort of stuff when he puts his mind to it. It would almost certainly be the best speech the committee would hear on Tuesday. She expands the section on 'the importance of my family in my life' as much out of black humour as any real need to say more on the subject, and emails the amended version back to him with a note saying how good it was. He replies thanking her and says he will see her as usual for breakfast on Monday. She decides not to reply to this invitation for the moment. A text from the journalist at the *Telegraph* interrupts her thoughts.

Lottie. Thanks so much for all of the help on the J.Lomax piece. What a sweetie he is. So helpful and charming. Thanks again. Lucinda x

She smiles to herself. He really can't help himself. Realising that she hasn't eaten much apart from cake in the last twenty-four hours, she opens the fridge and chooses a favourite but complex supper to make. It's the sort of time-consuming recipe that she wouldn't normally make for just herself but she enjoys the experience, chopping and preparing a variety of vegetables whilst half-listening to Radio Four. She thinks to herself that this is how her new independent life is going to be and she had better get used to it. Although she was under the influence of a chronic hangover when she vowed earlier in the day to eschew men going forwards, she remains determined that any future relationship with a man will have to be very, very different from the one she has just exited.

Chapter 28

At a little after two on Sunday, Lottie parks her rented Zipcar on Lord North Street ten or so houses down from the Cressley residence. She reckons the anonymous grey VW Golf will be a sufficient disguise for her and she puts on her headphones to listen to a series of TED talks whilst she settles down for what she expects will be a long afternoon of waiting and watching.

Jonathan arrives just after three, walking down the street from the far end towards her. She pulls out her camera, fitted with the longest zoom lens she owns, and photographs him crossing the street, waiting outside the Cressley's door and then being admitted by Anna Cressley herself. Once the door is closed, she checks through her pictures and sees she has what she needs, each one time and date stamped and most of them in clear focus. She puts the camera down and returns to her talk on the future of artificial intelligence. She suspects she will have time for a couple more TED talks before Jonathan re-appears.

It is almost four thirty when the door opens again and Jonathan re-emerges onto the street. She starts to photograph him again and her heart almost stops when he crosses the road and seems to stare right at her, but the moment passes and he turns his back and walks away towards Parliament Square where she presumes he will look for a taxi to take him to his normal Sunday afternoon editorial session at the channel. There had been several occasions in the recent past when he had called at her house on a Sunday afternoon and they had made love before he went on to work. It had all seemed so right then, whereas now she could see it for what is was: a squalid, secret affair, hidden from the world outside.

Lottie catches up on her sleep on Sunday night after a Netflix binge and heads off on Monday morning to meet Jonathan for breakfast as usual. He is there when she arrives and she sees his winning smile light up as she enters the cafe.

'Hello, Lottie, how are you? I've ordered you some porridge and tea.'

Instantly she is angry with him; how dare he presume she would want porridge for breakfast? She calms herself. She had thought through this meeting and she wants to keep everything perfectly cool and professional.

'Morning, boss. How are the revisions to your speech going along?'

'I sent the draft speech to Adam last night and I'm going off to see him after this meeting to get everything ready for tomorrow evening. Thank you for your changes, they all made good sense to me. We will be there most of the day tomorrow, is that OK with you?'

'I will come up later in the day but I will be there in plenty of time for the committee meeting.'

'Will you be able to stay the night?'

'I don't think that would be a good idea, Jonathan. Anyway, I have some stuff I need to do down here on Wednesday. I can come back up again later in the day.'

'Thanks. It will be good to have you there. We are planning to stay up there for the week, assuming we win. I think the *Telegraph* piece today read really well, thanks for all of your help on getting that one out there. There's not much more we can do. Let's stay quiet on the social media front so we are not seen to be self-promoting, OK? It's good we have everything so well prepared, I'm sure the other challengers will be scrabbling around behind us. On the work front, I have some bad news, however. I had a call from Dwight Stevens last night – he's the head of Sympatico – and I'm pretty sure he wants to close the channel.'

'My God, are you sure?'

'He says he's just socialising his ideas. You know what these Americans are for not saying exactly what they mean. He loves the two police action channels, they are cheap as chips and make money but says he can't get his head around what Catalyst is trying to do and how it will ever make money. I think it's a typical drip-drip strategy which will eventually lead to closure or changing it into another library channel. I'm supposed to be meeting him on Wednesday so I will find out more.'

'What about all of the staff?'

'They won't be needed in Dwight's new model so major redundancies, I guess. No-one should ever go into TV these days without expecting to lose one's job every so often.'

'But we are doing something good here. The viewing numbers are improving and the advertising revenues are on the way up, why are they doing this?'

'I can't get to the bottom of that one. He rambled on about strategy and the McKinsey review but I suspect they are just asset-strippers and want to slash and burn costs before selling on the investment. These hedge fund guys are really animals and they don't care about the businesses they own, they just exist to turn over a quick profit and pay themselves fat bonuses. Of course, don't say a word to anyone at the office; nothing is confirmed. It may be just as well that you and I have a political future together given the shaky prognosis for the channel. Remember, not a word to anyone.'

'Of course not.'

Lottie is fuming inside. He really doesn't care about all of the people who will lose their jobs, who had worked around the clock to make the channel the success it was. He was on to the next thing and had already rationalised the channel closure in his own mind.

They finish their breakfast and Jonathan's new driver is waiting outside to take him to his meeting with Adam. Lottie walks the short distance to the office and calls Angie asking if she and Ben have time to get together to discuss something important. They meet some fifteen minutes later in Lottie's office. Amber is there too. Lottie briefs them all on the Mali cover-up and takes them through the whole story, right up to and including Jonathan being bought off by the Prime Minister and then bedding Anna Cressley. She shows them pictures of Jonathan entering and leaving the Cressley residence on her iPad. There is one shot in particular where Anna's welcoming smile on the doorstep leaves little doubt as to the purpose of the meeting. They all sit quietly listening to this story and it is only when Lottie finally finishes speaking that Angie unloads her feelings.

'Jesus, Lottie, what a bastard he is. He has the story of the decade that could bring down the Government and he coolly allows himself to be bought off by the buggers and then cheats on his own wife to compound the crime. Why am I always so disappointed by men?'

'Angie, that's not all, I'm afraid. It looks like these new hedge fund shareholders – Sympatico – they want to close the channel. They don't get what we are trying to do here and they just see the losses. Nothing's confirmed but it doesn't look good.'

'So, just as Ben and I get the chance to take over the channel, the bloody rug gets pulled from under our feet and we are out on our arses. What a fucking disaster.'

'Nothing has been confirmed and please don't say anything outside of this room. If we are going to go down, I want us to go down with a big bang, not a whimper. I want to tell the whole Mali story on the channel, from start to finish with nothing left out. What do you think?'

'Do we have all of the evidence?' asks Ben.

'I have all the documents and the audio tape of John Andrews talking to Jonathan. You've seen I have the photographs of Jonathan entering and leaving the Cressley house yesterday afternoon. We have everything we need to make the programme. Obviously Jonathan can't know anything about it. How soon could we get it on air, assuming you are up for doing it?'

'Well, it's a simple enough programme to make,' begins Angie, thinking on her feet. 'We would need to shoot it with a presenter to camera, some location shooting around London. It would be ideal for Melissa to front, she's still got the gravitas from her ITV News days and I think she would love to do it.'

'We would have to tell her the full story.'

'I know, but she's not as indiscreet as you might imagine. She's been courted by the BBC for fronting their Sunday morning politics show so she would see this as a perfect job application piece. We don't have to mention the station closure issues, and for reasons I don't fully understand, she seems to have taken against Jonathan somewhat anyway. You may not have noticed but she's as thick as thieves with me these days.'

'When could we get the show on air?'

'If we start today, we could get it on air by Thursday evening. Would that do?'

'That would be great. We can leak the show to the papers late on Thursday and get them to cover it in Friday's paper. Everyone sweats all day on Friday and we dominate the news. One of us will have to front up for interviews on Friday.'

'In that case, it has to be Melissa. You know she will love to take credit for the journalistic scoop. To be fair, she will also be the best person to promote the story.'

'Agreed. Amber, will you put together a plan to push the story? All to happen just before it goes to air so it can't be pulled. What about lawyers? We need to show we have been through the proper legal due diligence before we go to air with this story.'

'That's fine. I will handle all of that with the lawyers. Assuming we go for an 8pm start time and make the show available on line at the same time, that will give everyone the time to pick up the story for the 10 o'clock news and the Friday papers. Is that the way you want to play the news?'

'Yes. That's great. The main news will be able to report the story, but won't have time to get comment, and the serious newspapers can have a clear run at it and then TV can come back at the story on Friday morning. We probably need to clear our schedules for Friday too. We should also aim to re-run the show on Friday, assuming we don't get an injunction slapped on it, that is.'

'How do we keep all of this away from Jonathan?' asks Ben.

'He's going to be tied up with the selection committee for the next few days. I suspect he won't be back until Thursday, so that becomes the problem day.'

'Don't worry,' says Angie. 'By Thursday, the show will be in edit and he won't have a clue that it's going on. More to the point when do we tell him it's going to air?'

'When it's gone to air and the credits have rolled. I don't want him to pull the transmission.'

'Jesus, Lottie, you're not taking any prisoners on this one, are you?'

'Angie. For too long I've been blind and now the time has come to do the right thing. Let's get to it. Can I help you brief Melissa?'

The meeting breaks up but Angie stays behind, lingering to get a moment alone with Lottie. She waits until the others have left the room and then shuts the door behind them.

'Lottie, I'm sorry that it's all ended up like this for you.'

'What do you mean?'

'Lottie, this is me, Angie, the woman who knows everything. I've seen the way you look at him when you think no-one is watching you.'

'Angie, I ...'

'Lottie, it's OK, I get it. I could too. I just want you to confirm to me that you are not doing this because he's left you and taken up with that Anna Cressley woman.'

'No, it's really not. I've realised he's just like all the rest. I didn't think he was, but now I know he's no better than all of the others I despise for their lies and double standards. Angie, for three years I have loved a man who it turns out doesn't really exist. He's just a cheating husband and shallow and craven and he's joined the crooked establishment he claims to despise and I want to expose all of that, not just him.'

'OK. That's fine. I had to ask – and I'm still sorry it has worked out like this for you. Well, let's do it. Who knows, it may be the best show this little channel has ever made.'

Jonathan returns to the office after a lunch date and Lottie is keen to keep her distance from him as long as possible. He comes by her office late in the day to brief her on his political developments.

'Hi. Just to let you know that we've got a bit of a problem. Bruce, my agent, tells me that some of the selection committee are proving very sticky. This local woman, Megan Smith, is running strongly and I've a real fight on my hands to make the nomination. It seems an edict from the PM's office is not the knockout punch we thought it would be. I've got Adam looking at information on her.'

'What do you hope to find out?'

'Anything that she would want to remain in the dark. There's some stuff about local planning permissions that looks positive and her developer husband seems like a slippery fish so we might dig something up there to throw her off. Time is not on our side however. Can you give him a hand? I wouldn't normally ask but if we are to get something out there it needs to be by lunchtime tomorrow.'

'I will speak to Adam and see what I can do.'

Lottie thinks to herself that she will absolutely not do anything to help destroy this woman.

'Thanks.' He pauses. 'Are you alright Lottie? You look stressed.'

'I'm fine. I've just got a lot on and I'm feeling under the cosh.'

'You are not still cross with me about Amber, I hope?'

'No. That ship has sailed,' she says and turns back to her computer as if to dismiss him from her office.

'I was hoping we could celebrate together on Tuesday night...'

'I told you this morning that I've got to get back to London after the vote.'

'But I will need you there on Wednesday to help me organise the next steps.'

'And I will come back up by lunchtime Wednesday.'

'I'm hoping Ellie will be up there on Wednesday evening now that her court case is coming to an end. Hopefully, we will all be having dinner with the local bigwigs and getting stuck into the by-election.'

'I'm sure we will. Now, I really must get on, especially now I have to call Adam as well.'

'I'm on my way. No breakfast tomorrow, I'm afraid. I'm going straight up to the constituency. I will see you there later in the day?'

'I will be there just after lunch.'

He smiles widely and they look at each other for what seems an age – and then he is gone, leaving Lottie alone with her thoughts.

Chapter 29

Lottie pauses outside the elegant Richmond house and looks at her watch. It's 10:45am. She thinks to herself that this is a time and a moment in her life she will always remember. What happens in the next thirty minutes will irrevocably change several people's lives and, having endured a sleepless night agonising over this moment, she draws a deep breath and then strides forwards and rings the doorbell. After a short delay, Ellie opens the door. She is wearing her running gear and looks as if she has just come back in from a morning run.

'Lottie, what are you doing here? How nice to see you. Has something happened to Jonathan?'

'No, Ellie, nothing like that. I'm sorry to disturb you at home but there's something important I need to talk to you about.'

'Come in, come in. Would you like some coffee? I was just about to make myself a cup.'

'Thank you, that would be good.' Lottie follows Ellie through the hall and into the kitchen and waits whilst Ellie loads the coffee machine. Lottie looks at the clock on the wall. Time seems to be standing still at 10:45. Ellie fusses around the expensive coffee machine whilst it hisses and steams and, after what seems forever, offers Lottie a cup of coffee and they sit down together around the dining table. They are both silent through this process.

'Well, I must say this is a real surprise. Has Jonathan sent you to harangue me into attending his confirmation meeting tonight?'

'No. He doesn't know I'm here.'

Ellie looks puzzled. 'Tell me then, Lottie. Why are you here?'

'Ellie, I have a long story to tell you. I want to tell you the whole thing and then ask for your advice. But first, I have to start with a confession. And that's not easy for me to do but I have to tell you that Jonathan and I have been lovers for the last three years. There's nothing I can say to make that any better and...' She looks up from her coffee to see Ellie, hand over her mouth, frozen in a state of bewilderment, eyes darting from her to the window outside. 'Ellie, before you say anything just hear me out. I fell in love with your husband and disregarded the fact that he was married and nothing can make me despise myself more than I already do...'

'Get out of my house! How dare you say these things! He wouldn't do this to me. I know he wouldn't.'

'Ellie. I'm so sorry. But you need to hear this. I'm not the only one...'

'Stop. Stop. Get out of my house...'

'Ellie, I can't imagine how hard this is for you but you need to hear the truth.'

There is no response from Ellie who is now staring into her coffee cup and avoiding looking at her so Lottie ploughs on. 'There's nothing I can say to make my behaviour more excusable but I want to...'

'And now I suppose he has thrown you over for someone younger and you want to get your revenge on him, and me.'

'No. It's not like that. I have ended it. But yes, he is seeing someone else and no, I was not the only one he was seeing whilst we were sleeping together. I was his mistress, I suppose, and I turned a blind eye to his flings in the office so I didn't lose him. How pathetic was I.' Lottie's self-loathing is all too evident, even to Ellie. 'I was the other woman and how I hate myself for it; the hurt I have caused you and the hurt I have caused myself. I haven't come here to tell you this to hurt you, although I know you will be, but to ask your advice and I can't do that unless I tell you the whole story. I'm not going to tell lies anymore and most of all I don't want to lie to you.'

There is silence in the room. The only sound is the slow tick-tock of the large Victorian wall clock. Lottie thinks she should wait for Ellie to say something before she speaks again. Seconds pass by slowly as they both avoid making eye contact. Eventually, Ellie sighs heavily and looks hard into Lottie's eyes.

'Why are you telling me this, Lottie? Why didn't you just retreat hurt into the darkness from where you obviously came and let me get on with my life? Do you think you are helping me by destroying my family's life? Does it make you feel good? Does it give you power?'

Her voice hesitates and then she buries her face in her hands and quietly sobs. Lottie watches, horrified. What had she expected to happen? She had just destroyed someone's happy family and now she is watching it crumble in front of her. She sits silently, not knowing what to do and desperately wishing she was somewhere else, anywhere else. Eventually, Ellie stops crying, looks at her again and wipes away her tears.

'You said you wanted advice. You're not pregnant, I hope?'

'No, nothing like that.' Lottie opens her briefcase and takes out large black and white prints of Jonathan arriving and leaving the Cressley house with the time and date stamped on the bottom right corner. 'This is him entering and exiting Anna Cressley's house on Sunday afternoon. As you can see, there's ninety minutes missing between the two events.' She then takes out a colour photograph of Anna Cressley taken at a society event, looking fabulous in expensive couture. 'This is Anna Cressley...'

'This proves nothing other than the fact he went to her house on Sunday afternoon. You don't even know what went on inside.'

'No, the photos don't prove anything, but this does.' She passes over her phone to Ellie. It is open at the messages page with the texts between Anna and Jonathan highlighted. She sees Ellie's face twitch as she reads the texts.

'You could have faked these two texts. How do I know they are genuine?' Lottie says nothing. 'This is the same Anna

Cressley who heads up Cavendale? The company Jonathan was investigating for the illegal arms sales to Mali?'

'The same. Jonathan has been bought off by the Prime Minister. The whole fix up of Sir John's seat, the promise of a cabinet post, it's all a thank you to get Jonathan to drop the Mali investigation. You know the Government could fall if it goes public. They bought Jonathan off to close down the story. I don't know where sleeping with Anna Cressley comes in but I suspect it's more complicated than just her physical attractions.'

'You took these photographs?'

'Yes.'

'The revenge of the spurned mistress?'

'To some extent you are of course right. I realise that I too have been lied to over the years and I feel a fool. But even more than that, I'm sick of all of the lying that I've been party to and I want to tell the Mali arms story even if Jonathan now doesn't want to.'

'How do you propose to do that?'

'We have put together everything on the story from the beginning of the investigation right up to the confirmation of Jonathan as the Tory candidate later tonight. We still have a stringer in jail in Mali and I'm hoping the publicity and the fuss will help get him out. Jonathan knows nothing about this but we are planning to run the programme on Catalyst on Thursday evening. We will cover the original arms sale, the dodgy export licences from the Government, the cover-up and Ministers lying to Parliament, and Jonathan being bought-off with the promise of a Cabinet post.'

'You know that in doing that you will destroy him?'

'Yes. I have thought it all through. That's the advice I need from you. If you want me to bury the story, I will do it. Everything will go away and I promise you the story will never surface. Only a few trusted people in the company know the facts. I owe you, not Jonathan, you, that much at least. If we go public his candidacy will collapse and, as he might have told you, the channel looks doomed anyway because the new owners hate it...'

'No, that's another thing he has omitted to tell me. There are probably plenty more things too.' She pauses and takes a deep breath. 'Tell the story, Lottie. I will deal with all of the consequences.'

'It could mean the end of all of this,' she waves her hand around the room. 'Everything could be at stake. You must know this.'

'I know. That's fine. I don't want him anymore and I don't want his money. Or at least no more than is rightfully mine.'

'Ellie. I think you should think on this decision for a while in case you think differently when you've had a chance to consider everything. We can stop the programme right up to transmission.'

'Lottie, I'm a lawyer. Much of what I do is thinking logically on my feet and making swift decisions on complex issues. I will not be changing my mind. You know, when I first met him and we were going out together I always felt that I was never quite good enough for him, that he was always looking for something I couldn't provide...'

'Ellie, don't do this to yourself. It's not you, it's him.'

'Maybe. I don't know anything anymore. My whole world has turned upside down this morning.' She pauses, breathes deeply, and when she continues, the lawyer in her has taken over. She is now matter-of-fact and precise. A mask has come down and her former vulnerability has vanished. 'You are right of course. It is him. Let's tell the story. You want to put it out on Thursday? What time?'

'Eight o'clock. Obviously, I need you not to say anything to anyone. Jonathan could halt transmission if he gets even a whiff of the programme going out.'

'I understand. I will talk to my own lawyer but that will only be to get divorce proceedings underway. A Friday morning delivery of divorce papers should hit him when he's at his weakest.'

'You don't have to do this, Ellie.'

'Oh, but I do, Lottie. I really do. Just promise me you won't ever forgive him and have him back.'

'Never. I promise you. Never.'

'I think I believe you. I also feel a bit sorry for you. How bizarre is that.' The two women stare at each other and Ellie continues, 'I think we have both loved someone who was not who we believed he was. Thank you for coming and telling me this. It must have taken some guts.'

She holds out her hand to shake Lottie's. Lottie hesitates and then reaches out to accept.

'Ellie, I'm so sorry...'

'No more. Are you going up to the hustings tonight?'

'I am. Just a flying visit this afternoon and back on the late train tonight. I need to keep up the pretence that everything is normal for a little while longer.'

'You must be a whole lot better at hiding things than I am.'

'Practice, I guess. I'm sorry. If you change your mind about the programme, here's my mobile number. We can pull the transmission any time if you want us to. But remember, if you want to go ahead with this then complete secrecy is the key.'

'Don't worry, Lottie, I haven't forgotten. Exposure by television seems the right way to tell his story. Poetic justice I suppose. Now, I need you to leave me alone, I have to finish my legal arguments for taking on Hounslow Council this afternoon and you've set me well behind.'

They both get up from the table and Ellie shows Lottie to the door. As she opens the front door she turns and asks, 'How many women?'

'I don't know, Ellie. Must be double figures but I only know some of it.'

'The bastard. How could he do this to me and the boys?'

Lottie leaves the house without answering Ellie's final question and strides quickly away as she hears the door shut behind her. After a minute or two, she stops walking and begins to physically shake. Tears fill her eyes and she blinks them back and wipes the back of her hand across her face. She had blurted out her story to Ellie and knew that if she had lost control of that conversation she would have broken down in tears and not recovered. If she hadn't given up smoking this would have been the moment to light up. She looks around for a shop to buy cigarettes from but fights the urge and decides if she can get through today without a smoke she will definitely have cracked the habit. She struggles down the road and finds a gaily-painted cafe where she orders a double expresso, and only when that is finished does she start to feel a little calmer. The bastard, she thinks, the smug fucking bastard, how did he think he could play around with so many people's lives and care nothing for the consequences of his actions?

Chapter 30

Lottie is on the train to Northampton when Adam calls to tell her he has found some skeletons in Megan Smith's cupboard.

'If you look hard and long enough you always find something,' he says, sounding as if he was smirking at his own cleverness. She realises that she has always disliked him and had only agreed to work with him because of his importance to Jonathan's career. His sense of self-importance and arrogance was unbearable.

'What have you found?'

'Nothing to destroy the foundations of our democracy, but a nice little document that shows that she did indeed lean on a planning officer to get a granny flat built in her garden, even though it had been turned down twice by the planning committee.'

'That's it?'

'Believe me, Lottie, it's enough. Even a whiff of scandal can sink a candidate at this time.'

'And how will you use this tonight?'

'I will be using it before we go into the hustings and that's why I need your help.'

'What do you want me to do?'

'As you know, we've got a bit of national media interest in this selection so I will send you the information and you can then leak it to the *Telegraph* and see if they can get it up on their website later today? I can then spread some disinformation about it and just muddy the waters enough to see off any potential challenge.'

'But the story is really a fake?'

'No, it's true, but we need to embroider it and give them no time to hit back. That's why we need to get it up by no later than 4pm. Can you do it for me?'

'Sure. Send me the stuff.'

She hangs up. So this was how her career in front-line politics would be, she thinks to herself. She would be using her media skills to knock down a thoroughly decent woman and give her no chance to appeal or fight back. She watches the landscape flash by from the speeding train and tries to gather her thoughts. If Jonathan was forced to step down at the weekend after the programme went out, then Megan Smith would be the most likely candidate going forwards. A local planning scandal would make that less straightforward and could open the door for that pumped-up idiot John Andrews and that would play everything back into Anna bloody Cressley's lap again. Lottie decides that she will bury the story and just blame the *Telegraph* for not running it. No-one would want to put the story out on social media today for fear of being seen to have planted it. She will just have to tough it out with Adam.

By the time she arrives at the hotel, there is a measurable sense of crisis in the hotel bedroom they are using as a campaign headquarters. Mobile phones are ringing and Jonathan, Adam and Bruce are all talking on their own phones simultaneously. She sits down and waits for a break in the activity. When it seems clear nothing would be slowing down anytime soon, she calls reception on the hotel phone and orders tea and sandwiches for everyone, correctly guessing that no-one will have eaten. When the food arrives it creates a natural break in proceedings and the three of them all bring their calls to an end and silently munch on the sandwich selection. Lottie uses the opportunity to ask on progress and receives confusing answers. It seems the race is going to be a lot closer than anyone had predicted. Megan Smith has syphoned off quite a constituency who are all keen to give Tory high commend a bloody nose and vote against Jonathan. John Andrews has also picked up more support than expected, and although unlikely to win, his support complicates the picture making it difficult to predict the outcome. Bruce has a long list of voters he thinks could be influenced and the three of them are slowly working their way through it and marking off the results on a white board propped up against the wall.

'Well, Lottie, this is it. Democracy in the raw. Not a pretty sight,' says Jonathan as he helps himself to another sandwich. She gets the full-beam Jonathan smile. 'Did you get anywhere with the story in the *Telegraph*?'

'They are not biting so far. They think it's a fake story or a nothing story but I'm still working on them so leave it with me. I will get it away.' She can hardly bear to look at him as he sits back eating his sandwich – master of all he surveys.

'We really need some dirt to stick if we are to win this,' said Jonathan, chewing away and helping himself to some crisps. 'Lottie, try them again and call in whatever favours you need to and get this story away for me...'

'I don't want to worry you guys,' said Bruce draining his teacup, 'but there's still a whole heap of calls to be made and not much time to do it - so let's get back to it, shall we?'

The three of them return to their phone lists and start dialling again. Lottie watches in silence and then takes out her own phone and scrolls through her emails – more to look busy than to do anything real.

***

By the time they arrive at the selection meeting, the room is already full of local Conservative members. There is a small gaggle of reporters and one camera crew but they are kept outside the meeting room by an officious marshal wearing an orange hi-vis tabard to show his importance. The tabard proclaims "A Conservative vision for the future" which seems an oddly vacuous slogan, thinks Lottie, as she follows her team into the room. John Andrews pointedly refuses to shake

Jonathan's offered handshake but Jonathan just smiles and turns to greet the other candidates. The four of them are lined up on the stage alongside the local party chair person who opens the proceedings. She tells the audience that the candidates have drawn lots for the order of speaking and reads out their names in that order. Jonathan is last. Lottie listens to the first three speakers who were all, in their own way, impressive and sincere. Even John Andrews, who is third, makes a decent fist of his speech, although Lottie has to hide a smile when he speaks of the tremendous support his wife gives to him and how he depends upon her so much. Anna Cressley is nowhere to be seen, although she suspects that the glamorous older woman in his camp is Lady Annabel Cressley and that is confirmed in a whispered exchange with Brian, who obviously has no time for the society hostess and interior designer.

Although she had edited Jonathan's speech and is a little biased, it is instantly evident that his presentation is head and shoulders above the competition. He flashes his winning smile carefully but it is obvious to her that his charm is winning over some of the undecided, especially the women. His voice breaks a little when he apologises for his wife's absence and tells how she is absent only because she is taking on the might of the Tory council in Hounslow over their inflexible housing policy and suggests that this independence is typical of his humane approach to politics. This is an addition to the speech that Lottie doesn't recognise. He goes on to praise Ellie in glowing terms as a wife, mother and activist lawyer before saying how much she is looking forward to putting down family roots in the constituency and leaving the chaos of London for a better quality of life for their boys.

He hits all the other notes that Brian had suggested to him. He is, he says, a kind man but couldn't accept that immigration could continue unchecked and he wants to see more money go into education and the health service. He says he doesn't want to make local hospitals a political football but he will argue for a stay of execution on closing any local hospitals until a thorough and independent review is completed into local needs. He is, by turn, sincere, passionate, and even occasionally funny. He is in his element, thinks Lottie, this was what he was born to do; charm an audience and then leave them behind without a second thought: a born politician.

Questions from the floor follow Jonathan's presentation. The questions are courteous, and under the pre-agreed rules, aimed at all of the candidates. No-one excels and no-one falls over. Lottie admires Megan Smith's coolness under pressure when she steps out of Conservative mainstream policy on schools and the other candidates round on her. But no real points are won or lost in this section of the evening and Lottie suspects to herself that most of the voters have already made up their minds.

After the questions are finished, the candidates are ushered off into a large anteroom where they and their advisers and families huddle together in small groups out of earshot of the others. Eventually, the different whispered conversations in the room fizzle out as the minutes continue to tick by and all that can be said has been said. She catches sight of John Andrews scowling in their direction but thinks it is unlikely that he knows anything more than they do about how the voting is going. The room is silent for several minutes before they are finally ushered back into the main hall where the candidates again take their seats upon the stage. The chair stands up to announce the results and an expectant hush falls upon the room. She says that after a re-count the voting is incredibly tight but the winner of the contest and the Tory party candidate to fight the by-election is Jonathan Lomax. This announcement causes an outbreak of boos from the back of the hall and as Jonathan stands up to take applause from the rest of the audience, several party members walk out of the hall in a silent protest. Jonathan approaches the lectern and smiles at the audience.

'Thank you all for putting your faith in me to fight this by-election. I promise I will not let you down and I will, if successful, faithfully represent your views in Parliament.' He pauses for effect. 'I know some people in this room see me as a blow-in from London and wonder if I will be true to you all. Have no doubt: this is now my adopted home and I will fight for you in this election and future elections to make sure this wonderful part of the country gets everything it needs from Westminster. I will work for you so that you can thrive and deliver an improved quality of life for yourselves and for your children. Now, together we need to go forward and win this election. Again, I must ask you for your help. We start from a strong position but let's take nothing for granted; we need to win every vote we possibly can. Thank you all and thank you particularly to my fellow candidates: we were competing against each other tonight but now let's work together to ensure a Conservative is elected to represent us in Parliament. Thank you.'

Applause greets his impromptu speech which, Lottie thinks, is less than completely successful and shows his limitations when he has to improvise. She watches as he shakes hands with the defeated candidates and sees the extremely awkward body language as he shakes the hand of John Andrews. She wonders if Andrews already knows that Jonathan is sleeping with his wife.

The Lomax party returns triumphantly to their hotel headquarters down the road and Adam orders Champagne to be sent up to help them celebrate. Jonathan receives a text from the Prime Minister congratulating him and other messages follow. Lottie is quickly busy co-ordinating responses and putting out new messages on social media. She is surprised by the volume of reaction, especially upon Twitter; Jonathan's move to political candidate has cranked up the interest significantly.

Offering her a glass of Champagne, Adam says quietly to her, 'That was a lot closer than it needed to be, Lottie. Still, all's well that ends well, as the Bard says. It was a great shame you couldn't get that piece out to nail Megan Smith. That would have made it all much more comfortable.'

'As you say, Adam, we won. That's all that matters.'

'I suppose so. I'm just saying we could have made it easier on ourselves if we had got everything in place that needed to be in place. Anyway it's done. Now you have to really step up to the plate, Lottie. We are a bit of a shoe-in for the by-election but you have to help to build this man into what he can be. I have never had any doubts that he can go right to the very top of whatever ladder he chooses to climb. It's your job to help him get there and stay ahead of the marauding pack. Are you really up for the challenge?'

'I'm up for the challenge, Adam. Have no doubts.'

Lottie returns to her social media feeds and starts firing off responses to the many comments coming in. Before long, the hotel reception rings to say her taxi to the station is waiting and she quietly leaves the room, promising Jonathan she will be back by lunchtime tomorrow. She spends the train journey continuing to work across a variety of social media platforms and responding to requests for interviews with Jonathan. As usual, her quiet efficiency means the hour's journey is extremely productive, although she thinks to herself that she is really working on autopilot after the stress of her morning's meeting with Ellie.

By the time she arrives back at Euston station, her phone battery is flat and so is she. Pausing by one of the station bars, she walks in and orders a gin and tonic. She sits down and sips it slowly, looking around at the late night travellers heading out of the capital. Everyone looks so focussed and here she is with her life falling apart around her. Her day job is about to disappear, she is about to destroy her lover and put herself out of work in her new job too. She feels incredibly alone. What a bloody nightmare this has become, she thinks to herself. How did it all get so out of hand?

Chapter 31

On Wednesday morning, Angie holds a short meeting with Ben, Amber, Lottie and Melissa to discuss the Mali production. Everything has been going well with the show and all of the location shooting would be completed that day. Ben had done a great job re-arranging the story to make a compelling piece of television and Melissa is revelling in the role of investigative reporter. Angie had found some good library footage of Sir John and Anna Cressley but they were struggling to find any footage of John Andrews. They were trying to get something from Sky News from last night's selection meeting but were struggling to get any co-operation. Lottie says she will take care of it as she has lots of contacts at BBC News and they surely must have something that could be used. The lawyers have approved the script and would review the finished film before transmission. They agree that they would all share executive producer credits on the film to show they are all on the same side. They are interrupted by Lottie's phone ringing with its special ringtone – Jonathan is calling.

'Hello, Jonathan. How are things this morning?' Pause. 'Yes, I will be on the lunchtime train and around until early evening.' Pause. 'No, I will be coming back to London tonight.' Long pause. 'Well, I will warn Angie and the team and get everything ready for Friday. Is there anything we can do other than tidy up and be prepared for questions?' Pause. 'OK. I will see you later, bye.'

'As you might guess, he's keen to get me up there to help so I will have to get my skates on and head for the train. More importantly, two representatives of the new shareholders plus three people from McKinsey are going to be here on Friday afternoon at about three. They want to meet us all as part of their review into the whole of the group. I suspect by the time we are ready to sit down we might have some different things to talk about. Is everyone still happy with our plan?'

Everyone agrees they are still committed to their course of action and the meeting breaks up as the team return to their tasks. Amber and Lottie agree that they will work very late and maybe even through the night on Thursday to deal with journalist enquiries. Lottie orders an Uber and collects some things from her office whilst she waits for it to arrive. Once she is in the car, she calls Ellie. This was going to be a difficult call but one she needs to make.

'Ellie, it's Lottie. I hope I'm not interrupting your work.'

'No, it's fine, what can I do for you?' Ellie's voice is clipped and businesslike.

'We are nearly ready with the film and I just wanted you to confirm to me that you still want it to go ahead.'

'Yes, nothing's changed.'

'You are sure? It's not too late to pull it.'

'Lottie. Put the film out tomorrow as agreed.'

'We will. Ellie, there's more I need to say to you. When the film goes out, the media scrum will be intense. There will be camera crews camped outside your house and your phone will ring off the hook. Why don't you take the boys out of school for the day and head down to your cottage on Thursday evening? Get a new sim for your phone and don't take any calls on your old number.'

'That's good advice, Lottie. I don't want to put the boys through more than they need at this moment. Jonathan will want to talk to me though, how do I handle that?'

'Ellie, I of all people can't advise you on that. You can send him your new number...'

'No. I don't want to talk to him. I will text him telling him it's over after the show goes out and then switch off my phone. My lawyers will issue divorce proceedings on Friday morning.'

'Ellie, this is all happening very quickly.'

'There's no reason to delay, Lottie. I haven't thought about anything else since we met and my mind is made up. You won't change it. I must get back to work; the council lawyers want me to discuss a new deal.'

'Ellie, before you go I just wanted to say again...'

'Lottie, don't say anything. In another life we might have been friends, you and I, but I suspect that we will not speak again. It would be too weird. We've both ended up looking stupid through our love for the same man and in our own ways we have both been let down horribly. I don't hate you, I feel sorry for you. Take good care of yourself. Goodbye.'

She hangs up and Lottie stares at her phone vacantly wondering again if she is doing the right thing. It is too late now, she thinks to herself, as she exits the car and makes her way into the station.

When Lottie arrives in the constituency, things have already started to change. Jonathan has taken a lease on a flat in the city centre which will be both his required residence and their new campaign office. Lottie is immediately involved, using Jonathan's credit card, to buy beds, desks and basic furniture for the flat and then she spends an hour haranguing BT into the speedy installation of broadband. By the time she has done all of this, the three men have left the flat for a meeting elsewhere and Lottie looks around at the unfurnished flat and wonders what will become of it on Friday.

When the three of them return, flushed with the success of a meeting with a local developer who has promised to financially support their campaign, Lottie takes Jonathan to one side and runs through the important items that have emerged during the day and suggests a whole list of local interviews he should consider before the election campaign really gets under way.

'Yes, Lottie, let's do them all. Can you organise them over the next few days so that we we can keep this momentum going? I'm going to lose Adam now he's done the PM's work so it's important that you spend more time up here. Now we've got this flat it will make it easier for you to stay over too.'

'I don't think that's such a good idea, us sleeping under the same roof. You are public property now and it will get discovered.'

'You're right, of course. But we can be discreet and careful and no-one will catch us. Why don't you stay over tonight and we can make a start?'

'Jonathan, you don't even have a bed here so I don't think so. You need to be back in the hotel and I need to be back on the train. It's not a difficult commute and I can get lots of stuff done on the journey.'

'Lottie, I want you to resign next week so you can be full-time on my staff. Adam's found me a backer so I can afford to employ you at your current salary and you can concentrate on politics.'

'From what you told me this morning, perhaps I should wait and be made redundant first.'

'Maybe that's not such a bad idea. Anyway, one way or another I need you here full-time from next week.'

'OK. On that note however, I can't come up tomorrow at all. I will be able to do stuff remotely but I have things on in London that need me there.'

He looks disgruntled but doesn't push back and Lottie turns back to her laptop so that she doesn't have to look at him.

Chapter 32

Thursday dawns cold, bright and sunny and Lottie makes her way into the office early to view a rough cut of the Mali programme. She had found yesterday's meeting with Jonathan hard and she had spent most of the night tossing and turning as she thought through the possible permutations the next forty-eight hours might bring. She also realises that she might never see Jonathan again and although her anger towards him is intact, she still feels an emptiness inside at the loss of him in her life. She takes a last swig of her take-out coffee and pushes her office door open. Let it begin, she thinks to herself, let's see who is the strongest.

The rough cut of the show is strong but Ben wants to change some of the narrative structure and will spend the day supervising further editing. Jonathan is profoundly damaged by the programme: he is seen to be dissembling and dishonest and just another politician on the make. Melissa is perfect as the on-screen presenter, her silent looks to camera almost as damning as her narrative. The clever use of Lottie's doorstep photographs and the text exchanges between Jonathan and Anna seal the deal and condemn him completely. The lawyers were squeamish about this part of the film but Angie had argued back saying that Jonathan was in no position to sue and as long as they are safe from the Cressley's lawyers they are OK. The lawyers, having formally noted their concerns, were mollified and afterwards seem more compliant. Ben promises another version by mid-afternoon and goes off to find his editor, leaving the others alone together. They discuss how they will promote the show to the rival news media operations and maximise its impact.

Lottie returns to her office but struggles to concentrate upon her work. Promoting Jonathan to his constituents seems a complete waste of her time and instead she catches up on some work emails and other assorted paperwork. The morning drifts by, and after a quick sandwich at her desk, she re-joins the others to watch Ben's second version of the programme.

This second version is much tighter and more narrative led than the first cut and uses Melissa's on-screen skills more prominently. Ben also incorporates a previously unseen piece to camera by Melissa and this tilts the show slightly, making the conclusions about the Government slightly less convincingly than before. Lottie jumps in when she sees this.

'Why have you given those guys any wiggle room here, Ben?'

'I have to play fair, Lottie. This is the bloody Government we are taking on. We only have one dodgy conversation between Andrews and Lomax to try and seal the deal. I want to be honest and as we haven't asked the Government to comment we have to be scrupulous here. The implication is still strong and obvious, but remember: we still don't have any documentary proof. It's as far as the lawyers want us to go and I think they are right.'

'I always thought you were the one to go out on a limb,' said Angie. 'Let's put the original piece back in and damn the consequences.'

'Angie, we can't do that. I will not put my name to it. We can't lose our journalistic standards when we don't have the proof just because we want to nail the Government.'

'Well, maybe we can compromise here, Ben. Let's use this second piece but take out the opening phrase Melissa uses so it's tighter and more direct. That implies everything we need but does not actually say it. Can we agree on that?'

Ben grudgingly agrees to alter the introduction and leaves the room to oversee the changes.

'I'm worried we may just have given them room to get away with this,' says Lottie.

'Yes, you might be right. However we play this, the story of Jonathan and the Cressleys will always give the Government something to hide behind. I think we have to live with that and hope it's enough to bring the PM down too.'

At just after seven-thirty, the conspirators convene to discuss progress. Ben's final version of the programme is a little closer to the first cut and more damning of the Government. They have teased the programme primarily to journalists across social media for the last few minutes and can do no more until it goes to air; they are still worried that any definitive statement might allow the Government a chance to file an injunction and stop the programme. They sit around nervously watching the clock slowly tick around. The show is uploaded and ready to go out on YouTube, Vimeo and Facebook Video on the stroke of 8pm. Angie has also run off some DVD copies so they have some physical copies if they need to distribute those too. Amber has selected clips from the show to send directly to news journalists and has written a lengthy news release to go to national newspapers at 8pm precisely.

'Is everyone happy?' asks Angie, looking around the room.

'It's all ready to go,' says Ben. 'I wonder what tomorrow will bring.'

'The sun will still rise. It's just another political scandal amongst many others,' says Amber. 'It's just important we maximise our impact. Remember, we might all be fired tomorrow so our next jobs might depend upon our success tonight.'

'I'm sure that won't happen,' says Melissa.

'From what I hear, you are ready to sign for the BBC so there's only upside for you, Melissa.'

'There's no deal done yet, Angie, but yes I am talking to them.'

'We all should be talking to people,' says Lottie. 'Our new shareholders will be furious with us. They might have us thrown out of the building later tonight.'

'Who will Jonathan call first?' asked Ben.

'Lottie, then his wife.' says Amber.

'I won't take his call when he rings,' says Lottie. 'I've already blocked his mobile number. He will get me eventually but I don't want to talk to him anytime soon. I've also changed his Twitter password so although he will see his Twitter feed he won't be able to interact with it. I'm not sure he knows how to do it anyway. Ellie has switched off her phone and moved out to their cottage in the country so she can avoid him and the media. You won't be surprised to hear that she's going to file for divorce tomorrow.'

'It's nearly time,' breaks in Angie. 'Good luck everyone. Here we go.'

Lottie and Amber's phones start to ring a few minutes into the show as their press releases are picked up by news desks around London. They field calls at the back of the room whilst the others watch the show play out in real time. By the time the show credits roll, everyone is on the phone and half a dozen staff members have wandered in trying to make sense of what is happening. The media scrum intensifies and calls start to stack up. They switch to Sky News and see the story is running there; five minutes later, it is being reported on the BBC News Channel. Twitter is going crazy and the Amber inspired hashtag #Malibombshell is amongst the highest ranking of UK tweets. It isn't long before Angie has a call from Drew Smith who asks her what the hell she is doing running a programme besmirching a board member of the company without telling him first but simultaneously congratulating her for a great journalistic scoop. He tells her his editors will want exclusive access to any unpublished material and when Angie tells him that everything they had was on screen, he laughs and says he would expect no less of her. Lottie sees that amongst her many missed calls there are eight from Jonathan.

The frenzy intensifies and BBC News does a live cross from the front of the Catalyst studios as the second story in their 10pm programme. Newsnight are demanding a spokesperson for their show but, as previously agreed, all requests for interviews are politely turned down even though Melissa is heartbroken by the exposure she is allowing to go by.

By midnight, the scrum is dying down a little and the team munches through cold pizza and warm white wine whilst they share war stories and gossip from their calls and emails. They are sent an email from Group Publicity in which Drew announces that Jonathan has been suspended whilst an investigation is carried out to see if he has broken any of the corporate governance rules laid down for directors, and naming Angie as his interim replacement at the channel whilst this review is conducted. Number 10 puts out a carefully crafted release just before 1am in which they deny any involvement of Number 10 in selling or supplying arms to the Mali Government or army and blame the story on the two bitter and misinformed individuals with personal animosity towards the Prime Minister. It re-hashes the story that Jonathan and the PM had fallen out when Jonathan was briefly an adviser to him and suggests an enquiry into Cavendale's activities in Africa is required. It is clever and cunning and a deliberate attempt to put Jonathan and John Andrews squarely in the frame whilst distancing Number 10 from any malfeasance. This release is quickly followed by one from Conservative Central Office expelling both Jonathan and John Andrews from the Party with immediate effect. It further announces that there will need to be a new vote to select a new Tory candidate for the upcoming Northamptonshire South by-election.

It is almost one-thirty when Lottie finally answers a call from Jonathan who is using a different telephone so that she doesn't recognise the number.

'Lottie. It's me. Why, oh why, have you done this to me? I can't believe it. You bitch, you absolute bitch. You must know that this will finish me. I'm besieged by journalists all demanding answers. Even Ellie won't talk to me. Why did you do this to me?'

'Jonathan, you still don't get it do you? It's not all about you. It's for everyone that you have lied to – especially all the women. Not just me but Ellie, Amber, and all the interns you've used without a thought for the consequences. It's for Megan Smith and all the other women you were ready to besmirch. You and Anna Cressley are well suited to each other, although I suspect she'll kick you out now you are of no use to her. It's for Joe, who is still in prison and it's because Mali is a story that needs to be told and you were just too ready to be bought off. Before you think of firing me, by the way, I've already resigned. Goodbye.'

She hangs up before he can reply and switches off her phone so he can't ring back. Clutching her dead phone to her chest she fights back tears for thirty seconds or more whilst the group around her look on in silence. Angie smiles at her and holds up a thumb in approval. Eventually she smiles back at them all, claps her hands together and says, 'Right, well, there's that call dealt with. Who else needs a briefing tonight?'

Chapter 33

By Friday morning, the Government spin machine is in full gear and it is transparently clear that the PM intends to hide behind the human shields of Jonathan Lomax and John Andrews who have been clearly left to spin in the wind and take as much flak as possible. Government briefings off the record are describing Jonathan as a flawed character with a secret grudge against the Prime Minister. Whilst the PM had been taken in by him and had promoted him standing for Parliament, it was now obvious to all that the man is a complete scoundrel. Andrews is more simply dismissed as a low-level banker already under investigation for insider dealing. Commentators agree it is touch and go if the Prime Minister can survive through the weekend.

The Catalyst team decide that Melissa can start giving interviews but rein her in to ensure she does not stray beyond the known facts of the story. She strides out of the office in full make up and her favourite presenter outfit to meet the camera crews gathered outside the studio and is, of course, magnificent and gives even more mileage to what is already a sensational media story. The others keep their heads down and try to avoid any further comment. Jonathan, John Andrews and the Cressleys have all gone to ground and by Friday lunchtime the media are reduced to raking through the story and fronting endless commentator speculation. This inevitably means they start reporting on each other's speculations and opinions, and disaffected MPs and media commentators have a field day discussing endless permutations of how the Government might or might not cope with what everyone agrees is a crisis. The team from Sympatico and McKinsey cancel their afternoon meeting but Angie gets a supportive email from their boss Dwight Stephens. They all agree it means nothing.

Lottie heads home on Friday afternoon by foot. The story is now in the machine and being digested by both media and public alike. There is no way to tell where it will end up. She no longer has a role in its development. Once safely inside her own home, she pours herself a glass of wine, kicks off her shoes and sinks back on to her sofa. It had been an extraordinarily long week and she is exhausted by it all. She takes a long drink from her glass. Now she has lost her first job in politics, probably her last job in television, and her unfaithful and duplicitous lover. She had better start thinking hard about what she would to do next.

***

Four weeks is a very long time in politics and media, and four weeks to the day after that momentous Thursday, Lottie is sitting on the same sofa with a different glass of wine in her hand pondering the changes that have happened.

Another EU-based crisis has replaced the Mali story from the front pages and the Prime Minister has survived to fight another day, although commentators continue to discuss his diminished prestige and authority. It is unlikely that he will lead the Tory party into another election and he could well be gone from office before the summer recess. Lottie is hard pressed to care one way or another; she has no anticipation that a change in Premier will make things any better or any more honest.

As forecast, Catalyst has been closed down by its new shareholders and Lottie and the rest of the team are working through their statutory redundancy period. The two police chase channels have been sold off to Liberty Global but the Catalyst channel itself has gone off air and the channel frequency sold to an East European home shopping network. The staff turn up from time to time between interviewing for other jobs but there's a gloomy air that hangs over the building – especially when estate agents are there showing off the studios to potential buyers.

Joe, the stringer in Mali, was freed shortly after Jonathan's fall from grace and Lottie suspects that pressure from the Foreign Office helped smooth things out and placate the Mali Government. She's grateful for this at least, and has exchanged several Skype calls with Joe and his wife. Joe seems unfazed by his incarceration but his wife is much more anxious about their future and how he will find new work in Mali.

Lottie herself has had just one abortive meeting with a headhunter. He told her that her treachery was the talk of the industry, with everyone amazed how a senior PR could have shafted her boss so completely. It was now impossible, he said, that she could hold down any senior position in the PR business. She accepted this statement without a murmur of dissent. She was determined to escape the vanities of television and media anyway, and just because she was good at PR didn't mean she couldn't be good at something worthwhile – she just had to decide what that thing was and then apply herself to doing it. Her small redundancy package would buy her a little time to think. Lottie had no doubt that, as her career was in tatters, she would have to sell her house and part of her was keen to leave London behind as well and strike out somewhere else where she could make a fresh start and re-invent herself.

Amber and Ben and Angie were all in the process of interviewing for new jobs and didn't seem to be meeting the resistance she was finding, so that was good. She was quite happy to be the only sacrifice in the downfall of Jonathan Lomax. Some social media commentators had described her as a hero but she didn't feel like a hero: more like a fool who had been completely taken in by her lover's honeyed words and carefully constructed lies.

She has been asked by Ellie's lawyers to detail the terms and duration of her relationship with Jonathan and, having done this, she was embarrassed to be sent a copy of Jonathan's Amex card bill covering the weekend in Budapest. She is then asked to identify which of the purchases shown were presents for her and she dutifully does so, carefully crafting her reply so that she does not have to reveal she bought the items without Jonathan's actual knowledge.

And Jonathan? Well, he was emailing her most days. She had begun to look forward to his rambling, sometimes angry, sometimes sad, emails to which she never replied. He had managed to get through to her on the phone once more but she had hung up as soon as she realised who it was and now sent all unknown callers straight to voice-mail. He managed to leave several messages but she deleted them without listening to them. His emails told her that he was staying at David and Caitlin's place in Devon, although it appeared that they had disappeared in their camper van on a long-planned expedition to explore Europe about a week after he had arrived, so he was left alone looking after their three miscreant dogs. Reading between the lines, it would appear that he had maybe bedded or tried to bed and then fallen out with Caitlin in that first week. Jonathan sleeping with his best friend's girlfriend didn't surprise Lottie at all, but she wasn't sure if she was reading too much into his ramblings or if it had just happened inside his head.

Mostly, his emails mixed anger towards her and Ellie with occasional expressions of love and affection for his former mistress, along with a large measure of misery and regret. This was coupled with regular complaints about his lack of money and how he was reduced to driving around in David's fifteen year old Ford pick-up and shopping in the local Co-Op for bargains in order to feed himself. Ellie had earned his anger by pushing hard on the terms of their divorce settlement – one of his more memorable lines was 'never marry a lawyer because when you divorce they return to type and charge you by the hour for every day of your marriage.' Ellie's legal team had discovered the identities of several of his previous lovers and Eddie the driver had earned his special wrath for detailing his late night trips to Amber's bedside. Lottie is, of course, named as the lead infidelity. He complained that Ellie wanted to take everything and he would be left with nothing and he could never find any sort of proper job again. Ellie had also refused him access to see the boys until the divorce settlement was agreed. He was obviously drinking hard and several of the emails suggested they were written when he was in his cups; these ones tended to be full of self-loathing and demanding affection from Lottie – the only woman he had truly loved.

Now, four weeks on, she decided it was time to block his emails too. Everything about Jonathan – his addiction to sexual conquest, his ambition, his charm – was always just about exerting power over others. He didn't have that power over her anymore and he was beginning to bore her. He was a shallow, vain and selfish man and she wanted nothing more to do with him. She modified her mail settings to send his emails straight to junk and put her iPad down. It was time to turn the page.

Acknowledgements

As ever I am indebted to many friends who have offered encouragement as I started to write this book. Most of all thanks to Jan, Poppy and Harriet for your support, enthusiasm and positive criticism. You are my heroes.

About the author

A Very Modern Hero is Mark Cullen's first novel. After spending most of his career working and running broadcast and media companies in London, he has finally sat himself down and written his first book. Mark lives on the Hampshire coast and tries to combine writing with sailing. You can find out more at www.markacullen.com or on twitter at @markacullen.